I0718237

PRINT EDITION

Far, Far Away: 7 Stories in 7 Realms of Science Fiction and Fantasy© 2021 by Mirror World Publishing
Edited by: Justine Dowsett and Robert Dowsett
Cover Design by: Justine Dowsett

Published by Mirror World Publishing in June 2021.

Mirror World Publishing
Windsor, Ontario
www.mirrorworldpublishing.com
info@mirrorworldpublishing.com

ISBN: 978-1-987976-79-3

FAR, FAR AWAY

7 stories in 7 realms of science fiction and fantasy

mirror world publishing

Foreword

It's 2021. The pandemic drags on and we're all stuck inside. Blegh. Reality sucks.

So why not take this opportunity to escape into fiction?

A year ago we ran a contest and we asked writers to submit stories set in other times, places, and versions of reality. Then we had our judges pick the best ones to include in this anthology.

Therefore, the seven stories you are about to read are windows into other worlds, but also into the minds of eight extremely creative and talented individuals. We've included their bios and a few words from each of them so you can get to know the people who have created such imaginative stories to take us far, far away, if only for a little while.

So pack your bags, or don't, because you won't be needing them for this journey. Instead, sit back, relax, and turn the page to find distant galaxies, alien cultures, mysterious magical islands, unknown planets, the value of colour, the fragility of time, and the fickle nature of fate.

Justine Alley Dowsett

Publisher, Mirror World Publishing

Itinerary

Piece of Mind by L.R. Braden

With the imminent collapse of Earth, humanity sends out the seeds of civilization aboard an interstellar Ark to find a new home among the stars. But as the voyage drags on, the passengers lose themselves piece by piece to the limbo in which they are forced to travel, begging the question: what will be left of "humanity" if and when they reach their destination?

Songs and Superstitions by Shana Scott

Hired to exterminate the beasts roaming the newly-discovered ancient tunnels, insectoid alien Krem and human Max get trapped kilometres beneath the surface of Krem's home planet. Together they search for a way out, but first they must escape the creatures lurking in the darkness.

Black Spire Isles by Barend Nieuwstraten III

The infamous Black Spire Isles are known for wrecking ships, though few know what becomes of those marooned there as none are willing to mount a rescue that would only claim more ships. One small group of survivors is about to discover answers that none within the known world could have ever hoped to discover.

Field Notes from the Unknown Planet by Brittni Brinn

When Idylwild finds herself in a dry jungle under strange constellations, she must survive the resident predators, humanoid and reptilid, as she searches for a way off-planet. A story of human versus nature, "Field Notes from the Unknown Planet" chronicles one surveyor's experience of a strange and dangerous world.

The Colour of Roses by Kelly D. Holmes

All the colour from your sight is gone in an instant. In a world where only Soulmates can see colours, what would you do if you suddenly got them back?

The Prime Crusade by Buddy Young

Temporal voyagers on history's most infamous airship find themselves tangled in a struggle to save reality itself.

Fatestorm by Justine Alley Dowsett and Murandy Damodred

Praefecti Alton Rendall is tasked with subjugating the Lumen people for the glory of Rome. Deneige Audra wants nothing more than to see her people free. They're on opposite sides in a devastating war, yet their coming together may have the power to change everything.

Humanity has long held the dream of being an interstellar race with colonies spread among the stars, but to travel those vast distances would require more than one lifetime—unless we redefine "life". In this story, people have been scanned and uploaded as digital copies of themselves so they can voyage aboard an interstellar Ark. Once the ship reaches its destination, clone bodies will be grown for each person based on their original scans, and the person's consciousness downloaded.

However, every system has its quirks. In order to prevent file degradation, each consciousness is temporarily downloaded into a template body and allowed to "live" in a physical sense for three hours. But it takes several months to cycle through all the passengers, and the trip is taking longer than anticipated. Despite the scientists' best efforts, the digital passengers are starting to lose their minds, piece by piece.

Without their memories, will what reaches their final destination still know what it means to be human?

L.R. Braden

Bestselling author of *The Magicsmith* urban fantasy series, LR Braden makes her home in the foothills of the Colorado Rockies with her wonderful husband, precocious daughter, and psychotic cat. Her debut novel, *A Drop of Magic*, won the Eric Hoffer Book Award for sci-fi/fantasy, the First Horizon Award, and the Imadjinn Award for Best Urban Fantasy Novel. With degrees in both English literature and metalsmithing, she splits her time between writing and art.

To connect online, visit her website at: https://www.lrbraden.com

Piece of Mind

by L.R. Braden

For David, who makes all things possible.

Stale, slightly ionized air flooded my lungs, bringing with it the scent of disinfectant and…something else, sharp, sweet. Panic flitted around the edges of my exhilaration. I exhaled. I'd been dead another eighteen months.

The scientists didn't like us using that term, but what else could I call it? Hibernation? Dormancy? Suspended animation? None of those were strong enough to fit the empty silence of the limbo where we waited.

What piece of myself have I left in that cold, dark place this time?

"Back with us, Mr. Thompson?" A voice floated out of the darkness, but not the inky void of that other place. Not even close.

I opened borrowed eyes, blinked.

Dr. McCarthy perched at the edge of her steel stool, watching me, waiting to see if I remembered how to speak, how to move, who I was. The gray at her temples was more pronounced than I remembered. Skin sagged from her cheeks like deflated balloons, silent testament to the time that hadn't passed for me, proof of her indispensability.

One hand poised over the tablet in her lap, she leaned closer. "How do you feel?"

I raised one smooth, pale hand, translucent skin bright under the ceiling lights. It tingled as motes of dust brushed against it, asteroids pummeling my senses compared to the nothing that came before. Purplish veins swelled when I made a fist.

"Alive." My lips snapped closed, cutting off the deep baritone voice I didn't recognize as my own.

"Do you know where you are?"

I blinked twice, slowly, relishing my control over the flash of light and dark as the room flickered in and out of existence. Medical tools lined the otherwise bare walls. An endless vibration thrummed through me, and I dug into my memory for the cause.

Interstellar thrusters.

"Still on the Ark." The unfamiliar voice cracked, shattering the last word.

Her mouth twisted to one side. "I'm afraid so. What do you remember about your life on Earth?"

"I lived in…an apartment, in…" I wracked my brain, sorting through labels until I found one that felt right. "New York."

"Very good." She smiled and nodded encouragingly.

"I—" More images flitted by, but I couldn't hold them. "I was a—" My fingers tightened on the chair as I groped for some way to end that sentence, but all I found was a gaping hole where the information should have been.

Liquid trickled down the side of my face, and I was momentarily distracted by the need to identify it.

Tears. Crying.

"It's all right, Mr. Thompson." Dr. McCarthy set one cool palm over the back of my clenched fist, and the low moan I hadn't realized I was making subsided.

"I can't remember what I did before," I said, waving my free hand, "this."

Her smile returned, small and sad. "You were a writer, Mr. Thompson."

I tried to fit the word into the blank space in my mind, but it was swallowed by the emptiness.

"What did I write?"

Her cheeks colored slightly. "To be honest, I don't know. I never read your work." She lifted her tablet. "I can look it up if you'd like."

I shook my head, a hollow feeling settling in my abdomen. "Never mind." We'd gone through this dance before. No amount of recited information would fill that void of lost memory.

She puckered her lips into a tight frown, tapped a note on her tablet, and set it aside. "That's enough for today."

Dr. McCarthy leaned across me. She smelled like lilacs and industrial cleaner. I breathed deep, pulling the scent into my lungs like a drowning man coming up for air. Wisps of hair sprouted from her haphazard bun to dance in the ventilation currents like seaweed on the ocean floor.

There was a pressure on my wrist.

"All set." Dr. McCarthy sat back, crow's feet digging into the skin around her eyes. "Enjoy your time."

A black band circled my wrist, angry red numbers glaring from its surface. 02:59:52...02:59:51...02:59:50...

The seconds were already eating away at my three hours of freedom.

Muscles stretched and contracted under translucent skin as I pushed out of the reclined chair and pressed my bare feet against the cold tiles of the floor. The room shifted, and my stomach heaved. Plastic creaked under my fingers as I clutched the seat.

Vertical. Upright. These were concepts from the physical world, so different from the cloud of nothingness in which I'd floated for so long.

"Take your time." Dr. McCarthy's lips turned down at the corners.

My eyes slid to the black bar with its red countdown. 02:59:38...02:59:37...

Looking past it, I found ten toes peeking out from the bottoms of loose, pale green pants.

Neurons fired, muscles coiled, my weight shifted. One foot shuffled along the floor. Then the other. The third step felt almost natural. It's amazing how fast it all came back, like that other place was just some terrible dream from which I'd finally woken.

A loud hiss shattered my ears when the door slid open, and a shift in the air currents fluttered the coarse fabric of my clothing like sandpaper across my skin. Three more steps took me into the curved steel tube of the hallway. A strip of light traced the ceiling like a glowing spine in either direction. Another hiss cut me off from Dr. McCarthy.

Three hours to live. I knew exactly where to spend it.

The door to the observation deck whooshed open and I took two steps inside before registering the startled eyes staring at me over the back of the viewing bench.

I froze mid-step, stumbling awkwardly to catch my balance.

Except for Dr. McCarthy, other people stuck mostly to the staff side of the partition, busy with running the ship. But this woman wore the same green pajamas I did, the same translucent skin. I stared into pools of liquid blue, similar to the ones I knew would greet me if I dared look in a mirror, and swept a hand over my own close-cropped hair. She was my counterpart.

"Sorry." I retreated, trying not to look at the body that echoed the lie of my own.

Jumping to her feet, she stretched out one hand as though she could arrest my motion from across the room. "Please, stay."

I was already halfway through the door.

Behind her, the endless expanse of space called me, colors swirling through its depths. I glanced over my shoulder. I'd used too much time getting here already, wandering empty halls that looped back on themselves and all looked the same.

Fingers drumming my thigh, I took in the too-wide eyes and downturned mouth that had invaded my sanctuary, and sighed.

She sat as soon as I reversed direction, but her eyes never left me as I crossed the room and settled on the far side of the bench. Slouching back, I laced my fingers over my stomach and tried not to fidget under the woman's close regard.

She perched at the edge of her seat, ramrod straight, practically vibrating.

I tried to focus on the view.

"What's your name?"

My own saliva nearly choked me as I jerked up in surprise, pounding my chest to clear the airway.

"I know we're not supposed to ask." She continued to stare, unrepentant. "It's just—" Finally those unyielding eyes slid away. "It's gone," she said in barely a whisper.

Breathing steadily once more, I turned to face her. Her previously piercing gaze now skittered around the room like a frightened creature.

"What's gone?" I asked.

"My name."

I sat up a little straighter. "You don't remember your name?"

She shook her head.

Mouth dropping open, I glanced toward the darkness on the other side of the glass, then turned to look at her again. "Surely the doc could tell you."

"She did, but—" She shook her head, and it spread until her whole body was quaking. "It isn't mine anymore."

"What do you mean?"

"I can't remember ever being called that. It doesn't have any connection for me. No emotion. No relevance." She finally looked up. Tears glinted at the corners of her eyes. "If someone suddenly gave you a name, a name you'd never used before, would it feel like yours?"

You were a writer. Dr. McCarthy's words taunted me from that missing chunk of myself they'd been unable to fill.

Shaking my head, I pressed my lips tight and leaned back against the bench.

"I just thought, maybe—" Again, her piercing gaze slid away. "Do you—did you have a wife?"

I squirmed in my seat as a hazy image of dark hair, smile lines, and freckles in the sun drifted through my thoughts. Was it a wife? It could just as easily have been a sister, or a friend, or some random woman in the protesting mob that swarmed the launch pads the day I boarded the Ark. It could have been the face of the woman sitting across from me.

"I don't know." Quiet as my response was, it was a scream compared to the silence that followed.

"They told us what might happen. But they didn't, not really." Her hands came together in her lap, and she slouched back against the bench as if all the tension had left her at once. "A little memory loss, a few gaps that could be filled in once we reached our destination. That's what they said."

"It's taking longer than anyone thought." My voice sounded hollow as I recited the empty words.

"I don't even know how long anymore, how many times I've gone under and come back."

I sat forward, elbows resting on my knees. *I shouldn't have come here. I should have turned and left as soon as I saw her.*

Pushing to my feet, I stepped up to the giant window that made up one wall of the observation deck and rested my forehead against the smooth, cool surface that protected and caged me. I looked out at the universe, and the endless expanse of the universe looked back— space and time stretching out in a ribbon of patchwork memories eaten through by my time in limbo.

Staring at that beautiful, terrible vista, words bubbled up from some long forgotten place in my soul. I turned them over, tasting their flavor, learning their shape. Then I let them wither away, unspoken.

Pushing against the emotions welling inside me, I forced them back to their prison.

"What's the point of surviving if we can't remember who we are?" Her words hung in the room like a toxic gas. I cringed, both from the intrusion on my solitude and the uncertainty those words carried.

"Do you think—"

A high-pitched buzz split the air.

My muscles cramped. My eyes darted to the tiny red numbers on my watch. A hollow vacuum twisted my stomach into knots.

02:02:48.

Not me. Not yet.

Guilt rode the wave of my relief as I spun to face my companion. Her knuckles were white on the edge of the bench. I took a step, my hand hovering as though I wasn't completely useless. Balling my fingers into a fist, I let my hand fall and ground my teeth at the pain written on her face.

The sound cut off.

A shuddering breath rippled through her. Tears streaked her cheeks. We stared at each other for one long second, my horror mirrored in her too-wide eyes.

"I have to go." Her words dropped into the space between us like a pebble tossed in a pond and I rocked in their wake.

I glanced again at my watch. Ten seconds had already passed. She wouldn't make it to the med bay before another twenty were gone. The alarm would hit her again. It would keep sounding until the clone was back in the operating room, until the doctor shut it off, until the woman huddling in on herself at the edge of the bench was dead.

All I could feel was relief that it wasn't me.

Sweat glistened on her forehead and glinted like diamonds in the peach-fuzz of her colorless hair.

She pushed to her feet, swaying slightly.

My body leaned toward her, but I held my place.

"Goodbye." Her voice broke on that single word.

She waited another precious second, but there was nothing to say. I had no comfort to give, so I scrunched my eyes closed and huddled around my cowardice until the door hissed open.

I looked up in time to see a flash of pale green cloth disappear around the corner before the door slid closed, sealing me into the solitude I'd wanted—a solitude that now echoed the emptiness of the limbo to which we would both be returned.

I took a shaky breath, gagging on the taint of guilt and the lingering smell of the dead woman.

Wiping my eyes, I glared at the bright red numbers floating on the inky surface of my watch. Was I crying for her? For myself? For the whole human race? I couldn't tell anymore.

A high-pitched buzz filled the room once more, shaking me to my bones. Every muscle pulled tight, my lungs froze mid-gasp, and a dull ache spread through my temples and settled in the base of my skull. When the sound cut off, I blinked until the observation window came into focus, then rolled my eyes to the watch below my clenched fist.

-00:00:05. The angry red numbers flashed in time to the seconds I'd exceeded.

Already? Looking back at the swirling kaleidoscope of darkness beyond the window, I caught a glimpse of my own pale reflection and jerked away before the details could register.

It can't be time already.

But the numbers continued to climb.

-00:00:27...-00:00:28...-00:00:29...

I hunched around the cavern in my chest and wrapped my arms around my head as though I could somehow protect myself from the blow that was coming.

-00:00:30.

The alarm echoed through my head, singing to the ingrained response in my treacherous body. Tendons and ligaments tensed, pulling me apart. Pain lanced through my temples, setting off my nervous system like a chain of fireworks. Bile raced up my throat and I spit burning tan sludge onto the polished floor.

It will only get worse.

The siren hit me twice more as I stumbled down the corridors, searching for the only person who could make it stop. The first time I clutched a wall for support and managed to keep my feet. The second saw me crumpled on the floor, panting.

I pushed through the med bay door before the pneumatic hiss stopped. Dr. McCarthy held the device that would remove the watch, but I was too late. Another alarm ripped through the air, flooding me with pain.

I grabbed for the chair, but my arm hit a tray of tools and scattered them across the floor a second before my knees connected with the cold tiles. Curling into a ball, I tried to fight the burning in my unresponsive lungs.

It will pass.

They wouldn't dare cause permanent damage to a body, not with so much at stake, but two seconds seemed to stretch forever before the alarm cut off, leaving only my quiet whimpers to fill the sudden silence.

My muscles went slack, and I sucked in a deep breath of antiseptic air.

Dr. McCarthy knelt over my wrist and grumbled, "I don't know why you all drag it out to the last minute, knowing what will happen."

Even if I had the breath to respond, there wasn't anything to say. No one who hadn't faced a thousand deaths that slowly ate away your being could ever understand. Dr. McCarthy, who spent every day of an extended life in her own body, would never know the horrors of the hell she'd created to save us all.

The black band fell off my wrist and Dr. McCarthy scooped it up. "Just look at this mess. I'll have to prep a new set."

Stepping to the cabinets that lined one wall, she reached for a box on the highest shelf. The heels of her white pumps lifted off the ground. She balanced on pointed toes, her body a taut line stretching to her fingertips.

Rolling onto my elbows, I found my reflection in the overturned tray and the weight of everything I'd lost overrode the lingering pain that had called me to my death. My fingers curled around the edges of the shiny metal.

Dr. McCarthy's hands wrapped around the box.

I pushed to my knees.

Her heels hit the floor.

I staggered to my feet.

As she turned, I slammed the smooth metal sheet into the side of her face. Pink spittle splattered the cabinet. The box hit the floor, empty syringes rolling free. Dr. McCarthy crumpled beside it. The tray followed with a clatter, one edge streaked red.

What have I done? A trickle of cold sweat slithered down my spine and I rubbed slick palms on my thighs.

I dropped to one knee beside the doctor.

Strings of pale hair hid her eyes. Any damage I'd done was pressed to the floor, invisible.

My hand shook against her neck. Was that a pulse, or an echo of my own racing heart?

Time stretched while my mind scrambled to make sense of the situation. Dr. McCarthy's chest compressed and a strand of hair fluttered near her lips.

My own lungs froze, as though there might not be enough air for us both.

Dr. McCarthy's ribs lifted slightly.

I let out a dizzy exhale.

Running both hands over the scraggly buzz of my hair, I squeezed my borrowed skull until the pressure dulled the needles still stabbing into my temples and the backs of my eyes.

Dr. McCarthy needed medical attention, and the small blue button on the wall behind the operating chair would bring it. I took a step toward it…and froze.

What about me?

No way they'd forgive me for attacking the woman responsible for maintaining the human race, cycling souls through limbo on this endless journey. The last sliver of hope that I would see the end of this trip snapped the second I swung that tray.

My head swung back and forth like a pendulum. No way to cover up what I'd done. Nowhere to hide on the ship. Nowhere to run.

The muscles in my neck tensed, jerking my head and spiraling thoughts to a stop.

I stared at the door, imagining I could see past the walls and rooms that lay beyond, all the way to the swirling expanse of that endless, dark sea. Somewhere beyond the security doors marking the area designated for clones were enough escape pods to save the few dozen people important enough to spend this trip in their own bodies.

Swallowing the lump in my throat, I rolled Dr. McCarthy onto her back, revealing a crimson puddle. The wound on her cheek started to ooze with enthusiasm when it found the open air. The cut was shallow, but my stomach heaved. I clamped a hand over my mouth, pulling deep through my nose until the sensation passed.

Yanking open drawers, I found a box of gauze pads and a roll of medical tape. I was no doctor, and every second I remained risked discovery of my crime, but I couldn't just leave her bleeding.

Blood stuck to my hands as I wiped her wound and slapped on a sloppy bandage. I tried not to look, not to feel the warm wet on my skin. I wiped my hands clean as best I could on another pad of gauze, then tugged free the plastic card clipped to Dr. McCarthy's lab coat.

Beep.
The hallway beyond the first security door looked identical to the one I was standing in, but my heart sped as I stepped over the threshold. Cold sweat pricked my forehead, and I wiped it away with a shaky hand to keep it from stinging my eyes.

The door hissed closed, making me jump.

Voices echoed like ghosts to fill the empty hall. All the people missing from the other side of the ship were here, somewhere.

Pressing my shoulder to the wall, I peeked around the first corner. Doors lined either side of the hall. Tracks of lights traced the edges of the steel floor and ran along the center of the curved ceiling.

Not a soul in sight.

The second corner offered the same view, except a large laminated image hung in the middle of one wall.

Stepping up to it, I studied the map of the only home I'd known since leaving Earth.

The section I was familiar with was highlighted in the same pale green as my clothes. I was now in the orange area, most of which was taken up by the label Engineering. The front of the ship was blue and marked Navigation. Along one side of the orange section were a number of small red dots. Lines traced from each dot to a single word: Evacuation.

A hiss to my left, and the voices that had been flitting at the edge of hearing flared like someone turned up the volume. A shadow spilled across the hall.

I glanced at the hallway behind me. *Too far to run without being seen.*

The door slid closed. Whistling merrily and swinging a large wrench from one hand, the man who emerged took a few steps before looking up.

Deep brown eyes swept over me. A crease burrowed between his brows. A frown puckered his salt and pepper beard. His lips parted.

I threw myself forward, planting my shoulder into the man's gut so his accusation came out in a breathy gasp.

We toppled backward and a heavy *clang* rang out. Grabbing the fumbled wrench, I swung it.

There was a sickening *crack*, and the man went limp beneath me. The bearded curve of his jaw was now sunk in on one side. A stream of blood and bubbles dribbled from the corner of his mouth.

I dropped the wrench—fighting the urge to vomit—and cringed at the racket when it hit the floor. My chest heaved, ribs aching. I sucked in the metallic flavor of blood with every gasping breath.

Unable to make my body respond, I stared at the door through which the man had come. He'd been talking to someone.

Seconds ticked by and I found myself looking at my naked wrist. A sick laugh twisted in my gut at the absence of those glowing numbers.

Someone would find him soon enough, him or McCarthy, and then I'd be done. If they caught me, I'd be erased for sure.

I pushed to my feet and ran.

I didn't bother to peek when I came to the next intersection. I didn't even slow down. A door slid open as I dashed past, and I briefly registered wide eyes and dark skin before skidding around the next corner.

Two more turns and I slammed into a solid wall. Red letters swam in my vision as I steadied myself on the cold steel of an escape hatch.

CAUTION. The word looked like it was painted in blood.

Fingers curling around a lever to my right, I split the warning in half. On the far side, a matching lever sealed the hatch behind me.

The pod was cozy. Six seats lined the walls, each with a dangling harness. At the far end, a swiveling chair faced the buttons and dials of the control console.

My breath caught, trapped by a weight suddenly crushing my chest. Could I pilot a spacecraft?

I ran down paths in my labyrinthine memory, cringing at every dead end. If I'd ever known how to fly…it was gone.

Dropping into the chair, I laid my hands on the console and looked over the puzzle of knobs, switches, and buttons standing in my way. The controls curved along the inner wall of the pod, surrounding me with choices. My heart sank as my eyes rolled over them. Then, at the far left end of the terminal, was a panel with the words LAUNCH PROCEDURE stamped across the top.

A smile tugged at my lips. Of course, escape pods were meant to save everyone, not just pilots.

"Mr. Thompson?"

I jerked, twisting half out of my seat to scan the space behind me. There was no one there.

"Can you hear me?" McCarthy's voice crackled through an intercom.

My shoulders relaxed. I sank back into the chair.

A small red light flashed on the console to my right and I pressed the little button below it. "Glad you're okay, doc."

"Better than Officer Jensen." Her voice grew faint, as though she'd turned away from the microphone.

"Is he—"

"He'll live, but he'll be eating through a tube for a while."

My head dropped against the chair's backrest. I stared at the rivets in the ceiling until they blurred. I hadn't killed him. "Good." My voice cracked. I wiped the back of my wrist under my nose with a cough. "That's good."

"Mr. Thompson…John, you need to come back."

I turned back to the launch instructions. "Sorry, doc. Can't do that."

I flipped the indicated switch and the engine hummed to life. Glowing gauges showed the thimble-sized fuel tank was full and the CO_2 scrubbers were active.

"Once you disengage, you'll have less than thirty-seven hours of air. Where do you think you can go?"

"I don't need to *go* anywhere."

"Then why are you doing this?" McCarthy's voice grew shrill with frustration.

With a sigh, I stared out the tiny porthole that was all the view the pod had to offer. I could just make out the other pods clinging to the side of the larger ship like parasites, umbilical cords siphoning what they needed.

"I don't expect you to understand, doc, but I can't go back to that place again. I just can't. I'd rather die with what I've got left than let limbo poke any more holes in me."

I flipped several gray switches marked with the numbers two, three, and four, and a digital schematic showed my pod's life-lines had been disengaged. My palm brushed the red button that would detach me from the ship.

"What about your son?"

Jerking to the side, my hand slammed into the console beside the release button.

"What did you say?"

"The body you're wearing, how long do you think it will take to grow another? How many memories will the men in limbo lose waiting for it?"

"I don't have a son." But I raced desperately down every memory I still possessed, looking for any indication, any hole where a son might have been.

Too many blanks.

"You do." A slight hesitation. "You haven't remembered him in three years."

I scrunched my eyes and shook my head, fists balling on the console.

No way could I forget a son.

But the woman on the observation deck had forgotten her own name, and I couldn't remember if I had a wife.

McCarthy's words looped through my mind. I pulled apart every nuance, every inflection. My eyes popped open. "Why did you hesitate?"

"What?" Her voice cracked.

I push back from the console. "You're lying."

"I wouldn't—"

"Of course you would."

Silence crackled over the intercom.

"Thousands of people are waiting for their turn in that body." Her voice was soft but even.

"I don't have a son."

A deep breath. "No."

I ground my teeth. "That was low."

"I'm desperate."

I snorted. "You don't know the meaning of the word."

"You think I don't know what limbo is doing to you?" A sharp edge crept into her voice. "To all of you? I know better than anyone the shortcomings of my technology. I'm there when each and every one of you wakes up with a little bit less of who you were, and you all blame me, but what choice do I have? What choice does any of us have with humanity itself on the line?"

"I'd rather die as myself than live as an empty specter of a human being."

My hand swung down on the ejection button, but froze with my palm just brushing the surface as the echo of my words slammed into me.

A century ago, I never would have pressed this button. Never even considered it.

But the soul that once sang to me of hope, and life, and adventure was nothing more than a withered husk pinned to the shell of a walking corpse.

"John? Are you still there? John!"

My hand slid off the console to lie loose in my lap.

"Not sure there's much humanity left to save."

McCarthy's sigh was audible through the speaker.

"I'll bring your body back," I said. "On one condition."

"You didn't do any permanent damage. I'm sure I can convince the captain to pardon you."

I shook my head and smiled at the pale reflection of my borrowed face drifting in the window. "Not even close."

"Then what do you want?"

"I meant what I said. I'd rather die than go back. But, I won't die a murderer." I took a deep breath, let it out slow. "I'll open the door. You erase my consciousness."

"You want me to *kill* you?" The speaker crackled at the higher decibel.

"Erase, doc." I ran a hand over the clone's peach-fuzz hair. "I died a long time ago, and there's nothing in your doctor's oath against erasing a digital file."

"It amounts to the same thing."

"Euthanasia then. I'm in my right mind, I'm in chronic pain, and I'm asking." An image of the woman whose name wouldn't have mattered even if I'd asked it drifted in my vision. "And I want you to offer the same choice to everyone. I doubt I'm the only one done with this journey. Besides, *someone's* son might last a little longer if there are fewer of us to cycle."

I eyed the launch button. "So, what's it gonna be?"

The silence stretched on. Then, "Okay, John. You have my word."

I spun the chair and stepped to the hatch, setting my hand against the cool metal. She'd lied about my having a son. She could be lying again. Probably was. For all I knew, we'd done this dance before and I'd simply forgotten. But after all the pieces of myself I'd lost in limbo, I'd finally gotten one back—a tiny sliver of humanity from a woman with no name and a child who never existed.

There are no guarantees in life. Only choices.

I pulled the lever to open the door, and smiled at the men who greeted me with matching glares and guns.

I created "Songs and Superstitions" to build upon another short story, "A Cure for Homesickness", which was published by the Escape Pod podcast in March 2018. In that, I wanted to write a happy, fluffy, space pet story, but I fell in love with the main characters Krem and Max, so I wanted to keep playing with them. In "Songs and Superstitions", I wanted to go to Krem's planet and find out more about my insectoid alien and his culture. I also wanted to explore Krem and Max's friendship more, which is really the heart of all their stories. They're the best of friends even though they don't always understand each other. I really love future stories with optimistic outlooks on the universe.

Shana Scott

Shana Scott is a digital archivist and content specialist with a Master's degree in Professional Writing and Publishing. She's a member of SFWA, and her work has been published in magazines, anthologies, and podcasts such as *Escape Pod*, *Gothic Fantasy: Footsteps in the Dark,* and *TulipTree Review*. Currently, she writes about the craft of world-building in her blog, <u>Woman in the Red Room</u>.

Songs and Superstitions

By Shana Scott

*To the best space pet in the universe, Commodore McFlufferton,
who was too fun to only have one story about him.*

Krem dropped the mangled gun onto his bunk. Torqu-style weapons were difficult to come by, as were the weapons of all insectoid species outside their territories. The rifle was the latest casualty to Commodore McFlufferton's teething.

Krem hated Commodore McFlufferton. The semi-sentient raok had been an annoyance when Krem could snap it in one claw and return it to Max, his human crewmate, whenever it tried to chew his leg. Krem never understood how humans saw these monsters as "adorable". Nearly a year old by the Torqu calendar, the full-grown vermin's furry red head reached waist-high when sitting back on its haunches, and it measured as one of the tallest creatures on the ship when standing on the backmost two of its six plate-sized paws. How such a huge species could travel without making a sound baffled him. Maybe all that fur insulated it. Add in the *two* rows of steel-sharp teeth in its massive maw, and Commodore McFlufferton was capable of ripping an individual of any species apart with unnerving ease—or, as in this case, tearing Krem's favorite rifle in two.

Krem grabbed the plasma shotgun—one of the few remaining survivors—and headed for the cargo bay to meet Del and Max. Maybe he could get replacement weapons after the mission, though he doubted any Torqu would sell to him. This might have once been his colony, but he hadn't left in the appropriate way, and Torqu didn't forgive easily.

"Ready to see home again?" Max called in greeting as they met in the scarlet halls that led to the exterior cargo bay. Commodore McFlufferton padded its six pillar-like legs serenely at Max's side, matching her pace precisely. While loose on the ship, the creature managed to sneak its substantial body unnoticed to torment Krem, yet when they left the ship it waited on Max's every command. Krem *knew* the vermin did so simply to prove that it targeted him on purpose.

"The colony isn't my home anymore," he said. "Each Torqu has a duty to the colony they must perform. A small percentage of Torqu don't agree with their placement in the colony. I've heard in a few colonies it's acceptable to request reassignment, but my colony doesn't function that way. You either fulfill your role or you leave. I left. Now, I'm an outsider, like you."

Max allowed sufficient time to pass in silence, and he was grateful. Krem and Max didn't always understand one another, being from vastly different species, but she comprehended his need to have things in their place, drilled into him from a lifetime as Torqu. That he'd chosen to leave the colony didn't mean his culture left him, and Krem sensed her respect for the difficulty of that decision.

Then, because she was Max, a wry grin played on her lips as she cocked a single brow his direction. "What was your job in the colony?"

Normally he'd have answered her honestly, as Torqu standards demanded and in order to avoid any misunderstandings deception caused between species, but he'd lived with this crew for nearly four years, and they'd rubbed off on him. In a serious tone and with no obvious malice, Krem replied, "Killing raok in the tunnels. I was very good at it."

Commodore McFlufferton growled, while Max laughed and hugged the beast around the neck. She, it seemed, had caught the joke.

Del waited at the exit hatch, his skin a shade of fluorescent red. Del's sweat produced a variety of colors and patterns that his species used as non-verbal communication in a way that didn't cross species barriers. Max had attempted to log all the colors and patterns in a "mood chart" for their captain and failed so spectacularly that Del hung it up in his room as a souvenir. Usually, Del produced green and blue hues. Red was interesting, like a star glowing beneath his skin.

Max followed Krem's gaze and a sly smirk lit her face with amusement. Red had been deemed "kerfuffled" on Max's mood chart, a word that no amount of explaining on Max's part adequately defined in a way that made sense to Krem.

"Let's go," Del said, leading the way to the drone who would act as the colony's representative.

"Captain," the Torqu representative said, ignoring proper introductions, "is this all of your crew? I was told to expect a larger party."

"Two of my best," Del said with a smile that flushed his skin with a yellow wave and was too friendly to have missed the insult of a failed introduction. "We haven't received a full report on what we're to do, so I left the rest on the ship until we've been briefed on the situation. No point having us wandering all over your colony."

"We don't normally allow aliens beyond the port's commerce area." The representative pointedly focused on Krem when he said *aliens*, as though Krem had changed species when he left.

He tried not to let that bother him. It did, but he tried nonetheless. Next to Krem, Commodore McFlufferton growled and the representative stiffened. Out of the ship, the raok rarely made a sound unless Max ordered it to intimidate someone or attack. Though she was silent, Max's lips pressed tight together, as if she wanted to say something she shouldn't. Perhaps the beast had picked up on her body language.

"Don't worry," Del continued in his overly helpful tone. "I've told Krem to keep us in line with Torqu protocols. I believe that was why your government hired us, since he's from your colony."

At Del's last sentence, Krem smelled the representative's repulsion at their presence like a miasma wafting out on the wind. "Better to risk aliens and tarqkot than our own drones at this point."

Max looked to Krem. "What the hell was that word? All my translator gave me were clicking syllables."

Del appeared just as confused. If it had been another word, Krem might have been pleased that for once it wasn't his translator that had difficulties parsing alien languages.

"It's from an old Torqu language. It means," Krem paused, trying to figure out how best to explain, "outsider, but more than that. Traitor. Dark crawler. Without colony. It's only used to refer to Torqu who leave their colony."

"It's an insult," Max said sourly, narrowing her gaze on the representative, who didn't appear apologetic at all. Not that any Torqu in the colony would call Krem differently, but not all would be vicious.

"Yes and no," Krem amended. "It's my designation now, my title."

"It's the only title you deserve, tarqkot. If we didn't need someone to help them navigate the tunnels, you wouldn't be allowed back."

Commodore McFlufferton clamped all its razor-sharp teeth deep into the representative's leg. Given a Torqu's exoskeleton, this was accompanied by a great deal of cracking. After a few seconds longer than she'd normally wait to react to Commodore McFlufferton acting out, Max tapped the raok on its back and it immediately released its victim.

Max pulled it back into what appeared more like a hug than a restraining hold, and admonished her beast. "Bad boy. No attacking the nice Torqu. Yes, you're a bad boy. Yes, you are."

Krem noted that Max's voice was the high-pitched cooing that she normally praised the raok with, and not her deeper scolding voice, and she gave it a quick kiss atop its fluffy head. Since the colony representative didn't appear very familiar with aliens, Krem doubted he knew the action was affectionate and deliberate.

Not that the representative focused on much beyond his own leg, now spiderwebbing with cracks and two sets of large holes where the raok's teeth had punctured his exoskeleton. Max had been bitten many times during the raok's training, and had only required a little patching of muscle and skin. The Torqu would be laid up for weeks while they replaced the leg plate and fused it with the rest of his exoskeleton.

"I'm so sorry," Max said, not appearing contrite at all. "He's normally well behaved."

"Vermin," the colony representative hissed, and he backed away three unsteady, hobbling steps. A few fangs must have reached the muscle or the Torqu would have only suffered a limp. There were no nerve endings in the exoskeleton to cause pain.

Del placed himself between his crew and the representative, offering a helpful arm to redirect the Torqu toward the colony.

Once Del and the Torqu were far enough away, Krem addressed Max. "Did you order Commodore McFlufferton to do that?"

"Did I?" she replied with exaggerated shock. "Boss wouldn't be very happy with me if I did. We haven't been paid yet."

"Why?" As enjoyable as it was to watch, Krem didn't understand why the human had bothered. The representative was only acting Torqu.

Max cocked a single eyebrow at him, a sign she was just as confused at his not understanding as he was confused with her actions. "Only family gets to insult family without consequence."

"It's what I expected," Krem explained, "but thank you for the sentiment." Torqu didn't have families the way humans and other birthing species did, but Krem appreciated the concept.

Upon reaching the port interior, the colony representative acquired a replacement and hobbled off to the nearest medical facility. The new representative, a younger, female Torqu, kept a safe distance from Commodore McFlufferton as she led them into the colony proper and explained the mission.

"During routine maintenance and expansion on the northern border, roughly six kilometers underground, our engineers encountered a series of ancient tunnels not marked on any map."

"The Seket colony allowed expansion into the border area?" Krem asked, surprised that any outward expansion could happen. The space between borders provided a much needed buffer between territorial colonies.

"Yes, tarqkot," she said, though her tone held no malice. "After much negotiation both colonies agreed to minimal expansion at different depths. We obtained the deeper levels and to find any ancient tunnels at that depth that hadn't collapsed caused a great deal of excitement. Unfortunately, when our engineers tried to reinforce them, something attacked. None survived. Soldiers were sent in, but none returned. A second squad followed and we found their bodies torn apart near the entrance to the ancient tunnels. After the third squad failed, leadership agreed to seek outside help. Torqu tactics do not appear to work against whatever lives in the tunnels."

"Do you have any idea what it could be?" Del asked, his skin flushing a dark indigo with blue and green spots shimmering here and there.

"Communication not wired into the tunnels is blocked that deep underground, and we had the entire level cleared to avoid any more casualties. By the state of the bodies we were able to recover, it's believed that raok are breeding down there."

The representative's mandibles twitched with nervous energy as she glanced down at Commodore McFlufferton. As if to reassure the Torqu woman, Max took a firm grip on the ruff of her pet raok's neck. Max was in no way strong enough to stop the vermin from getting free, but the gesture settled the Torqu.

"Raok don't normally go more than a kilometer down," Krem said.

The representative nodded. "We believe that there must be a way higher up, and the raok may be using these ancient tunnels as a nesting area, which would explain why they've become so vicious to protect it. Your job is to eliminate any and all threats in the tunnels."

Max sighed over-dramatically. "I don't understand why no one in the galaxy likes raok. They're so cute." As if in agreement, Commodore McFlufferton yipped a loud, booming sound that echoed over the wide tunnel walls and sent several Torqu scurrying away.

"You mean, besides the tearing-creatures-apart aspect?" Krem asked.

"There is that. But I don't hear you complaining when he's tearing up people trying to kill you. Besides, how can you hate that face? Commodore McFlufferton, smile." The raok politely raised its head to the group, dropped its bottom jaw to expose all fifty-six of its enormous teeth, and lolled its tongue to the side, looking delighted.

"Vermin," Krem muttered, and the raok's jowl curled away until they could see where those teeth attached to the gumline.

Whether from their interchange or the raok's name, the colony representative stared at them without even a whiff of emotion drifting from her for several moments. She wasn't rude like the first one but showed no more proficiency with aliens. She didn't know how to respond. Krem knew that feeling well, though not as often anymore. He'd gotten better at accepting their strangeness without question.

"I assume you'll want to survey the area before gathering the rest of your crew," she finally said, falling back on the protocols necessary to prepare them. It was a Torqu reaction.

Max pulled out her assault rifle and performed a quick check to make sure everything was in order. "No need, Boss. Krem and I can go down and make a plan of attack while you go get the others. Sounds like we'll need everyone, anyway. We won't go far."

Krem nodded, approving of the plan. He'd be able to navigate the tunnels to make sure they didn't go too deep without backup. Del agreed, but the colony representative smelled hesitant. After a moment during which her mandibles twitched intently in Krem's direction, she nodded and told Krem sparse directions only a Torqu who'd grown up in the colony could follow.

"Before we go," Max said once Del had started back to the ship with the colony representative. She untied a red cloth from around her arm, a good luck charm she'd called it, and ripped it in half. She tied one half to Commodore McFlufferton's collar so the cloth lay like a flag across its back. "If we're hunting raok, I don't want anyone shooting him by mistake."

"Of course not." Krem didn't entirely bemoan the sentiment, but Max laughed anyway. Then she tied the remaining half of the cloth around his wrist. "What's this for?"

Max grinned. "So I don't lose you in there. No offense, but you all look alike. I thought here at least there'd be more variety. How do you tell each other apart?"

"Torqu only have four or five breeding pairs at any one time, and we hatch in groups of hundreds. I suppose that doesn't offer as much genetic diversity as humans." He himself had marveled the first time he'd seen his second human. She'd been so vastly different from the first that he questioned whether they were the same species. "Generally we know one another by scent more than sight. Deeper in the colony it won't be well lit, so visuals aren't as important to us."

Krem stared at the cloth around his wrist. It was certainly meant as a joke, though he wondered if she sincerely couldn't tell him apart from the rest. He found he didn't like that idea. Perhaps more genetic variety wasn't a bad thing. That or humans needed to evolve more sensitive olfactory abilities.

Max and Commodore McFlufferton followed Krem through the maze of tunnels that took them deeper underground. Nearer to the surface, lights kept the tunnels bright and drones regularly cleaned any debris that might impede the traffic of countless Torqu scrambling with clear intention to their destinations. A surprising amount of open space formed around them as they travelled. Was it the raok or the alien causing the fuss?

After a few more identical tunnels and a long elevator ride down six kilometers, they exited into a dim tunnel as silent as the earth around them. Max turned on the flashlight attached to her visor and a narrow band of bright light swept back and forth over the terrain. At her side, Commodore McFlufferton sensed the change in her demeanor and waited at the ready. She made a wide sweeping motion and the raok leapt forward, bounding down the hall in a steady lope that turned the beast into a shadow moving in the distance. It returned a moment later, ears up and tail high. It hadn't found any dangers.

Max raised her assault rifle at a relaxed but prepared stance and nodded for Krem to lead on. "Let's see what this old tunnel looks like."

Most of the tunnel resembled all other tunnels in the colony—clean floor and walls built for traffic—until they reached a tangential path blocked off from the rest with a metal barricade, which lay knocked on its side as if Torqu needed it out of the way in a hurry. Krem could smell old blood and dark splashes marked the floor.

They continued their silent patrol down this tunnel for several minutes, dodging abandoned equipment as they went, before they reached the rupture into the ancient tunnel. And it *was* ancient. Not yet leaving the modern tunnel, Krem ran a claw over the edge and listened to the way the tunnel felt to him.

"This isn't Torqu-dug," he said with certainty as he attached his own flashlight to the top of his plasma shotgun. Just because he had four arms to use didn't mean he needed to hamper one with a flashlight—with raok, every arm might be necessary. He passed the light over the walls of the ancient tunnel. Rhythmic markings lined the dirt walls in even, equidistant strokes unlike anything Krem knew. "It's too big to be raok-made, even for a nest of them."

"The raok could have stumbled on the tunnel, right?" Max asked, waving one hand sharply down to signal Commodore McFlufferton to stay close. The beast obliged, teeth bared and fur bristling.

"Yes, but that leaves the question who built this if not the Torqu. It *feels* different. The way the vibrations move through it is," Krem fumbled to put into words the sense a Torqu had while moving underground, "organic. Like this area was always meant to be a tunnel, but it obviously was created by something." Krem shined his light onto a mound of dirt that had fallen from the ceiling above, probably when the engineers broke through.

"Earth has places like that. No one knows who really made them, they've just always been there."

Commodore McFlufferton dropped its tail, arched its back low to run, and growled a rumbling noise that vibrated the ground. But not just Commodore McFlufferton. Krem felt the other creatures' paws digging into the soft dirt further in. Raok.

"Fifteen meters, maybe less," Krem whispered, shifting his gun so the light noted the direction where he had sensed the movement.

Max's light joined his, and while Torqu relied more on other senses in low light, it still benefited a raok to be brown against dirt tunnels. They only saw the first one when it leapt from their field of vision, disappearing in the surrounding darkness.

"Defend!" Max yelled and Commodore McFlufferton slammed its massive body into the darkness before them, a yowl of pain echoing against the tunnel walls.

Max swept the tunnel with her light and a flurry of motion further in the tunnel ended with the sharp crack of her gun. Another raok skid into the ground—motionless—even as a battle ensued in the darkness nearby. Without light, there was no way to tell if Commodore McFlufferton was winning, but by the howling shriek, one of the raok was injured. Krem pushed Max to the other side of the ancient tunnel so she didn't accidentally move into his line of fire and shot above the thrumming mass of writhing raok. White hot plasma struck the tunnel wall, illuminating the two raok, both red with blood, and sent the wild one scrambling to escape deeper into the tunnels. More used to the sound of gunfire, Commodore McFlufferton leapt after the fleeing raok and crushed its hindmost leg with a fierce crunch.

The raok weren't the only things that moved from the force of the plasma's strike. The tunnel cried a shuddering warning to Krem's senses. He could have escaped into the modern tunnel, but Max moved further in to finish the raok Commodore McFlufferton had subdued. There wasn't enough time to get her and the vermin out, and Krem refused to leave her. When the tunnel entrance collapsed, encasing them in total darkness save for the slight illumination of their flashlights, Krem pulled Max down to cover her fragile flesh from falling soil.

When the collapse ceased, Krem clawed out from beneath the dirt encasing them, keeping two arms firmly around Max to ensure he didn't lose her in the shifting soil. Max sucked in a gasping breath the moment her head escaped and he paused to allow her to squirm free of him. Max's visor light swung widely as she searched for Commodore McFlufferton, who, after a moment of Max's panic and Krem's hope, dug itself to the surface. The other raok didn't emerge, so either Max had killed it or the collapse did.

"That's not good," Max said, her voice shaking in a way Krem didn't recognize as she stared at the wall of earth that had once been the tunnel entrance. She knelt down to cuddle against Commodore McFlufferton, using the action to check it for damage. The raok tucked its head under her chin and made a sound no wild raok produced. It whined, a long, high-pitched reaction to Max's mood more than the raok's own distress.

Krem placed all four claws against the dirt wall and scratched around, feeling how the vibrations moved through the earth. "It's packed too tightly to try to break through, and the ceiling isn't stable yet. Digging ourselves out could bring the rest down. Excavators will have to do it."

"And they won't get here until Del and the others arrive, 'cause communication is crap."

"Del won't arrive for another fifteen minutes, then thirty more for the excavators. It may be hours before they can safely make an opening. I don't think it would be wise to wait here for more raok to find us with no escape route."

"Because going into tunnels where trained Torqu ended up butchered is so much better an idea." Max checked her weapon. It was a nervous habit, a ritual to collect herself. Krem approved as it was a useful way to deal with stress. That she was visibly stressed was odd. Max normally ran headfirst into danger with a smile.

"Are you all right?"

Her fingers clicked against her gun. "Let's just say being buried alive and then lost in the dark six kilometers underground with no way out makes me very unhappy. Don't worry, I'll deal with it."

Ten minutes later, after walking in the glorious silence only the deep tunnels could produce, with darkness enveloping them like a cool wind, Krem learned how Max "dealt with it". She sang. Not a real song, but she definitely sang—softly, with a melody that changed with each verse. And—for reasons Krem couldn't fathom, though the singing itself made no sense to start with—she sang of their coming deaths.

Krem stopped, his befuddlement so entire that all he could do was stand there. In the weak side-illumination from his flashlight, Max's serious face remained half in shadow.

"*Why* are you singing?"

"I'm in the epitome of a horror movie. Humans don't like being trapped, buried alive, in the dark, underground, with killer aliens. Pre-contact we had tons of those movies. You know what they don't do in those movies? They don't sing. So if I sing, I can't be in a horror movie."

Krem abandoned any belief that he had obtained a semblance of understanding about humans. They were far stranger than he'd given them credit for. "That makes no sense."

"Call it a superstition," she replied, humming under her breath.

"What's a superstition?"

"You don't know?" Max cocked her head to one side. "A superstition is the belief that something unrelated to a situation has the ability to affect its outcome. Hence, singing keeps monsters from killing me."

"And you *believe* that?" He wasn't trying to be cruel. The concept simply didn't make any sense.

"Whether or not it's true, it makes me feel better. And if I'm calm, I'm better prepared when the monsters attack." With that, Max continued her song about them dying, and them not dying. Their future livelihoods were dependent on the verse.

Krem considered her explanation as they walked. The idea of a superstition baffled him, but he didn't need to understand to comfort Max. To him, the darkness and the weight of the earth around them reassured him. But if those things were instinctual fears—manageable ones before they were trapped without aid or exit—then a superstition provided the necessary stress relief to keep Max steady. That seemed an adequate trade for some singing. He'd never seen her this flustered on a mission before and wished to put her at ease.

Krem singing wouldn't help, though. In the past, the crew decided that Torqu singing was not for the rest of the galaxy. Apparently, it made their "skin crawl". He'd thought it was a metaphor, but several spent the following hour scratching at their arms or legs, so he wasn't certain. He did have one musical option, and it would have absolutely no impact on their present situation. That fit all the requirements of a superstition.

Krem arched his back until the two plates that made up his torso's posterior exoskeleton split roughly an inch apart, raising up to hook on a notch below his neck. He flexed the wing-like membranes beneath the plates until they vibrated in a steady rolling cadence. Accompaniment, rather than singing.

This time, Max stopped. "I didn't know Torqu could do that. It sounds like cicadas back home." There was a wistful quality to her voice and she smiled.

"Most can't. Only breeding males have enclosed wings to produce this sound."

Her soft smile turned into a shocked guffaw. "Wait, wait, wait, wait, wait," she said all in one hurried word. "You're a *breeding* male? *That* was your job in the colony?"

"It was a very dull job." Krem didn't know why she was so surprised. "Breeding females only lay eggs twice a year. Breeding pairs can take on administrative duties between layings if they wish, but nothing I'd consider adventurous. So, I decided to leave."

"Damn. I take it breeding isn't as pleasurable for Torqu. Every human man I know would love to do nothing but breed. Women, that's different, we don't have the luxury of laying eggs and walking away, though the process is quite fun."

"The song isn't unpleasant, I suppose, but I wouldn't call breeding pleasurable. It's more instinct."

Max laughed. "You're telling me there are hundreds of little Torqu out there that you fathered."

"Thousands, more likely."

Max shook her head. "I have a new appreciation for you, Krem. It must've been really hard to leave the colony with a job like that."

"It was," he said, turning down a new tunnel. He kept the hum of his wings going as it seemed to help her and wasn't difficult to maintain. "I'm in the wrong era. Before, new colonies formed when a breeding pair became tarqkot. Back then tarqkot meant wanderer, not as an insult. Other tarqkot gathered to protect a breeding pair, and a colony began.

"Our colony has the best creation story. Our founder couldn't convince a breeding female to leave with him, and without one, no other tarqkot would join him. He wandered alone for years until he met the..." Krem paused, not wanting to confuse her translator again. However, when the correct meaning came to him, he realized it answered an earlier mystery. "Tunnel Maker. They were ferocious, territorial beasts that hunted unsuspecting Torqu in the deep tunnels. They were supposed to be stories.

"According to the tale, our founder found a way to lead the Tunnel Maker. No other Torqu managed to tame one. He built the entire colony this way. When word spread, tarqkot from all over joined him, as did *two* breeding pairs. Once I knew I was a breeder, I wanted to be like him."

"As much as I'd love to let you fulfill childhood fantasies," Max said with little chuckle, "I'd rather not run into a beast more ferocious and territorial than a raok that can create tunnels this big."

Krem nodded, though Max probably missed it in the darkness. "Speaking of raok, I would've expected to run into more by now if we were near a nest. And for the amount of damage they caused, we must be near a nest."

They continued on. Max set the rhythm of her song to match the rise and fall of his wings' hum. She was calm, even if her verses now included tunnel monsters ripping them apart. Commodore McFlufferton joined in with a yowling growl here and there.

Eventually, they stumbled not upon a nest, but a lake. The cavern was enormous. How did no one know of it? His planet didn't have oceans, making underground reservoirs crucial resources. Colonies went to war for water sources, and here one was, as if waiting for them to find it. The Seket colony would be furious when they discovered the kilometers they'd given to his colony included a reservoir. They would demand to share.

"Water," Max said with a sigh as long as the darkness around them. She pulled a chemical scanner from her belt and dipped the top antenna into the water. Her voice brightened after the beeps. "And I can drink it!"

Max dunked her entire head into the still lake for several seconds before pulling it out with a laugh. "Damn, that feels good." She ran a hand through her short hair, spritzing water all around her to halo in the flashlight's beam. Her laughter signaled Commodore McFlufferton it was safe to leave his guarding post, and the raok bounded into the lake with a much noisier splash.

"The gravity's getting to me," Max said, cupping her hands together to bring water to her mouth. "Just a bit stronger than the ship. And where are all these raok? I can't imagine we missed them all."

"Wasn't your superstition supposed to keep you safe?"

She laughed. "Yeah, but I didn't expect it to work. By the way, thanks for...indulging me. Humans weren't meant to be down here. It didn't bother me until the tunnel collapsed. Never realized I was afraid of being buried alive."

"Technically you *were* buried alive. It makes sense that would trigger a primal fear."

"Yeah, but I like being a badass mercenary."

"Not even fear can stop you from being a 'badass.' You *were* singing about our gruesome deaths."

Max let out a brusque guffaw. "What other kinds of deaths do you expect us to have?"

Krem scanned the area while Max refilled her canteen, which had gone dry an hour earlier. It didn't make sense that this reservoir went undiscovered when it was located so close to two colonies. Torqu were masters at seismic tracking. Most of their off-world trade came in mining and tunneling technology. Even back when the colonies first grew, surely someone should have noticed the markers of a cavern as massive as this one and claimed it. Perhaps they thought it an empty cavern too dangerous to tunnel near, or maybe the water seeped down from another source after the colonies set their boundaries.

"Krem." Max waved her light to show where she was, a few yards from the other side of the lake. "Commodore McFlufferton's found something."

The fluff of the raok's mane now hung in a thick, dripping mass matted to its body but failed to make the vermin appear smaller. Raoks were solid muscle beneath the fur. It shuffled back and forth, whimpering low in its throat as it sniffed and then recoiled from a nearby pile of...something. Krem added his light to Max's own.

"Bones. Raok bones," Krem said, squatting down to pick at the long-since scavenged remains. There had to be dozens of full-grown raok in the pile.

Max put a hand on Commodore McFlufferton's head to calm it, and the raok's wet tail sloshed heavily against the ground. "Is this the nest?"

"No. Raok don't let dead creatures anywhere near a nest. It would draw too much attention from other animals. And they don't normally eat their own unless desperate. The raok we saw earlier didn't appear starving to account for so many gnawed bones." Krem held a long bone, probably from a leg, close to the light to see the damage better. It wasn't gnawed exactly, more like clamped over and over with something sharp.

Max's light shifted to follow her sodden raok as it searched further along the lake's perimeter, head to the ground, only to vanish.

It popped back into view before either of them could move, or its head did at least, happily yowling a high-pitched sound to call them to follow. Max hurried—carefully—to her pet to see what happened, while Krem did the same, except he closed his eyes. It was easier for him to sense the cavern without the light drawing his attention to only the visual.

He felt the thickness of the cavern beneath his free claw trailing along the wall; heard the padding of wet paws move back and forth from the softer, moist dirt around the reservoir to the hard-packed earth of a well-traveled path; and smelled a dry breeze dispersing the humid air of the cavern. Krem didn't need Max's confirming call of, "He's found another tunnel," to understand why the raok had disappeared. More than that, though, Krem knew this tunnel had been used by someone or something for a long time.

"Don't go far," Krem called, pleased when both Max *and* the vermin obeyed, though given their situation, the raok wouldn't stray far from Max.

Krem stepped into the new tunnel and examined the patterns on the ground. The story was all in the dirt. Aside from the now muddy prints left by Commodore McFlufferton's soggy paws, the dirt was smooth and pressed as hard as stone. The tunnels they'd traveled through earlier had seen traffic recently—that much made sense since the colony had tried to clear the tunnels, but the dirt there was looser and easily kicked up.

What made Krem nervous was the size of the path. Travel only hardened so much ground. Six massive raok paws running back and forth would eventually form a distinct path, and one only so wide. This path almost reached both walls of the tunnel. Could even a Tunnel Maker be that enormous?

"Something uses this tunnel," Krem explained to Max, who made an involuntary check of her weapon at the comment. "It's probably what killed the raok near the lake."

"And maybe the Torqu who found the tunnel, and the soldiers who came thinking it was done by raok. Maybe a terrible monster capable of making giant tunnels." Max guessed his thoughts. As strange as humans were, they weren't stupid, especially not Max.

Krem made a sound of agreement and assessed his crewmate. Humans were one of the toughest species Krem had met since leaving the colony. Not physically; he was average for a Torqu and still outweighed her, stood a head and a half taller, and possessed an exoskeleton that protected him from most physical damage. Yet, for all his physical superiority, Max would gladly jump in front of him if she saw danger nearby. And had, in fact, done so before. Humans were resilient and fiercely loyal, or at least the ones he'd met had been. They could wear down or panic the same as any other species, but they adapted and coped with remarkable ease.

Commodore McFlufferton was one of Max's ways to cope with mental strain, as confusing as it was to Krem and the rest of the galaxy that a human would not only emotionally bond with a less sentient life form but one as grotesque as a raok. And now, after struggling to deal with being buried alive and the fear it incited, Max remained ready to fight a creature possibly out of Torqu legend with nothing more showing than a tight jaw and a hip touching Commodore McFlufferton's wet body. The dark hadn't abated any more than her fear, but the danger being a real thing rather than her imagination prioritized her fear beneath the need to survive.

There was something he could do to not only help ease her fears but also keep her from being the most vulnerable choice to the Tunnel Maker should they encounter it. Krem shifted the plates on his back again and let his wings hum to life. Max glanced up at him, perplexed, then her jaw unclenched a little and she smiled, returning to her cautious scan of the area as they walked deeper into the tunnel.

He'd been right. The hum comforted her. It would also cause the Tunnel Maker to sense him easier than her. Anything that lived in here felt its way through the tunnels—not saw—and to a creature like that, his vibrations were as glaring as the burning light of a fire. At least Max didn't sing along this time. That would have ruined his protect-the-squishable-human plan completely.

The tunnel led to another cavern, smaller than the reservoir and without water, but still far more expansive than the tunnels. On one side, the ground was packed into a wide mound with deep gouges around all sides.

"We found a nest after all, didn't we?" Max asked, moving her light over the torn up ground.

"Not a raok nest. If this is a Tunnel Maker, there should be only one. The stories say they defended their—" Krem paused, focusing on the feel of the earth. Was it trembling? With his wings active, it was difficult to sense more minute shifts in the dirt. "Something might be coming. Go over there." Krem flashed the beam of his flashlight toward the far end of the cavern, where he'd sensed another connecting tunnel.

Max readied her weapon and made a hand sign that set Commodore McFlufferton poised to fight. "I'm not leaving you, Krem. You know I won't do that. Everybody comes home."

Humans were loyal. Foolish, but loyal.

"It's better if we're not together. Two targets are harder to hit than one. I can't tell where it's coming from." He could have stopped his wings, but that might lead the Tunnel Maker to attack Max first, especially since Commodore McFlufferton guarded her, and a raok was familiar prey.

Krem felt a rhythmic thud join the tremble too strong to mistake for his own wings. It rumbled closer to him, but he felt several other tunnels connecting to this cavern for it to appear through. The thudding was strange. Not the quick lope of running raok, though it did get faster the longer he felt it. The problem lay in the rhythm. It wasn't isochronous.

Two quick. One. One. Two quick. One. Three slow. One. One.

What kind of creature produced a walking or running pattern like that? What did the stories say a Tunnel Maker looked like?

Krem's claws trembled as he felt the pressure of the air displacing behind him and three hard thuds sounded as legs with hook-like thorns caught the entrance of the tunnel wall to heave an enormous body into the cavern. The creature was as big as the tunnels, with six long double-jointed legs hefting it high enough so Krem couldn't touch it even as it stood over him. Commodore McFlufferton lunged forward a step with its tail and body low to the ground but a snarl on its face, as if torn between protecting Max and running away.

"Tell me that's not a Tunnel Maker," Max whispered, slowly raising her gun. The creature was so massive her flashlight beam caught only two or three of the spike-like appendages that covered its torso.

It *was* a Tunnel Maker, and they were going to die in a way far worse than Max sang about. They wouldn't scratch it before it tore them apart with its four Torqu-sized curved mandibles, which explained the notches in the bones they had found. The Tunnel Maker rocked, rotating its body forward so those mandibles snapped at Commodore McFlufferton. Though, like the raok, it didn't move to attack—only to threaten.

That didn't make sense. Nor did the fact it ignored Krem completely despite him reverberating with far more vibrations than either Max or Commodore McFlufferton.

No, it didn't ignore him completely. Krem forced himself to turn and locate all six of those monstrous legs. They surrounded him. More than that, they contained him beneath the Tunnel Maker. Krem could have fired up at the creature's underside. The same thick, stone-like spines covered there as well, and not even his plasma rifle would do much damage. Yet, despite knowing of Krem's presence, it made no attempt to force him out where its mandibles could snatch him.

Something felt familiar about the Tunnel Maker, beyond childhood recollections of stories and legends. Something *comforting* in this great beast. It unnerved Krem—and drew him closer.

"Where do I shoot it?" Max said in a calm tone that spoke volumes to her experience in life-threatening situations. "It's too dark for me to find a weak point."

"Don't shoot," Krem said. The Tunnel Maker hadn't attacked yet, and everything he knew said it should have torn them apart the moment it caught them in its nest. Instead it refused to move, just as Commodore McFlufferton snarled and snapped but never budged from his protective place in front of Max.

Protective...

Was the Tunnel Maker *protecting* him? Was that possible?

Krem was struggling to place all the stories of the Tunnel Maker into this new perspective when it crouched its massive body down to gouge deep treads into the ground in warning to the harried raok. And Krem felt it. They were synchronized. Deep in the Tunnel Maker's body it vibrated with the same thrum as Krem's wings, matching his song with its own. Closer, Krem could feel the vibrations echoing through his body. It felt...natural.

"Max," he said, more hopeful than certain in his course, "trust me and do what I say. Pull Commodore McFlufferton back and step away."

"I'm not leaving—"

"*Trust* me," Krem repeated.

Max hesitated for a moment, then called out to Commodore McFlufferton, "Heel." The obedient vermin backed away from the Tunnel Maker to stand ready at Max's side.

Krem took a deep breath, fortifying himself. He took a tentative step. Then another. And another. He reached out and clamped his claw lightly around the hooked thorn a third of the way up the lower part of its leg.

With Max and the vermin making no attempt to threaten it, and Krem's claw creating an audible clicking against the stony hook as they quivered together, the Tunnel Maker folded the rest of its legs under itself to curl around him. Cautiously, Krem ceased vibrating his wings, and the creature stirred restlessly. When he restored the song, the beast thrummed, spines contracting and relaxing in a contented rhythm.

Krem now understood why the founder of his colony had been the only Torqu to tame a Tunnel Maker...until today. It took a breeding male, and breeding males weren't allowed on adventures. If Max hadn't sung her superstitious song, he wouldn't have hummed along with her or thought to distract the Tunnel Maker by using his wings.

Krem exhaled a breath he hadn't realized he held. "Max, I officially believe in superstitions now."

Max soothed Commodore McFlufferton with steady petting between his soppy ears and stared dumbfounded at the creature. "Honestly, even when you believe in superstitions, you don't *really* expect them to work. Do you have any idea what just happened? Did you just become the founder of your colony?"

"Like him, it appears. I believe it's safe to say his stories are true."

"Wait, you said your founder used this thing to make the colony. Can we use it to open the tunnel that collapsed?"

"We can try. Let's see if it'll follow me." Krem stepped toward the tunnel leading to the lake. The Tunnel Maker's body rippled and a cascading clicking sounded from the scale-like spikes coating it. It lumbered up, and when he continued in, the creature followed with Max and Commodore McFlufferton trailing at a safe distance.

It filled the tunnel almost perfectly and used its double-jointed legs to snake around its torso and hook the wall to pull itself forward. Whenever a malformation in the tunnel appeared, it rolled so that the spikes covering its torso dug and collected the dirt, then shifted it through the spikes to deposit the sediment behind itself.

"I can't wait to see the look on all those Torqu when *you* bring in a monster of legend. I bet they'll beg you to come back," Max yelled in a happy voice.

Krem considered this. "They might, actually. Tarqkot aren't given second chances, but this story will spread through the colonies. They might not risk other colonies offering. I am a breeding male after all."

"Do you want to go back?" Max's voice sounded strange. Was that anticipation of his answer?

The static of the comms blared noisily, interrupting Krem's reply. "...better not be dead! Answer me. Krem! Max!"

"Del!" Max cried out. "Damn, it's good to hear you. We're okay. Mission's done, by the way."

"What the hell happened?"

Krem glanced back at the Tunnel Maker following him. "You'll have to see to believe. I assume excavators are trying to re-open the tunnel. Tell them to move away. We have a way through. And don't shoot what comes out. It's docile now."

There was a pause as Del took in that information. "This sounds like quite a story. Is it going to give me a headache?"

"It's going to get you paid," Max answered.

Del bellowed a thick, gurgling laugh. "Now that's the kind of story I like."

Krem sighed, pleased to be back on the ship. As tarqkot, leaving the colony should have been simple, but the discovery of the Tunnel Maker altered his colony's view of him. Their insistence that he remain to control the Tunnel Maker was transparent and expected, but any breeding male's song could pacify the creature. Krem wondered what had caused their founder to start the song and attract the Tunnel Maker in the first place. Did he hope to find a breeding female wandering as well, or did it comfort him when he was alone in the tunnels?

"Welcome back," Max said as he entered the commons area. At her feet, Commodore McFlufferton lay on its side, tail thumping. "I was starting to wonder if you'd decided to stay."

"No, I'm glad to be back," Krem said with a certainty that surprised him. "I'm too much like our founder. I left my colony, had adventures, and ended up in a colony of my own. I don't think I'm ready to wander from it yet."

Max's face broke out into a bright smile. "Sounds good. Come on, I got a present for you."

She led him back to his bunk to a new weapons trunk, complete with a polished chrome lock that gleamed in the artificial light. She unlocked it and revealed a slew of new Torqu-style weaponry. He tilted his head, curious. True, he hadn't had time to go buy any replacements for himself, but with his newfound relationship with the colony arranging for a shipment didn't seem difficult.

"Commodore McFlufferton was the one who destroyed them, so that makes them my responsibility to replace. The guy I talked to at the dock said they're top of the line for Torqu. I think I got a deal when I said they were for you."

"Strange things have happened since we arrived."

Krem paused. Gift giving among Torqu was reciprocal, and he bristled to receive so much from her without giving anything in return, even if the vermin was at fault. His mandibles twitched in satisfaction as an idea came to him. Krem moved to a small storage set that acted as a nightstand next to his bunk and retrieved a single greenish-black ornament a few inches long and carved with decorative lines on its surface. There were plenty more in the drawer, though not as many as when he lived in the colony and had more room to keep them. He'd taken only a few dozen when he'd left, mostly out of sentiment.

"It's part of my first exoskeleton," Krem explained as he handed it to her. "Caretakers shatter them and make these ornaments for us to give to those close to us."

"That's both creepy and awesome. I like it. Thanks." Max turned it over in her hand, and then her grin brightened as her eyes dropped to the raok sitting at her feet. "I know just what to do with it."

She squatted and pulled at the vermin's collar for several minutes before standing up again, hands empty. The ornament hung loose at the raok's neck, tied by wire around the collar.

She had given his gift to the vermin. Krem was less than pleased.

Max reached out to cuddle the raok's big head. "Doesn't he just look handsome now?"

Commodore McFlufferton didn't appear any happier than Krem at the addition, and it shook, trying to dislodge the dangling ornament. Disgruntled with Max, Commodore McFlufferton padded from the room and a strange thing occurred. Krem heard it move. The ornament at its neck clinked softly with every shift of motion.

Max teased a smirk at Krem. "No more sneaking around for him. Not on the ship, at least."

Once again, Krem knew he preferred this colony to the one he'd left.

Welcome to the world of Theseolyn. A world once governed by the twelve gods, known as the Avanar, who ruled from the great city of Avantolis. Upon raising their city to the clouds, they raised many mortals to gods of a lower pantheon, the Etheri, to rule in their stead. Over the next millennia, the first gods divided existence into four realms. Their great city became the highest realm of Avantolis where the Twelve and their people remain. Then Etherius was made, where the new gods crafted their own kingdoms and afterlife for the mortals who worship them. Between them and the final realm, the physical world where mortals dwell, a void that became Nihrius was brought into existence. Populated by the dreams of those gifted with magic, it is a strange and warped reflection of the world that most know. In it, the demigod children of the Etheri dwell as well as the creations of nightmares. In the physical world, men, elves, dwarves, and orcs live in their tribes and kingdoms, and even empires as they rise and fall.

Amongst their lands, especially within the southern continents that surround the Middle Sea, dwell the twelve wizards of Avantolis who stayed behind when the first gods left the waking world. With them, ten of the Greatwyrms stayed behind. Guardians of the first god's city who spread apart, creating the dragons and subsequent races such as the drakes and wyvern, and lesser known beings shrouded in secrecy and lost in forgotten times.

The continents around the middle sea are separated from other lands by great oceans that can only be traversed by four elven ships that make trips too seldomly to benefit most mortals. But within the Middle Sea there is a place perilous to all ships known as the Black Spire Isles. Prone to storms and populated with long jagged rocks that tear through the wooden hulls and bows of any vessel unfortunate enough to pass too closely.

Barend Nieuwstraten III

Barend Nieuwstraten III has been working on a collection of works set within a single fantasy world, currently working on stories ranging from flash fiction and short stories to stand-alone novels as well as an epic series.

He has worked in film, short film, television, music, and comic formats. His writing experience has mainly been in comedy (sketches/comics) and music (lyrics), but is now focused on High Fantasy that sometimes delves into horror.

He grew up and lives in Sydney, Australia where he was born to Dutch and Indian immigrants.

Black Spire Isles

by Barend Nieuwstraten III

Black rock rose jagged and steep from both the sand and sea in dark, rocky spires and ridged cliffs, rendered lustrous by the brine crashing from the Middle Sea. Elaeni staggered onto the beach amidst explosions of sea foam and the slapping of splintered wood on the sand around her.

The ship carrying her had been ripped asunder and its broken fragments scattered violently upon sand and rock. One of the sails had torn and stretched, flapping against the rocks ahead of her with the rope and netting whipping about in the wind.

Familiar crewmen were impaled high upon sharper rocks, like soldiers raised on pikes in some thwarted battle charge. She clutched her stomach where the sea had hurled her into a mercifully blunt rock before she surfaced. The blow had made her take in water, brine that she had just finished violently expelling. Her lungs and nostrils still burned from it as she passed more crewmen lying dead on the sand with split heads and broken bodies, while their lifeless flesh was accosted by washing reddened waves and pink foam.

In the distance, people scurried to collect the debris and flotsam, but she could not see them clearly through her green eyes turned half red. It was too soon for her to call out, her mouth full of salt and her own matted black hair, and it seemed no one had even noticed her. Elaeni collapsed onto her hands and knees, and allowed herself the luxury of rolling onto her back. She began to fade as she looked back to the crashing waves where sailors dragged their fellow crew and passengers onto the sand from the sea. The ship's severed bow stood upright in the shallows, propped up by rock like a temple, with its prow serving as a spire and the seadrake figurehead upon it facing its belly to the sea and its maw to the sky.

The ship's first mate ran towards her, crunching the wet sand as he dropped to his knees while his drenched clothing flapped in the wind. He leaned over her, dripping the sea onto her face as he called out her name, lightly slapping her cheeks while she drifted into darkness. There she dreamt a memory of four men standing side by side as ropes were placed around their necks. She was sure she stood before them the last time, but this time she was being effortlessly carried away as the first mate's voice assured her that she would live.

When she awoke, Elaeni found herself in a strange village with huts made of fragments of old ships thatched with reeds and vines, supplemented by turtle shells and grey clay bricks. One stood taller than the rest, a hall by hut standards, built into the side of a rocky rise where it seemed a shallow cave would have made up half the dwelling.

Survivors of the now destroyed Saltdrake were gathered about her. There were eleven including herself, though two did not look well. There was a middle-aged man whose leg was broken and another passenger, unconscious, with bloodstained cloth wrapped around her head.

Upon noticing Elaeni rise, a short bald crewman with a bristly black beard brought a small turtle shell to her. It was full of a cloudy liquid. "Here, miss," he said, "the locals put this aside for you."

"What is it?" she asked as he held it to her face.

"Couldn't tell you for sure," he shrugged, "but I think it's meant to be good for you. We've all had some and lived to tell the tale. It's a little strange, but drinkable. It'll at least wash the taste of the sea out of your mouth."

She sniffed at the liquid, which had an oddly grainy smell to it, almost woody. It had a strange savoury taste, though she struggled to liken it to anything she might normally eat or drink. Either way, it was refreshing.

She took the shell and rose to her feet, making her way to the first mate. He stood on a cliff overlooking the beach far below, where locals were still frantically retrieving what they could of the ship. From their high vantage point, it was easier to see how unsafe this place was for ships, for the black rock could be seen just below the surface of the water for what seemed a mile in every direction.

"How do you feel?" the first mate asked, pulling his long, damp brown hair from his face as the wind flapped his empty scabbard, still hanging purposelessly from his belt. His grey eyes looked her up and down as she imagined he would examine an injured sailor.

"Too early to say," she said, clutching her pained abdomen. "What do you think of our hosts?"

"Too early to say," he huffed. "Friendly enough, so far. Delmur seemed to understand their tongue to some degree. He says the language they speak is Old Kestrian, from the actual empire era. He's the only one of us able to talk to them, and even then, he struggles."

"Which one's Delmur?" she asked as she gently rubbed her bruised stomach and tried to focus her foggy mind.

"The one with the broken leg."

"Imperial Kestrian?" she contemplated, looking to the injured man with dark blond hair turning grey. "Maybe they fled the fall of the empire in its final days."

"And ended up wrecked here," the first mate said. "Their leader wears a golden wreath, so it seems likely the case. But that means they've been here for centuries, trapped on this ship-rending nightmare of an island for many generations."

"Centuries?" she pondered as she looked back around. None of the locals seemed to be about; instead they were all down on the beach some considerable distance below.

"Enough time for everyone to become related," he grimaced with distaste, giving his otherwise flat face a little more depth. "Closely related, by the look of it."

"How many are there?"

"I don't know that I've seen them all, but about fifty, maybe sixty, including children. All with the same black hair, save for the old ones who've greyed, but the same small, wide-set dark eyes, that same curve in their nose."

"You knew my name," Elaeni recalled. "On the beach."

"Of course," he said. "I'm first mate, we run…ran a tight ship. It's my job to know the passengers' names. Elaeni," he said, pointing to her before turning his finger to the middle-aged man with the broken leg, "Delmur." He pointed to the slender red haired woman lying unconscious with a bandaged head, "Felina." Next, he pointed to a handsome man about his own age whose finer clothes exposed cuts and abrasions through tears but seemed otherwise unharmed, "And Edwuld Darrow. There were two more who made it ashore, along with several of the crew, but they did not make it further than that."

"I'm sorry. But what is your name?"

"Renald. First mate Renald."

"And the Captain?" she asked, but Renald shook his head despondently. "So, that makes you captain, I guess."

"Captain of what?" he asked, pointing to the fragments of the Saltdrake being dragged to shore. "Without a ship, I suppose I'm not even First Mate. So, it's probably just Renald."

"Well, just Renald, what do you make of our chances of getting off this island?"

"This island, these islands, and the rocks around them, are known as the Black Spire Isles. Sailors avoid going anywhere near them, being somewhat famed for wrecking ships. Just sailing close has been enough to damage and sink ships in the past. The way the rocks are, it must have taken a rare and considerable effort to get so close to the actual central island the way we did."

"It was a vicious storm," she recalled.

"Escape would require a seaworthy vessel that'll prove challenging to build."

"What do you mean?"

"Look around you. There are no trees on this island," he said, prompting her to check. "Though I did see them rescue a few barrels. So maybe, if we're lucky, they were ones full of apples or oranges and we can plant the seeds and sit around for a dozen to twenty years waiting for them to grow."

Elaeni grimaced sardonically. "And the wreckage?"

"There is enough sail and wood, I've seen so far, to perhaps build something that would float and ride the wind. Something that could carry enough food and water for eleven people…maybe. There's still the matter of getting it out past all the jagged rocks, which we'd have to do holding it over our heads as we swam through them, well beyond the walkable seafloor. That's a long time to tread water, especially encumbered so. Then, if the sea doesn't immediately throw us back into the rocks, we'd have to pick between sailing to Nordmeer, Westmeer, or Ohtylos, which are all about the same distance away. A long way, in any direction, to sail in wet clothes at sea level."

Elaeni looked back out to the water where ropes were being used to tie the bow to the rocks to secure it, presumably until the sea calmed down. "Well, seafaring's not really my area of knowledge, I'm afraid," she admitted. "So, I suppose it's up to you and the crew to think of some way out of this place."

"What is your area?" he asked.

"Being a widow." She shrugged, not wishing to list skills that had no application here. "I'd better check on the others."

Elaeni did not see the locals up close until they invited the survivors of the Saltdrake to join them for dinner. Though they ranged in age from infant to elderly, they did all look like siblings as Renald had observed. They sat in the grass, gathered around a wide fire that Elaeni stared at, wondering what exactly was fuelling it.

"A combination of moss, roots, grass, and other low things that grow, dried out and pressed together," Delmur informed her in her native Nordmeerian tongue. "The things people think of when forced to operate without the usual resources we take for granted, aye?"

"Indeed," she agreed. "How's the leg?"

"Still broken, lots of pain, but not as much as there should be thanks to our hosts," he said. "They gave me this oil, you see. A few drops on the tongue, a few drops on the leg. Hurt like death when they rubbed it in, but then it went all numb for a while, and now it hurts but not as much as I know it should. Or I don't care as much as I should. Hard to say. I've been in a bit of a daze for most of the afternoon, to be honest."

"I still feel a little dazed myself," Elaeni said. "I hear you understand our hosts' language."

"Oh, well, yes. Not exactly having a great time of it, but our landing here is a bit of a mixed blessing for me," he admitted. "A rare opportunity, as I'm researching the rise and fall of the Kestrian Empire, you see. That's why I was in Angvjaald. Looking for accounts of the departure of Sten to invade the continent, founding house Stenbrok, and the kingdom of Hjaanmar when his forces attacked the heart of the empire."

"I've yet to speak to any of them myself," she said. "I do speak new, or current, Kestrian, having lived in Umberdale for the last few years. Just how different is it?"

"Well, the basic building blocks are there, you see. It's just that New Kestrian has been seasoned by the old Nordmeerian of Westmeer, the Sond of Sondaal, the Angvjaaldi of the Hjaanmarians, the Ohtylosian of West Edenvaal, and possibly even a little peppered by the Elvish of East Edenvaal. Then this lot, you see, well, they haven't exactly stuck to the letter, themselves. Or, quite possibly, the way I've seen it written isn't meant to sound the way it has in my head. But if you speak New Kestrian, I think you could learn their language over some months. Edwuld in far less time I should think, being from Umberdale, and presumably of the faith of the Order of Light. Much of their holy texts are written in Old Kestrian. Being a noble he no doubt reads, so his capacity for learning will be better than most. Between my study of the old and his natural ear for the new we should hopefully get a grip on it all by the time I can walk again."

"Unless we find a way off this place first," Elaeni said hopefully.

"Well, I won't be leaving in this state. So, either everyone waits till my leg mends or you all leave me behind. So, either way, I must learn the language, you see."

A small group of the islanders brought large turtle shells full of fish and root vegetables served on a bed of what looked like vine leaves. They said words together with their eyes closed like a prayer before handing the food over.

"Thank you," Elaeni said slowly in modern Kestrian. The locals seemed to glean her meaning from her manner, and gave her a smile and a nod. "Well, it smells amazing." She looked to Delmur, who hesitated a moment before shrugging and digging in. "Oh, this is beautiful," she said, halfway through her portion.

"Yes…" Delmur agreed, looking around at the rest of their group enjoying the food as the sun slipped away.

"What is it?" she asked the injured man, who seemed distracted.

"Oh, just wondering how long it will take everyone to figure out."

"Figure out what?" she asked, chewing on the soft fish flesh.

"This fish was milk-poached."

"Yes," she hummed, delighted. "My husband and I were fond of this style."

"But I don't recall seeing any cows," he said, sucking in his sunken cheeks. "Nor goats, nor sheep…"

"No," she said, looking around after taking another mouthful. "No trees, either. But, as you say, these people seem to make do. They found something other than wood to burn and they found…" Her chewing slowed. "Something else to…milk."

"Someone else," he said, with an apologetic grimace," I should think."

Elaeni stopped chewing, her mouth full of the deliciously milky, steamy fish, and breathed heavily through her nose as she made the realisation. Now she also looked at the other survivors, wondering if they had put any thought into how their meal came about.

"Oh well," Delmur said, "when in Kestrus…" and took another mouthful with a shrug.

Elaeni slowly began to move her jaw again. She couldn't leave the fish in her mouth forever. She swallowed awkwardly.

"Look, if it's good enough for infants, it's good enough for us. We drank it when we were small," he reasoned. "And it makes more sense than drinking milk from a four-legged horned beast if you really think about it."

She nodded slowly and continued, too hungry not to.

"Though, the real question is how they have so much spare to poach what must be at least twenty fish," he pondered aloud. "Wouldn't the children be demanding such a resource?"

"One mystery at a time," she suggested, hoping to finish her otherwise enjoyable meal, evading any further revelations.

"Maybe it's a religious thing," he suggested. "They did give thanks to the 'great mother', probably referring to Aetheya, you see. Perhaps it's symbolic to them."

She casually watched the others, mostly crewmen from the ship, as one of them helped feed Felina, the injured woman. She was barely conscious but seemed to be enjoying the food.

"Wait, where's Renald and the other passenger?" she asked as she noticed their absence.

"The Empress wanted to dine with them."

"Empress?"

"Their leader," he said, acknowledging the absurdity of the title. "An empire of fifty-something islanders."

"Why them?"

"She had someone ask me who was the most important person amongst us," he explained, "They were looking for our leader, you see. I explained that Renald was essentially the captain, and therefore in charge of our expedition, but also that Edwuld was the only nobility amongst us, having a surname and serving the Lord of Fleetwatch. And so, she decided to dine with them both."

"Without you there to translate?"

"Just a matter of imperial courtesy, I suppose," he offered. "But, yes, I imagine an awkward evening of polite nods and smiles."

Elaeni grinned, amused by the thought of it.

"Over their breast-milk fish," he added, and the pair began laughing.

Elaeni grabbed her abdomen as pain reminded her of her own injury.

"So, what dragged a young woman from Nordmeer to Umberdale in the first place?"

"My husband." she said, her smile fading. "I was returning home because he died. He left me enough coin to live on for quite some time, but now it's at the bottom of the sea along with everything I ever owned and everything that reminded me of him. Well, almost everything," she said holding up her hand to show the silver ring on her finger. "My whole life, at least what was left of it, was on that ship."

"I am so sorry to hear that," he said. "I know it's not the same, but years of my work are all down there too, keeping it company. We'd have both been far better off if we stayed where we were."

"I think that goes for everyone," she said.

"Except the ancestors of the folk who live here now."

After dinner they were taken into huts where room had been made for them. Elaeni was given a small one to share with Felina. The injured woman from Angvjaald did not sleep soundly for someone who'd barely flirted with consciousness since arriving on the island.

By morning they were woken by the locals who brought them milk in a clay pot with two small turtle shells out of which to serve themselves. Elaeni tried to politely decline, but the two women who brought it seemed quite insistent. One of them stayed to watch them drink and served Felina, still too dazed to feed herself, though she showed more coherency than the previous day.

Drinking the milk, Elaeni realised it had not only been in the fish, but also the draught they were served the previous day. It was only now that they seemed to be getting it in its pure form, as if being weaned onto it. But as she was reunited with the rest, she realised it was only the injured that had been brought the pure milk. She wondered if they attributed some health benefit to it, while at the same time feeling herself somewhat invigorated by the drink. She found it thicker and sweeter than cow's milk, while tasting oddly wholesome.

"I could swear I tasted almond and vanilla in there," Delmur later observed. "I might wonder if they mix it in, were it not for the lack of orchids and trees on which to grow such things."

"If I didn't know what I was drinking, I might actually enjoy it," Elaeni said, as she sat down beside the injured man. "Though I suppose as long as they don't make us drink it from the source, I might be able to make myself forget in time."

"A prospect that disgusts you more than me," he cheekily admitted.

Elaeni shook her head and smiled as First Mate Renald approached them.

"How are you two faring?" he asked them.

"Quite well. Aside from the leg," Delmur said. "How was your imperial dinner?"

"Conversation didn't stretch far beyond learning each other's names. There were five of us and I was the only one without a surname," Renald said.

"Five?" Delmur asked.

"Yes, the Empress Octuria Verseidon, and her small council of two, Errius Duvandt and Vitius Vereno."

"Oh, that is most intriguing. I wish I had my books with me." The injured middle-aged man seemed quite excited. "Those are some very historically significant names that you just dined with. Verseidon was the ruling house of the Kestrian empire from their first emperor, Etyus, till their last, Hexavius. Some sources say he had a young daughter, you see, but I could never find out what happened to her. Most interesting."

"Isn't there a town called Duvandt back in Nordmeer?" Elaeni asked her well-read countryman.

"As there is also a Castle Duvandt in Westmeer," he informed her. "The two are connected, you see. House Duvandt's history is a little vague to me, as they fought for the empire but also swore fealty to the kings of Westmeer after the empire fell. I suppose some of them joined the emperor's daughter on a ship that must have crashed here. As for the Verenos, I recall there being a General Septus Voreno, but I can say little more about either house without my books, you see."

Renald's eyes moved about under furrowed brows as he lost himself in thought, reviewing the previous evening in a new context. "She really is an empress, then," he said.

"To what's left of her empire," Delmur added. "At least, having conquered these islands."

Elaeni instinctively put her hand over her stomach as she chuckled but found it did not hurt. She prodded and pressed her hand into her upper abdomen and felt little discomfort. "Delmur, you should think about teaching us all what Old Kestrian you know," she suggested.

"My dear, I'd be delighted," Delmur said enthusiastically.

"We're probably going to be here a while," Elaeni said, standing up. "It would be nice if we could all understand one another."

"Where are you going?" Renald asked.

"I need to walk around," Elaeni said.

"I should join you," Renald suggested. "I don't want anyone wandering off on their own."

"Do a little walking for me too," Delmur said, trapped on the ground with his broken leg tied to a splint.

"I won't be gone long, but I want to start learning my surroundings," Elaeni said, smiling at the injured man.

Renald followed Elaeni as she wandered the black cliffs that elevated the inhabitable land of the central island from the surrounding beach below. The north island came into view, a great black rocky hill emerging from the sand, speckled with lichen and vines. It lacked the great grassy plateau of the main island. Gulls were gathered on the eastern beach, picking away at dark slippery chunks scattered in the wet sand in a trail leading to what looked like a cave mouth.

"What do you suppose they're eating?" Elaeni wondered aloud.

"Probably bits of fish that smashed upon the rocks during the storm," Renald suggested. "It reminds me of when fishermen toss the innards of gutted fish."

"The storm was yesterday. I wouldn't have thought the birds would leave anything behind."

"Perhaps they only washed up on to the shore this morning," he speculated, "or maybe the night tides bring whole fish in so hard and violently through the rocks it beaches them in pieces."

"It's almost as if this place was created purely for stranding things."

"If fish can't navigate safely about it, there's little hope for anyone else."

"But have you thought of anything?" she asked with reluctant hope.

"I've considered a few possibilities, but the only realistic one is if I make a small boat and some oars with a small sail."

"A rowboat big enough for eleven?"

"A boat big enough for two at best," he said with an almost apologetic sternness. "The crew could hopefully swim it out safely past the rocks, where it could make east for Nordmeer, convince a ship to sail back this way, and anchor some safe distance away to slowly ferry people in a rowboat over several trips if they swim out to us."

"Didn't you say something about ships avoiding this area?"

"They all give it a wide berth, yes." He sighed. "Convincing someone to bring their ship this way will be the hardest part of the task. Meaning no offense, but there are not enough of us worth rescuing. Any captain worth his salt would have to weigh the value of his ship against his countrymen expecting liberation. A scholar whose studies lay in the sea, a coinless widow, and a handful of crewmen, the likes of which could be mustered from far less perilous places."

"That's a harsh assessment."

"These are not my thoughts on the matter, merely a reflection of how any captain out there is likely to appraise the venture," he explained.

"What of the others?"

"Edwuld serves a lord of Umberdale who might be willing to send a ship for him, but I'm not rowing three times the distance to Umberdale to find out. As for an Angvjaalder last seen bleeding from the head…?"

"So in the end, the boat built for two would only really serve to rescue the two who leave in it," she cynically summarised.

"That's not the intention, but it could very well end up the outcome."

She shook her head. "Then it sounds like we need a better plan."

"A better plan might be to build four, maybe five boats, with a Saltdrake crewman on each, only to drift apart when those accustomed to softer living fatigue during their turn to row, scattering us all to the wind," he said, taking the derision personally. "Not that we're likely to have enough material to build this small, doomed fleet."

"And I suppose you would be amongst the two who would take this small boat out."

"You're welcome to take my place if you think you've got as much row in you or sway with other captains."

Elaeni smiled, embarrassed by her own suspicion.

"It's only an idea so far," he said, stopping to place his hand gently on her shoulder. "And, trust me, being on a small, makeshift boat on the open sea is not for the faint of heart. Even in good weather we'd be lucky to make it, and the only food I've seen here is not stuff that keeps well over time. Even if we made it, even if I convince someone, I'd still need to pay them, which means I'd need to earn the coin. For I, too, was rendered coinless by the sea. We'd be gone for months and the rest of you would never know if we even survived the trip or not."

"So in the end, it would just be two fewer mouths to feed for the locals and a tiny thread of hope for the stranded."

"And, truth be told, a probable death sentence for those on the boat," he said, turning back towards the sea. "The best we could hope for is to run into a ship within a day or so."

"What are the chances of that? Nordmeer has a lot of trade routes by sea."

"None that would cross our path. Even other trade ships wouldn't really pass Nordmeer without docking there. It is, after all, a powerhouse of trade by sea. At best, a naval patrol ship might cross our path shaving a day or two, a week at best, off our voyage," he said, gazing past the north island, studying the sea. "This place really needs a tower. The high ground helps, but I can't tell from here how far out the rocky spires beneath the water go. If we build a boat, we should do it on the north island, I think." He turned back, hearing the locals call out something indecipherable.

When she looked back they were gesturing them over and miming the act of eating.

"Oh, sounds like lunch is ready," he said, turning to her. "Eating poached fish for the rest of your life isn't the worst fate the gods could have dreamt up."

"No, I'd like to think they ran out of terrible fate ideas after my husband died, the sea swallowed everything I own, and then violently threw me onto an inescapable remote island surrounded by ship-destroying jagged, rocky spears."

"I'm sorry for all the things that have happened to you," he said, as they walked back together, "but I wouldn't talk like that around the crew. They're a suspicious lot. You might just convince them that you upset the gods somehow and got us all thrown here as part of some curse."

"I'm not completely convinced that isn't the actual state of things," she huffed.

A few days passed, and they stopped bringing the pure milk to Elaeni. Now it was brought only to Delmur and Felina, who continued to mumble in her sleep as if in conversation, while being quite docile in her rare moments of vague consciousness.

The local people were accommodating hosts and did not assign tasks to the stranded, giving everyone time to learn what ancient

Kestrian they could from Delmur, who translated their hospitality as being in thanks for bringing "tree-flesh" and "something to do with gardening" to their island.

Some of the locals began to sit in on these language sessions to interact and assist, confirming their own pronunciations with Delmur's, both compromising their versions of what they knew in order to understand each other a little better.

Renald, a ship hand Eramir, and the other crewmen, began salvaging what wood they could, as the locals used the larger fragments of ship to build shelter for their stranded guests. They seemed to assume all were staying but allowed the pair to tax what materials they could.

By the end of the first week Delmur was mobile again. He had a painful limp and couldn't get far without assistance from another, but Renald looked upon his progress with suspicion.

"That's not natural," the first mate observed. "I've known men to take months to heal from such a wound. Young, fit men, that is, not men halfway to a hundred like that dusty bookworm."

"Maybe it's the milk," Elaeni suggested, rubbing her hand over her abdomen as she followed him to the place where he worked on his boat with the crewmen. "They stopped giving it to me once I felt better."

"What milk?" he asked confused.

"The milk they use to poach the fish. The milk they use to make the draught. The milk they still feed Delmur and Felina each morning. Did you not notice?"

"I didn't even know you could poach fish in milk. I was wondering how they cooked it."

"And so, we come to the question Delmur and I asked the first night here," she said with an expectant grimace.

Renald did not get there as fast. He furrowed his brows, huffed through a frown, and looked about with his hands on his hips a few moments before straightening his neck. "What do they milk?"

Elaeni gave him a congratulatory pat on the shoulder and smiled.

"Walruses? Seals perhaps?" he bargained, avoiding the inevitable conclusion, though the creativity of his guesses shamed Elaeni for not thinking of them that first night herself. Curiosity washed across his face, instead of the disgust she had expected and gleefully anticipated. He looked to the north island again, his eyes darting about, juggling information she clearly didn't have.

"What is it?"

"Each morning the lads and I watch…noticed," he corrected, "a group of the local women wade to the north island upon a shallow path that winds between the black spires. They take large pots during the low tide of early morning. They walk around the east side and, I think, into a cave. The pots have lids, so I've not seen what's inside when they return. I thought perhaps they gathered cave moss or lichen but, for the increased weight, a fluid would make more sense."

Elaeni smiled cynically. "What do you mean watch them?"

Renald gave the embarrassed grin of a mischievous young boy. "Well, the thing is, it seems they don't want to walk about in wet clothes for the rest of the day so…"

"They cross naked?"

He nodded slowly and bit his lip a little shamefully as a couple of the crewmen within earshot turned their faces away from her.

"So, you and your dirty sea dogs watch these women disrobe and wade through water for your pleasure and amusement?" she asked, scandalised. "From your safe vantage point up here, spying on them."

"No spying about it. They usually wave back to us," he said, giving a little demonstrative wave.

Elaeni shook her head, lost for words.

"But if you've finished judging men who don't see women often, especially like that, for not averting their eyes, I think you'll find a much bigger concern has presented itself."

"What cave-dwelling beast produces milk?" she asked, stepping past him towards the north-facing cliff.

"Perhaps a ship transporting cattle was wrecked here?" he offered, "But then why are they in a cave?"

"It is not cow's milk."

"Of that, you're certain?" he asked. "When did you come to that decision?"

"First night," she admitted.

"So, what did you think it was?"

"Well, we presumed it came from some of the women," she said through her teeth, as his face twisted between disgust and amusement.

He pointed at her. "Oh, I see. So, we're a bunch of dirty sea dogs for looking at naked untamed women's breasts, while you've been happily quaffing pints of what you were certain was milk from them."

"Alright," she said, covering his accusatory finger with her hand, pushing it down. "I think the oil was for the pain and the milk has some…property to it."

"Something that unbreaks a man's leg in a week?"

"Perhaps?"

"I've heard of no beast whose sucklings enjoy such benefits." He looked to the north island again, as the crewmen with him rethreaded salvaged rope by hand. "I'll send someone to have a look before nightfall. Though a morning sun would light the way better, I don't want to upset the locals."

"They've imposed no restrictions so far," Elaeni pointed out. "Maybe your naked milk maids would even enjoy the company."

"If they do, it'll slow down work on the boat," Renald said quietly.

"Though, maybe we should wait till we can properly understand each other. When we learn more of their language, perhaps they'll just tell us what's in there."

"You think they would?"

"As far as they'd be concerned, we live here now. From what Delmur's been able to learn, we're not the first people to crash here since their imperial ancestors first arrived."

"And what happened to those who crashed here?"

"They settled here. You're looking at their great, great, great, grandchildren or beyond," she explained. "Delmur seems to think, with their limited breeding stock, they'd have been glad of the new blood."

Renald's brow tightened as he pondered something. "Gods, that's why the empress had Edwuld and I join her for dinner."

"The empress is looking for a husband," Elaeni said, with a devious smile, as she playfully slapped his shoulder. "Someone to father a little island emperor."

"Don't know why you're looking at me. Edwuld's the one we don't see much of anymore. I assumed it was because they understood each other a little better, well, slightly more than not at all. But there you have it."

"So, either way, less reason for them to keep secrets from us," she suggested. "So maybe rather than wandering about without warning, let's get to know our hosts a little better to learn what we can from them."

Renald nodded. "I suppose it makes little difference to the task at hand."

When Elaeni returned to the settlement, Felina was walking about freely. Her long red hair flowed in the wind as she moved about with a rare grace and elegance of posture, with high cheekbones and plump lips on her long angular face. She recognised Elaeni and approached her, smiling peacefully with her hands out. "Elaeni," she said and took her hands in her own. "I've only seen you in fleeting moments, but it's good to finally meet you."

"You speak my language?" Elaeni asked, surprised at hearing her own Nordmeerian tongue. "I thought you only spoke-"

"I do not speak your language. This is merely a spell at work."

"You know magic?"

"I am a sorceress, studying under the wizard Kai Vjorgan. I was sent to Nordmeer as part of my final trial. When I returned, I would have been able to call myself Tor Felina. So yes, I know magic".

"How is your head?"

"Much better. It's kind of you to ask, but this spell does not last forever, so we need to be mindful of what we choose to talk about."

"So, what do you wish to talk about?" Elaeni asked, complying with the constraints.

"How much do you know of magic and those that use it?"

"Not a great deal, why?"

"Know you of Nihrius?"

"Is that a place?"

"Sort of. Most uninitiated call it the void, though the term is thousands of years out of date. It is a place where sorcerers and warlocks visit when we sleep. A reflection of this word shaped by the dreams of those touched by magic. When our bodies rest we can travel into it, and sometimes we meet others of our kind there as well."

"That's quite fascinating, but why are you telling me this? I don't understand."

"While my body rested from my wound, I have explored these islands from the other side. In Nihrius, the void."

"And...?"

"There is a…woman who wants to meet us in person," the recently recovered sorceress said.

"Us?"

"She asked to meet the women who survived the wreck."

"And where is this woman?"

"She dwells within the north island."

Elaeni took a step back with a cynically nervous smile.

"What's wrong?" Felina asked.

Elaeni found it odd that she was being invited to the north island so soon after discussing it with Renald. Had this elusive figure used her magic to gain some special insight or was it mere coincidence? Either way, she realised she couldn't share any suspicions with a woman who had spent more time unconsciously speaking to this stranger than consciously with her fellow survivors. "Nothing," she said, shaking her head. "When do we go?"

"She said we're to follow some of the island women in the morning but wait till they've done their gathering before entering the cave."

Elaeni winced as she imagined the crewmen standing on the edge of the cliff, watching her cross the black-spired lagoon naked.

Over dinner that evening, Elaeni made a point of suggesting Renald and his crew find elsewhere to work on their vessel. She provided little explanation beyond an opportunity to unlock the mystery of the north island.

At dawn, Elaeni found herself looking over her shoulder, back towards the cliffs above, as the milk maids began to disrobe on the beach. Felina, conserving her magic, did nothing to dissolve the existing language barrier between the pair that morning. The sorceress tied her red hair into a knot to keep it dry after allowing her dress to slide off her long, slender, freckled body. Elaeni, confident her own shoulder-length black hair would remain dry, simply pulled her dress and shift over her head, and began to roll them tightly into a small bundle she could carry above the water. She didn't feel that civilisation was so lost to her that she was ready to explore a strange cave and meet some mysterious woman without being covered in garments. However, she did feel slightly liberated standing on a beach naked, as a late summer breeze brushed her bare skin. There was nowhere she'd ever lived where she could imagine doing this. It made her feel like she was part of a group of wildfolk women bathing in some river or lake.

The soft sand pushed between her toes as she waded in. The water was cool but she wondered how the milk maids managed carrying their ceramic jugs and pots across this water in winter. It seemed likely she'd be here long enough to find out.

As they emerged from the water, the local women continued into the cave while Felina and Elaeni brushed and danced the excess water off before eventually redressing. Elaeni couldn't help but look again to the northern cliffs of the large central island, but Renald had done as requested and was nowhere to be seen.

When the other women returned, it was time for the two stranded women to enter the cave around the east side of the island. The dark rock climbed high above the beach and the morning sun lit the mouth of the cave from behind them, sending their long shadows in to scout ahead.

A heavy breathing echoed deep within the dark rock; something large dwelled inside, by the sound of it. As they passed the first chamber, beyond the sun's reach, the way ahead was lit in pockets of blue light, as long fungal spores grew with luminescent bulbs in corners of the cavern while shafts of daylight shone from above through occasional cracks in the rocky ceiling.

Something heavy dragged through the sand and against the rocks, out of sight. Elaeni was sure she saw something move in the dark corners and around the edges as batches of the glowing plants began to appear, uncovered by something shifting out of their way. The noise was all around them at first but slowly receded to some spot ahead until only feet in the damp sand could be heard. A woman in white-layered garments stepped out of the darkness into a shard of light that illuminated her long, straight, white hair and made it glow.

"Welcome to my home," she said, with her arms outstretched to beckon them forward. "Felina, I recognise. It is good to finally meet you in person."

"And you," Felina smiled.

"And you must be Elaeni."

"I am," Elaeni said, realising she was not quite speaking her native tongue, nor Kestrian, yet understanding everything. "What language am I speaking?"

"This is the language of Ancaraug," the white-haired woman said. "Not too dissimilar to your Nordmeerian, for it was settlers from your homeland who came to mine. But I have put a spell about us so that we may all understand each other as I told Felina I would."

"How strange," Elaeni smiled as she marvelled at the foreign words coming out of her mouth.

"It is for your benefit, for I speak all languages," the mysterious woman declared. "My name is Aekestyr and I have lived in this place so very long."

"Were you also wrecked upon these shores?" Elaeni asked. "You do not look like the others who live here."

"I was here long before the ones who call me Great Mother arrived, leaving their empire as it collapsed behind them."

"Great Mother? Delmur says that's who they give thanks to before each meal," Elaeni said. "He assumed they meant Aetheya, but it's you. They worship you."

"Aetheya?" Aekestyr said nostalgically. "I've not heard any of the first gods named in a long time. I often wondered if my father made me with their blessing," she said, seemingly to herself. "But yes, they worship me. For it is I who guides fish to their nets when the sea is not feeling generous, it is I who strengthens them against the cold of winter when it comes, and it is I who now asks you to breathe new life into my children."

"What do you mean?" Felina asked.

"The last emperor of the Kestrian Empire sent his daughter with his general and a handful of trusted men who brought their wives and children," Aekestyr said. "They took a small ship that tore upon the rocks when they found these islands and they settled here, welcomed nowhere else in the lands around the Middle Sea. That was eight centuries ago. At first it was easy. Three noble houses and a handful of imperial officers. Good stock to preserve an empire, all but wiped out. But as time went on and families were joined again and again, too few options were afforded later generations. But the sea provided a ship of new blood before their seed corrupted. Then again and again, each time barely in time. My children have need of you. Their empress has already chosen one of the men among you, but there are two men of noble birth of similar age to you who've yet to take wives, and more than enough women who would gladly take the rest of the men amongst you."

"You're asking us to stay and…breed with the people here?" Elaeni asked.

"You haven't been here long, so I know escape will still be fresh in your hearts, but you will not find a way home and no rescue will ever come," Aekestyr said with a sympathetic look on her pale face. "The sooner you embrace a life here the easier it will be for you."

"No one has ever left in all this time?" Felina asked.

"None. From each wreck some have tried, but in the end they saw the fruitlessness of their efforts. They settled and grew content, even happy," Aekestyr replied.

"I was on the verge of becoming Tor Felina," the sorceress said. "That's a hard thing to turn my back on."

"What would you have done with that title?" the white-haired woman asked. "Become advisor on the council to the jarl of some city? You can be the arcane advisor to an empress here."

"I suppose," Felina reluctantly agreed. "Though I'd have no library to consult."

"You need no library, you have me," Aekestyr said, taking her hand, "There would be few questions you could possibly have about the arcane arts that I could not answer. In fact, there would be few questions on most topics that I could not answer, for I have lived such a long time and I saw much before I came here. Even here I have seen beyond the sea that surrounds us. There is so much I can teach you."

Felina looked enamoured by the promise, as if she knew every word was true. The pair turned to Elaeni.

"And what of you?" Aekestyr asked. "What calling are you hoping to return to?"

"There is nothing waiting for me. Just my homeland," Elaeni said, slowly pacing through the cool, damp sand. "Without my husband there was little reason to stay in Umberdale, and now with everything I own at the bottom of the sea, I'd have little choice but to return to my parents' home."

"Then why not make a life here?" Aekestyr asked. "You still mourn for your husband, I understand, but no one is pushing you to move on so fast. Take what time you need, but do you truly mean to be alone forever?" The white-haired woman gently grasped her arm, sliding her hand down to take Elaeni's. "Grieve for as long as you must. But you can be loved again, be whole again, have children, and know that no one will harm them here."

Elaeni tilted her head as mild suspicion grew in the back of her mind, "How do you know someone did harm to him?"

"When you're as old as I am you become a scholar of grief," Aekestyr said, as she pulled both women's hands to her heart. "Every tear tells a tale. I know not the details, but I sense a vengeance that failed to fill emptiness."

Elaeni remembered watching the brigands hang at the front of the crowd, looking them all in the eye before, during, and after the life was choked out of them.

"Join us. Plant your hearts here and we can be as sisters," Aekestyr said, looking to Felina. "My sister in magic," she turned to Elaeni, "and my sister by heritage. My ancestors on my mother's side were from Nordmeer." She smiled at them both with hopefulness in her eyes.

"We have many questions," Elaeni said.

"And a lifetime in which to ask them. But for now, I grow tired. Come see me again soon now that you know the way. Later in the day, so I can talk longer." She released their hands.

"Very well," Elaeni agreed, with a polite smile. Still seeking answers, the invitation to return appealed to her, while the proposed time in which to do it did not.

"Yes, of course we will," Felina added.

"It was a great pleasure to meet you both," Aekestyr said, backing away from the light and fading out of sight, somehow allowing her pale skin, her white hair, and bright flowing layers to be consumed by the shadows as she retreated into the darkness.

It wasn't until Felina and Elaeni settled in to sleep for the night that Felina used her magic to enable the pair to understand one another again. "There is much to discuss," Felina said, sitting up and taking Elaeni's hand.

"Why does everyone keep grabbing my hand?" Elaeni asked.

Felina smiled, "Aekestyr was being affectionate. I am being opportunistic."

"How, exactly?" Ealaeni asked, concerned.

"People who use magic have a pool of energy from which they draw upon to cast what spells they know. The more you learn, the larger the pool. When we sleep the pool refills, but if the pool is full or nearly full when we go to sleep, it's a waste of potential. Enchanting, as you may call it, is how we remedy that. Pouring our unused magic into a wand, a staff, a sword, an amulet, a ring," she said, holding up Elaeni's hand, which bore the silver wedding band.

"What are you doing to it?"

"I'm going to put my left-over magic into it each night and keep doing so until there's enough magic to sustain the spell I'll put into it."

"What manner of spell?"

"The one I'm using now, letting us understand each other, seems a practical choice," Felina said. "Most are slowly picking up bits and pieces, but if there was someone who could understand everyone more of the time, here and there, for a while at a time, I think it would be helpful."

"But why me?"

"Because you have a silver ring. Precious metals make good vessels for magic. I had a necklace that I put the same spell into. It worked quite well, allowing me to use this spell without drawing from my own pool, until it ended up somewhere out there in the greatest pool of them all," Felina said, pointing in the vague direction of their wreck and out to sea.

"I have a few necklaces and pendants down there myself, probably being worn by some crab."

The pair laughed.

"Well, it's your ring so you get the job of translator," Felina told her. "Well, at least eventually. This will take months." She closed her eyes and mumbled to herself a moment.

Elaeni felt a strange warmth about the ring for a fleeting moment.

"So, while we can understand each other," Elaeni said, "what did you make of Aekestyr?"

"She seemed sincere," Felina said with a shrug, "but there's more to her. I felt her power. Whatever she truly is, she has a pool far deeper than mine. Though, I think she had us leave because she was struggling to appear the way she did."

"She said her mother was ancestrally from Nordmeer," Elaeni recalled.

"And lived in Ancaraug, the dragonlands."

"And that she's been on these islands longer than these imperial Kestrians. So, what, a thousand years or more?" Elaeni pondered. "How has she lived so long?"

"There are more young gods and demigods than I know the names of, but Aekestyr is not a name I have come across before. It sounds like the name of a dragon."

"You think she's a dragon?"

"No," Felina said, shaking her hand in the air dismissively. "Dragons are proud creatures. She would not have taken human form when her true stature would humble us so. She conceals her true shape for some other reason, even in Nihrius."

"And what of this plan to marry us off to the island nobles?" Elaeni asked. "Where does that sit with you?"

"You still grieve for your husband and I still desire to complete my training, but she put no real pressure on us. However, we are trapped here, and we seem to have a choice. Do we stay untouched in our sorrow and grow old alone, or do we admit that the life she offers is far from terrible? The men of which she speaks have made no attempt to coerce us, patiently allowing us time to decide."

"Maybe they should," Elaeni said. "I understand that these are unusual circumstances, but if I'm to move on from my husband, I would have the man intending to replace him at least desire me enough to approach me, rather than allow another to make a pitch about improving his stock as if we were cattle."

"We are the only women on the island who don't look like their mothers, sisters, cousins, or neighbours," Felina said. "I think we can assume the desire would be there."

Elaeni laughed. "Well I have dark straight hair, like the rest of them, but I suppose you're right. Though as a tall, pale, red-haired sorceress you're certainly the more exotic choice."

"You have green eyes," Felina said, releasing Elaeni's hand as her eyelids grew heavy. "At least they won't get us mixed up once we're wed," she slurred sleepily as she faded off.

Elaeni looked to her wedding band and lost herself to memory as she laid back. She hoped to dream of happy moments with her husband, but again her mind took her to the hanging. She resented that her grief seemed to commandeer every attempt to go back to him, and instead showing her those men in that grim act of justice.

The next morning Elaeni ate with Delmur, who seemed to be limping about with minimal assistance from others.

"What do you know of Ancaraug?" she asked.

"Little. Like most, I've never been, but oddly enough it did come up in my research," he said.

"In relation to the rise and fall of the empire?"

"Mostly in the fall," he said, breathing heavily through his nose in recollection as he chewed. "Sten Stenbrock, the first high king of Hjaanmar. Most thought he came from the frozen wastes, south of Angvjaald, you see. Though he did spend time there in his early adult life, I've found evidence that suggests he originated from Ancaraug, for he spoke the language that enabled him to tame and train a frostdrake he named Groek. It was on this creature's back that he rode into the northern parts of Angvjaald and inspired followers. For half a decade he led assaults on imperial outposts, before rallying an army to follow him across the sea to Greater Kestrus to topple the empire."

"He must have been quite a man."

"Yes. Accounts in Angvjaald tell of a man of impossible strength, who did not suffer the cold, first making himself known in little more than rags as he rode out of the frozen wastes on the back of the white-scaled beast, armed with only a dagger. He had long white hair and, some accounts say, two small white horns, high on his brow, that curved backward like those on frostdrakes and white dragons."

"And he brought down the empire."

"Well, he began their downfall. He took the heartland, and the surrounding kingdoms were inspired to overthrow their imperial masters. Overseas outposts were withdrawn from all the other kingdoms to restore their hold on the continent, but they were fought to extinction, you see. Why do you ask?"

"I met a…woman with long white hair who claimed to be from Ancaraug. Her name is Aekestyr," Elaeni told him.

"Oh? When was this?"

"Yesterday."

"Yesterday?" he asked, startled. "You met her here? I have not seen such a woman on this island."

Elaeni explained her meeting with the mysterious woman on the northern island. "But do not speak of this to others for now," she asked. "I intend to find out more. She did invite Felina and I to return."

"Then you must go back and learn more," Delmur agreed. "Learn all that you can."

It was a few days later when Elaeni and Felina returned to see Aekestyr again. As before, something quite large moved through the dark before the white-haired woman stepped into the beam of light that poured through the largest crack in the dark cave's ceiling.

"It is good to see you both again," she said, smiling warmly at them. "Felina tells me there has been some agricultural activity over the last few days."

"Yes, the barrels that were recovered from the ship," Elaeni confirmed. "One was full of grain, the other oranges.

"It will be interesting to see crops and trees grow on these islands," Aekestyr said.

"It will be many years before we could truly call them trees," Elaeni said with a shrug.

"Things worth waiting for always take time," the white-haired woman said, raising her nose as if sniffing something. "I seem to sense the faintest trace of magic about you, Elaeni. Nothing tangible, but something."

"I have been putting magic into her silver ring," Felina volunteered. "I intend to give it purpose."

"What sort of purpose?" Aekestyr asked.

"Translation," Felina answered.

"I see," Aekestyr said contemplatively. "A practical endeavour. Though, by the time you have enough magic in there to sustain the spell, Elaeni will have had sufficient time to just learn the old Kestrian tongue."

"I also need to learn Angvjaaldi if I'm to speak to Felina outside this cave," Elaeni said.

"If I might offer a more beneficial solution?" the white-haired figure said as she extended an open hand. "Leave the ring with me. One week. But you will not be able to visit me in that time. Not physically, nor in Nihrius." She looked to Felina. "But that is where I will find you when the ring is ready. I have a longer accumulation of knowledge from which to channel a far more powerful enchantment. When I am done with it, you will be able to speak, read, and write any language you come across. Not in increments of time, but as a constant, as long as you wear the ring."

"That's most kind of you," Felina said, turning to give Elaeni an encouraging nod.

Elaeni jostled the ring from her finger, loathe to part with it, and she held it to her heart a moment before stepping forward to place it in Aekestyr's awaiting pale palm. The white-haired woman sealed it in her fist. "I will keep it safe," she assured Elaeni, who nodded and stepped back.

"There is a question on your mind," Aekestyr observed of Elaeni.

"Well, a curiosity," Elaeni admitted.

"Go on, then," Aekestyr said.

"I was talking to Delmur about the fall of the Kestrian empire," Elaeni continued. "He told me of a man, Sten Stenbrock, who he believes came from Ancaraug. A powerful man who was unaffected by the cold of the frozen wastes of Angvjaald and rode a frostdrake into battle. He said that he had white hair like yours."

"We are related," Aekestyr admitted, "though he died just over seven centuries ago. His great, great, grandfather and my father were one in the same. He was one sixteenth of what I am one half. He'd have died of old age, around a hundred-and-twenty years, while I have endured for twenty of his lifetimes so far. And while he was no progeny or descendant of mine, he would not have existed had I not come first. Stenyksil was his name by birth and his bloodline rules Hjanmaar to this very day. That is why I feel responsible for those who are stranded here. Their empire ended at the hands of my own blood."

"You know of these things, but did they not all happen while you were here?" Felina asked.

"They did," Aekestyr continued. "There have been few here who came to talk to me in the time I have spent here, leaving me free to explore the lands about the Middle Sea in my sleep, through Nihrius. There, sorcerers and warlocks sleep also, and project themselves into the realm where I have spoken to them and been kept abreast of the outside world."

"You can contact people across the sea?" Elaeni asked.

"Those touched by magic only," Aekestyr said.

"But you could send for a ship," Elaeni said.

"From where? Have you forgotten who I harbour here? The last descendants of an empire wiped out. An empire who conquered kingdoms all about the Middle Sea. Who would come to their rescue and who would house them?" Aekestyr asked. "If someone came to you and asked for a ship to rescue those who killed your husband, trapped on some island, what manner of rescue would you launch?"

Elaeni contemplated her words and understood her fear.

"Bringing a ship would either condemn my children to death or those aboard that ship to be stranded here with them. In a thousand years only two ships have wrecked here yielding survivors before yours. Ships have sunk after being wounded upon the black rocks when storms brought them close and those who survived rowed away in the lifeboats, taking their chances with the sea rather than risk coming here. All who come to sea avoid this place. No rescue will ever come. You need to understand that," Aekestyr concluded.

Elaeni slowly wandered about the cave as she took in what Aekestyr had said.

"The men you spoke of have not approached us," Felina said, changing the subject.

"As I said, they understand you have yet to let go of home. They will not pressure you," Aekestyr assured them, as Elaeni neared the cave wall, looking at the glowing spores growing in the corner. Her toes kicked a ridge of piled sand before the ground sank into a ditch. She felt a strange pattern carved into the sand as she prodded gently about with her bare feet in the dark. "Elaeni?" Aekestyr called after her.

"Sorry, I was miles away," Elaeni replied.

"Yes, you have much to think about," Aekestyr said. "Perhaps we should leave it there for today. The sooner I get started on your ring, the sooner we can see each other again."

"You are most fortunate," Felina said to Elaeni, as the two stood naked on the beach of the northern island, rolling up their dresses to cross the water again. "The spell she will cast upon your ring will be so much more powerful than the one I could have applied."

"You'll not have to conserve your magic, once I've the ring back. We'll be able to talk to anyone," Elaeni said, rubbing the place where the silver wedding band belonged. "Though there's nothing to read from nor write upon."

"So which surname do you think you'd rather have?" Felina asked. "Duvandt or Vereno?"

Elaeni rolled her eyes, resting her furled clothes on her head. "I've not really thought about it."

"I think Felina Vereno has a very musical sound to it, don't you think?"

"Sure."

"And Errius and Elaeni Duvandt has a nice ring to it."

Talking about how her name sounded next to that of a stranger's, in place of the man she'd lost, while wading between islands the rest of the word avoided, made her recall the men that she had watched hang. She loathed to think of them now, naked, at her most vulnerable. She had looked them in the eyes as they danced at the end of ropes because they had destroyed her life by taking him away. If only she'd known how much more she'd lose, she might have begged the local authorities for a far more drawn out execution.

Felina voiced the alternate name combinations and continued talking as Elaeni's mind went elsewhere, until Aekestyr's name came up. "She's so fascinating, don't you think?" Felina asked.

"It's strange talking to her. She tells me things that raise more questions, but I feel almost compelled not to ask more," Elaeni observed. "She seems to control just how much we learn each time."

Felina stopped as they reached the shore of the central island, her ankles still in the lapping water as she held her rolled clothes in front of her, waiting for the water to drip off her pale, freckled skin. "We have the rest of our lives to ask her questions," she reminded her, echoing Aekestyr's words. "You just have to remember them for next time."

"That's a week away."

"That's a week to ready your questions. By then, you'll have the ability to ask anyone anything you like."

"I don't know if I have many questions for the rest," Elaeni said, shrugging as she stepped from side to side to hasten the run-off.

Felina watched her little drying dance, amused as she stood still. "I think I enjoy this, you know. Being naked outside."

"Really?"

"Oh yes. Angvjaald doesn't really have a summer worthy of the name. Nor does it have hot springs like Ohtylos. Walking outside naked is something only done by those who feel they've had enough of living. I'm surprised these islanders went to the effort of making clothes at all. This is breathtaking, feeling the sea breeze on every part of my body at once. I feel so alive."

"You really just get into the spirit of things, don't you?" Elaeni cheerfully observed. "I can't help but admire it. But, to me, this feels weird. Especially knowing there are around sixty people getting about, who aren't all that far away."

"That should make it more exciting," Felina said, winking as she let her clothes unravel so she could put them on again.

"The pursuit of magic must just make you more adventurous, I suppose," Elaeni said, as she slid back into her garments with relief.

"I chose a far less adventurous path than most, when it comes to magic. More practical, safer magic. I've seen the odd fool set themselves on fire or cause themselves some other manner of harm."

"Though, magic fire would probably come in handy here, come winter. I can't imagine crossing between islands like this during the later months of the year."

"Well, we can probably build a bridge with all the trees that are getting planted," Felina suggested.

"Perhaps," Elanei said, as they began to climb the path leading up from the beach. "Though trees that bear fruit are far more valuable in one piece."

Elaeni parted from Felina's company to visit Renald, where she found him and only one crewman working on their boat.

"How goes the boat?" she asked him, as he sanded the edge of a piece of wood with an abrasive rock.

"Slowly," he said, with reserved resentment.

"Didn't you used to have more crewmen?" she asked jovially.

"I did. Five more to be precise," he said, as he stopped work and looked back at her. "Then someone suggested I move them away from the place where they could see the women who shamelessly abandoned their clothes every morning. A short daily distraction from their efforts, that gave them the morale boost they needed to toil ahead the rest of the day. Missing them, they sought them out to meet them. Now those women distract them all day, every day."

"But you're their captain. Don't you command them?"

"A grounded captain who took away their only vice," he said. "I've no coin to pay them, no wine to sway them, no ship to house them, and I don't feed them. So why should they work on a boat that doesn't have room for them?"

"They aren't crewmen no more," Eramir, the remaining ship hand, said. "They're just men what live on an island now."

Elaeni was unable to imagine an apology capable of reconciling the loss of his command for the sake of her modesty. "I didn't mean for-"

"No. it's probably for the best. We're the only two who truly mean to leave this place, it seems. Why should anyone else waste time on our deliverance when they can start their new lives?"

"Deliverance? So, you don't mean to send a rescue?"

"The boat could probably take four, if that many actually wanted to leave by the time it's ready. Survival is not guaranteed. Hells, even getting this thing out to sea isn't guaranteed. Nor is even finishing it at this rate. Not with the tools available to us," Renald said, angrily throwing the rock on the ground as he stood up to face her.

"Look, I am sorry about the men," she said.

"Don't be. They're much happier now," Renald said bitterly. "Hand fed by women they've seen naked, they're going nowhere. They're a part of this place now. This is where they want to be, so this is where they can stay."

Lost for words, Elaeni just looked at him apologetically. He'd lost the last of what had made him everything he was. She gently nodded and took a few steps back as he turned his back to her, dropped down, and resumed work.

Eramir gave her a gentle nod as he continued to work on their vessel.

"Stenyksil?" Delmur said, astonished as he ate again with Elaeni. The middle-aged scholar had listened to his young female friend recount elements of her conversation with the mysterious woman of the north island. He wriggled his fingers in the air, clasping at nothing. "Gods, if only I still had my books and notes. This is most interesting. And she claims to be related?"

"I think she said her father was Sten's great, great grandfather."

"My, she raises so many questions."

"I found that," Elaeni agreed, "but it will be a week before I see her again."

"Yes, aside from the milk maids, only you, Felina, and the empress seem to venture that way," Delmur said. "Part of a privileged few."

"You saw the empress go?"

"Well, it's a bit of an assumption, but one of the first nights here my leg was keeping me up during the night. I saw her make her way north. Obviously, I couldn't follow her, but she was gone some time and her clothes seemed damp upon return. I thought at the time that maybe she had gone for a late dip, but for the time she was gone, the direction she went, and the clothes…after seeing you and Felina, and those ladies who fetch the mystery milk, it seemed to add up. Though I only noticed it the once."

"Might be interesting to see what Edwuld has to say," Elaeni pondered.

"I've barely seen him. He hardly leaves her side and she's not terribly sociable herself." Delmur shrugged. "Audience with her seems strictly an invitation-only affair."

"And the two noblemen seem an elusive pair."

"Yes, they don't wander out of the turtle-shell palace terribly often either, do they."

"Well, I think I have a way in, but it's a bit of a commitment," Elaeni said sourly. "I'd rather save that option for an emergency and preferably later than sooner."

"Understandable."

"Though Felina seems more open to the notion. So maybe she could have a word with our missing passenger."

"But then perhaps she'll become as elusive herself," Delmur cautioned.

"How late do you think it was when the empress went?"

"Hard to say, I'd been asleep, you see, and everyone else still was. The fire pit outside still glowed, though," he recalled. "I fear the only way to establish her window is to stay up late each night until it happens again. An exhausting undertaking, but an effective one, assuming I can stay awake."

"I shall try the same," Elaeni offered as a thought occurred to her. "How old would you say Edwuld is? I've only seen him once or twice since we arrived, I can barely remember his face."

"Mid-thirties?" Delmur shrugged. "Why?"

"Seems a bit of an old age for a man with a surname to reach without being married off."

"Seems like he got here just in time then, no?" Delmur said, with a chirpy shrug.

"In time or too late?" she wondered aloud.

Delmur tilted his head like a confused dog. "What do you mean?"

"I'm not sure, just a thought." She squinted, turning thoughts over in her head. "Something to query Renald about if he ever feels like talking to me again."

Elaeni waited a few days before approaching Renald again. Her commitment to staying up late left her tired and she would return to sleep after breakfast each morning, rising again sometime in the middle of the day. Renald and Eramir's boat was slowly taking shape but still looked far from being seaworthy.

"Permission to come aboard, Captain?" she asked as she approached.

Renald sunk his head before looking to her with a reluctant smile. "I think it'll still be some time before I can grant you entry to her," he said.

"So, it's a she?"

"All ships are, miss," Eramir informed her, as Renald gave a conceding gesture towards his one remaining faithful crewman.

"So, does she have a name yet?" Elaeni asked.

"Not, yet," Renald said. "Why? Did you have something in mind?"

Elaeni pondered a moment, with her elbow in one hand while the other drummed fingers over her pursed lips. "Well, let's see. She was made from the remains of the Saltdrake. Birthed even. So, how about the Salty Hatchling?"

The two seamen looked to each other with tilted nods, frowning impressed.

"Clever," Renald said. "Though we can't officially name her until she's ready. Which is still a long way away."

"I wanted to ask you something," Elaeni said. "Edwuld Darrow. Was he married?"

Renald stroked his now quite whiskery chin, furrowing his brow as he struggled to answer. "I never really spoke to him, on the ship. When he dined with the captain, I was at the helm. There was a noblewoman at the docks the day he boarded. One of a few people seeing him off, though." He rubbed his temple as he tried to recall, "She seemed quite affectionate towards him, but I only remember him crossing gangplank alone."

"Affectionate like a sister, or a wife?" Elaeni asked.

"I didn't stand there and watch them kiss or anything. I just noticed her. She held his arm a lot, she talked to him for a long time before he boarded. Why do you ask?" Renald asked.

"Was she young or old?" Elaeni continued.

Renald shook his head. "I really can't recall her face to be honest."

"Eramir has a wife, doesn't he?" Elaeni questioned.

"Aye, miss. How'd you know that?" Eramir paused as he was tying two planks together.

"Because you're still here trying to get home while the other men were lured away," Elaeni replied.

"I don't have a wife," Renald pointed out. "But I'm here, working at this wooden hatchling every day."

"You're a career sailor. Married to the sea. First mate, a step from captain," she said, "You can't stomach the idea of being stuck on land."

"Least of all land that produces no ale and serves no mutton," Renald admitted. "So, if Edwuld's married, why is he spending all his time with this empress instead of helping us make this boat?"

"I think she's been able to make him forget," Elaeni concluded.

"How?" Renald asked.

"That's what I mean to find out," Elaeni said, determined.

A week after their last visit to the north island, Felina woke up informing Elaeni that they had been summoned by Aekestyr. They crossed to the northern island where the regal, pale, white-haired figure stood before them once more within a shaft of light in the great, dark cave. She held out her hand towards Elaeni to reveal the silver ring in her palm.

Elaeni stepped forward and cautiously retrieved it, expecting a spark or heat from the magic, but it felt like a normal hand-warmed ring. She put it on, where it belonged, where her husband had first placed it. Her eyes moved about, as she expected to feel different.

Aekestyr smiled at her. "I have made it so that we can all understand each other already. You won't notice anything until you talk to those who were born here."

"Thank you for this," Elaeni said, not wanting to bombard her with questions so soon after such a gesture. But her face was twitching as she tried to think of a way to tactfully transition.

Aekestyr smiled, knowingly, "You have much you wish to ask?"

"There are many questions, yes," Elaeni admitted.

"Then ask them," the white-haired woman invited.

Elaeni shut her eyes tightly as she unleashed her questions. "How did you come to be here? How did you get here? Why did you come here? What is happening with Edwuld? We have barely seen him since he first dined with the empress. Where does the milk come from? Why does it heal us so fast? How is there so much of it?" Elaeni took a deep breath. "That's what I can remember to ask right now."

"Much to get through," Aekestyr said, with an amused smile and raised brow as Felina just looked surprised.

"I'll forget otherwise," Elaeni explained. "I always seem to."

"My kind are the forgotten," Askestyr explained. "Early attempts by creators whose expectations could not be reached until they perfected the art of what they intended to make. The first of our kind took us in, sharing our lost purpose of living in a legacy of failure. Events unfolded, a forgotten rebellion brewed in resentment, that saw many of us scatter. I crawled into the sea to find somewhere cold on the southern continent, but when I passed these empty islands on my way I swam ashore, fighting my way through the hostile surrounds onto the beach, and taking this form to explore before settling in here. I chose solitude but, as you know, that was not to be, when exiles wrecked upon these shores. I took pity on them for they were like me in many ways. The emperor's daughter, Atavia, the last of a bloodline descended from that which I was intended to be. House Duvandt was also the progeny of a different breed of the same kind. Both exiled and defeated at the hands of one who shared my blood. I almost felt I owed them my protection."

"That's what the milk is for," Felina realised.

"Yes. My milk provides for them where the islands' minimal vegetation fails them. My milk makes their bodies heal faster, resist the cold, and make their blood resist the lack of variety in their breeding stock."

"But if you produce milk, you must have children of your own," Elaeni reasoned.

"I was made to breed men and women who would raise and fell kingdoms and empires, but my parents were not of similar kind to one another. Magic was required to fuse the two but, as I was amongst the first of my kind, I was nothing more than a deviation from the path to success. My womb does not bear fruit, but my existence relies on it doing just that, so I have two redundant things in great excess: motherly instincts and life-sustaining milk. I provide both to all that the sea casts upon this hostile cradle and name them my children."

Elaeni again felt herself burdened by Aekestyr's cryptic honesty, which concealed as much as it revealed. The mysterious woman's voice carried an intensity and passion that weighed like anger but washed like sorrow. Elaeni felt emotionally drained hearing it but wanted to see all that she could ask answered. "And Edwuld?"

"Everyone who has come here has accepted their fate sooner or later," Aekestyr said. "Some fought it, clinging onto hope of escape into old age, even encouraging those born here with tales of civilisation. Others took one look and knew they were here for life, quickly adapting. I do not rush nor deter," she said, stroking Elaeni's hair on either side of her face, "for that is what a good mother must do. Let her children find their own feet in their own time. Edwuld had a life he's accepted he cannot return to. He chose happiness over a life of mourning. He did so in mere days. Most of the crew of your ship have accepted this. I know that Renald and Eramir refuse to give up, but their drive to escape gives them strength they're not ready to find elsewhere, so I must let them have that. I think Delmur is too fascinated by his surroundings to know what he wants, but this is probably the happiest he's ever been, and you and Felina will make your choices in your own time. I know that the sooner you embrace this family, the sooner you'll feel you belong, and the sooner you'll find new purpose. But I must let you both mourn for your old lives for as long as it takes. Perhaps now that you can talk to anyone here, you'll ask them of their lives and tell them of yours. Get to know my children before you commit to a life of distancing yourself from them."

Elaeni nodded. It seemed a fair request.

Upon talking to the locals, Elaeni soon found herself one of the most important people on the island. She was able to bridge the communication gap that existed between the shipwrecked and the locals. She offered the service, allowing the five wayward crewmen to offer marriage to the milk maids. Renald was able to get better materials with which to complete his boat, and Delmur was able to learn so much more from the people as Elaeni also passed on education she received from Aekestyr.

Before long the empress wished to meet with the two women who had come to her islands. They were escorted to her hut-palace made of shipwrecked wood, turtle shell, reed, and mud, built against the side of the rocky rise to extend its natural shelter. Ancient imperial armour hung on display from the walls as well as several gladiuses and spears. The empress wore a far finer garment than most, made of dark red silk. She also wore a golden pendant shaped like a wreath around a ruby while wearing a matching golden circlet styled into leaves over her short black hair.

She sat on a cushioned stone throne carved out of the rock as the elusive Edwuld Darrow sat, draped in loose silk, on a lower stone bench by her side, almost like a pet. He barely took his eyes off the empress, utterly enamoured. Though she looked much like everyone else on the island, something did set her apart. As it did the two men introduced to them, Errius Duvandt and Vitius Vereno.

"Felina and Elaeni," Edwuld said, "allow me to introduce Empress Octuria Verseidon."

"Well, it is time we finally met," the empress said. "When the great mother told me that she had bestowed upon you the gift of tongues, I was excited."

"It is an honour to finally meet you too, Empress," Felina said, implementing her own magic to understand as Elaeni simply bowed her head.

"Do you speak to the great mother often?" Elaeni asked, in the old Kestrian tongue, after small talk had run its course.

"Of course, I take audience with her weekly," the empress said as food was brought in. "She's taken quite a liking to you, as have my advisors." She pointed to the noblemen on either side of her. "What great additions you would make to my small council. A sorceress and a translator."

"Felina is quite capable of translating as well," Elaeni suggested. "I'm not sure I'd be bringing all that much to the table."

"I think you're being far too modest," Errius Duvandt offered. "You have lived on two continents, I am told, while we have lived only here. There is much you could teach us about the world and how it has changed over the centuries from how it was in the stories our ancestors passed down to us."

"I suppose so," Elaeni conceded.

Conversation for much of the night seemed to fall to her, telling them of the societal structures of Umberdale and Nordmeer, and what the continent of Kestria was like nearly eight centuries after the departure of their empire. Errius seemed to devote much of his attention to her as Vitius Vereno gave his to Felina who was only mildly reciprocating, but far more so than Elaeni.

Similar dinners happened more and more, and Elaeni found herself immersed in the island village as they all had similar queries about the lands beyond the surrounding sea. Delmur was delighted to learn what he could from them through her.

As days passed and even weeks, curiosities and doubts that had been pushed to the back of her mind fought their way back to the surface, for the more she saw Edwuld Darrow sitting by the side of this empress, the less natural his affection seemed. He did not seem like a man who had moved on from his wife, but like a man utterly enamoured by some spell. If magic could be placed on her silver ring, then what spells could be put upon the golden ornaments the empress wore? These were not queries that she felt comfortable asking Aekestyr, and with each passing day, as Vitius's charm wore Felina down, Elaeni felt a declining desire to confide in her any suspicions.

As the crewmen would marry the milk maids over the weeks, it occurred to Elaeni to befriend one in the days leading up to her ceremony. She offered to take her place the following morning as a means of a wedding gift.

Elaeni took the large ceramic pot, made from the ash grey clay of the southern island, and carried it with her down to the shores before the northern island. She buried her ring in the sand beneath her clothes, remembering how Aekestyr had sensed the magic when Felina had only just begun to enchant the ring.

She followed the women naked through the water for the first time without her clothes above her head. She made sure to stay at the back of the group, keeping her face low as they entered the first cave.

Entering the second cavern where she normally met with Aekestyr's white-haired, white-robed, womanly form, there was no woman. Instead something of tremendous size filled the cavern with the deep echoing of its loud, heavy breathing. The pillar of light that would shine down at noon was angled by the low rising sun into the back wall, where large white scales covered an appendage of some kind and the flesh behind it.

The sand scraped to her right as she entered behind the other women. In the place she had previously felt a deep indent in the sand, she saw a great scaled tail fill it, as her eyes adjusted to the limited light. Though she had never seen a dragon, she knew that what she was looking at was not one, but not so far removed from one either.

Soon she could discern the entire shape. Some huge wingless reptilian beast, covered in scales with patches of skin in no natural pattern, curled around the cave's edges. The hind legs reminded her of a stocky woman or dwarf in shape while the forelegs resembled human arms of different lengths. The head was a nightmare of a human face distorted with that of some great white lizard or crocodile. White hair fell to the ground from the creature's scalp, long and coiled upon the sand, with white horns that curved back over the skull.

At the approach of the women, the massive beast twisted in rotation, maintaining its horseshoe position, exposing all four appendages and an underbelly with two great breasts. One, smaller, seemingly restricted by its covering scales. The other, fleshier breast was veiny and engorged to the size of a great shipping barrel.

The women continued towards it as the forty-foot-long beast let out a gravelly idle sigh that filled the cave with a chill. Two women pressed into the breast from either side, putting their whole bodies into it, as a third collected the expelling milk into the first pot and the others stood ready to pass the next vessels. It poured into the ceramic container with force as warm, white vapour rose in contrast to the chill that hung in the air.

There was something about the half dozen naked women gathered about the underbelly of this beast collecting milk that made Elaeni think of young pups feeding at their mother's teats.

One woman filled the vessels while the others left their empty ones on one side, collecting filled ones on the other. Elaeni kept her face hidden from Aekestyr's true and monstrous face, enveloped by her enormous and twisted form. She showed the same calmness and reverence as the others, while driving the dread and horror she felt deep within herself to focus on the task at hand, though the deformed monstrous sight made her want to run.

She collected her pot as soon as they were done, now heavily filled, and pressed it against her bare chest, surprised she could even carry such a weight. She followed the others out again, leaving the terrible sight behind her and fighting the compulsion to look back, lest she be recognised.

They held their pots high as they again traversed the water and placed them on the flattest part of the beach, before brushing as much of the water from their bodies as they could and then climbing back into their clothes. Elaeni fished her wedding ring from the sand and slid it back onto her finger, followed by her garments.

She delivered the milk with the rest and excused herself, only taking the opportunity to react as she walked alone to Renald. She found her breathing panicked as the horror of the twisted creature she saw sank in. No wonder she chose such a beautiful form in which to appear when receiving Felina and herself.

She described what she saw to Renald, who didn't know what to make of the image she conjured.

"Forty-feet you say, scaled like a frostdrake or white dragon, robust, wingless, and mixed with human flesh?" he summarised. "Some horror created on Ancaraug by the ancient wyrmkind that govern those lands."

"Some horror, wider than people are tall, that swam ashore through those black spires. She herself described the moment as fighting through the hostile surrounds and spoke of later taking her human form to explore the islands."

Renald pondered on her words a moment.

"Bloody hells," Eramir said, standing up after listening to the conversation. "Don't you see what she was saying?"

Renald looked back to his faithful crewman and smiled, confused.

"That bloody big monster swam here," the bald and bearded crewman explained. "Smashed her way through the rocks with her hard scales. Probably along the south coast of one of these islands."

"So, there's a cleared path somewhere," Renald realised. "A way out. A safe way out. We just need to find where."

"I'll not ask," Elaeni said, "I suspect she only told me as much as she did because she never expected me to see her true form. For if she truly supported the notion of anyone leaving, that detail would have certainly been included."

"So how do we find it?" Renald asked. "I've not seen anywhere that looks like there could be a clear path."

"I think it's on the southwest island," she said, with a cunning grin creeping across her face. "That's where they get their clay from and that clay makes the water murky around its shores. Hard to tell what's going on in that water. So perhaps I should go for a swim each morning down that way until I find a clearing."

"We'll have to start moving our work, then. Once we're done, we might not be able to get the boat between islands without damaging it," Renald said. "But this friend of yours on the north island might realise we've figured a way out if word gets back to her."

"I could tell her that you wish to make pots that fit into the grooves of the boat to store water and food," Elaeni suggested.

"Clever," Eramir nodded approvingly. "You're a sharp one, miss, no mistake."

"Though, we should probably actually do that," Renald admitted.

Elaeni rose earlier each morning and swam between the south and central islands to begin with, slowly making her way around each as she expanded her search. She kept the sessions short, in order to return before most rose. On the sixth day, as she swam further along the coast, determined to find the clear path she believed to exist, she found her wide strokes failing to be stopped by the underwater forest of long rocks that surrounded her. She swam back and forth to confirm the width, then out as far as she dared before returning to the shallows with her hands outstretched to either side. She laughed as she waded back, thrilled and proud.

She left the water, bountifully scooping up clay in her hands, and scurried across the muddy beach directly to the rock formation that raised the greener land several feet above its shores. She squeezed excess moisture from the clay and began crafting a circle on the rock to mark the path.

She smiled triumphantly as she stood back and admired her handiwork with her clayed hands upon her hips. Standing there quietly, she realised she could hear Renald and Eramir working on the boat some distance away. Excited she called out to Renald somewhere over the ridge.

"Elaeni?" he called back, as she heard him approach.

"Yes, I found it," she said, excited. "Look, I've marked the…" she trailed off as he appeared on the higher ground above the marking she'd made. His face was pale and stunned.

"What's wrong?" she asked.

"Uh, well," he said, swallowing nervously and pointed at her.

Eleani's eyes bulged as she remembered she was standing naked before him and quickly spun around to face the sea. "Bloody hells." She quickly ran back into the water and squatted in the shallows to cover herself. "Sorry, I got so lost in the moment…"

"No apology necessary," he said turning away in delayed politeness, "I shan't forget the spot now."

She realised her clothes were rolled up on the shores of the central island and had some distance to swim before she'd be near them again.

"Well, I er…I better get back to work on the boat," he said, sounding as embarrassed as her. "Well done, though," he added, to recapture some of the lost celebratory moment.

Swimming away, she refrained from looking back until well after he'd left the spot.

"Where have you been?" Felina asked, when Elaeni returned to the village.

"Morning swim. Got a bit carried away this time," Elaeni said innocently, rubbing her thumb on her silver ring as Felina's native language poured out of her mouth. "Why? Have you been looking for me?"

"Yes, there's to be a ceremony this evening for Edwuld and the empress."

"I think he's already married."

"The Saltdrake is well overdue. His wife back in Umberdale will have probably received word by now that he's considered lost at sea," Felina reasoned. "How long should he wait, trapped on an island he can't escape?"

"What if he could escape?" Elaeni challenged. "You've seen how he is around our empress. Do you truly believe he would take a way out at this point?"

"I think that if there was a way off this island, it would be getting dangerously close to being too late to bring it up," she suggested.

"What about you?" Elaeni asked. "If we could leave tomorrow, would you?"

"Can we?"

"No."

"Then I suppose you'll have to ask me the day before we actually could, if that day ever comes. You've been talking to those two sailors too much. They're filling your head with dreams of home, but this is your home now." Felina gently brushed her friend's arm. "I know it's hard for you to let go, but if anyone here has reason to move forward and embrace a life here, it's you."

"Because I have nothing to go back to?"

"Like Edwuld, I'm losing a life of prestige. Delmur's lost all his work, but he has his studies to go back to. A name to make for himself. Renald and his crewman are just being stubborn men of the sea. That life is in their blood and they refuse to let go, for now. But you? You're a pretty woman and you're still young. Yes, you could rebuild your life, if you made it home somehow, but that same opportunity is here, only without the peril. I know the grief is still near but in time, you'll want to be loved again, held again. When you've had time to heal."

"When I boarded the Saltdrake it had been a year since my husband died. In the time I've been here, a year has passed since I watched those responsible hanged," Elaeni confessed to the sorceress. "It's been long enough that I can no longer recall his face. Yet the loss still feels so recent. So, yes, if anyone should embrace a life here, it's me. But if there was a way out, I would take it. I no longer believe you would," Elaeni said sadly, raising her hand with the enchanted silver ring. "Do you remember how Aekestyr sensed the magic you had put into this ring?"

"Yes, of course."

"Can you sense such enchantments?"

"I'm not so sensitive that I would notice something as preliminary, but an article that had been imbued with magic, yes, if I was looking for it. I wouldn't just…smell it the way Aekestyr did, but I can cast a spell that reveals such things to me."

"Can you tell the nature of the spell?"

"Not always precisely, but yes. Why?"

"Next time you're near the empress, I want you to see if there's anything on the gold she wears," Elaeni requested.

"You believe she's using magic on Edwuld?"

Elaeni shrugged, underplaying her conviction.

"I'll see what I can discern," Felina said, pondering.

With Felina and Aekestyr communing in the place they called Nihrius, Elaeni didn't feel as confident as she'd like trusting Felina with knowledge of guaranteed escape. How she reacted to confirmation of Aekestyr's influence over others, through this empress, would settle the matter.

That evening Elaeni attended the ceremony binding Edwuld Darrow to Empress Octuria Verseidon in the ancient Kestrian custom. Elaeni was invited to stand in the front with Errius Duvandt while Felina stood with Vitius Vereno. The six of them were adorned in the well-preserved imperial garments and armour of those who first landed on the islands. Delmur was utterly thrilled to witness the occasion. The priest held a golden gladius out before him as the pair being wed swore their oaths with their fingers on the blade.

Elaeni watched the ever-enamoured Edwuld the whole time. She did not know him well enough to know how naturally he was behaving, but as one yet to recover from losing her husband beyond a year, watching this man wed another, while his own wife must be pining for him across the sea, churned her stomach.

Elaeni paired off with Errius as the hut-palace was left to the wedded couple for the night. She found herself forcing small talk as he walked her around the central island, while Felina, now given a chance to complete the task Elaeni had given her, was somewhere else being escorted by Vitius.

She did manage to query her companion about his family history, which she thought would at least delight Delmur, having gaps in his understanding of the origins of house Duvandt and how there came to be a Kestrian house named after a place in Nordmeer.

Connecting his family name origin and her place of birth allowed Errius to attempt to press the issue of the two of them seeing more of each other, skilfully evading a direct conversation about the future he intended for her. She felt unkind doing so, but wilfully misled him to avoid suspicion about what she hoped was an impending departure. She left him with the impression that over the next few months she would make more of an effort, but still maintained that she needed time.

Eventually she was able to part ways for the evening but found that Felina had not managed to shake off her own suitor. Realising she'd have to wait till later, Elaeni sought out Renald instead.

"Uh, hello," Renald said awkwardly, suddenly reminding her of their last encounter.

She could feel her face redden. "Oh, right. I was so caught up in what I was doing, and I've gotten so used to getting about…well, I wasn't thinking."

"If you were embarrassed by what happened this morning, I should probably warn you of the harsh realities of sharing a small sea craft with others over several days or weeks with no lower decks," he warned her. "Everything you have to do in a day you will have to do with others by your side. There'll be no privacy, modesty, or dignity in the voyage ahead."

"If that was an effort to lessen the burden of my embarrassment, it did not work out the way you might have hoped."

"Not so much, just that compared to what you'll have to endure, me seeing you…well, me seeing you as you were will seem like nothing."

Elaeni realised he was equally embarrassed by what had happened, for however the sea had hardened him, his lack of time spent around women had rendered him quite shy. It made her smile, as she found it endearing that such a tall, strong, determined man was so flummoxed by the sight of a naked woman, at least when it was one that he knew.

"I think we should make for Ohtylos," he said after she let the conversation slip into silence. "When we leave, that is."

"Why?"

"For a start, the way out is south. The southward clearway off the southern beach of the south-western island."

"That is a lot of south," she agreed.

"If this Aekestyr doesn't wish us to leave, then sailing past the other islands might be risky, especially past hers. That is time we could spend putting distance between us. The important thing is to reach land, any land, in lieu of a ship. As you can speak any language now, we should manage far easier, though I do speak a little Ohtylosian."

"If you think that's best."

"The goal has changed from escape and rescue to simply escape now. Finding work on another ship and seeing you home is far more an achievable task than I originally thought. If the crewmen want to stay, then let them. The best chance I had at arranging rescue would have been for Edwuld, and he seems to have made his choice, so anyone who wants out has to come with us."

"How many can we take?" Elaeni asked. "There's you, me, and Eramir. I'm sure Delmur would come, but I'm uncertain about Felina."

"Four would strain our chances, but five could make staying seem favourable. We can only store so much water. Rationing it will be sufficiently difficult without more people draining it and adding inexperienced contrary voices to discussion of its rationing. However, there's a good chance the sea will just claim us regardless."

Elaeni twisted her heel into the grass as she began to realise how limited her options were for saving the others.

"There's other things you need to be ready for," Renald warned. "We'd have to leave almost as soon as everyone retired for the night. The more travelling we do without the sun above us the better. We also need to cover ourselves from the sun like the Northern Heruusians do in their deserts. So, as much cloth as can be gathered should be."

Elaeni nodded and heard all the things Renald had to say about surviving the trip as he listed them.

By the time Elaeni returned to the village she found Felina alone in their hut and already asleep. Elaeni sat up on her own bedding, parallel to Felina's, and watched her for a while. Had she done as she asked or was she right now repeating Elaeni's doubts and suspicions to the great twisted creature in the northern island, doubtless appearing to her as a white-haired beauty? Would she still be loyal to it, if she knew what Aekestyr truly was? An unnatural crossbreed forced into existence as a horrifying monstrosity by magic.

Then again, Elaeni wondered if she was being fair in doubting the intentions of such a tragic creation. Unable to bear her own offspring, she adopted those who crashed upon her lost corner of the world. Her heart began to fill with doubt. Did she even know why she was so desperate to leave? To put cobbled stone beneath her feet again and do little more than mourn in more familiar surroundings? She mourned because she had suffered loss. She mourned because love had been taken from her. So why was she so reluctant to open her heart to those who meant to refill it? So much so that she was willing to risk her life on a makeshift boat in open seas even after Renald had outlined the dangers and indignities that awaited her. But to answer would be to understand her own sadness and doing that would surely mean being able to defeat it. So far, she had not.

Felina woke up startled, as if from a nightmare.

"What is it?" Elaeni asked.

"You." Felina slapped her knee in retribution. "Do you know what it's like drifting awake in the middle of the night to find someone leaning over you, staring?"

Elaeni smiled. "Sorry," she said. "I wasn't leaning over you, nor staring. I was just thinking, and there was little where else to gaze."

"Well, it's very alarming," Felina said as she pushed herself up to sit. "What are you thinking about?"

"Everything."

"That's quite a bit," Felina said with a gentle smile and rubbed Elaeni's knee apologetically.

"Promise me that whatever is said tonight, in here, is just between us."

Felina nodded in agreement.

"If I found a way off this island, but it was a dangerous way, and I couldn't guarantee success, would you want to come? Or would you rather live out your life here, knowing you were safer?"

"My journey was to complete my training, not that the study of magic has an end, but at least I would have had a title of prestige and used that title to counsel important people who paid generously," she said. "But there is an ancient being inside the north island here. I could learn so much more from her. I could become so much more. It's a surprisingly hard choice."

"If I found a way and left you behind, would you be angry? Would you be hurt?"

"I would be sad. I have grown fond of you. But I would understand," Felina said, framing her friends face gently with both hands, smiling again. "I'd think you were completely mad, but I'd understand."

Elaeni's eyes glazed but she let out a small laugh.

"If you left without saying goodbye, I'd never forgive you, though."

"Would you keep that farewell to yourself?"

Felina furrowed her brows, her hands sliding from Elaeni's face to her shoulders as she leaned back. "What do you mean?"

"If I did leave, I don't think Aekestyr would approve."

Felina seemed almost scandalised by the notion for a moment. But then, something seemed to sink in. "The empress's circlet and amulet have magic in them. A charm enchantment exists on both. There are a few specific spells in that field, and seduction is one of them. If I had to guess, from what I sensed and what you've said, I'd say the circlet has something to aid with command, and the amulet seduction," Felina whispered. "No person could normally make such a compelling enchantment, but Aekestyr is ancient and powerful. She probably made it when the second ship wrecked upon these shores, allowing emperors and empresses over the centuries to take their pick of the survivors."

"Then Edwuld Darrow is a prisoner," Elaeni said.

"If you know a way off these islands, you cannot take him with you," Felina warned, grabbing Elaeni's wrist. "If Aekestyr truly wants us all to stay, your best chance of escape is to leave him be. You would have to separate him from the empress for days before you could convince him to come with you. She would be suspicious before the first day passed."

"He has a wife," Elaeni argued. "She would be waiting for him."

"Then she must suffer as you have. She will mourn her husband, lost at sea, and one day move on," Felina said. "If you try to rescue him, I fear you'll change nothing for her."

Elaeni thought desperately on the matter. She could not easily reconcile sacrificing a man's free will and marriage for her own escape to no one. "That's a terrible cost."

"An offering, just about," Felina said with a grimace, "but he is wanted here. He is a sacrifice you must be willing to make."

Elaeni squinted bitterly.

"Renald and his shipmate have made no effort to blend in or settle," Felina observed. "If they jumped on that boat they've been working on, I don't think anyone will try to stop them. Delmur is past fifty. The women here his age have had their children, and all those available have been taken by the other men of the Saltdrake. It will be years before Delmur has a mate of birthing age. So, if he escaped, I think it would be forgiven. Especially by the local men left out by the milk maids pairing off with our ship hands." Felina gave her a sorrowful look. "You might have to make a bigger sacrifice than Edwuld, though."

"How do you mean?"

"There are two men of importance here, and two of us. It has been made clear that they and Aekestyr want us to pair off with them. Both of us going would be an issue. Even one of us, I fear. Those three men's best chance of escape is if you remain."

Elaeni stared wide-eyed at the ground between them as she contemplated the truth of what Felina had said. "Gods, you're right."

"Something to sleep on." Felina patted her on the knee and laid back down.

Elaeni stretched out onto her bedding and stared at the low ceiling, framed by wood and rope that once belonged to a ship, digesting the complexity of the decisions ahead.

The day finally came when the boat was ready. Elaeni had spent the last several days skilfully evading her would-be suitor, and she'd had two more visits with Aekestyr, where she bombarded the vision of a white-haired woman with questions about history that she knew would interest Delmur.

Delmur had been instructed by Elaeni to meet with Renald and Eramir to extend him an invitation to return home, or at least to civilisation where he could finish his work. Work that had now been supplemented with knowledge he could never have hoped to find elsewhere, as well as direct exposure to the actual culture and spoken language. His broken leg was nothing but a memory.

When all had retired for the night Elaeni watched Felina grow tired and waited till she seemed too settled in to rise again. She said her name and kissed her on the forehead. "It's time," she said. "I'll miss you."

Felina wrapped her arms around her and squeezed her tight. "I wish you wouldn't, but I hope you make it. I'll miss you forever." She put her hand on Elaeni's cheeks and wiped a tear away with her thumb. "And if you ever find yourself in Angvjaald and have the opportunity to meet the wizard, Kai Vjorgan, tell him I won't be able to complete his task."

"I'll get word to him," Elaeni promised. "When the others figure it out, assure them we won't mention this place to anyone. But in the meantime, if anyone asks where I am, tell them I've gone swimming."

Felina huffed a gentle quiet laugh and let her friend go, watching her sneak out of their hut and her life.

It was a mercifully clear night, allowing the moons and stars to guide them. Aekestyr's milk allowed Elaeni to wade through the water at night without suffering the cold. As she dressed on the beach, she looked back over her shoulder to make sure none saw her. Then, looking at her silver ring, she felt guilty for leaving, having been gifted the powerful enchantment upon it, a resistance to the cold, and a fast recovery from her injury.

She found Renald, Eramir, and Delmur waiting for her on the beach, ready to push the boat into the water where she had marked the safe passage. They cautiously sent the vessel into the water and climbed into it, pulling each other aboard the stocked boat of salvaged wreckage.

They stealthily rowed their way out with crude makeshift oars, pushing against the rocky spires in the water that framed their path. Reflections of the stars danced on the dark waves lapping against their crude craft.

The islands were some distance away before the sail was unfurled and caught the night wind. With nothing to contribute to the journey, Elaeni settled into a corner and rested her head against the inner hull.

"You should try and stay awake for as long as you can," Renald suggested.

"Why?" she asked.

"So, you'll sleep more during the day," he told her as he handed the keel over to Eramir. "The less you do while the sun is out, the less water you'll need during the trip west."

Eramir gave a nod of agreement, and so Elaeni kept herself awake sharing the things she'd learned from Aekestyr with Delmur. He listened in fascination, comparing the new insights with what he had found in his studies. The pair bounced information off each other into the night as Renald slept so that he could steer the boat during the day.

Elaeni didn't remember falling asleep but she woke all the same, buried under cloth made from plant fibre, as pinpricks of light made their way through. She tried to stay asleep as instructed, but she could not. She peeked out to see the sun high in the sky but leaning in the direction in which they were travelling. Early afternoon.

Renald sat at the stern controlling the rudder with the sail inflated by the wind. The boat rose and fell in the water, bumping against waves. Eramir and Delmur were somehow sleeping through the turbulence under the additional cloth they had gathered. A gull was sitting atop the mast like a small-scale crewman in the crow's nest, only several feet high.

"How long before anyone starts to wonder where we are?" Elaeni asked.

Renald looked ahead at the blue sea. It looked identical in every direction, but he looked at it as if it was a road with a clear path ahead. "The central island was about the size of a kingdom capital," he said. "That's a lot of room for people to miss each other. Have you ever been to Varekuin?"

"No," she said, of the capital of their home kingdom. "I grew up in Vanport."

"Even in Vanport, imagine sixty or seventy people getting about in that space. It's easy to avoid others. So, with a north island the size of a large town that very few visit, and a south one none visit, I'd like to believe that no alarm has been raised. People have grown accustomed to not seeing Eramir or myself about. With Delmur's leg healing at such a rate it's only fair to assume he's making up for lost time by walking the beach. We all skipped breakfast often enough, but by lunch time, they'd probably have started seeking us out," he said, glimpsing at the sun. "I dare say they've realised something isn't right in the last hour or two. They might have started looking for us. But it won't be until they check the south island to see the boat we spent the entire time building is neither on land nor in pieces washing up on their shores."

Elaeni looked back towards the east, her face riddled with concern and doubt.

"How long do you imagine it would take for word to make it to the north island?" he asked

"Milk would have been gathered before significant suspicion was raised. Felina and I saw Aekestyr yesterday, so we wouldn't be expected back too soon, and she'd have to wait till night till Felina was asleep to contact her if she wants to press her for information. The empress had her weekly visit only a few nights ago, so it depends how urgent she considers our absence. Though I'd like to think that as a recently married woman with an obedient husband, she'd have better things to focus on."

"How certain are you that this Aekestyr could or would do something that should concern us?"

"She would see it as a betrayal. But she managed to keep seven of eleven of us. Six willing."

"You have to make peace with leaving Edwuld behind."

"Felina said saving him would have meant no one escaping. At the very least I can tell his wife he died so that she'll move on."

"If we don't run into a ship, we're bound for Ohtylos. When we arrive, if we arrive, we do so without coin. I wouldn't issue myself too many errands when getting home again is going to be enough of a challenge."

"Well, ships need first mates and crew, so you and Eramir should land on your feet."

"What will you do?"

"Perhaps I'll help Delmur with his work," she suggested, "now that he has to write it all down again."

Renald smiled. "There's a lot of people who could use your newfound skill. Merchants, lords, even kings. I've heard some of the finer ships keep a translator on board."

"As long as those finer ships give the Black Spire Isles a wider berth than the last one." Renald's smile faded and he looked away. "I'm sorry, I didn't mean…"

"No, it's alright," Renald assured her. "Though, it was a rare storm we tried to evade. The crew fought hard to veer away from the isles but no matter what we did we seemed to just keep heading deeper into it. It was almost as if something took hold of us," he pondered aloud, looking into the distance and reliving the loss of his ship. "Try and get more rest."

Elaeni nodded quietly and nestled back in, allowing the rocking, as erratic as it was, to sway her back to sleep.

Elaeni roused later as the falling sun tinted the western sky orange. Renald's shirt was wet with sweat as he rocked back and forth, rowing while the sail sat lifeless.

"I thought we weren't supposed to exert ourselves in the sun," she said.

Eramir, sitting at the keel, leaned to one side to see her past Renald. "Aye, we need more water when we work, and we've only got so much," he said. "But if we sit still when the wind's gone, we run out without getting near more. Don't forget, we got no anchor. So, sitting still might be the same as going backward."

"How long are we likely to go without wind?" she asked the crewman.

"How long are we likely to go without rain?" Eramir shrugged, as Delmur returned from the edge of the boat to bring a soaked rag to Renald's brow and hang it twisted around his neck so the brine would cool him down.

Delmur took the keel sometime later when the sky began to grow dark and Eramir took over the rowing. He worked away well into the night, taking breaks at Delmur's suggestion while he and Elaeni took over. Neither of them could come close to sustaining the work, but together lasted long enough to give the crewman a decent breather from time to time, postponing Renald's turn.

Soon it was dark again. Though the uncertainty ahead should have filled her heart with fear, Elaeni felt relief and calmed by knowing she had put a day between her and the islands. The place carried an intangible dread for her. She felt as though she had escaped a city cell but felt guilty for the sensation. She had been looked after, fed, welcomed, and accommodated. But more than that, she felt as if she had left a part of herself behind somehow.

As Eramir rowed well into the night there was a strange noise accompanying his strokes after a while. A strange jingling in the water.

"What is that?" Delmur asked, looking over the edge, squinting at the darkness. "Is there something in the water?"

"Sounds like ice," the rowing crewman said, as more shards clinked off the wood and chimed off each other. "We're a bit far north for that."

A crackling sound started to surround the boat as everyone began to breathe clouds of white vapour. As Eramir raised the oars out of the water, there were chunks of ice stuck to the paddles, glistening in the moonlight.

Renald awoke as the boat jolted violently.

"Something bloody hit us," Eramir said, concerned as he pulled in the oars. "Something big."

The four of them looked over the edge into the water.

"A seadrake?" Renald guessed.

"A frostdrake, I'd reckon, sir, what with the ice," Eramir suggested. "Though I've never heard of one hiding in the water like this."

"Here," Delmur called out, pointing past the boat. "I saw something."

"What?" Renald asked.

"White scales," Delmur confirmed.

Elaeni closed her eyes in dread and felt the boat rock forward as they were showered in cold brine from behind. Something huge had launched out of the water and hit the back of their vessel. Everyone was forced to grab the boat to stay onboard as the wooden craft violently thrashed about like a bucking horse.

When Elaeni turned back the boat was rocking from side to side, rebalancing itself in the water. Everyone was looking up as water still showered them from above.

"What the hells was that?" Delmur demanded.

"What the hells was what?" Renald asked.

"Something came out of the water," Delmur said, looking up and down, searching the night sky and dark sea. "Something huge shot out of the water, but it never came back down."

"It was white-scaled like a frostdrake but my eyes got sprayed," Eramir said, "I didn't get a good..."

The others looked to see why the crewman trailed off. He was staring at the back of the boat where a white female figure sat by the keel in flowing pale layers of cloth.

"You didn't even say goodbye or tell me that you were leaving for that matter," a familiar voice said. "Did I do something to offend you?"

"Aekestyr," Elaeni said, somewhere between fear and pity.

Eramir picked up one of the two wooden spears they had taken for fishing and pointed it at her, while Renald did the same.

"If you're considering attacking me," the white-haired figure said, "it won't end the way you think it will."

"Only one way to find out," Eramir said defiantly, as he lunged forward before Elaeni could stop him.

Aekestyr raised her hand, brushing the shaft aside as the point came towards her chest. She turned her hand and grabbed the weapon, guiding it past herself, and grasping the crewman's wrist with her other hand. A white glow washed over his forearm as his fingers released the weapon. A harsh cold crackle issued as he yelled in pain. His arm turned white, consumed by frost, as she tossed the spear into the sea. She pushed him back towards the others, where his frozen arm hit the mast and shattered like pottery. His hand and chunks of his forearm hit the wood of the inner hull with deep clunks like rocks.

Eramir fell on his back, screaming in pain as he cradled his frozen, shattered arm.

"Drop your weapon," Aekestyr commanded Renald, who complied, confused, and let the wooden shaft drop inside the boat. She looked to both men who were still standing and commanded again, "Both of you drop to your hands and knees," and they did so, compelled as if by some magic.

Elaeni dropped also, but to wrap cloth around Eramir's frozen, jagged stump. "We did not leave," she told their visitor, "we escaped. We were prisoners, not guests."

"What an ungrateful assessment," Aekestyr protested.

"And who is appropriately grateful?" Elaeni asked. "Edwuld Darrow? Bewitched by some spell to forget his wife and marry another? Or everyone aboard the Saltdrake who was drowned or impaled upon rocks as their ship was hurled by some great force beneath the waves, hiding in the storm."

"What?" Renald asked, struggling against his own compulsion to be knelt on hands and knees.

"You brought us to those islands," Elaeni accused. "You brought us there for the ones you call your children."

"I did not mean for so many to die," Aekestyr said with remorse in her voice. "My children needed new blood, else their children would soon be born deformed and defective. I don't understand why the first gods made people with such limiting rules. Such a small breeding pool is so easily corrupted, but then my own parents could not have been further apart."

Elaeni thought of the unfortunate shape she saw when she had spied Aekestyr's true form.

"Your children had their time," Delmur said, caught by magic in a motionless crawl, "a thousand-year reign and they pushed outwards until others pushed back. A handful fled, refusing to face their end, and you've watched over them. But to take lives from the world that moved on, to preserve a faint trace of what your children once were? No. History made its choice."

"And my children, the remnants of the last great empire, have not bothered history since. So what if I take a few souls every few centuries to replenish their limited number?" Aekestyr reasoned.

"How many ships broke upon those islands without your interference?" Renald asked, still struggling against the spell that held him down.

Aekestyr did not answer, but her face did. She had crashed them all.

"We all agreed we'd not speak to anyone of your children," Elaeni reasoned, "but one day you'll bring the wrong ship to its doom, and either those that survive will take the island from them or you'll strand someone too important to forget. Others will come. And what you fear most will come to pass by your own hand."

"And those who came, meaning harm to my children, would be smashed upon the rocks," Aekestyr informed her, as her defensive pride consumed her guilt. "Facing storms made not to gather but to destroy."

"There are those, of course, who would be willing to come," Delmur said, to everyone's intrigue. "It's commonly said that the ancient Kestrians were wiped out, but that's not strictly true."

Aekestyr's eyes widened. "Go on."

"Wildfolk," Delmur continued, "some of them are tribes that fell through the cracks of history, evading the rule of kingdoms and empires, living in remote, uncontrolled, places. Mountains, gorges, and whatnot. Some are outlaws who settled down, deserters, or even cults. But it is believed that many imperials adopted the wildfolk way of life, surviving extinction by creating hidden settlements and enclaves throughout the continent of Kestria. I'm quite sure they would be willing to seek this place out if they knew their empress lived."

"And if you can find sorcerers and warlocks across the sea in the place where they go when they sleep...?" Elaeni offered. "They would probably help you in exchange for the kind of knowledge you promised Felina."

"Yes," Delmur agreed. "They could be sent in ships packed with boats that could safely ferry them through the safe path of the southwest island if you kept the sea calm and clear."

"You are certain of these groups?" Aekestyr asked Delmur.

"I devoted my life to studying the Kestrian Empire," Delmur assured her. "Of little else could I be more certain. I'd stake my reputation on it."

"What about your life?" Aekstyr asked, with a cold menace. "All of your lives?"

Delmur looked to the others, uncomfortable making such a wager, but nodded all the same.

"Then I trade your lives for this knowledge, and this shall become my new pursuit," Aekestyr said, holding out her hand to Elaeni. "I set you free."

"Thank you," Elaeni said, taking her hand.

"Know that I regret what I have done to you," Aekstyr said, tightening her grip on her hand, "But promise me, when the fog in your mind clears, you will not return. Promise me."

"I promise." Elaeni held her gaze, wondering what made her think she'd attempt such a thing after all the effort that went into escape. It seemed as if Aekestyr wanted to say more but held back.

"I do not think the wind shall return anytime soon, so allow me to give you a parting gift. One that will aid you and hopefully help fill the void of what I have taken from you." Aekestyr smiled apologetically, further confusing Elaeni. "When it comes, you will be afraid, but remember you speak its language now." Aekestyr released her hand and stepped back. "In the meantime, you should start fashioning as long a rope as you can manage." She stepped back again, past the stern, and pin-dropped into the sea. The boat shook as Elanei saw something large and white beneath the water travel westward with great speed. Not back to her islands, but towards their destination.

"Has she gone?" Renald asked, grunting as both he and Delmur collapsed.

"Yes, but she's passed us," Elaeni said, confused. "She went the same way we're going."

Renald quickly went to Eramir's side while Delmur looked towards the west with Elaeni.

"To fetch this gift of yours, perhaps?" Delmur wondered.

Eramir's wound was dressed and tied off without fear of him bleeding to death, ready to halt the blood flow when his arm thawed out. Then the other three spent the rest of the night tearing to strips the material that made the blankets that were supposed to protect them from the sun. All three men sacrificed their shirts, as Elaeni gave up her dress, leaving her only in her shift, and they plaited them into ropes.

Making the rope made her think of the men she watched hang. The brigands who killed her husband. She had stood at the front of the crowd and looked them all in the eyes. But now, as she went back to that place in her mind, the memory she most visited, she could no longer remember their faces.

Elaeni closed her eyes a moment. She focused until she found herself there again, standing before the gallows as the bound men stepped up onto the bench. As she strained to raise her own head to see their faces, she noticed the crowd was silent for the first time. When she turned back, she found she was the only one standing in the city square. She took a few steps into the missing crowd and felt about the air before hearing the crash of the collapsing bench and the deep tug of the four nooses tightening under the weight of the dropping men. When she turned back the nooses swung empty in the air. She was alone.

"How right do you think she was about the wind?" Delmur asked, snapping Elaeni out of her trance as he helped Renald tie the last segments together.

"Uh…I don't know," Elaeni said, hovering over Eramir, remembering that she had come to the bushy-bearded crewman to check on his wound dressing, "but she seems to understand things beyond most."

As the sun began to peek over the east horizon a screech was heard in the sky from the west. All looked to see a white-winged creature in the distance, heading towards them.

"A frostdrake, that's definitely a frostdrake," Eramir exclaimed. "Hells."

"All we have is one wooden bloody spear," Renald said as he pulled in the oars.

Elaeni looked to the creature flying towards them, the sun of the breaking dawn illuminating its white scales, a lesser dragon with curved backward horns upon its head, no forelegs, no speech, no spells. Just a creature that could freeze men with its breath and tear them apart in its maw.

"The spear will do nothing," Eramir said. "You'd have to get it square in the eye and even then, you'll never throw it hard enough to get through to where it needs to get."

"It's all we've got," Renald argued.

"Sten," Delmur said to Elaeni.

"What?" she asked.

"Sten Stenbrok tamed Groek, a frostdrake, because he spoke their language, the dragon tongue," Delmur said.

Elaeni looked to her silver ring, enchanted by Aekestyr. "What do I say to it?"

"Perhaps…hail friend?" Delmur shrugged. "Hear my words…accept my command? Don't eat my friends."

As the frostdrake drew close, Elaeni yelled commanding words, hearing herself speak a tongue she did not know before. Aekestyr had spoken in the language of Ancaraug's people but this was different. The others looked at her, recognising no word that she used.

The white-scaled flying creature harkened to her, hovering before them, screeching back as its large flapping wings whooped the air while the tip of its tail flicked at the water below.

"I am your master now," she declared, earning another screech that sounded like one of submission, or at least so she hoped. The ring made her able to speak to the creature in a tongue it understood, but it did not have speech itself. It could only communicate with compliance. "Can you bring us to land?" she asked awkwardly, picking up one end of the messy rope that seemed to match the patchwork style of the boat.

The creature backed away as Renald tied one end of the rope to part of the bow framework and the other to the middle of an oar he tossed into the water. The frostdrake took it in its talons and slowly flew ahead until the rope tightened.

Everyone fell into the boat as it jolted and began to move forward. The creature's wings skimmed the seawater as it flew low a few dozen feet ahead of them. It struggled at first, adjusting and turning, unaccustomed to the task it was attempting. Eventually it found a harmonious position and increased its velocity, pulling them far beyond rowing speed.

Elaeni's new companion towed them tirelessly for hours, moving the vessel faster than was usual for a craft with a closed sail. Those onboard speculated as to how long it could stay in motion encumbered so.

Delmur assured them this would be the most anyone could hope to observe such a creature so close and for so long. "It would be foolish not to use this rare opportunity to make a study of it," the scholar said. "I'm quite sure someone would be most willing to put coin into such an undertaking."

Elaeni smiled at him and nodded in agreement.

By the time they saw a ship, everyone on board was leaning over the railing, marvelling at the sight of some makeshift sailing boat being dragged across the sea by twenty or more feet of white winged beast. Renald and Delmur waved to the gawking crew high above them, several of which raised their hands back in confusion and wonder.

Eramir laughed. "They're more like to reckon it's dragging us off to eat."

The creature dragged the boat right onto the sand on a beach just southwest of the Ohtylosian capital of Horkhund before releasing the rope. It landed on the grey damp sand, curled up, and promptly took to sleep.

Folk from a nearby fishing village stood staring at the group; three men with no shirts, one missing an arm, and a woman in only a shift, patting a sleeping frostdrake that had dragged them to shore from over the horizon. They were hesitant to approach.

"Frostdrakes are almost never seen in northern Ohtylos," Renald informed Elaeni as she ran her hand over the white scales of its long neck. "And they are notoriously hostile. I can't imagine what the locals must think of you, or indeed all of us, but I need to take Eramir into the city. His wound must be seen to properly."

"I can't come with you to translate," she realised. "I need to be here in case he wakes up."

"I think pointing to half a missing arm is the same in all tongues, miss," Eramir said, as Renald helped him to his feet.

"So, what are you going to call your new companion?" Delmur asked.

"My husband and I had always planned to name our first boy Rheatt," Elaeni replied.

"Not a very wyrmkind-sounding name," Delmur said, pointing to the beast. "How would you say the name to him in his tongue?"

"Gheleg," she said to her own surprise before whispering it again to the resting creature. "The only question now is how we're going to make enough coin to get clothes, food, and a ship," Elaeni sighed.

"Ship?" Renald said, pointing to Gheleg's wings. "I'm not sure you need worry about ships anymore." He put an arm around his crewman and the pair began to walk towards the city. "I'll return soon," Renald promised.

"I think we'll be safe enough," Delmur reasoned.

Elaeni thought about Aekstyr's words as Renald began to walk away. She said she had taken something from her. At first, she assumed she meant her possessions, her coin, and the things that reminded her of her husband. Then she remembered talking to Renald. The first mate who knew all aboard the Saltdrake by name. "Wait," she called out to him before the pair could get far.

Renald and Eramir stopped in their tracks and turned back to face her.

"Sorry, I just…" she realised there was no detail of the brigands' execution left. Like a dream that had faded, leaving behind only an impression and nothing of substance. "I have to ask you again."

"What?" Renald stared at her.

"You saw a woman with Edwuld. Edwuld Darrow. Before he boarded."

"Yes, what about her?"

"What did she look like?" Elaeni asked, as a shadow grew in her mind and doubt sank in her heart.

"Why are you asking this now?" Renald asked, as he gestured to his injured companion.

"Aekestyr was powerful and ancient. Yet she could only maintain her form for so long, as if her power was being drained by something else. Some greater enchantment or spell that she needed to maintain. I think."

"What's this to do with Edwuld Darrow?" Renald shrugged dismissively.

"What did his wife look like?" she asked.

Renald shrugged again. "Pale, slim, dark shoulder-length hair…" his shoulders sank as something terrible occurred to him.

"The first day on the island you said you knew the name of every person on that ship," she said. "At least every passenger."

"I do."

"Then without hesitation, as if you were reading the ship's manifest. What's my name?"

Renald smiled at the absurdity of the question. "Elaeni," he said, but as he thought of the day of boarding, his smile fell. "Elaeni Darrow."

Elaeni grabbed Delmur's arm for support as she staggered. Aekestyr's spell had faded, for she was too far to be influenced by it now and her mind was correcting itself. Her husband hadn't died, not a year ago, not now, and Edwuld's wife, the woman she had been so worried about, was herself.

"I'm so sorry," Renald said, stepping back towards her. "Why didn't I remember that?"

"She put a spell on us," Elaeni explained. "She made us forget. She probably made Edwuld forget that he'd even been married, and with the empress putting her own spell on him, keeping us separated…"

"Gods, that's why we hardly ever saw him," Delmur said. "Your mind was made to forget, but your heart wouldn't. That's why you felt so bad about leaving him behind. That's why you weren't willing to move on."

"I'm really so very sorry," Renald said, putting his hand on her arm as she began to tear up, "but I must take Eramir to be seen to."

Elaeni nodded. "Go, it's alright."

"I hate to leave you like this, but I'll be right back," Renald promised as he reluctantly left her.

Delmur nodded to him as he sat Elaeni down, leaning her against her sleeping frostdrake. He sat next to her for some time, letting her weep and took her hand to comfort her. "Do you know why you were on the ship, then?" he wondered.

"He had business in Noordmeer," she remembered, now that the spell had lifted like a fog. "We were going to visit my parents while we were there, but I wasn't returning to them the way I'd been fooled into believing. Just visiting." She shook her head.

"Hardly fooled," Delmur assured her. "Powerful magic was employed and not just on you. All of us. But, if it's any consolation, you probably didn't lose everything to the sea after all."

"Just my husband," she said miserably. "No wonder she made me promise to never return. Even if I did, she'd probably make me forget why I had."

"If that's all she did," Delmur warned. "But look at it this way. You lost your husband at sea, as so many women do. It will take some time to recover from that. But remember, you've gained some interesting friends. This great beast, chief among them," he said, looking back at Gheleg's sleeping head, "to whom I'm not ashamed to take second place. And I suspect the affections of the captain of a ship recently docked not a thousand miles away. Not a grand ship, I must admit."

Elaeni was confused until she looked to where the Salty Hatchling sat half dragged up onto the shore. "But a vessel worthy of the name," she said, wiping away her tears with a sad laugh. "A widow, of sorts, who speaks every language and commands a beast most feared in the southern kingdoms."

They sat on the beach as the locals stared and the gulls waddled away, waiting for Renald to return. Elaeni wondered, rubbing her enchanted silver wedding band, where her life would lead now. She considered Delmur's words. For all that she had lost, she had gained also. She could not go back for her husband. Aekestyr had the victory there, and Elaeni would have to make peace with not having a parting word on that matter. But she now saw new opportunities and perhaps new happiness ahead with her current companions. As long as they stayed clear of those Black Spire Isles.

I always find titles difficult. Usually, I write the title last so I can draw off of phrases or images that appear in the story. For "Field Notes", there's a part where Idylwild, the surveyor protagonist, thinks about her field notebooks. The ones she had when she was a kid travelling around with her grandparents, and the one she has now. These kinds of notebooks were inspired by a journal I was given for a sailing trip in junior high. It was pocket-sized with a bright yellow cover, and the paper was more like plastic: waterproof and durable. It's a touchstone object from my life that somehow made it into this science fiction story, and became the inspiration for the title!

Brittni Brinn

Brittni Brinn (she/her) is the author of *The Patch Project* and *A Place That Used to Be*, post-apocalyptic novels about survivors searching for a place to belong in a desolate world. She has a M.A. in Creative Writing from the University of Windsor. Her interests include rocks kicked up by the ocean, books from friends, and comfortable sweaters. You can read more about her work at brittnibrinn.com.

Photo by Sarah Kivell

Field Notes from the Unknown Planet

by Brittni Brinn

For Nico and Zach, my fellow spacefarers.

Yar had been stalking the mammaloid for half the day, her right hand clenched around a sharpened stick, her left hand clenched over her belly. Her last meal had been the day before, a reptilid the size of her fist. She was hungry, sharply, like there was something inside digging at her stomach lining with razor-thin fingernails.

The mammaloid lumbered through the dry grass a few metres ahead. It was about half her size and was covered in thin, dun fur. A short ridge of multicoloured hair ran from the nape of its neck along its spine. She followed, crouching behind a screen of vines as it paused to tear at a patch of lichen. It chewed thoughtfully, turning slightly so she could see for the first time a bulge along its underside. The mammaloid was pregnant.

She clenched her teeth, the grip on her spear tightening. "Doesn't change what I have to do." The mammaloid's head drifted up towards her, bits of lichen stuck in the beard of fur around its maw. It turned back to eating, methodically stripping the rock bare. The mammaloid ambled off through a copse of leafless trees, its belly swaying as it went.

She stayed behind, her stomach growling in protest.

"Your children will feed my children," she promised the mammaloid as it pushed its way through a patch of brush and disappeared from view.

She lowered the spear to the ground and pulled open the mouth of her satchel. Tucked into an inner pocket were a few shrivelled berries she had picked from a bush near her camp. She placed one in her mouth and sucked on it for a while before breaking the skin. She savoured the pulp; the juices had long dried out, leaving gritty seeds behind. She was about to pluck a second berry from her bag when she heard movement in the rushes behind her.

Grasping the spear, she turned towards the sound. The yellow patch of rushes remained still. She stalked towards it, staying low. A stray seed lodged itself in her throat; she endured it silently.

As she got closer, she noticed something green and scaly sticking out from the brush. She stopped, heart racing. A full-grown reptilid could tear her apart. She'd only seen one that big in all her time in the dry jungle, and realizing that she was this close to one now brought a wave of nausea. If she could get close enough, she might be able to stab it through the leg, retake her spear, and make another plunge into its chest cavity. A reptilid could provide enough meat for weeks. She had to kill it.

The reptilid had a strange foot. No claws, a different colour from the green leg, more of a brown. Strange lateral markings up to the ankle. And she'd never seen any creature with treads in their soles before—

She ran the rest of the distance to the brush, pushing the dead reeds aside. Laying on the ground was a humanoid, unconscious, blood and muck splattered over their tan face, a long tunic tangled over their green leggings and laced boots.

She grit her teeth as her hand tightened around the shaft of the spear. The humanoid looked well-fed and the fresh blood was enough to stir her hunger into a rage that demanded satisfaction. She lifted the sharpened stick, bracing a hand on her abdomen.

She remembered the pregnant mammaloid and stopped. She lowered the spear.

Surveying the jungle around them, Yar reached down and took hold of the humanoid under the arms. She staggered as she dragged them out of the reeds.

"Wake up!" she commanded, but the body lay still. It took her the rest of the afternoon to fashion a mat using the tarp and rope from her backpack. She tied the guide ropes across her chest, and headed into the brush, dragging the unconscious humanoid in her wake.

Idylwild smelled woodsmoke, pungent and strange. With the smell came memories of Boreal, one of the first worlds settled after Earth's collapse one hundred and fifty years ago. Boreal was big, nearly twice the size of Earth, with most of its landmass covered in rugged forests. Her grandparents said that their ancestors would've lived in a place just like it. They hadn't stayed long: a couple weeks of tents and canned food before taking off to find the next world and uncover its secrets.

The smoke curled into her darkness. She breathed in the charred smell and exhaled out through her mouth. She opened her eyes. She was in a hut of some kind, though 'hut' was a generous descriptor. A see-through tarp flapped against a skeletal frame of branches tied with vines between four living trees. More dead grey branches were woven into the walls to keep out the wind. A campfire burned outside the mouth of the hut, and she could make out a hunched figure through the flames.

Tired from the exertion of looking around, she lowered her head, comforted that there was something soft underneath it. Wherever she was, whoever had found her had cared enough to make the ground beneath her more comfortable. How did she get here? The memory was fuzzy...they drugged her...there was a *humming*, she didn't know where—Vyan, was he—? No, she remembered. He wouldn't be here. Not where she was.

She gathered the strength to push herself up, a covering falling away from her as she stood. Her clothes were filthy, and she winced, seeing a deep red stain on her shirt sleeve. Feeling steady enough on her feet, she took a step towards the figure. Another step closer, and the figure looked up, dark brown eyes reflecting the flames between them.

"Are you the one who helped me?" Idylwild began, then stopped. This might be first contact with this person. Maybe they'd never seen a human before. Starting over. "Hello," she said clearly, holding up her left hand with the palm forward, a standard greeting. "My name is Idylwild, she/her. I'm human." She placed her left hand on her chest, where personhood resided. Then she held out her hand, and waited.

The figure stood slowly, both hands resting on a swollen abdomen.

Idylwild tried the greeting again in the Old Earth language, in case the person was from one of the inner planets.

The figure grinned strangely then held up a right hand. "I'm Yar, she/her. Human."

Idylwild was relieved: she hadn't botched first contact after all. "I think I owe you thanks for getting me out of a dangerous position."

"Your clothes," Yar said, "where'd you get them?"

"My clothes?" Idylwild considered her tunic, armoured leggings, and laced up traveller's boots. Compared to what Yar was wearing, they did look a little strange. How far had the Council sent her? "This is what I wear at home on Qua'Suth."

Yar stared at her.

"Qua'Suth, do you know where that is?"

"Never heard of it."

Idylwild released the friendly smile, her face dropping into a neutral expression. Never heard of Qua'Suth? "Oh well, uh, that's..." Not a good sign, she sighed to herself. "What planet are we on?"

"Mulch," Yar said, rummaging in her bag and taking out a handful of something.

"Mulch..." A strange name. Not a place Idylwild had heard of or been to that she could recall. Idylwild lowered herself to the ground, a sharp pain running up her right arm as she tried to lean back on it.

Yar came around the fire, holding out a closed fist. "Here." Idylwild opened her left hand and Yar dropped a handful of shrivelled berries onto her palm. "That's all the food I have."

Idylwild registered the berries, and the next moment they were between her teeth as hunger took hold of her. They were gritty and bitter but she swallowed them anyway.

Yar went back on the other side of the fire and huddled around her swollen belly.

"Are you alone here?" Idylwild asked quietly. It had just dawned on her why Yar's stomach might be distended the way it was.

Yar studied Idylwild through the flames the way a hunter studies their prey. "Not anymore."

Idylwild kept track of the days in her field notebook. This one was a far cry from the flimsy thing she used to take out when surveying planets with her grandparents. Instead of thin sheets of microfibre paper, this was a pocket-sized two-hundred-page volume of plastic-enforced data paper. It was water-proof, only reacted to the tip of the stylus, and could not be erased. She had just bought it the week before, intending to use it for a short visit to a nearby moon. At least the Council hadn't taken it.

She flipped back a couple pages to her first entry on Mulch: it described the wasted jungle and what little vegetation she could make out from inside the hut. Yar had insisted she rest for the day and had gone out hunting. She'd returned with two chameleon-like reptilids, which Idylwild sketched as they roasted on a spit over the campfire. Yar didn't talk much, and only answered a couple of questions those first few days.

The entry from the night before was the one Idylwild wanted to look over. Yar had been drinking from the water reclimator, a tiny one obviously meant for backpacking where rain was plentiful. Unfortunately, water was the one thing the jungle seemed to lack. Probably the reason the plant life surrounding the camp was sickly and dying. A drought.

"Milky Way," Yar had said, gruff and curt, her usual tone.

"What about it?"

"You know where that is?"

"I mean, of course I do. The galaxy where Earth is."

Yar's expression was hard to read. "Earth, yes. How far away is it?"

"I don't, I don't know where we are—"

"Mulch," Yar yelled, exasperated. "Mulch, Mulch, Mulch!"

"I don't know where—"

"Do you see the stars? Figure it out!"

Idylwild craned her neck. Of course she saw them. They looked out of sync to her. That cluster could be the Pleiades, and the elongated 'L' could be a wedge of Cassiopeia seen from a different angle. There was no North Star. Nothing to take her bearings from. "If I had a ship—"

Yar stomped the ground, her long brownish-red hair flailing around her shoulders. "No ships, I checked. No crashes, no pods, no tracks through the jungle. Where the hell did you come from?"

"I could ask you the same thing," Idylwild said, Yar's frustration digging under her skin. "Did the People's Council send you here too?"

Yar didn't seem to hear her. "It's your turn to hunt tomorrow." Yar threw the stick she used as a spear, bloodied up to the hand grip, at Idylwild.

"I can't kill something with this."

"You will." Yar crouched down next to her. "Or we'll stave." Both of her hands went to cover the sagging pouch where an approximately eight-month-old fetus was growing.

Idylwild snapped the notebook shut, securing the stylus in the clip that kept the pages together. She tucked it into the pocket on the side of her left leg. Strange that the Council had dropped her here, wherever here was, without taking the stuff she had on her. The only things they'd removed were her knife, a gift from her grandparents when she started her own survey mission, and a pendant Vyan had given her. Maybe leaving her other possessions untouched was a way to highlight what was missing. To remind her that she had been stripped of her relationship to their people, and to Vyan.

She stood up from the sleeping mat. Yar had slept in the hut that night, leaving the spear at the foot of Idylwild's space by the fire. Idylwild picked it up. Would she be able to kill anything with the crude weapon?

Her eyes caught on the material wrapped around the wound on her arm. Yar mumbled in her sleep and turned away from her, curling around her belly. Idylwyld faced the brittle jungle and headed out to find breakfast.

Three weeks later, Idylwild picked her way through the green undergrowth. The rainy season had arrived without warning a few days ago, and already the plants were taking advantage. Idylwild rubbed a deep maroon leaf between her fingers and smiled. She'd have to come back through this way to make notes after delivering the spoils of the day's hunt: two neon green birds with white and yellow accents over their eyes and wings.

Yar was sitting on a low tree trunk by the fire, weaving vines together. She'd braided her hair back from her forehead, her beige skin blotchy with old sunburns. Since Idylwild had taken over hunting, Yar had become more sedentary, spending most days doing small repairs around the campsite and resting in the hut. Still, she often met Idylwild's return with a kind of wariness, a predatory gleam lurking deep in her eyes.

Idylwild dumped the two dead birds on the ground in front of her.

Yar's eyes widened. "Where did you find these?"

"Up by the waterfall, I hid in that big tree next to the pool—"

"Birds, with feathers." Yar picked one up by its wing, studying its plumage. "I haven't seen birds in a long time."

"Migration season." Idylwild sank down next to the campfire, her hands crossed in her lap. She'd spent hours waiting for the birds to land close enough to catch in a vine net, and now all she wanted to do was relax.

"They'll do." Yar started to stand, a hand braced on her abdomen. She froze, her face contorting in surprise. "Dammit."

"Is it happening?" Idylwild sprang up, hurrying over. "Yar?"

A weird smile overshadowed Yar's face. "We'd better get ready."

Nearly a full day into labour, her face a mess of tears and sweat, Yar looked over to Idylwild who was kneeling next to her. "I almost killed you."

Idylwild gripped her hand. "Do you mean the day you saved me? Don't worry about the bumps and bruises. You got me back to camp, that's what matters."

"I almost killed you." A spasm wracked Yar's body, but her gaze stayed on Idylwild.

"Don't worry about this now," Idylwild said. "Worry about the baby. Push, Yar!"

Yar pushed and pushed, then locked her red-rimmed eyes on Idylwild again. "I was hunting a mammaloid that day. When I saw it was pregnant, I let it go. And then I heard something in the bushes. I thought you might be a reptilid—"

"It's understandable that you'd be defensive." Idylwild brushed a piece of hair from Yar's face.

"I saw a humanoid. *You.* I saw your fat face and your meaty arms and I almost killed you."

"But you didn't," Idylwild soothed. "You had compassion, just like you had compassion for the pregnant mammaloid."

"Compassion!" Yar hurled the word in a stream of laughter and spittle as she strained against the ground. "You think it was compassion!"

Idylwild was at her knees now. "Are you sure you don't want to stand for this? I can catch the baby."

Yar grit her teeth. "You know why I didn't eat that day? The animal will give birth to a litter of ten or so, baby mammaloids who will grow up to be food—"

"I can see the head—"

"And I spared you for a selfish purpose as well—"

"Push! Push! You're almost there—"

"—I let you live only because I didn't want to have this baby alone!"

"Oh, Yar. It's a girl. Yar?"

The blood ran with the afterbirth, and Yar lay on the ground, never to move again.

Before burying Yar's body, Idylwild went through her things. Underneath the mammaloid fur vest, which was tied closed with lengths of dried sinews, Yar's clothes were worn to almost tatters. Hanging around her neck was a pocket that had been ripped free from what probably had been a coat of some kind; bundled inside was a plastic envelope. Idylwild slid open the resealable tab. She took out a letter and a carved wooden tower, perhaps an old children's toy. She set the object aside and, with the newborn supported in one arm, held up the letter with her free hand.

Dearest Nayar,

I'm afraid the orders have come through: I'm to leave tomorrow on the next transport ship. I tried to convince them to let me stay, just one more year.

But if I don't get on that ship tomorrow they might come looking for me, andfind you. I can't have anything happening to you, now can I? Everything inmy body tells me to deliver this letter myself so I can give you a proper goodbyeat least, but I can't risk it. I'll leave it with our good friend, who'll deliver it onceI'm off. Don't try to follow me

Nayar, I beg you. We travel through dangerous space. Even if you catch up, our ship is a warship, don't forget. They may shoot on sight. That's another risk we can't take. Our baby should grow up on Earth, where we met, fell in love. I love you Nayar. Please, think well of me. Speak myname often to our child, and maybe the gods will hear you and send me back.

In desperate hope, and endless love for you,

Ferra

Idylwild lowered the letter and sighed. "We had more in common than I realized," she said to Yar's afterimage.

The newborn slept in the crook of her healed arm. Idylwild transcribed a copy of the letter into her field notebook and replaced the letter in the envelope. She set the carved tower aside, intending it for the baby. Finding no other clues to Yar's past on her body, she scoured the campsite for anything that would give her an idea of how Yar had arrived on the planet she had called Mulch. Nothing came up apart from scraps of old ration packaging.

Idylwild set the infant on her bed mat and began digging. She buried Yar, along with the letter, and then set about the task of figuring out how to take care of a newborn.

The day it happened, Idylwild was waiting in the courtyard outside of the administrative building where Vyan worked. Two uniformed members of the People's Council approached her, wearing traditional grey robes, a red flower hanging from a gold cord around each of their necks. She stood from the public bench and nodded to them, careful to keep her teeth from showing as she smiled. They nodded back and informed her that she was under arrest.

They brought her to the hearing room, where all of the People's Council meetings were held. She shouldn't have been surprised, but Vyan was there as well, held in an alcove across from the one where she sat. The glossy floor stretched between them like a perfectly round lake. Members of the Council were seated on raised platforms around a tiled island in the centre of the room.

"Vyan'Ahl," one of the Council members began from their seat, "please come forward."

Vyan did so. As he moved from the shadowed alcove, Idylwild noticed with a stab of fear that his wings were bound behind him. She tried to catch his attention, but he stood on the island with his side facing her, his smooth white face angled up at the Council member.

"You know why you are here?" another Council member asked, and Vyan turned to face them.

"I have seduced a human, one not from our people."

"And you admit freely that it was an ongoing seduction, not a one time affair."

"Yes," Vyan said evenly, repositioning himself to face the next Council member.

"Is there anything you would like to say in your defence?"

"The human was innocent of the consequences of my attentions, and did not know that I was breaking our laws—"

"That's not true!" Idylwild tried to call out, but was quickly shushed by the Council member standing at her side.

"Stay quiet," they said in a quick whisper. "Don't you see he's saying that to protect you?"

Vyan turned fully away from her; she couldn't hear his response to the next Council member's question.

"Are you aware," the final Council member asked as Vyan wearily came full circle, "that any intimate relationships with outsiders are forbidden, and are to be punished most severely?"

"Of course I am," he replied in a pained voice, "but there is no law that says the partner of the trespasser should be punished."

The Council member pressed their six fingers together, three to three. "The human will not be harmed. However, we will need to ensure that this crime does not transpire a second time."

Vyan did look over to Idylwild then. The intensity of his gaze was unbearable; he looked at her as if he would never see her again.

A Council member escorted Vyan off the island, through the gap in the Council circle, and across the glossy floor. They passed through an archway, and were gone.

Idylwild knew from bits and pieces that trespassers on Qua'Suth were not imprisoned; prisons were unknown in their society, as was the death penalty. Depending on the crime, trespassers were rehabilitated through group therapy and moved to communities far from where their crimes had taken place. But she also knew that engaging in romantic entanglements with outsiders was one of the worst crimes of all. They would send Vyan far, far away. Where to, she didn't know.

She kept her eyes on the archway Vyan had passed through, feeling herself become unrooted, tilting between reality and dreams. Surely this was a dream. Vyan hadn't been taken away, not really. She had to keep watching the archway, otherwise he would never be able to find his way back.

The Council member next to her asked her to follow them into the hallway. She barely noticed when they exited through the small door behind her.

The circle of Council members came down from their seats and drifted out through the main doorway, the light whoosh of their wings rustling their robes. The time for decisions was over. The archway remained empty.

The Council member was waiting for her by a brightly-tiled pillar. They were average height, a few feet taller than her, dressed in the grey robes of the Council. Their skin was distinguished by ivory patches, a rare skin condition that Vyan had told her about.

"Where are we going?"

They glanced down, and then led the way through the dimly-lit hallway. "They're sending you off-world, probably out of this system. To protect themselves from your wiles." The Council member made a clicking noise, a short laugh. "You're a surveyor, aren't you? I'm sure you'll find your way back home, wherever you end up. Might even be a planet you know."

"What about Vyan?"

"About as far as they can send him. Beyond that I can't say."

The door at the end of the hall hissed open and the Council member motioned her through with their long three-fingered hand. Idylwild sat in the room's only chair, her mind kicking into motion as she considered the windowless walls. The Council member stuck a patch onto the back of her hand and moved to stand outside the door.

"What about my ship? There's an AI onboard—"

"I'll make sure everything's in order. Wait here," they said, "and good luck." The door hissed shut.

Idylwild barely had time to rip the drugged patch from her hand before she passed out.

Idylwild stared into the campfire, her mind wandering back to Yar's letter. It had been a long time since she'd heard Earth mentioned, and in the old language, too. It sounded like there was conflict in that system—warships, conscription. Had Yar gone after her lover after all? And how did she end up here?

"Lots of questions," she said to the baby sucking on a corner of her tunic. She'd managed to wash her clothes in some rainwater a couple days ago, after a thundering deluge that ran off the clear tarp overhead in a stream and drenched the soil outside the hut. The baby had screamed the whole time, cries blending into the storm.

"Maybe your name should be Screamer-in-the-Storm," Idylwild teased.

The baby looked up with dark brown eyes, mouth releasing the fabric and staying open as if in surprise.

"Well, we can think of another name if you don't like that one. How about Caterpillar?" The baby did look like a caterpillar, swaddled in a ripped off portion of Yar's old bedding, a round head massive on the tiny body.

The baby made a *hmm* noise, and then sneezed.

"Gods, you're adorable." Up until today, Idylwild couldn't bear to name the baby. Parents were supposed to name a child.

Obviously, no chance of that tradition here. But she couldn't keep calling her 'baby.' Not a name to grow into.

Idylwild stood, supporting the infant against her shoulder. "Well, it's up to you, baby. What do you think about Nerra—a bit of both your parents' names?" Idylwild took the wooden tower out of the side pocket of her legging and held it up where the baby could reach it. The baby's tiny fingers curled around the turreted edge, her big eyes serious.

"Alright," Idylwild said. "Nerra it is."

She fed Nerra whatever she could. Meat broth, mashed pulp from an apple-like fruit that had sprung to the trees after a couple weeks of rain. Now that it was the rainy season, Idylwild found herself missing dry ground. Mud sucked at her boots when she hunted and although the blooming foliage allowed for better cover, the closed-in vegetation made her nervous. Visiting species passed through—birds with vibrant and strange plumages, snakes and other reptilids the size of great danes, insects that if disturbed would billow into an angry cloud. But hunting was better, and she enjoyed testing the sweet or bitter fruit that developed in the seed husks and cactus crowns and vibrant green bushes, noting them in her field journal as she went.

Nerra still rejected solid food, her tongue pushing out, a survival reflex to prevent choking. Idylwild chewed her food for her. She soaked a cloth in fruit juice and let her suck on it. The baby seemed okay for never having known the benefits of milk. If only Idylwild could find a goat or something—milk was important for babies, wasn't it? Idylwild didn't know how to train a goat even if there were any in this biosphere. Still, Nerra seemed happy, and only screamed if the weather was bad.

She had to find a way off the planet. She suspected that Yar had a ship somewhere, or a landing pod. Even if it was damaged, there would be more hope of fixing it than waiting for a passing ship to find them. Still, it was worrisome that Yar had abandoned her only way out of Mulch, which she had clearly hated. Maybe it was destroyed beyond repair.

Idylwild was a thorough surveyor; she'd learned from the best. In this situation, her grandparents would do the exact same thing she was doing: survive, take care of others, and find a way to safety. She kept detailed notes and mapped out areas as she explored them. She took Nerra with her, bound to her back with a carrier made from the rest of Yar's bedding. She used a spiral search pattern, striking out further and further each trip.

After weeks of searching, she came across the first hint of what may have happened to Yar's ship. A section of trees had been knocked over, a couple of dead trunks scarred with burns. Not a forest fire. She followed the trail of broken trees.

Nerra began to fuss against her back. *Shh, shh,* Idylwild soothed. Nerra continued her small cries. When Idylwild turned her head to see what was bothering the baby, she caught sight of a full-grown reptilid stalking behind them. She turned to face it, Yar's spear ready at her side. She shouted and waved her arms above her head, hoping it would scare the reptilid into retreating. But this repilid had the steady gaze and sharp grin of a predator—not to be put off by a challenge.

It lunged at her and she staggered back, swinging the spear in front of her. The reptilid dodged clear and lowered itself in preparation for another attack. Idylwild used the pause to her advantage, rushing the reptilid so it had to reposition itself. It was agile for such a large predator and twisted around Idylwild's attack, moving behind her. She spun sharply, putting herself between the reptilid and the baby. The reptilid struck, sinking its teeth deep into her right calf. Before it could move away, Idylwild rammed the spear between its shoulders and wrenched it down, the tip breaking through the skin between its ribs. Gnashing at her leg, the reptilid struggled, held in place by the battle-hardened spear. Slowly, it died.

The reptilid's jaw relaxed as its body slumped to the ground. Idylwild pulled the spear free and limped away from the growing pool of blood. She leaned her shoulder against a tree, her senses buzzing. She checked on Nerra, relieved to hear her soft breathing. "Thanks, little one. Wouldn't have heard that coming."

She looked down at her calf. The armoured legging had taken most of the damage; it was ripped open around the wound, an oval of bloody teeth marks. She was aware of the pain but somehow disconnected from it, as if the injured leg belonged to somebody else. She made a quick bandage with a rag and braided twine from her pocket.

Before heading back to camp, she used a stone knife from her other pocket to cut a chunk from the reptilid's flank and wrapped it in fern leaves. "Guess we'll call it a day," she said to Nerra as if nothing was wrong. "Hungry?"

Idylwild couldn't sleep. She took deep breaths, focusing on the shadows flickering across the ceiling of the hut. The wound in her leg throbbed under the fabric bandage. It had been awhile since she'd been physically injured; she'd forgotten how much things could hurt, and continue to hurt. How long would the wound be tender for? Would it scar? But the question keeping her awake was more insidious than these simple questions of healing.

Her last inoculations had been almost three years ago, right before setting out to Qua'Suth. It was customary for surveyors to update vaccines and other medical precautions before heading out on any new mission, with planet-specific conditions in mind. She had not prepared her body for a new planet. She knew nothing about Mulch, its diseases, or its treatments.

What if the reptilid had a kind of rabies? One that would co-opt her nervous system and break down her ability to reason, to survive? When would the hallucinations start? How long would it take her to die?

The armoured legging had kept the bite at surface level, leaving teeth marks about a half an inch deep. The area around the bite bruised almost immediately, swelling into a yellow and purple bulge. She'd limped to the waterfall pool on the way back to camp and rinsed the bite as thoroughly as possible. The water numbed her skin enough that she was able to walk all the way back before the pain returned. She bound her calf in fabric strips she'd prepared in case of injury. After cooking the meat over the fire and feeding Nerra, she lay down in the hut, completely exhausted.

"Nerra?" Idylwild turned her head to where the baby lay on a mat next to hers. The baby's dark brown eyes opened. "I know you're too young to understand. But if something happens, something bad, you stay here, okay? If I leave and don't come back. If I...get sick. This is the safest place for you. The only place someone might find you."

Nerra didn't respond. Her eyes shone for a moment and then drifted closed.

Idylwild turned back to the ceiling, wincing as the movement jostled her leg. If the reptilid had given her some kind of disease, there wasn't much she could do about it now. She'd keep the wound clean and make sure that she ate well so her body could do the hard work of healing. She hoped that would be enough.

Finding a way off-world would be her surest bet at recovery, but being down a leg wasn't going to make that easy. She'd have to put off searching for Yar's ship, at least for a couple of weeks. If she could make it until then—well, she'd just have to wait and see.

She took a few more deep breaths, settling into the jungle sounds of rustling leaves, creaking branches, and night birds cooing gently in the dark.

The ship was a wreck. The hull was twisted and there was a strange smell coming out of the open door. Idylwild hesitated at the base of the entry ladder. "How would you feel if I set you in that tree while I check this out?"

From her back, Nerra yawned.

"You're acting nonchalant, but there may be reptilids around." She'd given the clearing with the reptilid corpse a wide berth on the way in. "Guess you'll have to stick with me."

Idylwild leaned her wooden crutch and spear against the hull and gingerly climbed up the five rungs. She slipped through the door, jammed open by a branch thicker than she was. "Definitely a fixer-upper."

Inside was in no better shape. The cockpit window was cracked and one of the panels had completely shattered. A smear of old blood caked the navigational screen. Easing the weight from her injured leg, Idylwild sat on the edge of the captain's chair, dead screens angled towards her at eye level. A sense of peace came over her. It felt better sitting here in a scrap heap that would probably never fly again than it did in the hut. A stab of yearning cut through her defenses, the wall that had not let her miss anything since she'd woken up on this unknown planet.

She thought of her old ship, *The Erebus*. But thoughts of her time spent aboard brought her to Vyan: his contemplative smile, the warmth of his arm against hers, the rush of his wings embracing her. She missed their quiet evenings on the *Erebus* watching classic Earth movies and listening to music from Ikks, a planet the next system over.

Focus on the Erebus, she told herself, moving away from the more charged memories. It had a swivel chair and an AI so advanced it was listed on her crew manifold: Keir. "He's probably pissed," Idylwild laughed to herself, thinking of the ship locked up in some cargo bay. Thankfully, the People's Council took AI personhood very seriously. They wouldn't deactivate him, even if the ship was condemned. They'd transfer him wherever he wanted to go. "Safe travels," she said to his memory, saying goodbye to more than that.

It was obvious from the moment she'd tried to activate the power system. Yar's ship was dead. She wasn't going anywhere. "*We aren't going anywhere*," she amended, as Nerra shifted against her back.

The next few weeks were spent ferrying all the supplies she could find from the dead ship to the camp. The ship's food stores were empty, but she found a bottle of vitamins high on a shelf. Some tools were in the lockers along the walls, but no weapons. A handheld welder, some wire, a small hammer.

The next step was to see if there were any portable power sources, but her search came up empty. She did find a self-powered beacon under a hideaway panel in the floor. She could use it to send out a distress call. Why hadn't Yar?

"I think your mom stole this ship," Idylwild told Nerra that night at camp. "The beacon wasn't that hard to find. Maybe she didn't want anyone from Earth to know she was here. If her people found her with stolen property...I mean, it did sound like a war was going on. Probably not a great thing to take off with a perfectly good ship that could've been refitted for battle."

Nerra slept, small breaths.

"We're in a different boat, though, or ship. You should be with your family on Earth." Idylwild fidgeted with the beacon, typing in a distress code in the four languages she knew, and a couple more that she only knew how to call for help in. "There," she said, and set it a dozen steps from the campfire. "Now to forget about it. If someone shows up, we'll be pleasantly surprised, won't we?"

After a while, Idylwild forgot about the distress beacon. She did her best to make the most of her time while her leg continued to heal. She kept detailed field notes, recording star positions, the path of the sun, and the segments of the two moons. When the dry season returned, she had a stock of dried food squirrelled away in a shed made of scrap metal from the ship.

Occasionally, Idylwild remembered her fight with the reptilid. Whenever she had a headache she would wonder, is it the disease? Whenever she felt light-headed from hunger, she would sit down and rewrap the reptilid bite with shaking hands. The wound healed slowly, leaving purplish scar tissue behind. An oval tattoo, embedded in her skin and her memory. She'd killed full-grown reptilids since then, but that encounter continued to hang over her. She'd spent many sleepless nights, wondering if and when the reptilid's disease would manifest. How would she survive if that happened? How could she protect Nerra?

Nerra was growing quickly, a dark-eyed, red-haired baby who was slowly developing an aversion to being tied to Idylwild's back all the time. She crawled around like a machine, getting covered in dust, always careful not to get too far away. Idylwild appreciated Nerra's discretion. Other babies might've wandered into the underbrush by now, but Nerra seemed content with the small circle of their camp. Nerra also seemed to know when a predator or hungry bird was around and would head straight for the hut when danger appeared. Idylwild kept the handheld welder attached to the end of her spear where it would melt a creature's flesh before it could reach her. That was usually enough to deter them from coming around for a second visit.

She grabbed for her spear when she first heard the ship. She scanned the withered bushes around the camp before remembering that the sound was an engine, and the wind on her face was caused by a landing sequence. The ship touched down behind a screen of bare trees and withered vines, out of sight.

Idylwild strapped Nerra to her back and, still holding the spear, waited for the visitors to approach.

It was agonizing, the wait, though it couldn't have been for more than an hour. *They're probably observing us*, crossed her mind, and with a great effort of will, she made a show of lowering her spear and holding up her left hand palm out—the long unused greeting that was as universal as she could muster.

When they pushed through the dead trees, she nearly burst out in tears. There were four of them, skin colour ranging from rosy purple to cerulean blue. Each of them wore a variation of a one-piece jumpsuit. Their four back limbs carried them along, their front two limbs held at their sides. Their torsos rose into long muscular necks supporting angular heads that tapered into short snouts. Dauphines.

"Greetings!" she called in their language, and they answered back, subdued but friendly.

"We followed your beacon," one of them said, the others swaying in agreement. "Do you require assistance?"

"Yes, myself and the child." She turned slightly so that Nerra's eyes were visible. The Dauphines were big on eye contact. "I was stranded here, and the child's mother...passed away. Would you give us passage on your ship?"

They gazed at her and the baby and then at each other.

"We would like to hear more, on the way," one said.

Another met Idylwild's eyes. "Don't you want to know where we are going?"

"It doesn't matter. Anywhere away from here. Where I can find a ship and return the child to her mother's family."

"Hmmm," said the one who hadn't yet spoken. "It seems to me that the child does not require return, for the child has already arrived."

Idylwild smiled, thinking that her Dauph was rusty.

"Where would you like to go?" asked the first.

Asking them where the Milky Way galaxy was located wouldn't get her anywhere—the Dauphines didn't organize the universe into types and groups and sub-groups. Everything was considered equal, designated only by numerical coordinates, not based around their own planetary system, but reckoned from the centre of the universe, where everything began. Idylwild tried to bring the universe grid to mind, but it had been too long, and her mind was muggy with hunger. "I only know that we want to go to Earth."

The Dauphines swayed thoughtfully but offered no guidance. "Is there anything you need before we depart?"

Idylwild looked back at the camp, the tattered blankets, and the hut that looked more like a card house than a shelter. The campfire had burned down to coals. "I'll put out the fire and disable the beacon to prevent any further visitors."

"Join us at the ship when you're ready." The Dauphines moved off, the curtain of vines rustling behind them.

The stillness of the dry season settled around her. She'd had a hallucination. There was no ship of Dauphines. The reptilid's disease had finally reached her mind.

"Were they real?" she asked, and Nerra replied with a forceful push on her back. "Right. Might as well have a bit of hope." Idylwild scattered a bucket of dust over the fading coals. She walked over to the beacon and switched the power to off.

Carrying Nerra with her, she followed the Dauphines through the bare trees and was welcomed with an open door, a meal, and a warm sleeping place, where the question of real and imaginary melted into dreams as the ship carried them away from Mulch and into the stars.

Soulmate alternate universes were a big discussion amongst readers and writers on the web a few years ago. When I thought about revisiting those concepts last year to stretch my writing muscles, I never expected to have the story I ended up with, let alone that it would get published.

When writing about a world of greyscale, I had to figure out how to distinguish between those who saw colour and those who didn't. This is where the "Hueys" and "Shaders" were born, an on the nose set of terms that I felt brought a richness to the story. How do things like art work differently for Shaders? How is a society changed by such contrast? These were some of the questions I had to ask myself when constructing this world.

I can say the last few years have been full of loss and heartache for me, and I connected deeply with my main character's journey through her grief and the fear of starting over. And I think that's something we can all relate to in some form or another. Just as Francis in the story discovers a new kind of true love and restoration, my greatest desire is that this story leaves the reader with hope for the colourless days.

Kelly D. Holmes

Kelly D. Holmes is an avid reader of all things sci-fi, spec fic and fantasy. She's been writing ever since she was ten years old and has worked on everything from comics to songwriting. She lives in London, Canada, and can be found curled up by the fireplace with a good cup of tea. This is her premier publication.

The Colour of Roses

by Kelly D. Holmes

"That which we call a rose, by any other name would smell as sweet." - Shakespeare

"It's only been a year but I have found that my eyes ache for the colour of roses. I never knew that flowers were so beautiful until I knocked into him on the street thirteen years ago. It was a breathtaking, silent explosion — shades of light I had never seen before, bleeding into the simplistic monochrome of the world. And I knew from the same awed, wide-eyed expression on his face that he saw it too.

"Green. That was the name they told us to call the colour of his eyes. We learned many things that summer, none more important than that we were Soulmates. My mother had always told me that Soulmates were everything in this world — that our view of life was complete because of them. And nothing made that statement more poignant than the morning the crimson roses in my garden turned back to grey.

"Like lead injected into my body, my lungs drowned in horror as the vibrant blues and purples of our house drained out of existence. The worst part was knowing what it meant…knowing with certainty that the heart which fuelled the beauty in my sight had stopped beating. The colour being stripped from my world only served to remind me, every moment my eyes were open, that I was alone. At least my dreams still granted me mercy, the brilliance of the love we once shared.

"I've adjusted. I don't panic anymore when the sun comes up and I can't tell whether the sky is pink or orange. I've stopped asking strangers what colour my clothes are. It's been a year that I've been blind to pigments, and while I'm used to it again, I still miss the colour of roses."

I take a deep breath and put the notebook in my lap, smoothing the edges with deliberate attention, unwilling to meet the twelve pairs of eyes fixed on me.

It was too much — the story of my past. I felt it as I wrote it out earlier, but now I know it with certainty.

Which, I have to admit, is quite on brand for me. Too much too soon.

The spacious study holds their silence like a blanket over my head. While I figured what I'd written would probably be too dark and depressing for a first book club meeting, I hadn't expected things to feel this awkward. After all, we were asked to participate in the exercise as a way to break the ice and get to know each other — write a page about the most defining stage or decision of your life. But the sharing now feels much more intimate than is appropriate.

My face burns under the weight of the cloying silence.

Someone clears their throat and I can't lift my eyes in time to see who.

"Well, Francis, that was certainly a moving piece. We're so sorry for your loss," says the squarish man who is co-hosting our gathering. An echo of agreement sweeps the sloppy circle following Doug's sympathies.

I dare a glance at my fellow book club members. Some eyes meet mine with tight, hesitant smiles as they attempt to uncouple their interlocked fingers from my view, like the sight of Soulmates will wither my heart. Others meet with such aching empathy that I can see the wraiths of colour haunting their gaze. The rest just stare at the ground, distancing themselves from the pain of losses they have yet to experience.

The healing of a year and my mother's raising prompt the edges of my lips politely heavenward. "Thank you, Doug. Thank you all. It's been a rough road to getting things back in order, but I'm strong and I'm ready to move forward."

I take a slow, steadying breath, noting the sweet pea scent of the candle burning on the coffee table. It reminds me of spring on the prairies.

Other voices draw me back to the meeting. Someone at the other end of the circle asked a question that I didn't hear, now sparking a discourse amongst the members about whether we'll be studying books exclusively by Hueys or if Shader authors are included in the roster as well.

I rise, taking the moment of general discussion to get another glass of juice. Tugging down my shirt, I leave the circle with quick apologies until I reach the card table where refreshments are set up. The gingham tablecloth draping over it is slightly frayed at the edges. The urge to ask what colour it is bubbles to the surface, but I push it down.

Not the right time.

Instead, I guess it's probably yellow or baby pink, since the shade of the pattern is light. A fitting choice for such a sunny day. I catch myself smiling at my imaginings as I return to my seat, lemonade in hand.

Doug's wife, Serena, turns her attention to the young woman next to me. She introduced herself earlier as a violinist. "Danielle, you're up next. Do you need some juice or water before you start?"

Smokey eyes peer back at her from charcoal skin and Danielle shakes her head with a smile before raising her paper to read. She tells us a memory of growing up on a houseboat with her parents on the East Coast, likening her childhood experience to that of a pirate princess sailing the seven seas with her siblings and their fluffy white cat, Percy. Everyone smiles and giggles, and I'm relieved that the group has such a fitting follow-up to my tragic downer of a tale.

"That sounds like such a beautiful adventure to grow up in," Serena says. She places her hand on Doug's knee and gives a squeeze. The small smirk that tugs at the corners of his mouth make her eyes sparkle. They are a genuinely adorable couple and it warms my heart to see two Soulmates still flirting in public at their age. I let myself wonder for the briefest of moments if Miles and I could have been like that.

The next two people to share their stories are short and concise, one seeming bashful at how little he wrote. Everyone smiles and gives encouragement regardless.

Lost in my thoughts, I almost miss the next speaker until she is in the middle of her story. I go through the names of my fellow book club members in my head. I'm usually bad at remembering these things but we literally introduced ourselves an hour ago.

I force my brain to work.

Sarah. I'm pretty sure her name is Sarah.

Her voice, crisp and clear, holds the confident steady note of someone who speaks to groups regularly. A teacher, I think, by her corporate slacks and breezy blouse. I zone into what she's reading.

"And that was the day I decided I wasn't going to wait for my Soulmate. Daniel loved me and we were best friends. He said 'let's jump' and I said 'what an adventure'. He could no longer see colour, so I didn't want to either. I didn't care so long as he and I were together. We would make our path, trailblazing the less-traveled. I don't know if I would have ever found my Soulmate to begin with, but I'm glad I never did, because then I wouldn't have Danny." She folds the ratty and torn cover of her notebook back over the page she read from and grins at all the surprised faces around the room, including my own.

Very few people do that — choose not to wait for their Soulmate before getting married. And it's brave of her to tell all of us so openly and unabashedly, considering how Jumpers like her are not very well-received in society in general. I suppose it's normal in some parts of the world, where famine, war, and disease take so many young lives. But here? Very bold. And rather inconsiderate to their Soulmates, who would go without.

And here I thought *I* was the one rocking the suburban boat.

I can't say I'm surprised when Doug and Serena exchange looks, a silent 'what should we say?' Serena beams through the awkwardness and smoothes her skirt. "You must be a very adventurous and…kind person to give up colour for your husband. He's a very lucky man. Thank you for sharing, Sarah."

The words are sincere, I think. Serena doesn't strike me as the type to be two-faced. After all, it's a book club, not an election.

I just hope Sarah will still be happy in the years to come. People who don't pair with their Soulmates often end up breaking apart over time. Having the experience I've had, though, I'm not sure whether that's worse than being plunged into grey by tragedy. At least Jumpers never know the breath of colour.

I stand at the bus stop just down the street from Doug and Serena's, waiting for my steel chariot to cart me home. The sun's heat begins to dissipate behind a roll of thick, dark clouds, an ominous sign of weather I'm not prepared for. The wind suddenly turns on me with the edge of a chill and I silently curse myself for not checking the forecast before I left. I close my eyes when a cold, wet drop falls on the back of my hand.

Seconds later, the sky unzips and lets out a shower that soaks through my clothes miserably quick. I let out the breath I'm holding while the shocking torrent breaks around me, and I wipe the precipitation from my watch.

Of course, the bus is late. Why should I expect any different?

I check down the street both ways, scanning and listening for some evidence of the throaty-engined vehicle, but all I can see is an old, crew-cab pickup in a misty shade coming towards me. I stand back from the curb, shielding my frigid hands under my arms, hoping I'm far enough away from the pavement not to get splashed as the truck passes.

To my curiosity, the pickup halts in front of the bus stop, the wipers squeaking as they glide along the windshield. The passenger window rolls down and I peer in from the distance. Sarah's bright smile beams at me.

"Hey! You need a lift home?"

I smile and wave her off. "Oh no, it's okay. The bus should be here any minute. I can wait. Besides, I'll get your seat soaked and everything."

Sarah leans far over the passenger side and pops open the door. "Get in. You're going to catch your death. My seats will survive, I promise."

I try to reaffirm that I will be fine waiting, but my shaky breath and quivering lips betray my independence. I just want to be warm.

I attempt not to look so hesitant as I climb into the truck and shut the door.

"There," she says, rolling up my window. "Now you can get home without freezing first. Nothing worse than getting caught in the rain on a day like today." She shifts the truck into gear and we leave the bus stop behind.

"Thank you. The bus usually isn't this late. I feel like an idiot for not bringing an umbrella. It was just so nice out this morning," I say through chattering teeth.

"No need to explain, hun," she says as she pats my frigid arm. "I'm happy to take you home. Where do you live?"

"This side of Upper West. Blake Crescent."

Sarah smiles and gives me a quick glance. "That's not too far from me, actually. I pass that way to get to book club. Hey, would you like to carpool with me? It would save on bus fare and getting caught in crap weather."

Her forwardness takes me a little by surprise, but if we're going to be at the same event every Saturday, why not?

"That would be amazing, actually. I don't really know the people in that group, so I appreciate the offer."

"That makes two of us. I just moved here with my husband to fill the principal position at Shoreland Secondary this semester."

Teacher. Principal. Close enough, I think.

"Oh…well, welcome then! I would have said something sooner if I had known you were new to town." I place my hand near the heating vents, absorbing the thaw right down to my bones. "So, your husband got a job here, too, I assume?"

She gives me a sly look. "He will. He's a journalist, so Danny's waiting to get on with the local paper. He's freelancing right now."

A writer. That's cool. A Shader journalist who is formerly a Huey? Interesting. I scold myself for drifting off during her reading. I have to fess up if I want to satisfy my curiosity now.

"I hate to admit this, but I was a little distracted when you first started your story. I apologize for that. But…but I missed the part about how Daniel lost his Soulmate. If it's not too much to ask, could you tell that part again?"

A hint of coarseness lines her voice, though she smiles. "Oh, Danny's Soulmate was one of my closest friends growing up. That's how I met him. They found each other at a community dance when we were all ten years old. They were together all through high school but at the end of twelfth grade, Darla got sick. Lymphoma. She passed away before our second year of college, two months away from their first anniversary. Danny and I got very close after she died and I just couldn't see my life without him in it, I love him so much."

A stab of old grief washes over me afresh, reminding me what it had been like to lose Miles. "I'm sorry for both of you. I'm…sure she was a lovely person." My consolation fumbles off my lips, knowing how those words never seemed to make it any better when they were directed at me.

"Thanks. It's been long enough now that I don't really feel the pain of it anymore. Just brings up bittersweet memories. I know you're not at that stage yet, but I have a feeling that you'll heal enough to feel that way too, one day." She shoots me an empathetic glance.

I'm not so convinced. Even after a year, the ache in my spirit has only just become dull enough for me to be functional in everyday life again.

"Do you go by Francis or Fran?" she asks at the next stoplight.

"Francis, usually, but you may call me Fran if you'd like. I don't mind. Just no 'Franny'. My mom calls me that and it's beyond irritating." A small laugh escapes me.

"Alright then, Fran, are you in a hurry to settle in at home right now?" Her tone hints at plot.

My eyebrow raises automatically. "Uh…just for a change of clothes but other than that, not particularly. Why?"

Sarah beams, her inky eyes almost luminous in the sunlight. "Cause I think a steamy cup of hot cocoa and some good conversation would do us both good. I found the cutest little bistro just down from my house that has the best cocoa I've ever had. You game?"

Well, it's not like I have anything better to do.

"Yeah, I'm game," I say as we pull into my driveway, where dry clothes await me.

We spend four hours sipping cocoa and chatting like a couple of reunited sisters. Everything from our favourite hockey teams to swapping gardening tips. After the first hour, I have to apologize to her for holding onto my old-fashioned mindset — like a miserable crone — that Jumpers are selfish. She's not who I thought she would be. Sarah is kind and understanding about it, which is more than I deserve. She makes me laugh in a way that I haven't laughed in eons and it's the most refreshing coffee social I've ever had.

When I get back to my house that evening, I busy myself with the chores I neglected the night before — dishes, tidying, and the like. Lost in thought, I happen to glance down at the polka-dot plate I'm washing and my heart jumps. It's only a quick flicker but I drop the plate into the sink with a clatter. It's a wonder that it doesn't break.

The polka-dots are *red* — bright, cherry red like they were when I first bought that dish set three years ago.

My heart continues to leap nearly out of my body, both terrified and excited. I stare at it, wondering if perhaps I'm dreaming that I'm awake. After all, the only time I see colour is in my sleep. Wild with adrenaline, I rush through the house searching for any other traces of colour — anywhere — just to make sure it isn't a fluke.

A tube of scarlet lipstick sits on the vanity. A single half-ripe apple in the fruit basket, the small patch of red dappled over dusty grey. Miles's old toothbrush hanging abandoned in the sink holder where I left it for the past year is also red. They all pop out at me in the dazzling hue, bright and crisp.

I stand for the longest time, staring at the objects like they are curiosities out of a circus. I bite my fingernails and can't seem to stand still without moving *some* part of me. I can't see any other colour but red, which means that things I remember as not being distinctly red from before are showing up muted, where purple or mahogany or coral should be. It's the oddest thing I've ever experienced, but still…

It's colour.

Feeling the excitement turn to old, raw emotions, I drop onto the square ottoman and cry. I cry until I'm too exhausted to cry anymore.

When I wipe the snotty mess off my face, my cheeks and eyes burning from being rubbed raw, I begin to wonder things I never thought I'd wonder.

What does this mean? Do I still have a Soulmate? How?

The next morning when I call my mother before work, I notice that several other things around the house are now in colour, too. Blues and purples greet me from the monochromatic world around them and their novelty to my thirsty sight leaves me in awe. The flowers in my garden even wink their vibrance at me from the windows, swaying side to side in the breeze.

I thought I'd never see this again.

"I'm telling you, Mum, it's true. I don't see all of them right now…but…but slowly, they're coming back!" I say to her, my voice trembling.

A short silence and then, "Dear, I don't know what to say. Are you sure that you weren't just dreaming this?"

I roll my eyes. "Yes, I'm sure. I'm seeing them right now and I'm wide awake. I just don't understand it. How could I be seeing colour again? That never happens…Miles is gone…I don't know."

Another silence, this time so long I have to check the call is still connected. "Mum? Are you there?"

"Yes, I'm here. I was just thinking. What you said about seeing colour again not happening? That's not entirely true. I've heard over the years of a few people who ended up with *two* Soulmates. It's extremely rare, mind. But it does happen."

"*Two* Soulmates? Are you suggesting that I have another one out there close by and I don't have a single clue who it is?" I sigh heavily into the receiver and rub at my temples. "Well, that's a jagged pill to swallow."

"I know, dear. I can't imagine how that must feel," my mother coos. "But despite all the things that this is going to drag up, you have been given the chance to see colours again. What an incredible gift, Francis! Whatever you do, savour it. Take it in. Enjoy it. And whoever it is, cherish them."

I wince at her words. Like *I* need to be told to cherish a Soulmate.

"I will, Mum. I have to go get ready for work now. I love you. Bye!"

"I love you too, Franny. Bye."

I sit the phone back on the hook with a gentle hand.

A second Soulmate. I don't want another one.

An ugly bitterness, old and acidic, flares up in my heart, scorching a sore wound into the scar that's already there. Miles was my Soulmate and he is gone forever. No one will ever — could ever— take his place, Soulmate or not. I want him back. And I would give up this so-called gift in a heartbeat for the chance to have him alive again. I refuse to let my heart open up to someone else. I mean, what if they're ripped from me in a few years too, the same way Miles was?

A sick sensation bubbles inside me. I can't go through that again. I can't wake up to a world of grey knowing that I've lost someone else. It's far too empty — too excruciating. I put my hand to my stomach to try and soothe the choppy waters. I inhale deeply, hoping it will calm the panic.

But it doesn't help all that much.

What about the other person? How will *they* feel about having a Soulmate who doesn't want them? The rejection of knowing their most compatible companion in all the world is still clinging to the love of the one who came before — would that not be even more painful? But maybe they will feel the same way. Maybe they don't want me either.

I can't just ignore this. My conscience won't let me rest if I do. I have to figure out who it is so that we can work this thing out together.

I grab a sheet out of my notepad and begin writing down the names of all the people I had met recently. There's the touchy new guy at work, Jerry. And the barista who accidentally brushed my hand at the bistro when Sarah and I went for hot chocolate. Two guys had bumped into me on the bus but I don't know their names. So "Bus Guy #1" and "Bus Guy #2" go on the list. Then there's the four men at the book club who shook my hand. I quickly add them as I try to recall their names.

Markus, Todd, and Jason? And…Phil? Bill? Something along those lines.

I go up and down the list, trying to intuitively make the connection of who it might be, until my eyes sting from the concentration. But as far as I can remember, none of them had shown even a small fraction of the awe and amazement that normally accompany a Soulmate revelation. Colours bursting from grey always warrants a shock. But then again, my return to the world of Hueys is gradual this time around. It happened right under my nose and sneaked up on me when I least expected it. Perhaps that's the case for them also.

I take a breath and shake my head free of all the manic thoughts running amok. There is only one way to find out for sure who my new Soulmate is, but for now I'm going to be late to catch the bus if I dawdle any longer. A good plan begins hatching in my brain as I rush through brushing my teeth, and I grab my messenger bag off the foyer hook before heading to my stop around the corner.

If I just pay attention to the people on my list, hopefully I'll see a sign of the Soulmate bond by the end of the week. I only have to retrace my steps.

But my tired heart flutters at the thought of confronting them. I don't know what path I'm going to take when I do. Can I open myself up to another Soulmate for their sake? Or can I bear the look of devastation on their face as I reject them? A world of colour is still a world of colour even without the love of a Soulmate, right?

By the end of the week, I'm functioning on caffeine and a strange mixture of relief and disappointment. I went out of my way every day to run into each person on my list, hoping for even a tiny glimmer of secret colour in their gaze. But not a single one of them showed any sign that they were suddenly struck by a new form of sight — exasperating and hopeful all the same. Perhaps I won't have to make any heartbreaking decisions after all. If my new Soulmate is content to live in colour without his counterpart, then who am I to ruin that for them when I'm not sure I want to embark on that journey again anyway?

I let out a sigh as I walk out to Sarah's pickup. She reminded me about our carpool to book club this afternoon when I called her to finally tell someone else about my sight and my plan. I don't know why I decided to tell her, out of all my other friends. Sarah just seems like the person who is least likely to be scandalized by my situation, considering the beautiful scandal of her own life. But though she seems excited for me, there's trepidation in her voice that I can't understand.

I've only known her a week, but somehow it feels like we've been friends our whole lives, and I don't see how my news should change that. Perhaps she feels left out, now that I'm no longer a Shader too. Or maybe it's a touch of envy. Or, more likely than not, perhaps I'm just overthinking it.

That seems like a typical 'me' move.

She rolls down the passenger window, grinning. "Got your book and notepad?" she asks. I wave them both before her and hop up into the truck. It smells like men's cologne and warm leather. I wiggle myself more comfortably into the heated seat, cherishing the sunbeam on my thighs as it washes away the chill.

"Okay. So the first three chapters…wow! I mean, I read way past them because they were so scintillating, but I was really impressed that this was Carle's first novel. She's blowing me away already! I can't wait to discuss it with the group," I say, flinging my hands around more animated than necessary. Sarah smirks at my literary excitement.

"Aw, right? I loved the terrace scene. So raw and real, but also so truthful of society. I hope Robert figures out what he's going to do about that empty house before he jets off to go see his aunt. It'll be such a major let down if the city ends up destroying it because of his lack of decision making skills, I swear." At this she rolls her eyes and pulls away from my street.

"Oh yeah! I didn't think about that," I say, trying not to spoil the big reveal in chapter eight. "I'm more concerned with how he left things with Nancy." I close my eyes and place my hand over my heart. "I have only known her for two and a half chapters, but I feel like she needs to find her Soulmate by the end. Robert is determined to find his, so why not bring her along so she can do the same? Missed opportunity if you ask me, Rob." I slap my knee to add emphasis to my point and Sarah laughs. Then she falls quiet with a suddenness that makes me wonder if she's having a stroke.

She doesn't say anything again until the next stoplight.

"So, speaking of book club and finding Soulmates, are you looking forward to your grand discovery today? Which one do you think it is?" She slides me a sidelong glance and raises her dark brows.

My fingers won't stop fiddling with the hem of my lilac sweater. By now I've regained the full spectrum of colour, which is a soothing balm to my bruised soul. Like a crisp breeze on a humid summer day. I try to block out the dread of what revelations await me at Doug and Serena's.

Because if he's not there, then I don't have a clue who he is or where he is.

"Well, to be honest, I'm nervous. I don't want to hurt anyone but I don't think I'll ever be ready to live my life with someone else.

We're so conditioned to believe that we only get one true chance at love that I'm just not prepared for what a second chance looks like." I give a sigh, pushing myself to be resigned about whether or not I'm going to take that chance. "But," I continue, with a grin that I can't help despite my turmoil, "I bet you it's Mateo. I remembered that he did shake my hand twice last week when he introduced himself and then when I left. Although, he's a bit younger than I expected."

Sarah is silent again. Then she gives a small smile and adds quietly, "Well, I hear Soulmates are certainly a surprising thing…you never know who you're going to get."

I nod absently as a flash of brilliant yellow catches my eye on the corner house as we approach Doug and Serena's street.

"Oh!" I turn my body towards the window to take in the full view of the bright cornucopia of hues that are in the garden. "I had no idea that they were growing *yellow* roses. That is such a rare thing to see! I thought maybe they were lemons…but they're definitely the roses I was admiring last week. And here I imagined they were pink. Huh." I tap my chin as Sarah slows the truck down to a crawl in front of the house. "You know, I was thinking that they're out awfully early this year, don't you agree? Roses shouldn't be out for another few weeks yet."

"Yellow…yellow. So that's what it's called."

She speaks so quietly and casually that I nearly miss it in my engrossed admiration of the flowers outside my window. It takes me a moment too long to process what she said. My heart stands still, freezing the blood in my veins.

"What?" I say, as I pivot my head to face her, my eyes wide and incredulous. "What did you just say?"

The tip of her ear turns red where it peeks out from beneath her chocolate brown hair. She stops the truck and wrings the steering wheel until her knuckles turn white. She doesn't look at me.

"Yellow," she whispers. Clearing her throat, she continues, "You said that the colour of those roses is yellow. I've been wondering what that colour was called." She finally glances at me from under her brow, her signature boldness returning to her eyes as she cheshires. "Surprised?"

Her smile can't penetrate my shock. I sit there, my jaw dangling as if she knocked it off my skull.

She can't be…because I'm not…

"I started seeing the colours the night we had coffee. Danny came up from the office and I screamed. 'Babe, your eyes are *glowing*! Your *eyes* are glowing!'." At this she giggles to herself. "Took him almost a half hour to calm me down before I could explain what I was seeing."

The elated look on Sarah's face deepens my shock. I know that look. It's the expression of someone who's entire view of the world has exploded into a thousand pieces of sparkling stained-glass turning everything into a mosaic of splendour. I've been searching for that look all week and now that I've finally found it, I don't know what to say.

"I thought he was pulling an elaborate prank, but then the curtains seemed weird to look at too and I couldn't stop staring at them," Sarah continues when I don't say anything. "He kept telling me it was colour but I didn't know how it was possible." She clears her throat again and turns to face me with tears welling in great pools on her dark lashes. "Fran, Danny's eyes are *blue*. Pale blue with little hints of dark blue near the centre. I never…never thought in a million years that I'd get to know that…*see* that." She brushes the streaking moisture from her cheeks, wonder and joy dancing in her gaze like gleeful children as she focuses her sight just behind me — at the garden full of colour.

Still, I have no words.

"He's so excited for me, Francis. Said it was the best gift he wished he could have given me. He's been going over colour names of things he remembers from when Darla was still with us and helping find others who see colour to teach me properly." She gives a long sigh and glances at me, apologetic. "Of course, the biggest question was who? Danny was so nervous that I'd want to find out and that my Soulmate would steal me from him. But he didn't have to be so worried. I knew it was you."

I raise my brows heavenwards, finally finding my voice. "What? How?"

She gives a sly smile that falters at the edges. "I came late to book club so you were the only person I touched that day."

My mind shifts to the small, comforting pat she gave me back when she picked me up from the bus stop last week. Of course!

"I feel like I've known you forever and yet I don't even know if you have siblings or pets. And yet I've never had a friend like you." She swallows and looks me dead in the eyes, searching them like she's examining their pigment before she speaks again. Her voice is softer and smaller than I've ever heard it. "I…I know that you aren't ready for another Soulmate…that you may never be ready for another one. But if it makes you feel any better, I don't think this time around will be anything like before." She takes a shaky breath, as if I'm about to break something fragile and delicate within her. Her countenance shifts, and though she appears more like her usual unruffled self, an apprehension hangs about the downward turn of her eyes. "Still friends?" she asks, extending a trembling hand out to me.

In the few split moments I have to think about all that she's said, a sadness and outrage strikes me with her question.

Miles was my Soulmate for twelve years before he left my world in grey, and in the year that has passed since, I've never felt as alive and happy as I have the past week, talking with Sarah. No one makes me forget my grief like Sarah's friendship. No one makes me feel like myself again since I put the love of my life in the ground.

How could she for even a moment think I would walk away from that joy — walk away from her? I dreaded the arrival of a new lover, but my fear vanishes at the surprise of the truest friend instead.

Tears spill from my heart and down my face as I launch myself like a python, arms grappling her, across the storage console that divides us. I don't care how awkward and uncomfortable this position is. That doesn't matter right now. I smile into her tense shoulder, her figure still rigid with the shock of my rather violent embrace.

I don't blame her — I'd be terrified of my python hugs too.

"Not friends, Sarah," I manage through my emotions. "*Soulmates.*"

As the words hang in the small cab of the truck, she relaxes slowly until she, too, is wrapping me in an embrace.

And as we sit there, parked around the corner from our book club meeting, their neighbours' sunny flowers blowing in the late April breeze, I realize something that I will carry with me for the rest of my life.

When crimson roses fade to grey and bloom again in yellow, there's no point in fearing or agonizing over the blooms. After all, isn't a rose still a rose no matter the colour?

In the era of climate change, what person with an imagination does not look on plans for a new subdivision or a career or a family without often thinking, *What does it matter, ultimately? The world is going to end.*

This notion of finding purpose in the face of doom has always dwelled in a cold place at the core of the human experience, since every individual eventually asks themselves: *Does anything I do matter? I'll eventually be dust, forever.* To me, this has always suggested the ancient conceit of life as a voyage—a voyage that is typically long and comfortable and even wondrous, but which is slated to end in destruction as surely as though the port of disembarkation were stamped as 'Death' on one's boarding ticket.

What tale, though?

I did not want to write a story that only diagnosed this sense of doom. Too obvious. Yet, I also did not want to write a story with a pat solution. Too disrespectful. So the idea of a doomed voyage languished in my imagination for a time. Finally, I just wrote it and let the passengers find their own way on our behalf.

Buddy Young

Buddy Young is a staff writer and a writing educator living in London, Ontario, and the long-time president of the London Writers Society.

The Prime Crusade

by Buddy Young

All the passengers who emerged from the airship terminal into the morning mists reacted the same way to the sight before them: they stumbled to a halt, raised their eyes, and stared in awe. No matter their age or nationality, no matter how urbane and well-travelled, no matter how much the hyperbolic promotional literature had prepared them for what awaited them, they still stopped to marvel at this first sight of the silver airship. It loomed above the ground mists of the airfield, vast as a dinosaur seen by ants in the grass and yet as weightless and as silent as those mists.

"*Fantastisch!*" an elderly passenger holding his homburg on his upraised head whispered to his wife. "*Was für ein Wunder!*"

Behind them, Alice squeezed Joseph's arm and spoke loudly enough to be overheard by the other passengers around them and the soldiers standing sentry at the terminal exit. "This will be the best honeymoon any woman ever had." And then, smiling in the way of a new bride about to share an intimacy with her groom, she drew so close to Joseph that her fashionable veil adorned with flowers brushed the brim of his fedora. "If they intend to intercept us," she whispered, "it'll be here."

"You might wish that were true, in the end." As he whispered back to her, Joseph did his best to smile like a lover who had received a tender promise, but such fakery had never come easily to him. His mouth twitched between an unfamiliar smile and the habitual scowl that had engraved lines into his face over the years. "If they move on us here on the ground, it'll be because they want us alive. If they let us board and get underway before intercepting us, it'll be because they want us dead. There'll be no place to retreat in the clouds."

She squeezed the arm of his gabardine coat, the gesture one part acknowledgement and one part reassurance. Then they joined the flow of excitedly chattering passengers undertaking the long hike across the airfield to the airship—a trip, Joseph knew for a certainty, that would be the last time most of them walked the earth alive.

The walk from the Frankfurt airship terminal to the zeppelin appeared short if you measured the distance as three lengths of the great airship, yet it seemed to continue forever. Three lengths of the airship was three quarters of a kilometre. Like the other passengers walking in pairs or in family groups, he and Alice glanced back during the walk at the airship hangar, fascinated by the visual perspective of a building shaped like a simple shed but massive enough to house skyscrapers.

"Remember the pyramids?" Alice asked.

Joseph contemplated the airship hangar. "Yes, it has the same sort of alone-in-the-sky feeling. None of the other buildings exist, they're all too tiny to notice." He turned his attention back to the airship, now starting to loom over them. "Then you see *that*."

The largest thing to ever fly the skies of the world floated in a hush, the six-meter-long propellers of its four nacelles motionless. Joseph's mind insisted that something so huge must rest on a mighty foundation of steel-reinforced concrete, but only a single narrow boarding gangway connected the zeppelin to the world. The tethers didn't count—the scale of the airship reduced the thick hawsers to gossamer threads, the teams of ground crew manning them mere flecks of grit. This close, the airship's tail, nose, and topside disappeared behind its own canvas horizons. Tall as a sixteen-story skyscraper and vastly longer.

Hindenburg.

At the boarding gangway, a ship's officer greeted the passengers and checked their tickets, then a steward in a white coat helped them onto the gangway steps. But nearby stood a dark-uniformed officer who was conspicuously studying faces and listening to the answers the passengers gave. As they joined the queue at the gangway, Joseph took off his fedora and pretended to examine its rain-spotted felt in order to cover his mouth as he murmured, "That Nazi officer, is he supposed to be here?"

"I'd assume," Alice said. "Why?"

"I've seen his face before."

She had been holding his arm all the way from the terminal to keep her high-heeled shoes from sinking too far into the sodden grass field, so he felt the spasm that flashed through her. "Where?"

He eyed the officer's face. Sharp nose and cheekbones, skin pocked from youthful acne or perhaps chicken pox, active eyes. So familiar, but he had seen so many faces in so many places in his life. "A war. I saw him in a war." After a moment, he added, "He may have fought for the fascists in Spain."

Alice smiled and looked around herself like a tourist memorizing the historic occasion. "Are there supposed to be this many soldiers?"

Joseph did not need to look: he had already noted the airfield's security. In addition to the soldiers flanking the terminal doors in dress uniform, the roof edge of the titanic hangar had at each corner dark notches in the telltale pairs of a rifleman and a spotter. And here underneath the airship stood an honour guard of soldiers, standing with their swastika banners limp from the dampness, their rifles slung over shoulders. Not regular army: black uniforms, white gloves, and the double lightning bolt insignias. SS.

No, he didn't think there should be this many soldiers. But he did not say this aloud.

When their turn came to present their tickets to the greeter at the gangway, he read out loud, "Joseph and Alice Bernstein. American."

"'Bernstein?'" The SS officer stepped forward, his head cocked at a sharp angle of interest. "*Jude?*"

Joseph edged slightly ahead of Alice. "*Juden.* Jews, yes."

"I am Hauptsturmführer Hoffman. You will step this way."

The SS officer led them aside to a coal-hued Volkswagen command car parked about forty feet away, yet still under the airship's lee. The dew dripping from the flanks of the overhead airship fell in streamers of silver pearls just beyond it. The Volkswagen's trunk was open, and the officer gestured to an integral tabletop that had folded out. "Place your bags here."

"They've already been checked." Joseph held up one of the *Hamburg-Amerika Linie* tags that the inspectors in the terminal had attached to his valise. Alice's overnight bag and makeup case had an identical tag, with the picture of a zeppelin soaring over a sailing ship. "Our matches, lighters and camera flashbulbs—the inspectors confiscated everything that could cause a spark."

Hoffman unpacked Joseph's valise anyway. Clothes, shaving kit, a copy of *Brave New World*. All innocent. But then the officer removed his white dress uniform gloves and ran his fingertips along the interior of the valise, and the liner gave slightly under the pressure.

Joseph drew from his pocket his American passport, deftly taking out his money clip in the same motion, and held them both out so that only Hoffman could see the billfold of high denomination sterling notes he held under the passport with a thumb. "I carry only innocent family mementoes in that compartment, please leave them in peace."

The officer ignored the bribe and pried back the false bottom of Joseph's valise to reveal the hidden compartment's contents. A Mauser automatic, two loaded magazines, a miniature flashlight, two tight decks of currency (dollars and pounds), and a row of twenty-franc gold coins pressed between two strips of tape so they would not rattle.

"Curious heirlooms!" Hauptsturmführer Hoffman declared. "Quite the family you come from, Herr Bernstein."

"We have a proud military heritage." As he said this, Joseph looked to Alice with a smile, as though at a marital in-joke.

She smiled back, which meant nothing. He watched her eyes. Two fast blinks would have meant 'fight'. One slow blink meant 'flee'. But she simply stared at him for now.

"I must remind you, Herr Bernstein and Frau Bernstein," the officer said, "that it is nearly a kilometre back to the terminal. Please do not run. You would only die breathless and with mud on your fine shoes."

Joseph dropped the false smile. Nobody was being fooled.

"Perhaps you might care to explain something to me," Hoffman said, drawing up before him in a Prussian straight-backed stance.

"Yes?" Joseph said.

"This flight of the Hindenburg is full, all her passenger cabins filled."

"So what?"

"According to history," the SS officer declared in a dour voice, "the final flight of the Hindenburg was only three quarters booked."

Alice relaxed so abruptly that Joseph could feel more of her weight shift to his arm as she sagged. "'Wanderers wander…'," she declared.

"'…until the end of time'," the SS officer replied. He fit a monocle to his eye to disguise his wink. "Professor Denis Massieu, at your service. I started my wandering in 2051, out of Marseille. I am Hauptsturmführer Hoffman for this trip, if you please."

"Joseph Smith, 2046."

"Alice Banbury," Alice declared. "From Waterloo (the Canadian university, not the city), in 2040."

"2040?" said Massieu/Hoffman. "Truly?"

"I was the first time traveller out of Canada, one of the first twelve Wanderers overall."

"An honour, Madame. If the Natives weren't watching, I'd kiss your hand." Hoffman nodded permission for Joseph to repack his luggage. "It's my chronal signal that you will have followed here, but as host of the event it embarrasses me beyond measure to suggest that you might want to choose a different Hindenburg iteration." He executed a discreet bow in a sheepish apology. "I deeply regret the inconvenience this might cause."

Joseph waved off the thought. In one regard, there could be no such inconvenience, since the most striking, most mysterious aspect of time wandering had proven to be the fact that nothing anyone did while wandering ever affected the flow of history permanently. Hence, the theory of a single Prime Line plus an infinite number of transitory other timelines, which made it simplicity itself for a Wanderer to have any historical event to themselves if they so cared. It would require no effort for him and Alice to side-step into another iteration of the Hindenburg voyage that had no other Wanderers along for the experience. The 'inconvenience' that Hoffman was referring to was understood to be the post-insertion pragmatics. The subcutaneous time travel wet-web that allowed them to wander time could transport a very limited amount of extraneous matter; so if they jumped to another chronal iteration, they would have to set about the tiresome process of gathering identity documents, personal sundries, tickets, and weapons.

"How many Wanderers converged for the voyage?" Alice asked.

"Including we three, there are fourteen." But even as he said this, Hoffman made a sour face and shook his head. "As a historian by trade and inclination, I would normally be honoured to host that many guests on this voyage. But the Wanderers who followed my signal to this convocation are less and less the respectful tourists of history, and more and more the rich fools of the breed who in earlier ages journeyed to Egypt and climbed the pyramids to etch their names into the capstone." He asked Alice, "Were you a historian at your university?"

"Physicist."

"Ah." When the historian turned to Joseph and silently asked the same question via a facial expression of polite interest, Joseph let his own features slide into their default expression of stone and said nothing. Hoffman gave a little cough of discomfort. "I only ask because with this many feckless Wanderer tourists aboard, a true lover of history will likely find this voyage of the Hindenburg to be a wine of an illustrious vintage that has turned to vinegar. And it will be a dangerous voyage at that—even more so than you may understand. You may believe that once the Hindenburg arrives for her rendezvous with inferno in New Jersey, all you have to do is position yourself at the promenade windows just before landing and you'll guarantee yourself of escaping the flames, but this final flight of the Hindenburg is fully booked because of the Wanderers who have come along for the experience, so escaping through the windows will be more like the clawing rush for a lifeboat seat on the Titanic. Have either of you ever travelled on the Titanic?"

"No, neither Joseph nor I are thrill-seekers," Alice said. "We followed your signal to this gathering exactly because we know the Hindenburg will be full of Wanderers."

"Wandered time so long that you've become lonely for your fellow kind, have we?" Hoffman asked.

"Nothing could be further from the truth," Joseph said. "But we have news. News that all Wanderers need to hear."

"What sort?" Hoffman asked.

"The only real news," said Alice. "News from the Prime Line."

Hoffman nodded, but Joseph did not believe in the man's indifference. The Prime Line was the only resilient reality, as singular to historians as Rome to the Romans. Hoffman asked, "What news would that be?"

"The worst conceivable," Alice said. "News to end all news."

"Impossible. As they say, the Prime Line is eternal," Hoffman said.

But Alice shook her head, her veil rustling like that of a widow. "'Nothing', as they used to say and will now say again, 'is forever'."

At this, Hoffmann instinctually glanced around for eavesdroppers, and this Wanderer instinct served them well. "Careful," he whispered. "Native."

The greeter from the boarding gangway approached. He bowed to Hauptsturmführer Hoffman and announced, "'*Schiff hoch' in fünf Minuten, Herr*. Up ship in five minutes, sir and madam."

"*Ja, verstanden*." Hoffman waited until the steward had withdrawn. "You were saying?"

Alice opened her mouth to speak, but Joseph set his hand on his wrist and told Hoffman, "Our news is for all the Wanderers to hear."

Hoffman studied him. "I...I don't think I like your eyes, my friend. Perhaps I won't let you on my airship." A line of shadow appeared between Hoffman's eyes as they played along the planes of Joseph's face. "Why do I think we've met somewhen before?"

Joseph considered whether to evade the question or to argue that whatever chance encounter he and Hoffman had had in the depths of history was of no consequence when all of history now hung in the balance—a hard argument to make when he had no intention of explaining his mission just yet.

In the end, it was Alice who broke the impasse. Moving in front of Joseph, she said to Hoffman, "We've learned what the Wall is."

"Madame mustn't fib. It's impolite."

But Alice touched her fingertips to Hoffman's hand to make him look through her veil into her eyes, then simply repeated, "We have learned the truth of the Wall. We've come to spread the word to the Wanderers."

Hoffman looked from her to Joseph, who nodded. Still, the historian had doubt in his face as he declared, "Very well, you may board." He gave his boot heels a proper Prussian click. "If you do, understand that my authority upon the ship is absolute. I have provided the Native crew with forged papers ostensibly from Himmler himself, giving me complete discretion over the voyage in light of intelligence that agents will seek to sabotage the Fatherland's proud airship."

"Understood," said Alice.

"Most of all, you must understand the risk you are taking upon yourself." The Volkswagen had a strongbox with an eagle crest in its trunk, and Hoffman now opened it. Inside was an arsenal of weapons. Some were period-correct knives and guns, but there were also a dispiriting number of chemical sprays, palm automatics, and electrical stunners small enough for time travel. As he added Joseph's weapons to the trove confiscated from the other Wanderers, Hoffman continued, "As I was saying earlier, the Hindenburg has become popular with the 'extreme history' crowd of Wanderers. Danger enthusiasts. My lovely airship was already history's most infamous firebomb, and on this particular voyage it will have a belly swollen with moths. Do you still wish to board?"

"We do," Alice said for the both of them. "And the voyage will be far more dangerous than you know."

At her tone of voice, Hoffmann hesitated, as though he himself would decline to board the death vessel.

"*Schiff hoch*," a Native steward shouted. "All aboard, if you please."

They stared at each other for a moment, then Hoffmann sighed. "All of history at our beck, and we are out of time." He slapped the strongbox closed.

They boarded the airship together, the morning mists swirling like stirring ghosts all around them as the giant propellers thrummed to life.

The cabin Joseph and Alice shared was marketed by the *Hamburg-Amerika Linie* as futuristic, and he supposed it was. The slender bunk beds, fold-out writing desk, narrow sink, and aluminum trim around white walls were familiar to anyone who had taken a sleeper train later in the century. Cleaner, though. And instead of a train's spastic swaying, the crash-rumble as the tracks crossed roads, and the constant blare of the warning horn, the airship flew with a silky smoothness marked only by a low thrumming.

I don't think I like your eyes, Hoffman had said to him. As Joseph shaved for dinner in the cabin's mirror, he searched for whatever Hoffman had seen in his face. Years spent marching in the deserts of the Levant and Spain had burned a tale of sun and wind into his skin. The worst of the scars he had had removed at Alice's insistence, yet still his hard features bore a thousand lines, like a stone mask that had been heated in flames and then tossed into ice water over and over. But it had been his eyes Hoffman had mentioned. He studied them without pleasure. Light blue in a way that people had found pleasant in the young and cold in the old. Perhaps, he decided, Hoffman had recognized his eyes as the hollow pebbles of a used-up soldier.

'*Se fue*' the Republican nurses had said of Joseph's eyes as he lay unresponsive in a Madrid hospital during the last year of the Spanish Civil War. *Gone away.* Just another idealist from the International Brigades shell-shocked by the horrific reality of war and by the collapse of the grand socialist hopes for a brotherhood of humanity.

But when they had cut away his blood-stiff uniform, they had found a filigree of fine scars on his forearms. "*La espada marca?*" the nurses whispered. *Sword scars?* Some of the fascist officers carried ceremonial blades certainly, but in that war of the Mauser rifle and the Spandau machine gun and the Dornier bomber, an actual sword injury was not something they had seen. A torture victim, they decided. Someone the bastard fascists had carved. This explained his muteness too. But when they pulled off his uniform tunic, their whispers had turned to gasps. Blade scars crisscrossed his torso, front and back—not in the methodical order of a torturer's blade, but in the mad angles of a battlefield's frenzy of suffering. Seven crosses of thick scars graced him where incisions had been made to remove arrows.

The rumours of this brought Alice. Dressed in the bohemian uniform of a nurse who had volunteered to serve the cause, Alice took him as her personal charge, tending his wounds and shaving him and cleaning him. She recognized what he was, of course. When none of the Natives would overhear, she murmured to him, "Wanderers wander, don't they…. Wanderers wander, but they come back…. Come back sometime, Wanderer…." She tended him for six weeks, an eternity for a time traveller who could have invested that precious personal absolute time in any of history's pageants of wonder, glory, and iniquity.

Waiting for death, he had remained mute.

Inexorably, the fascist artillery had risen from a distant rumble, to thunder, to an earthquake that refused to stop. Eventually, he and Alice were alone in the subterranean hospital, the last two figures in a cavern that had once held hundreds. Bloody bandages still covered the floor. The blasts shaking dust from the timbers onto his face had not made him blink out of the dead rhythm his eyelids had observed for months. The sight of dust falling almost into his uncaring eyes had caused Alice to start throwing her body over his whenever a shell detonated nearby. Eventually, one blast dislodged the metal hood from an overhead light fixture; it struck her shoulder, making Alice gasp in pain.

Her gasp of pain made him finally blink. He worked moisture into his mouth, then spoke in a desert-dry voice to her for the first time. "Go away."

"No."

So be it, he told himself. He had chosen to die here, and now so had she. It did not matter. Nothing did, he had discovered in a lifetime of being defeated over and over again by a history that refused to ever change.

A short time later, an artillery shell struck directly above the hospital. Half the timbers gave way, the northern section of the ward collapsing. The dust had blinded them, choked them, and still she covered his scarred shell of a body with her own fragile one, as though that would matter when the earth itself crashed down upon them both with all the weight of the world. And again he spoke to her, this time in a stronger voice. "Go away."

"No," Alice had said. "Not unless you come with me."

After three heartbeats in which three more shells detonated above them, he allowed his wet-ware to accept the wireless handshake proffered by hers. He gave her control. And she had whisked them away to a safe 'when' in the future, where they became two dusty figures from history emerging after-hours from a museum exhibiting the excavated hospital filled with unblinking mannequins of heroic nurses and patients.

They had travelled history together for six years now, measured as absolute time.

When Alice returned to the cabin from the single shower facility on their deck, she found him standing motionless with the foam-dripping razor forgotten in his hand, staring into the mirror, into his own eyes, into memory. "Stay with me, Wanderer," she said, patting a cheek still covered in shaving cream. "It's the future we need to think about from now on, not the past."

He slowly stirred back into motion. They shifted positions in the cramped cabin, moving automatically out of a long familiarity with travel together. Alice, petite, moved in front of him to begin the process of applying her 1930s cosmetics; he, a Clydesdale of a man, was able to stand behind her and still shave in the mirror, his chin level with the top of her head. "Perhaps we should change our cover story," he said. "I don't look young enough to be on a honeymoon with you." He was only in his mid-forties and looked it, the ministrations of the future's cosmetic surgeons only able to stabilize a weathered body that would otherwise have appeared decades older. Though the same age as he, Alice appeared in her twenties.

"You look perfect for the role: a businessman who has been too busy making money to marry." She flashed him a merry smile in the mirror. "I'm the lively young minx who is going to bring joy to your existence and redeem your soul."

He kissed the top of her head.

"The story we tell the Natives isn't that important," she said. "But what shall we tell the Wanderers about who you are?" After a moment, she solemnly corrected herself, "I meant: were."

"I'll tell the Wanderers what I always tell them. Nothing." He pinch-wiped at the blob of shaving cream his kiss had left in her hair. "Amnesia from a head wound."

"They won't believe that."

"It's not a lie meant to be believed. It's a warning that says, 'I have no interest in dwelling on my past. Back off'."

She reached up, took his arm, and brought it down so it was around her chest. "It's important that the Wanderers believe us. They have to trust us when we tell them the truth about the Wall."

"Then tell them about yourself. You reflect well upon you." And when she started to protest, he gave her a fond hug but shook his head. "Telling the other Wanderers the truth about my life wouldn't encourage them to trust me. So leave it at amnesia. I do." He turned her and held her out at arm's length then, growing solemn. "But speaking of amnesia, you need to remember our deal."

"I remember," she said. "This one voyage, this last mission, and then you and I retire from history. It'll be just the two of us, somewhere and somewhen peaceful."

"Promise."

"I do." She kissed him as warmly as though she truly were a new bride on her honeymoon. "I do, I do, I do."

At dinner, Alice took in hand a familiar domestic task: that of sharing her delight in life with Joseph so that he could enjoy in her what he couldn't find in himself. She admired out loud the landscapes and exotic birds hand-painted on the silk wallpaper of the dining room, which had the feel of an ocean liner's amenities whereas their cabin had suggested an intercontinental train. Alice had studied all the passengers from historical records and now she discreetly pointed some out to Joseph: industrialists and writers, financiers and acrobats, Luftwaffe officers and correspondents. The men wore suits and ties, the wives pearls. In the way of the era, the children wore miniature adult hairstyles, but giggled timelessly.

Joseph glanced at them dutifully but mostly kept his eyes on the Zeppelin Company china. Food, art, history, people—he couldn't taste any of it anymore. But he listened in pleasure to Alice as they progressed through cream soup, smoked Westphalian ham with fresh Swiss Asparagus, veal cutlet farci, cucumber salad in cream sauce.

Just as they were accepting a dessert of mixed compote, Hoffman arrived in a pale SS dress uniform. "Herr Bernstein, Frau Bernstein, please join me on the promenade." Joseph put on a display for the sake of the Natives in the dining room, parting his lips to protest and heaving his chest, but then finally standing as though he feared Hauptsturmführer Hoffman too much to refuse this peremptory invitation. Alice played her part by lingering in her duralumin chair and only rising when Joseph tugged at her arm.

Hoffman guided them across the A-deck to the other side of the airship, where the white tablecloths and stiffness of the dining room gave way to a lounge of russet chairs and matching carpeting and relaxed bistro-style conversations. A large map of the world covered the inner wall. The ersatz SS officer drew them over to a promenade that ran the length of the lounge's outer wall, which featured a bank of windows mounted waist-high like museum display cases. Looking down through these, Joseph saw the emerald and dun countryside of northern Holland passing alarmingly close below. He could even see the expressions of surprise and awe on the faces of pedestrians and bicyclists who stopped to stare up the airship passing only a few hundred feet overhead.

"Is the ship in distress?" he asked Hoffman in an undertone.

"Not at all, the Hindenburg flies low to provide the finest possible view. Even at cruising, the Hindenburg remains at two hundred metres." The French professor kept his voice low so that none of the other passengers could hear them over the engines. "Please feel free to admire the scenery as we speak. The Natives watching us will assume that you're looking for an excuse not to meet my eyes."

At this, Alice and Joseph did indeed stare down through the windows at the scenes playing out below. When they recovered from their initial surprise, the Dutch waved hats and handkerchiefs at them. A boy raced into a stone farmhouse to reemerge on the run with his parents and brothers. The mother flapped her apron at the sky, the floral print discernable. Staring down at them, Alice whispered, "This is history in miniature, isn't it? Them down there, us up here."

"The privileged ones with awareness gazing down as we soar the sky above, the multitudes of the unaware staring up at us from the land below," Hoffman agreed, angling his face so that only Alice and Joseph could see his smile. Joseph made the fake fascist for a leftist.

Meanwhile, unlike Alice and Hoffman, Joseph kept his attention mostly on the other passengers inside the promenade. They had all given Hoffman and his SS uniform a wide berth, which allowed the three of them to speak in private. Yet, life continued. Suddenly, hay-scented wind snatched at hats and hair all along the promenade as a family of passengers opened one of the viewing windows so the family's teenage daughter could reach her arm out to wave back at the Dutch farmers below with a tissue.

"That family," Alice whispered to Hoffman. "They are the Doehners?"

"Yes. The girl, Irene, does not survive."

The sepia sunset glowed on Irene Doehner's face as the rushing slipstream tore her white tissue to tatters that rained down on the land like parade confetti. Her brothers laughed in glee.

Joseph stood silent. *Hold still, let the moment pass.*

Alice averted her eyes. "I hope when those farmers below recall the glory they saw soar overhead, they remember the little faces in the windows."

"So these Natives *are* real to you?" Hoffman asked Alice. "You don't believe they're an illusion, just a transitory kaleidoscopic reflection of the Prime Line?"

"I did at the beginning." Suddenly, she elbowed Joseph in the ribs in revenge for what she knew he was about to do.

The companionable blow gave Joseph a pleasure that the fine dinner had not. Smiling, he ratted her out. "Alice invented the term 'Prime Line'."

Hoffman lost his SS demeanour completely, becoming an eager Professor Massieu. "Did you? Did you really?"

"Not just me, my research team," Alice said. "During the theoretical phase of time travel, all the world still assumed that whatever we did in the past would impact the present. So, I was one of only seven Wanderers that the UN gingerly allowed back in time to conduct experiments. Finding myself in 1888 (our targeting was very uncertain on long jumps at first), I checked into the Banff Springs Hotel just as it was opening."

"I believe I've read of this," Hoffman said. "Something about champagne?"

"Wine at first," Alice said. "I ordered their finest Bordeaux from room service, poured myself a glass, then set it down on a table to breathe before an open window with a splendid view of the pristine Rocky Mountains. And then I time-jumped thirty minutes into the future, just enough time for a mature wine to properly breathe."

"But..." Hoffman said.

"But there was no wine. No Bordeaux on the table, the window was closed, and the bellhop who had escorted me to my room now had no recollection of me. I repeated the process a few times, but you know the result," Alice said.

Hoffman nodded. "You were the first to discover that whatever we do while time wandering never permanently affects anything, anywhen."

Alice nodded. "I posited the existence of a single immutable timeline. But it was someone else on the team who invented the term 'Prime Line' to describe it."

"I envy you," Hoffman said. "Your experiment meant that you were *part* of history, not just a Wanderer wandering through."

"Tell him about the champagne," Joseph prodded Alice.

She sagged against him in a show of reticence, but knew he would not relent. So she told Hoffman, "We had all been so terrified of the terrible disruptive effects of altering history in the slightest, only to suddenly discover that we could do *anything*. So I ordered the hotel's finest bottle of champagne to celebrate." Her face attained that hybrid expression of a smile and chagrin unique to people no longer young as they reminisce on fond mistakes of the past. "In fact, I ordered quite a few bottles of champagne over the next week, and put on quite the unladylike display with the handsome tycoons in the ballroom. And with two hard-as-oaks lumberjacks I found in a bar on the other side of the tracks. And with a poetess I found travelling alone in search of her muse."

"The party had started." Hoffman said this with Gallic ruefulness.

"I even gave the young bellhop who had forgotten me a special sort of tip that he would otherwise have remembered all his life," Alice said.

"Then naturally, you skipped out on the bill," Hoffman said.

"Why wouldn't I?" Alice asked.

At that moment, loud laughter barged through the conversational murmur of the promenade. They turned to look.

On the other side of the lounge, a tall blonde woman with the outdoor tan and muscle tone of a twenty-first-century health buff was laughing at a jarring volume at something her companion was saying. A joke about a Hitler portrait hanging on the wall, apparently. She wore a period appropriate chiffon evening gown of metallic lamé, but the shoes that peeked into view under the hem had a cut that would not crush her toes and an athletic sole rather than high heels. Her grinning beau wore an American gangster pinstripe suit that was more 1920s Hollywood than 1930s historical, and had artificially whitened teeth.

Wanderers, of course. Joseph had marked at least half of the fourteen that Hoffman said had boarded this flight of the airship. It was easy. Even in proper period attire, Wanderers had a certain aggressive and informal way of moving—pushing past Natives, calling across the room, and staring straight into people's faces. An echo, he supposed, of the accusation made by Europeans about American tourists in the past. The pseudo-gangster ass had wet-drunk eyes and was telling his girlfriend another joke in a too-loud voice, and Joseph caught a snatch of his conversation: "Just like the Titanic, but at least no hypothermia and no bloody band moaning about."

"Can't you shut that idiot up?" Alice whispered to Hoffman.

"It's no use, this new crowd of Wanderers are everywhere, ruining everything," Hoffman said. "When I last left the Prime Line, the cost of a set of displacement implants were down to the price of a private jet. If it weren't for time travel, that breed of privileged fool would be roaring in speedboats along pristine beaches and driving all-terrain monstrosities through rainforests."

Spotting Hoffman, the man in the pseudo-gangster outfit reeled over to him. "Top of the evening, host of mine," he said in an Irish accent. He turned his wet-drunk eyes to Joseph and Alice. "That must mean you two are part of the gang. 'Wanderers wander' and all that code shite. My name is O'Connor."

Joseph stepped between Alice and O'Connor. Seeing the glint of a silver torc inside O'Connor's open collar dress shirt, he figured O'Connor for the kind of Wanderer who would brag that he'd earned the torc from the hand of Brian Boru himself in battle or a drinking contest. The kind of Wanderer who had probably knifed the ancient hero in his sleep and taken the torc from his body, all on a lark.

Grinning, O'Connor held up a ballpoint and a *Weinkarte* stolen from the dining room. "Did you vote? Did you vote?" On the wine menu's cover, the Hindenburg soared over a globe with an eagle on the north pole and a swastika on the South Pole. Tally marks from the ballpoint pen in O'Connor's hand defaced the picture. "We Wanderers are voting whether or not to divert this gasbag from Lakehurst and set it down on the lawn of the White House instead."

"If you didn't want the risk," Joseph said, "why would you get on board?"

"Pull the cork out, boyo. Don't you want to see the look on Teddy Roosevelt's face when—" O'Connor began.

"Wrong president. And we *are* going to Lakehurst, sir." Hoffman snatched away the *Weinkarte*. "Lower your voice."

"Oh I see how it is, I do. You're old school. D'ye think these Natives will complain to history that they were denied their sovereign destiny to burn up?" O'Connor suddenly lurched past Hoffman, just as the Doehner family were passing, and he put his arm around the shoulders of the girl, Irene Doehner, and pressed a sloppy kiss on her cheek. As she squirmed, struggling to get free, he slurred, "Do you want to live a little, girlie?"

"Joseph," Alice said curtly.

Joseph instantly seized O'Connor by the tie and, using it as a leash, hauled him away from Irene Doehner over to the promenade windows. O'Connor's blonde companion, who had been listening passively, suddenly moved toward Joseph fast and with a purpose. When Hoffman moved to block her with an upraised hand, she seized him in a wrist lock and twisted, forcing Hoffman to drop to a knee to keep his wrist from being broken. Gasping, Hoffman drew his Luger from its holster and pressed it to her thigh. The woman hesitated.

Fist bunched in O'Connor's tie, Joseph forced him down until he was bent double over the angled windows of the promenade. Below, the sun was starting to set on the Dutch countryside, burnishing the fields of hay gold. Joseph asked Alice simply, "Yes or no?"

O'Connor giggled. "Yes or no what?"

Alice opened the window.

The sudden rush of hay-scented air into his face blew away some of the wine fumes, and O'Connor stopped giggling. He stared wide-eyed down the drop.

For his part, Joseph studied the window frame dispassionately. It would be a tight fit, but he had forced larger men through smaller windows.

Naturally, everyone in the promenade had fallen silent and were watching the drama, so Alice had to lean close to O'Connor and trust the howling of the wind to keep her words private. "For many of these Natives, these are the last three days of their lives. Are you going to let them enjoy their time with dignity?"

"Wh-what does it matter?" O'Connor's face was starting to go red as Joseph tightened his grip. "As soon as we leave, they all cease to exist anyway."

"You don't know that for certain. Nobody does," Alice said.

O'Connor hesitated, and Joseph knew what the man was thinking. A Wanderer's instinct in the face of danger was to slip away to some other time, but doing so in the context of the airship would only strand him high in some other era's sky—briefly. "Yes, yes, bloody all right!" O'Connor hissed. "I'll be canon, I'll be good."

Joseph did not release him until Alice nodded, which she took her time doing. When he did, the man reeled away along the promenade windows.

The blonde released Hoffman and stepped between Joseph and O'Connor. She whispered something sibilant to Joseph in Russian while giving him a hard glare, and Joseph suddenly understood what she was. A fair few Wanderers, rich as Mammon and aware of how dangerous history was, travelled with specialized bodyguards, and Joseph realized he had just embarrassed one. When the blonde turned away from him, she made sure to thump him in the sternum with her shoulder. Yes, a debt of honour to be paid there.

Alice, meanwhile, was helping Hoffman to his feet, undermining their drama of 'Jew fleeing Europe disguised as a new bride hounded by suspicious SS officer'. She asked him, "Are you all right?"

"I am not!" Hoffman holstered his Luger and gingerly rotated his wrist to test for damage. Doing so, he noticed the *Weinkarte* with O'Connor's straw poll on the floor. He threw the thing out the window in disgust. "I don't know why I host these excursions anymore, I just don't. I just want to sip absinthe in the sky all day while debating my fellow travellers about the tectonics of history and then drink wine at the setting of the sun as we toast *fin-de-siècle* tragedy, but instead I find myself trapped in this duralumin bird cage with a flock of ungrateful drunken vandals pecking away at everything. Vandals, thieves, and rapists." He waved a finger at Alice. "And may I say that I'm surprised by you, Madame Champagne."

Alice frowned at him quizzically.

Hoffman sputtered, "You were the one who discovered that nothing we do in the past affects the Prime Line, kicking off this...this perpetual chronal carnal *carnivale* in which Wanderers can behave as demons and angels and animals to our heart's content. So why does it matter to you what a Wanderer does to a Native?" Hoffman glared after O'Connor, who had moved away to accost another pair of Wanderers. "As that fool said, nobody knows what happens to the Natives when there is no Wanderer present. For all we know, this timeline is only a mirage that exists when we are here to behold it and vanishes when we mischievous Gods wander onward."

Alice gazed after Irene Doehner as the shaken girl's family shepherded her out of the lounge. "It's true that when I first discovered that the past could not be changed, I duly reported my findings with the thought, 'Now everyone else can share in the fun!' Then I flung myself in a celebration of life that spanned three millennia, or about ten years personal time. A life of freedom and indulgence that empresses could only dream of. I was never completely certain whether the past I was experiencing was just some quantum mirage or one of an infinite number of variations with infinitely tiny gradations of difference that could never be found twice. But, to my surprise—physicist or not—I found that such theoretical considerations didn't matter. Not when one is floating down the Nile on a pleasure barge with slaves fanning you with peacock feathers and sucking your toes."

At this, Hoffman looked at Joseph. "Is *that* how you met her?"

"Watch your tone," Joseph warned him.

"But eventually, even voyages down the Nile must end," Alice continued. "For me, the end of that part of my life's journey came at the feet of the Colossus. I found that I could indeed look up at the Colossus of Rhodes, into that gigantic bronze face of the sun god, and say 'I don't believe in you'. Yet, I also found that when I looked down from that face in the sky to the little faces walking past the Colossus's feet—the bearded sailors, pock-faced beggars, bent fisherwomen, hungry children—I couldn't disbelieve in them. They were just too human in their suffering. To believe that they were mere fleeting shadows was to believe that I was nothing more than a passing ray of light."

"I sympathize, Madame," Hoffman said. "Would you believe that I have never killed a Native? Except in self defence."

Joseph stared at him in naked disbelief.

Hoffman returned Joseph's stare defiantly even as he asked Alice, "So where did this epiphany of the little people at the Colossus's feet lead you?"

"To a life devoted to caring for people throughout the wretched times of history. I'd lie if I said that I wasn't plagued by the suspicion that I was wasting my time, and that I don't still somehow feel that Wanderers are somehow more real." She squeezed Joseph's arm. "But having burned myself out as a *bon vivant*, I learned that without caring for others, I couldn't care about myself."

On the other side of the lounge, O'Connor had gathered around himself a knot of like-minded Wanderers. The six of them were passing around a bottle stolen from the dining room, keeping it away from the hand of a scandalized Native stewardess in a white dress and nurse-style headkerchief who was trying to take it away, while a ship's officer was haranguing them with empty threats about prosecution upon the airship's landing.

"This can't go on," Hoffman said, stepping in that direction.

But Joseph took him by the arm. "It won't even go on until the end of this voyage. That's why Alice and I honed in on your invitation signal. The era of the Wanderer is ending, in disaster."

At dawn, Hauptsturmführer Hoffman marched through the A-Deck passenger corridors in his black SS uniform, banging on selected cabin doors. These cabins contained Wanderers, and they naturally recognized Hoffman as the host of the Wanderer excursion who had greeted them all at the airfield in Frankfurt. But they were confused by Joseph and Alice, marching at Hoffman's side— wearing Nazi armbands. Joseph could read the Wanderers' thoughts as they studied him and Alice. *Weren't they Wanderers? Or were they actually Native Gestapo hires all along?* Offering no explanations, Hoffman declared to the Wanderers in a stentorian tone that they and the other passengers responsible for the previous evening's unacceptable rowdiness would assemble: "A-Deck lounge, fifteen minutes."

Wanderers, being who they were, most arrived insolently late. But Joseph only had to go fetch two of them who outright refused to get out of bed. When he had pushed them into the lounge, bracing sea air was blowing through open viewing windows of the attached promenade. Below, the grey morning light showed the endless waves of the North Atlantic. While a Native steward refreshed a coffee service and platters of rolls, Hoffman harangued the passengers in German and English for their boorish behaviour the previous night.

When the steward left, Joseph locked the lounge's door behind him.

Now that the fourteen Wanderers on the voyage were alone, Hoffman dropped the charade. "Let us begin, then. Everyone, Alice

Banbury, out of the University of Waterloo, 2040. She has something you must hear."

Many of the Wanderers groaned or swore.

"She has come," Hoffman declared, raising his voice to be heard, "to reveal to us the true nature of the Wall."

This silenced most of the complaints, but not all. "The saints preserve us," muttered O'Connor, the loudmouth drunk from the night before. "Another fecking theory about the Wall."

Other Wanderers grumbled agreement with his disbelief. The Wall was time travel's most famous mystery. Nobody had ever met a time traveller from beyond September 1st, 2089, and nobody knew quite why. Theories abounded of course, but most had been discarded. One early theory held that some technological advance at that time would allow Wanderers to access even more minutely disassociated time streams, the streams becoming so infinite in number that the occasional meeting by chance between Wanderers would become statistically unrealistic. But that theory faltered because Wanderers could circumvent this problem by sending out signals, as Hoffman had done, allowing them to congregate within a single stream whenever the urge to socialize or cooperate took them. No time traveller past the Wall's date ever did so.

The most popular theories had been the bleakest. Something happened on September 1st, 2089 that ended humanity. Something sudden and unexpected, since Wanderers from very near that date reported that no wars had been imminent, no solar catastrophe had been foreseen. The environmental crisis had been dire of course, but that tragedy was only a slow motion genocide. One theory was that a secret scientific experiment involving a particularly potent technology, antimatter perhaps, had simply obliterated the earth.

The utter impenetrability of the Wall's mystery and the bleakness of its implications had made the topic a sour one among the Wanderers. Those who claimed to know the truth of the Wall were particularly insufferable, since none of them ever truly did. So as Hoffman moved aside to let Alice speak, many of the Wanderers rose from their seats and turned toward the exit with the intention of returning to their beds.

But Joseph stood in front of the door, arms crossed.

The sight of him and his hard face stopped most of the exodus, but four of the Wanderers took up the challenge and pushed through the others toward him. Two were O'Connor and his statuesque bodyguard, who Joseph had learned from Hoffman was named Zelfira. O'Connor had bragged that she had been a member of the Russian Spetsnaz before becoming a bodyguard. As Zelfira approached Joseph with a studiedly casual stride, he suddenly sniffed at the air. "The hydrogen in the Hindenburg has been treated with the scent of garlic to help make gas leaks noticeable."

Zelfira paused and sniffed too. "I smell no garlic."

"Me neither." With this, Joseph refolded his crossed arms so that the Luger in his hand became visible against his bicep.

The two other brave Wanderers moved off, but Zelfira—the start of a smile on her face—took a long, searching look into his eyes. He let her see what was in there. Her smile faded. Nodding, she backed away two steps, took O'Connor by the arm, and guided him to the other side of the lounge while watching Joseph over her shoulder.

Hoffman yielded his place in front of the Wanderers to Alice. She stood before the mural that dominated the lounge, a giant map depicting the routes and ships of famous explorers of the past. "I was a researcher in the earliest days of time travel. Some of you may have heard of me, if you know the history of Wandering."

Several of the Wanderers nodded. One murmured, "Our Lady of the Champagne."

This earned a few giggles, and Alice patiently waited while this joke was explained in brief whispers between the Wanderers, letting them establish her credibility as best they could. Then she continued, "Even when I retired to Wander, I retained contacts in the research community. A week ago in personal time, I attended the deathbed of a colleague who had remained a core member of the United Nations Chrono Displacement Authority for decades. It was she who whispered the secret of the Wall to me."

"This just gets more and more gammy," O'Connor muttered. "Another person who knows what the Wall is because Someone In the Know told them."

"I guess I'd have to prove I'm right?" Alice said.

"Da," said Zelfira. "Can you? Answer is no, I bet."

"Let's see if I can." Alice tapped the side of her head. "I want you all to access your database of historical troves." Everyone's wet-ware included a database of historical information ranging from maps to language guides to chronologies. All displayed invisibly within the wearer's vision. The database included a list of history's hidden troves of treasure that Wanderers could plunder for local operating funds in any given era. "Please put up your hand if you have an entry for the Paris 1944 Liberation Trove."

After a few moments in which everyone's eyes were distracted as the Wanderers consulted their database, half the Wanderers raised their hands into the air. This earned frowns from the other Wanderers.

"Those of you who originated from after 2072 and have the Paris 1944 Trove in your database," Alice said, "please keep your hand in the air."

Every hand dropped.

"All right, but so what?" said a Wanderer, a woman with tiny impressions on her nostril betraying a life with nose piercings. "The database is constantly updated. They just omitted that trove after 2072."

"The Paris '44 Trove?" a nebbish Wanderer exclaimed incredulously. He had blue contact lenses and some cosmetic surgery that somewhat disguised his Chinese ancestry. "There's no reason at all to take *any* trove out of the Wanderer database, let alone the crown jewel."

Murmurs of agreement rippled through half the crowd. That fact that this half were the Wanderers who had raised their hands earlier was not lost on anyone, Joseph judged. Those who had never heard of the Paris Trove were now looking uncomfortable, confused.

"For those of you who do not know," Hoffman said, "the Paris 1944 Trove was the non plus ultra of chronal insertion convenience. One did not need the toil of digging up buried Roman coins in a farmer's field and selling them to black market antiquaries and then cold-calling the purveyors of false identification documents. The Paris Liberation Trove involved a safe house in Paris where Resistance fighters were awaiting the arrival of an agent from Britain, whom unknown to them had not survived the parachute drop. For security purposes, they knew nothing of the agent—not age, gender, or race—so whomever arrived at the safe house with the proper code phrases was accepted. A photographer was on-site, as was a master forger of identity documents, along with a kit of currency, a Walther pistol, resistance letters of introduction, travel passes from both sides. Anyone could walk out of the safe house within two hours, completely kitted out. Even a local guide, if they so desired."

"And it was more than that," said the blue-eyed Chinese Wanderer, squirming in his chair in excitement. "That was the eve of the liberation of Paris, the greatest day of the City of Lights. Imagine it! The resistance battling the Germans across the rooftops, the allied tanks rumbling down the Champs-Élysées with the crowds cheering and flinging flowers. Battles on one street and mad dancing on the next. Hemingway liberating the bar of the Ritz, mademoiselles in short skirts with rifles, journalists everywhere, the frantic on-the-ground negotiations to save the city. And with your papers and guide, you could go anywhere you wanted, get as involved as you like, and...and anything!"

A Wanderer with Indian features nodded vigorously. "For years when I was working sixty-hour weeks to buy implants, I spent my ten-minute breaks reading everything I could about Wandering, and the Paris Liberation Trove was on every top-ten list of Must Visit." He smiled sheepishly. "Not only was it one of my first jumps, I swear I hit it a dozen times at least."

The Chinese Wanderer grinned over at him. "And the guide they give you? Mademoiselle Renarde? Did you—"

"Enough, enough, sold already, no spoilers," said a freckle-faced middle-aged woman to chuckles. "But why have I never heard of this ride before?" And several others murmured aggrieved agreement.

"Because," Alice said, "it collapsed."

For a few moments, the only sound in the lounge was the whistle of the wind at the promenade windows and the eternal thrum of the engines.

O'Connor, seated atop an empty buffet table, was the first to find his voice. "What does that bloody mean, 'collapsed'?"

"It means," Alice said, "that any of you who try to access the Paris Liberation Trove will find no safe house at all, just an address that does not exist. Natives will grow agitated at the name of Mademoiselle Renarde for no reason they can explain. And if you persist trying to attain the trove, you'll start to feel...off. The experience has been described as venturing into a building full of CO2 fumes. A sensation of confusion, numbness, inexplicable anxiety or anger, a deepening malaise. Those Wanderers who retreat to another stream soon recover, but those who don't are never heard from again."

Joseph left his guard position at the door. Nobody would leave now. He moved to a position near the front of the lounge, though off to the side, to watch the crowd for signs that any of the Wanderers already knew Alice's news. They would be an enemy.

"I started Wandering in 2072," a Wanderer said, "and I've never heard of such a thing as this...this phenomenon you're describing."

"The UN spooks call it a 'disruption'," Alice supplied. "History is full of attractions, but the Paris Liberation Trove's well-documented combination of convenience and excitement made it the most intensely travelled point for Wanderers. Almost all of the Wanderers took advantage of it at some point, and many made a habit of returning to it multiple times. For that reason, it wore out first."

"Wore out?" This came from Wanderer who had a 2060's neo-hanja tattoo peeking out of his period-correct shirt collar. "That's impossible."

"'Impossible' is history's most useless word," Alice retorted. "They believed it was impossible to log all the forests of the Western hemisphere, they claimed they could never fish out the teeming waters off the Northeast Coast of North America, they said it would be impossible to ruin the climate with fossil fuels. But history doesn't care what you think is impossible. Just as nature could recover from only so much pollution, history can recover from disruption only to a certain point. Nature and history both have a breaking point. And just as pollution doesn't create a new nature, historical disruption does not create a new historical timeline—it just eventually causes a toxic zone."

"I'm not saying I believe any of this," declared O'Connor, "but just so that I understand the claim: you're saying that's what the Wall is? A giant disruption?"

"No," said Alice. "When the United Nations Chronal Displacement Authority learned that history could be distorted—the Prime Line impacted—they knew humankind was about to repeat the same world-altering foolishness that had ruined the environment. So they immediately began secret programs. One covert program worked on an economic level, working discreetly to slow down private innovation that would have made chronal wet-ware more affordable, trying to restrict the population of Wanderers. Another program, massively complex but equally massively funded, worked to create a jamming network that would lock down time travel altogether. That system comes online without warning on September 1st, 2089. That's the Wall."

For a moment, a shocked hush reigned. Then suddenly, the Wanderers began to shout. "They couldn't get away with that!" someone called out. "In my era, everyone with the tiniest bit of courage and imagination is demanding affordable implants. The whole world is clamouring for them!"

"Which is why the UNCDA kept the Wall program a secret," Alice called over the shouts. "If the world knew about the coming lockdown, millions of people would do whatever it took to get implants and escape into history before the Wall went up. But now—"

"The public won't stand for it!" someone else shouted. "When the Wall goes up, the whole world will learn the truth. Then the people will—"

"When the public learns the truth about the Wall," Joseph roared, "they'll tear the Wanderers to pieces!"

His words and the thunder of his voice shocked everyone into silence. O'Connor's bodyguard Zelfira asked in her Russian accent, "What is this you are saying?"

Joseph moved to the front of the lounge to stand directly at Alice's side. "When the pan-national agencies who raise the Wall reveal to the world that history can be disrupted, all people everywhere will suddenly see the Wanderers as moles under the floor of their reality, gnawing away at the foundations. An invisible, unpredictable existential threat. Their lives, their children, their very reality will suddenly just be playthings in your lawless hands—the way the Natives have always been." He let this sink in, knowing that the Wanderers would imagine themselves being held accountable for their riotous behaviour in the past. When he saw guilt starting to beget fear in their faces, he continued, "When the Wall goes up, the governments will simultaneously broadcast the truth on all media— the truth that everyone's existence is in the hands of the Wanderers. And then any Wanderers caught by the Wall are going to die in the streets at the hands of hysterical mobs. No mercy, no escape."

The Wanderers greeted this vision with groans—and no denials. Everyone who had travelled history as privileged outsiders had developed a keen fear of the lynch mob, and this had naturally become married to a communal nightmare of what would happen if the masses of Natives suddenly became aware of the Wanderers in their midst and their parasitic, lawless ways.

"We'll...we'll fight," O'Connor eventually sputtered. "Tell us the names of the politicians and bloody bureaucrats who made these decisions about the Wall. I'll jump into their childhood nurseries as many times as it takes to smother them out of history. Assassination by disruption."

"You think the governments didn't anticipate that?" Joseph declared. "And what would you do in their position?"

The lounge grew silent.

"Now you're starting to think," Joseph said. "They're not going to let you and your sense of grievance wander time as human wrecking balls. The Wall is only the first move. The first move of a war."

Zelfira was the first to understand. "They will come. They will come for us."

Alice nodded. "The United Nations Chronal Displacement Authority secretly developed a cadre of special forces trained and equipped to scour the Wanderers from the pages of history."

For a few moments, nobody moved. Then some Wanderers stood up, getting their feet under them: high-tech travellers starting to feel the primordial instinct to fight or flee. Aluminum seats and their leather upholstery began to creak as other Wanderers turned in their chairs to eye one another.

"That's right," Joseph said. "The assassins are probably already among us."

Near midnight, Joseph sought out Hoffman and found him in the B-Deck smoking room, a small chamber with chairs and tables of black material and silver trim, and historical blueprints of lighter-than-air ships covering the walls. When the airlock-style door closed behind him, Joseph could feel a pressure on his eardrums due to the higher air pressure maintained in the smoking room to keep out any stray hydrogen for fear it would be ignited by cigarettes. The single-counter bar adjacent to the smoking room had closed up for the night, so the only other person in the room was a distinguished silver-haired ship's officer with whom Hoffman was having a low, intense conversation in German: Captain Pruss, the airship's commander.

Waiting for them to finish their conversation, Joseph leaned against a protective railing running the length of the curving outer wall and gazed down through the Plexiglas windows. Unlike the promenade's waist-high windows, these panoramic windows were mounted flush with the floor itself, so it seemed that he stood only a half-step from plunging over the earth's highest cliff.

At first, the world below was lost in the unbroken darkness of a moonless night. Were the Atlantic's cold waters fifty feet below? Fifty thousand? No way to tell. The uncertainty made him vertiginous in a way that the mere sight of the long drop could not have. But then, a strange double row of golden pinpricks appeared in the void far below. After a moment, he realized that these were the lights from the portholes of a passenger liner gleaming on the surface of the sea. The ocean itself was still invisible in the darkness, the liner seeming to float like another airship soaring at a lower altitude.

Captain Pruss eventually left the smoking room, casting an unfriendly glance at Joseph as he passed. Joseph found that he had lost track of who he was in the Native's eyes: a fleeing Jewish refugee, one of the clique of passengers who had behaved so boorishly, or an undercover SS officer. When the airtight door hissed sealed behind the Captain, he and Hoffman were alone.

Hoffman nodded after the departed Captain. "He will survive the inferno, but with a badly burned face." Hoffman circled a cigarette tip around his own sharp-featured face, a cameo frame of smoke forming briefly. "I've always had this ugly face, so I feel the tragedy acutely when I see a handsome one go to waste."

Staring at this face surrounded by smoke, Joseph was again forcefully struck by a conviction that he had seen Hoffman somewhere—somewhen—before. He now had a fleeting, fragmentary memory of that face surrounded by candle smoke, Hoffman's features lit by candle flames. "I was surprised," he said, concealing the moment of almost-recognition, "that you didn't want to take part in the A-Deck war councils." Since the revelation of the Wall's true nature in the lounge that morning, the Wanderers had adjourned to their cabins in the passenger section, turning the cabins into private, albeit cramped, meeting rooms for a series of planning sessions.

"I've been busy keeping the Native crew placated," Hoffman explained. "I told the Captain that all the passengers creeping from cabin to cabin are in discussions about lodging a complaint about my SS high-handedness, and so on." He offered Joseph a cigarette from a swastika-embossed holder. "So, are they war councils then?"

Joseph waved off the offer of the cigarette. "There are three factions. Some of the Wanderers have decided to return to the Prime Line and turn themselves in. Surrender their chronal wet-ware."

"They have family they don't want to be separated from, I suppose?"

"Some do. Some simply don't want to live their lives in fear." Joseph shrugged; their specific reasons were of no interest to him. "Of the other two factions, Alice leads the group that believes the Wanderers should scatter themselves far and wide through history to make it prohibitively difficult for the assassins of the Prime governments to hunt us down."

"'Us'?"

"Wherever Alice goes, I go."

Hoffman nodded. "I believe I'd be part of her faction. After having all of history arrayed before me as an infinite living Louvre, I could not return to a little university office redolent of the dust of books." He tapped some ash from his cigarette. "But you said there were three factions?"

"O'Connor leads the third. He wants to form the Wanderers into an army and fight the Prime governments."

Even as his eyebrows rose, Hoffman lowered his eyes to the burning tip of his cigarette. "Surely they cannot believe they can win?"

Again, the sense of deja vu struck Joseph. He had a flash of memory: Hoffman's voice saying, *They cannot believe they can win?* Except not in English.

This time, his reverie of near-recall stretched so long that Hoffman noticed. "Is something wrong, my friend?"

Stirring out of memory, Joseph considered how to ask Hoffman if he seemed familiar to him too, but did not want to give the game away until he remembered where he had met Hoffman before. He had made so many enemies, so he instead turned his attention to the matter that had caused him to seek out Hoffman in the first place. He removed from his jacket pocket the Luger that Hoffman had given him so that he could maintain order in the lounge that morning, and he held it up. "Give me the firing pin."

Hoffman took his time drawing on his cigarette and blowing a plume of smoke. "What makes you think it does not have a firing pin?"

Joseph aimed the Luger at an eagle on the breast of Hoffman's SS uniform and pulled the trigger. Inside the weapon, a spring uncoiled with a musical chirp to no purpose. "I checked."

"A prudent man. As am I." Hoffman started to turn the ashtray, one with the *Hamburg-Amerika Linie* image of a soaring zeppelin in the heart of the crystal, around and around on the table. "And I believe it would be imprudent for me to give you a working gun. That precaution about smelling garlic around hydrogen leaks is hardly foolproof."

"Give me the firing pin anyway."

"I decline. What does it matter if the gun does not work, if everyone on the airship believes it does?"

"It matters because I cannot use the gun to fire bullets into people."

"Why would you need to?"

"Alice. Now that she has taken up this...this crusade to warn the Wanderers, she will be a priority target of UNCDA assassins. She'll need to be protected."

"While she is on the Hindenburg," Hoffman said, "she is under my protection."

Joseph studied Hoffman's face. The professor had the delicate features of an academic. A very easy face to trust, Joseph thought sourly. "I have changed my mind, Herr Hoffman," Joseph said, putting the Luger down on the table between them.

"Good."

"Instead of a firing pin," Joseph explained, "I require you to give me your gun."

Hoffman raised an eyebrow. "What makes you think I trust even myself with a functioning weapon aboard this unparalleled gas bomb?" Hoffman said this with a sheepish smile and a lowering of his eyes, but Joseph noticed how this submissive gesture also allowed Hoffman to watch Joseph's hands and the language of his body, just as he himself had now started watching Hoffman's hands. One held the cigarette, making small movements that attracted the attention to its burning tip and the threat it could pose if, say, the cigarette were suddenly thrust at an eye. But Hoffman's other hand was still toying with the ashtray, spinning it, the ashtray migrating closer with every revolution to the edge of the table to his right side—nearer to the Luger holstered on his right hip. "One of the key lessons of history," Hoffman said, "is we need to trust each other if we are to survive."

"No."

"No?"

"No, history teaches us the opposite lesson. The exact opposite lesson. A real historian would know that."

Hoffman smiled tightly. "Perhaps you and I have simply lived two different histories then, my friend."

"If neither of our guns has a firing pin," Joseph said, "then you would have had no compunction in switching them."

Hoffman's smile flattened out now. The ashtray was now very near the edge of the table above his holster, and Hoffman's hand rested on the ashtray so lightly that the eternal vibration of the death ship's engines made the ashtray migrate toward the edge by itself.

Something clicked behind Joseph, causing him to twitch in surprise.

His own twitch was mirrored in Hoffman, and for a moment Hoffman's right hand left the ashtray and started toward his holster. But Hoffman, looking over Joseph's shoulder, almost instantly returned that hand to its former position.

"There you are," boomed the voice of O'Connor. The atmospheric hiss marking the closing of the smoking room's door confirmed that the click had merely been the lack of the airlock latch disengaging. "To which of you two fine gentlemen should I be addressing myself on this historic occasion?"

"Depends," Hoffman said. "Do you have a question about why the devil they ever put a smoking room on a hydrogen-filled zeppelin, or are you recruiting for a war?"

"Right then, I'll speak to you, Joseph." The room's tables were small, with three fixed chairs each. O'Connor joined them at theirs, and Joseph saw that the man was sober for the first time in the flight. Sober, yet animated, his eyes dancing and his mouth grinning. "Your woman Alice wants to give up and run for all time, but I say otherwise, I do. I say we take to the field." O'Connor noticed the Luger on the table. "Did I miss out on something?"

Joseph put the Luger into his pocket and looked to the door, wondering why O'Connor's Russian amazon, Zelfira, was not with him. "Where's your bodyguard?"

"She quit." O'Connor rolled his eyes at the foolishness of the woman. "I don't suppose a fierce fellow such as yourself ever had to consider hiring a chronal bodyguard, but it's a tangle of a profession, it is. If they could afford chronal implants, they wouldn't be offering up life and limb in the service of strangers, but if they're given the implants to do the job, why would they serve?"

"They could just blink away and wander free in history," Hoffman agreed.

O'Connor winked and nodded. "So they're fitted with wet-ware that has to be recharged every three weeks personal absolute time, back in the Prime Line. The power source is code-locked. Poor thing has to return to home and hearth with her client hale and happy or she'll be stranded in history."

"So she can't follow you in your proposed war," Hoffman said.

"She's been denied the honour and the glory, that is indeed the sorry truth." O'Connor took out a silver flask. "Understand that I can't get into specific operational details until I know who to trust— and that day will be a long time coming, I assure you—but here's a taste. Our general plan is to send messengers to gather up the Wanderers congregating at famous historical loci such as this ride, then direct them to a camp. A rebel camp somewhere in an era when they have just enough technology for us to produce chronal wet-ware of our own."

"Why would Wanderers need more wet-ware?" Hoffman asked.

"Recruits, you thick git. Native recruits!" O'Connor unscrewed his flask and took a swig that brought a smile to his face. "We'll smuggle tech from the twenty-first century back to the nineteenth."

"The nineteenth century?" Hoffman asked.

"The government intelligence agencies still work by written letter and telegraph in that era," Joseph guessed.

"And globalization hasn't squeezed the fun out of the world." O'Connor offered Hoffman the flask. "There are still regions in lands like Africa and Asia where an organization can operate in peace."

Hoffman ignored the flask. "Chronal colonialism," he said with distaste.

"With all the Natives for our Native porters." O'Connor offered Joseph the flask. "And for colonial troops as well. In the nineteenth century, there is enough science and science fiction for its Natives to be able to adapt their worldviews to the idea of time travel."

Joseph took a drink of the whiskey in the flask. "And to adapt to the use of automatic weapons, grenade launchers, and missiles?"

"Or even gas and biological agents," Hoffman said with a sour twist of the mouth.

"Maybe even a wee nuke or two, ultimately," O'Connor admitted without shame.

"But to make the chronal disruption permanent," Joseph said, handing back the flask, "you would have to commit the same act of sabotage thousands of times over."

"Then thousands of times it shall be, if they force our hand." O'Connor crossed himself as though he abhorred the idea. "But that's the way of uprisings, my brothers. You don't need to overthrow a government by force, you just need to demonstrate that you'll fight forever if they don't negotiate—and 'forever' is exactly the weapon that we Wanderers wield. The deal we will offer is that they let us live in freedom, we'll let them live in peace. We rule the past, they rule the future." He raised his flask again in a toast. "To the Wall. Good fences make good neighbours."

Joseph kept his expression neutral.

But Hoffman's distaste had him squirming in his seat. "And I suppose you'll form yourself into a network of cells, like any terrorist organization."

"We're not terrorists, we're the Resistance. And nah, nah, that's how we Celts made a right bag of our place in history." He tugged down his shirt collar to show his silver torc. "A mighty people we were, but as little peoples we fell. We were everywhere, but united nowhere. A thousand scattered tribes, we ended up the slaves and mercenaries of every empire between Africa and Eire. But the Resistance will learn from history, we will. We Resistance may have all of history, but we don't have much *absolute* time in which to fortify ourselves for the freedom struggle to come. So we'll band together to establish our humble techno-industrial complex as quickly as possible, then diversify into action cells only later."

"I see, I see." With two fingers, Joseph took the Luger from his coat pocket.

O'Connor stiffened. "Don't be playing with that firecracker. Hydrogen."

"It's safe in here," Joseph said. "The walls and roof of the smoking room are fireproofed, and the air pressure is kept higher in here so that no stray hydrogen can enter." Joseph handed the Luger to O'Connor.

O'Connor took the gun with a solemn nod. "You've got vision, brother, vision. And that's exactly what the times demand." O'Connor put down his flask and set about verifying that the gun was loaded, fumbling with the mechanism. "Uniting a band of freedom fighters on the fly is a sore enough trial without your woman convincing all the Wanderers to cower in caves across the millennia. Can your brothers and sisters count on you to talk sense to tender Alice?"

Joseph was nodding even as he took another drink. "Mmm, yes, talking sense to her is actually what is called for. I need to warn that we conceptualized the danger all wrong. We were watching for a Judas, but that was short-sighted."

"Do tell," O'Connor said in a distracted way, his frustrated attention on the gun. He had verified the loaded magazine in the Luger's handle, but was fruitlessly trying to check its chamber by tugging at the top of the receiver as though it were a standard automatic, rather than pulling back on the Luger's idiosyncratic jointed arm.

"Alice and I tried to anticipate how the Prime Line assassins would hunt down the Wanderers," Joseph explained. "Tracking down individual Wanderers across all of history? Almost impossible. So Alice and I assumed that the Prime Line assassins would instead rely on the classic counterinsurgency technique of ambushing groups at key locations."

"So you suspected me?" Hoffman asked.

"Of course. We recognized that the key danger was from the host who sent out the signal that gathered the Wanderers here. He'd be the most likely Judas." Joseph turned from Hoffman to O'Connor. "But now, listening to you, I realize we were thinking small."

A bit of tongue tip had appeared at the corner of O'Connor's mouth as he continued to struggle with the Luger's mechanism. "You've lost me, brother."

"Ambushing small groups of Wanderers at gatherings such as this voyage?" Joseph said. "It's better than hunting us down one by one, but it's still slow and it only needs to go wrong once. When an ambush fails, the survivors scatter and start warning other Wanderers, and then the hunters are back to having to hunt fleeing individuals across time." He took a swig from O'Connor's flask.

"But listening to you just now, I see the proper way to go about it. Instead of hunting Wanderers, the assassins would be smarter to masquerade as Resistance leaders and urge the Wanderers to gather together in one place so they could fight. A black flag operation, with all the trimmings: fine speeches, oaths of secrecy, and grand talk of freedom and brotherhood. They would even use naive Wanderers to recruit other Wanderers and send them to a central rebel base camp—and there, they'd put a bullet in the back of their heads."

Hoffman was breathing through his mouth now, staring in realization at O'Connor. "Not a Judas—a Judas goat."

At first, O'Connor almost seemed not to have heard, still absorbed in the puzzle of the Luger. But then, his fingers left off tugging fruitlessly at the top of the weapon and deftly snapped back the Luger's jointed arm, chambering a cartridge.

With a grunt of fear, Hoffman clawed clumsily for the flap holster at his hip.

But O'Connor moved with lightning purpose, the Luger in his hand rising up to fire a bullet into first Hoffman's forehead and then instantly tracking left to fire another into Joseph's head. The movement was so swift and so automatic—betraying long training—that O'Connor had completed the entire motion before consciously registering that the gun, lacking a firing pin, had not fired at all.

Joseph threw a punch across the table, rising from his chair as he did. But O'Connor, despite his momentary surprise at finding the gun dysfunctional, still rolled with the blow and almost dodged it altogether, Joseph's knuckles just grazing his cheekbone. Even before Joseph could pull his arm back, O'Conner grabbed his wrist in an aikido lock and twisted. Pain shot through Joseph's arm, and O'Connor pulled as he twisted, seeking to drag Joseph over the tabletop, the useless Luger already rising for a blow to the back of Joseph's head. But Joseph hooked his free arm under the table and violently thrust it upward with all the strength in his body. The four bolts affixing the table to the deck gave way, the table rising and jamming against O'Connor. The two of them went down in an awkward heap, gouging and striking at each other. Somewhere in the melee, Hoffman cried out in pain and started calling out for help.

The smoking room was cramped and its tables and chairs all bolted down, so the struggle that ensued had the frenzied brutality of men fighting in a siege tunnel. Joseph and O'Connor thrust thumbs at eyes and bit at the fingers that sought out their own, they head-butted at faces, they tore back fingers, they clawed, they clutched for testicles. O'Connor was faster and well-trained, but Joseph was bigger and horribly experienced. Eventually, he rammed O'Connor backward through the railing that guarded the chamber's row of viewing windows with such force that the railing broke. Even as O'Connor landed flat on his back atop a floor-level panoramic window, he snapped his legs outward in an acrobatic move to launch himself back to his feet.

But Joseph stomped on O'Connor's chest with the pitiless strength he'd shown crushing the faces of the fallen on dozens of battlefields.

The sternum stomp was a double paralytic: it not only drove the breath from O'Connor's lungs, it also cracked the Plexiglas sheet underneath him. He froze as spider web cracks migrated out across the window under him.

Joseph seized the broken ends of the railing and braced himself, his foot firmly planted on O'Connor's chest.

Even as he wheezed, desperately drawing air back into his lungs, O'Connor looked over his shoulder and through the cracked glass. The moon peeked out momentarily, touching silver to the storm-tossed black waves of the North Atlantic a thousand feet below. "Ease up," he gasped. "I'm not resisting."

Breathing hard himself, Joseph kept his foot on O'Connor's chest. His wrist throbbed, he felt blood trickling from his ear, and a dozen other places on his body felt as numb as dead meat. He glanced quickly around for Hoffman and saw the historian on his knees, blood gushing from his nostrils, trying dizzily to rise and failing. Joseph couldn't even remember how Hoffman got hurt.

"Gun," Joseph said to him. "Wake up! Gun!"

Eyes unfocused, Hoffman nevertheless nodded and fumbled in his holster for his Luger. He crawled a few feet closer on his hands and knees, and handed it to Joseph.

Joseph took the weapon and aimed it down at O'Connor. "Tell me your specific mission orders. Talk and I'll let you live, I swear."

O'Connor coughed out some blood, then said in a hoarse voice, "I'll do better than that, I'll give you my best possible advice: surrender."

"B-be realistic, O'Connor," Hoffman said, climbing to his feet by pulling on the railing farther along.

"'Realistic'," O'Connor mocked. "Reality is exactly what I'm all about, Professor Massieu. And I have a message for you."

"For me?" Hoffman said, puzzled by this and by the shock of O'Connor knowing his real name.

"Tell the other Wanderers this: if they think that the soldiers and warriors of the past were fanatical about defending a country or a faith, wait until they see the men and women of the present who have volunteered to protect reality itself. You and Joseph and Alice and all the rest of the Wanderers? You're on the wrong side of history in the most literal sense."

"All Wanderers are," Joseph agreed. "From the moment we turned our faces from the future and took our first backward step."

O'Connor nodded at him, but continued to speak to Hoffman. "You'll have to be the one to pass on that message to the others, professor, because Joseph and I have to *go!*" With this, O'Connor grabbed Joseph's ankle in two-handed death grip, then kicked upward—not at Joseph, but at the underside of the railing. This forced his body downward, the Plexiglas pane giving way beneath instantly—but as he passed through the window frame, he kept hold of Joseph's leg.

The shriek of the airship's slipstream and of the high altitude wind roared into the smoking room, and suddenly invisible demonic claws were tearing at everything. Coasters, ash trays, and cigarette butts shot like shrapnel against Joseph's back and shoulders on their way out the shattered window as he was dragged down to one knee, his other leg dangling through the broken window. Somewhere, Hoffman was screaming.

Clinging to his ankle, O'Connor was lashed back and forth in the bitingly cold slipstream below the airship. Flying bits of Plexiglas lacerated the assassin's face and other debris battered his head and shoulders, his mouth open in a long scream lost amidst the roar of the wind and the airship's engines. But still O'Connor kept his grip on Joseph's ankle, fingers gouging into Joseph's flesh like spikes into lumber.

Hugging the railing one-armed in desperation, Joseph aimed the Luger at O'Connor's silently screaming face and pulled the trigger. Nothing. He felt rather than heard the impotent striking of a spring bereft of a firing pin.

The end was ugly, of course. Joseph pumped his trapped leg up and down, trying to shake O'Connor off, Hoffman flung ashtrays and liquor bottles through the window at O'Connor, and as strain and cold robbed O'Connor's hands of strength, he sank his teeth into Joseph's calf to hold on with his jaws as well. Eventually, Hoffman scrounged an aluminum table leg, poked it through the window, and timidly pried at O'Connor's hands. Joseph tossed the Luger aside, snatched the table leg away, and speared it down into O'Connor's face until his features were a gory mush trailing horizontal streamers of blood in the slipstream.

Finally, after five hideous minutes, O'Connor's grip faltered and he dropped out of sight into the void, plunging toward the eternal sea.

When the airship's doctor left, Joseph glimpsed a knot of Wanderers with worried faces through the open door of the cabin, waiting in the A-Deck corridor to hear the full story of what had happened. But Alice slipped past them, pushing back the two who tried to follow her into the cabin, then shut and locked the door. He was sitting on the edge of the lower bunk in his undergarments, one of the undershirt's white cotton shoulders stained with blood that had leaked from his left ear. Bandages swaddled his ankle where O'Connor's fingernails had torn his flesh. A crescent of teeth marks stood out on the back of his hand beneath a shiny smear of antiseptic ointment.

"What did the doctor say?" she asked as she set down a folded bundle of clean linen.

"Messed up that metacarpal in my right hand again, bite lacerations, and my ankle—"

"Do you have another damn concussion or not?"

"Maybe, maybe not. A little dizziness and ringing, but I took a hit right on the ear." He rose to prove that he could do so without swaying, then stood before the sink and its mirror. Right eye bloodshot. He explored the cheek and socket around it with his fingers, but felt no displacement of the bones. "What about Hoffman?"

"Broken nose. Says it was you who clipped him with an elbow."

"Close quarters. It happens." He crouched a bit to help her as she started probing her fingers into his hair. He knew she was checking if any of the blood matting his locks came from a scalp laceration the doctor had missed—it was not the first time she had tended his injuries. "Did Hoffman have the wits to give the Natives a proper story?"

"A single glass of Château Lafite Rothschild and he steadied up enough to convince Captain Pruss that O'Connor was some radical Jewish saboteur that he had been hunting for all along. By the way, you and I are now Yankee fascist sympathizers he recruited for the mission." She filled the small sink with water. "Hoffman and I interrogated Zelfira."

Joseph shot Alice a scowl in the mirror. He had asked that O'Connor's bodyguard amazon be placed under arrest only. "I told you to wait for me."

"If she had been another Prime Line assassin, do you really think she was going to just sit around and wait for you after what happened to O'Connor?" She soaked a cloth in the sink. "When Hoffman and I opened her cabin door, a log pile of empty bottles rolled out into the corridor. It took us an hour to sober her up enough for her to say she knew nothing about O'Connor other than that he was a client her bodyguard agency assigned her to."

"All right."

His mild response made her pause just as she was wringing the cloth. "You believe her when she says that she's not a Prime Line operative?"

"Do I believe her because she managed to convince you and Hoffman? Of course not." He leaned his head forward as she began cleaning blood from the rear of his neck. "But when O'Connor was fighting for his life, she was nowhere to be found, and when you and Hoffman went to her cabin, she didn't twist your stupid heads off your skinny necks. *That* convinces me she's not on-mission. She's probably just a dupe O'Connor hired as window dressing for his masquerade as a Wanderer."

Alice nodded as she wormed a finger wrapped in the wet cloth behind his ear, cleaning out a seam of crusted blood. "The revelation that their leader was also their intended executioner sobered the faction that wanted to fight an insurrection against the Prime Line."

"The idea won't die that easily, though."

"Not as long as there are people who define it as a struggle for freedom, no," she agreed. "But now all the factions—those who want to surrender to the future, those who want to hide, and those who want to fight—are united behind the same immediate goal: to survive this flight."

He dropped his voice in case any of the Wanderers in the corridor were bold enough to put their ear to the door. "You didn't tell anyone the secret about the cargo hold?"

"Not even Hoffman," she whispered back.

He nodded and closed his eyes to luxuriate in the feeling of her hands washing away the blood.

She gave him a minute of this peace—a final minute—then said it. "I've agreed to be the leader."

He opened his eyes and stared at her. "The leader of what?"

"The rescue."

"You mean you'll lead the escape from the ship? That's perfectly fine with—"

"That's only the task of the moment, Joe." She twisted the cloth, blood droplets raining down into the sink's pink water. "I mean I've agreed to be the leader of the movement to warn all the Wanderers about the Wall and the Prime Line assassins. To warn all Wanderers everywhen."

For a few moments, the only sound was the eternal thrumming of the unseen engines that kept them all in the sky. He said in a voice low and hard, "We talked about this."

"We did."

"And we agreed we'd only warn this one group of Wanderers and tell them to spread the word." Their plan in coming to the Hindenburg was that they'd swear every Wanderer to warn ten other Wanderers about the danger of the Wall, then the two of them would retire to some peaceful and discreet nook somewhere somewhen. Would retire from history itself. "This would be it, you said."

"I know."

"And I told you—I *warned* you—that when you felt that Florence Nightingale compulsion of yours to do ever more to help, you'd have to stifle it."

She stood holding the cloth over the sink so that it dripped blood into the water and not onto the floor. "You did."

"And you promised that—"

"Yes! Yes, I'm breaking my promise."

Joseph tore the sink out of the wall, pipes briefly trailing out like a spinal cord behind a skull during a blunt force decapitation, then he threw it against the wall. Blood-tinged water splattered the pale wallpaper and touched watercolour petals to the bunk sheets. Then he rounded on the cabin door, fists ready for when the Wanderers hovering in the corridor burst through the door to investigate the sound of destruction.

But Alice explained, "They won't come in. I warned them there'd be smashing and yelling, and that they should stay outside because you'd be looking to hurt someone."

He turned to her instead, looming over her, breathing as hard as he had when fighting for his life against O'Connor, and hurting more.

But Alice just looked up at him, her eyes immensely sad on his behalf. "So. You've been betrayed again."

Dressed only in an undershirt and boxers or not, he went for the door, meaning to storm out. But Alice was right: if he went out into the corridor full of Wanderers, someone would say something or look at him some way or just...just *be*, and his hands would go for their face, his thumbs for their eyes. So he spun away from the door back to her. "Why fight for them? The Wanderers?"

"I'm not going to fight. I'm simply going to ensure they're warned."

"Which will put you in a position of being hunted down by soldiers in a war."

Alice calmly tore the cloth in half like a nurse making bandages. "Doctors and journalists get targeted in war all the time. That doesn't make them soldiers."

"But why die for *them*?" He punched a fist in the direction of the door and the Wanderers beyond it. "There are no innocents among the Wanderers. Even those who start wandering by telling themselves they're just tourists, eager to see and learn and grow, eventually end up jaded sociopaths who—"

"Yes, yes," she said with an impatient grimace. Everyone knew the Wanderers had subcultures of those who assassinated historical figures, burned down ancient wonders, and raped legendary beauties. "But not all of them."

He pointed a shaking finger at her. "I'll tell you what happened. You went into those war councils and told the other Wanderers that in return for you saving their lives with your warning about the Wall, you wanted them to warn ten other Wanderers in return. That's all. But then you looked into their eyes and you saw that they weren't going to do even that much—you saw that the moment they escape this death trap, they're just going to hide and let all the other Wanderers die in ignorance. Right?"

Low-pressure water was trickling forlornly out of two small pipes where he had torn out the sink. She set about plugging them with torn strips of linen. "*Some* will help."

"*Most* won't. So why the hell are you going to devote your life to saving people who wouldn't help anyone else?"

"For the same reason that doctors, firefighters, soldiers, and parents do." Alice began packing her single suitcase. "Some people deserve to be saved and some people don't. But I can't sort the undeserving from the deserving—and I thank God that I don't have that power—so I'll try to save them all."

She left, lugging the suitcase with both hands.

Joseph slept away the rest of the night in a blood-stained bunk, far from his first time doing so. He woke with a splitting headache that convinced him he had a concussion. Not the first time for that either. He considered remaining in the cabin for the remainder of the flight, even though it would mean going without food. He'd starved for longer than that on many occasions. But the cabin had no toilet.

After a visit to the passenger deck's toilet facilities, he decided upon a quick turn in the deck's single shower in the hopes the water would ease the pounding in his head. It did not. When he emerged, a cabin boy who could not have been older than fourteen presented him with a folded note from Hoffman inviting him to the bar. He considered ignoring this, but when he returned to his cabin, a huffy Native crewman was at work repairing the sink.

Joseph passed two Wanderers on the way to the bar. They avoided his eyes and pressed up against the pale papered walls to give him room.

He passed through the smoking room. The window where he had fought for his life against O'Connor had been sealed with a sheet of wood and canvas. Men reading magazines and writing letters smoked cigars and pipes, delicate coils of smoke floating languidly in air that had so recently been torn by a shrieking gale.

Despite the airship's massiveness, space was always at a premium, so the bar was a tiny affair about the size of a photographic darkroom. A barman stood behind a bar no bigger than a cinema ticket booth. Joseph ordered red wine in order to still the grumbling of his empty stomach. As the bartender poured, Joseph found himself staring at another of the hand-painted images that adorned the airship's pale walls. This one depicted a Spanish lady in a crimson dress dancing the Flamenco as a guitar player and a matador admired her. It occurred to him that the Spanish Civil War in which he had fought and lost was still ongoing at this very moment in history. Musing on the timeline of that tragic struggle, he realized that he was soaring the sky in comfort on the pride of the German aero industry only two scant weeks after the razing of Guernica by German bombers. The smiling bartender who gave him his red wine was dressed in a pale uniform that included a virginal version of a Wehrmacht side cap.

Hoffman was sitting at one of the bar's shiny black tables, which was no larger than a bookshelf. The wings of purple bruising that spread out under his eyes from his broken nose seemed to mock the proud eagle insignia of his SS uniform. As Joseph squeezed into an aluminum chair opposite him, Hoffman gestured at his crooked nose ruefully. "I haven't made up my mind what to do about this. Usually, I would simply go to a modern era to have it repaired at a cosmetic surgery clinic, but now I suppose I'd be gambling my life if I did so."

"Probably. But why not? Self-destruction by self-indulgence is at the core of the Wanderer zeitgeist."

"Alice told me about your fight." Hoffman's bruised eyes flickered in the direction of the nearby smoking chamber, and he clarified, "The fight between you and she, I mean."

"And?" Joseph said with a hint of warning in his voice.

The other man set a hand to his uniform over his heart. "Herr Hoffman admires her devotion to duty, as she sees it." He then raised his hand and tapped two fingers to his temple. "But Professor Massieu thinks you're right, and that she's being naive in trying to save the Wanderers."

"Is that what you wanted to tell me?"

"Tell you?"

"Why did you ask me here?"

"Simply to drink and talk. Travellers do that on voyages, even doomed ones." Hoffman took a sip of his cognac. "I hope you don't mind, I've reserved us a table for two in the dining room. I noticed you have not eaten."

"I have no interest in the company of people just now." In particular, he did not want to risk encountering Alice in the dining room. "You can have food sent to my cabin, if you like."

Hoffman made a hushing noise. "The table's not ready yet. Maybe you'll change your mind by the time it is." He cast a glance at the bartender, but the man was paying them no attention. "I still have O'Connor's bodyguard, Zelfira, under cabin arrest, but Alice says you don't suspect her?"

"I don't see the Wall assassins working in pairs. Militarily, they need to strike everywhere and everywhen they can while they still have surprise on their side, and working in pairs halves their offensive footprint on a battlefield the size of history itself. The safety factor of working in pairs won't matter to them—the stakes in their war are too high for them to care about taking casualties. You saw how O'Connor was. No, the assassins will be lone wolves until surprise is lost and an organized opposition coalesces."

"A concise analysis. A military man are you, then?"

Joseph just downed the rest of his red wine, eager to leave.

Hoffman persisted. "I'm curious because our occupations say so much about our beliefs, no? As a historian, I believe that combing the Wanderers from the hair of history like so much lice may well be the proper thing to do. So I don't understand why Alice—a scientist by training, a physicist no less—is so passionate about saving them."

The stem of the empty wine glass almost snapped in Joseph's tightening hand. "Let me explain to you a secret about people like Alice. They're scientific, rational, and progressive—yet, they all ache for a mad crusade. Right at this very moment in Spain, an army of socialist atheist free-thinkers is fighting and dying in an ecstasy of idealism that the clergy opposing them could only dream about."

At 'crusade', Hoffman leaned back as much as his seat allowed and started studying Joseph with an intensity that narrowed his bruised eyes. "I...I know you, my friend. We've met somewhen before, haven't we?"

Joseph considered ignoring the probe about his past as he always did, but throughout the voyage he had been maddened by the sense that he too knew Hoffman. "Were you ever in the Spanish Civil War?"

"No, but my first chronal academic grant was for a study of the Crusades."

It took another moment or two, but finally Joseph imagined Hoffman with a beard. Then it was his turn to lean back in his chair in surprise. "You were that map-maker. Arnould."

"Arnould, oui. A humble cartographer following the Crusader armies. Easy for a historian to play the ever inquisitive observer that way." Hoffman was studying him with eyes narrowed now in an ecstasy of frustration. "But I can't quite place you."

Joseph put a finger into the wine dregs in the bottom of his glass, touched that finger to a place above his right eye, then stroked it down all the way across the socket and cheek to the jawline, inscribing in red wine the path of a scimitar scar he'd borne for years.

Hoffman's mouth rounded in surprise and then remained open in horror. He started to rise from his seat as though he would flee, but then he recovered his sense of time and place just enough to sit down rather than make a scene. But he drew his legs away from Joseph's under the table and sat as far back from the table as his seat would allow. "You were him, the right hand of Bohemond of Flanders himself. His mail-clad fist. I don't even recall what name you used, men only ever called you 'le Loup de L'Enfer'."

"The only name I ever used was my own, 'Joseph'. But I believe men once also called me 'Heaven's Hound'."

"Not by the time our paths crossed at the end of the Siege at Antioch. By then, the other crusaders were calling you 'Hell's Wolf'."

"Then you should have been at the siege at its beginning, nine months earlier, when we were still united. To a degree." Joseph set about scrubbing away the red wine scar with a handkerchief.

Hoffman was staring at him in amazement. "I suspected at my very first glance that you might be a Wanderer, since you were as tall and as soundly built as a modern man. But then I saw you wage war." Eyes growing distant, he shook his head at what he had witnessed so long ago. "When the half-starved, plague-ridden, sun-crazed, thirst-tormented noblemen and knights and prophets and bishops wanted to give up the siege, you fought onward. No, I told myself, *that* is a crusader. *That* is a true believer."

"I was," Joseph said.

Hoffman stared at him in open doubt. "In what sense?"

"In the simplest, purest sense." Joseph shrugged to acknowledge the reasonableness of Hoffman's doubt and explained, "By the time that time travel became possible, Christianity had mostly degenerated from a living faith to a quaint genealogical adjective. But the Elders of one of the more fundamentalist sects, for all their resentment of science, still saw time travel as a boon from heaven meant for them—meant as the means to reinvigorate the faith. So they raised a final generation of children—all boys, of course—as holy warriors, training us in faith, in history, languages, oratory. And most especially in killing."

"And you were one of those children?"

"I wasn't just one of those children: I was The One." A corner of Joseph's mouth twitched in a bitter smile. "The Elders had the candidates who had survived the years of training prove their worth in the eyes of God in a final trial among themselves with live steel, and then I was The One. The Last One."

"My...!" Hoffman stopped himself before he could finish the inadvertent obscenity of uttering *My God.*

Eyes lowered, Joseph continued, "The Elders sold their property and emptied their savings as the religious do at the coming of the promised rapture, and outfitted me with implants. We all gathered in France, and there they knelt in prayer with me one last time. Then I went forth into the past."

"How old were you?"

"Eighteen." Joseph took a pass at his cup, not remembering that it was empty. "No armour, no sword, not even a gold coin or two in the mouth. The implants back then were so low yield in their carrying capacity that I could only travel into the past with nothing more than sackcloth and sandals. And that's how I arrived at the Council of Clermont to hear Pope Urban II declare the First Crusade."

"So early in the Crusade? Are you saying that you actually endured the entire journey from France to the Holy Land?"

"By foot, by donkey, by ship, by camel. Through forests, across rivers, over hills, across the stormy seas, through the deserts. Starving, thirsting, aching, burning, shivering, sick with disease. And then? To war."

Hoffman fetched an entire bottle of wine from the bartender and returned to the table. "But why? The Elders of your faith must have understood that you could not change the history of the Crusades."

Joseph took the bottle from him and set about opening it with impatient hands. "You don't understand. They didn't send me to the

Crusades to conquer the past—as Christian faithful, they believed in their minds that they already ruled the past. What drove them into a madness of bitterness was that they did not rule in the present."

"You're correct, I don't understand."

Joseph sloshed wine into his glass. "They gave me a divine mandate to triumph in the Crusades and then return to the Prime Line with the tale. Eyes ablaze, I would tell all the faithful and then all the faithless my story of self-sacrifice and glory and triumph—I would proclaim my testament that my faith in God had given me the power to cast down armies and raise up kingdoms. This tale, they believed with the fervour of desperation, would lead to a grand religious revival."

"Ah, I see. They did not seek to change the past: they sought to change the present in order to lay claim to the future."

"And so off I went to the First Crusade." Joseph downed half the glass at once, the wine aging his voice. "I marched, starved, bled, and killed, until we conquered Antioch."

"And slaughtered every man, woman, and child inside the walls."

Joseph downed the rest of the wine, leaving the glass once again an empty crystal ball with dregs in its bottom. "I was meant to avert two tragedies of that victory: the massacre of the inhabitants of the city and the falling out of the victorious Crusader factions. But it proved easier to breach the walls of a city than keep the blood from flowing through its streets."

"What happened when you returned to the Prime Line with *that* tale?"

"The Elders clucked their tongues and sent me off on another Crusade. The Second Crusade was my second chance." More wine went into Joseph's cup. "This time, older and wiser, I took a firmer grip on the reins of history. Instead of simply marching, praying, and killing, I also politicked, bribed, and blackmailed. But we failed all the same, even worse than we had in the First Crusade."

"And what did the Elders say to that?"

"Try, try again." The wine was starting to make Joseph's cheeks burn at last. "You must remember that though years of personal time had passed for me, an odyssey of suffering the length of the Iliad, for the Elders this all happened over a period of mere days. They had ensconced themselves in Clermont in a pleasant little country manor with a vineyard, a converted hermitage in fact. When I returned the second day to report failure again, they patted my calloused hand and told me, 'Back then. Try harder and have faith'."

"And you did?"

Oh yes, he could feel the wine burning in his chest too, now. "For a time, I even thought I had the Third Crusade won. In addition to politicking, bribing, and blackmailing, I assassinated, tortured, promised love, gave sex, and usurped. I defied Saladin's forces at the Siege of Jerusalem, forcing the inhabitants to fight onward whereas historically they surrendered. That stretched matters out from mere hunger to cannibalism, but in the end the walls still fell."

"So you fought in all three crusades?"

"I even cheated in the Third Crusade, repeating it several times."

Having tasted a bit of the suffering of those struggles, Hoffman shook his head in dismay. "What a wonder. And what a horror. How many personal years?"

Joseph swayed in his chair more than the wine could account for, staring a thousand years back into empty space. "Twenty-one years."

"You must not be serious. No man could survive that."

"Twenty-one years of crusading. Each day a trial, each week a battle, each month its own plane of hell. Twenty-one years? It was a hundred years. A thousand." Joseph's hand wiped at a line of sweat trickling down his face like an old scar reforming. "Eventually, I had to stumble back to the Prime Line to report my failure. My life of failure. This was only the third day of the Elders' pleasant vigil at the vineyard, you understand. So they sent me to bed, as adults do with children when they want to talk about grown-up matters, and when I awoke on their fourth day, they explained what I was to do."

"Lie?"

"Lie," Joseph said with a nod, filling Hoffman's glass with wine to reward his insight. "The grand publicity tour in which I would tell the tale of how my faith had triumphed would still take place. Why not? Nobody could verify my testament, since the wounds I had carved in history had disappeared like footprints on a tide-swept beach the moment I left. The past could be anything I claimed, the Elders pointed out, so the future could still be ours. By which they meant: theirs."

"And what did you say to that?"

"Nothing. I killed them in silence."

A twitch went through Hoffman as he raised his glass, a slop of red wine falling to the table. "You...?"

Joseph raised his hand into the air and curled his fingers as though grasping an invisible hilt. "The Elders had a collection of weapons on the wall. Those men of love and peace (and they were all men of course) had developed quite the fetish for the trappings of the Crusades over the years of the project. So I simply plucked down a flanged mace and killed them all. Once you have spent a lifetime fighting *askars*, slaying grey-haired children is little more difficult than snuffing low-burning candle flames." Joseph smiled with wine-stained lips, amusement entering into his voice. "But as it turned out, *their* deaths mattered. Oh, I had slain hundreds with my own hand—including my brothers— and thousands more with my commands, but apparently killing those men who had set me on my path of death was a crime. Isn't that odd? I had suddenly become a murderer. After that, I could never again return to the Prime Line."

Hoffman was now sitting with his arms across his chest as though against a chill. "What did you do then?"

"I was so lost that I made the grandest mistake ever possible for the faithful. Can you conceive what that is?"

Hoffman pondered this question for a time, then the bruised purple flesh under his right eye crinkled in a wince. "Galilee?"

Joseph nodded. "I went back in time to ask that carpenter from Nazareth what to do."

Hoffman pressed his legs together in the reflex of a man who sees another suffer groin trauma. "How could that have ever turned out well?"

"I was desperate. Would you like to hear the tale of what happened?"

"If you write it in a journal and bury it under a rock somewhere, I'll certainly dig it up eventually. But if I let you tell it to me here and now, I fear you'd find a reason to kill this witness before the ship returns to earth."

Joseph considered this and then let the accusation pass unchallenged. "Suffice it to say that after my trip to Galilee, I went in search of a place to die with the proper kind of fool. In the Spanish Civil War, when the Republican militiamen famously formed a firing squad to execute the statue of Jesus near Madrid, I was one of the riflemen. And in the Red Terror that followed, I joined in serving justice to the clergy who had trampled the people, though I personally only killed a few dozen of the thousands who died." Joseph made a dismissive gesture with the same hand that had feigned plucking a mace from the air. "My heart wasn't in it, really. For me, killing was no longer the point—dying was. Eventually, I just laid down. After surviving all those Crusades, I simply laid down. I was in my death bed at the siege of Madrid at the end of my final lost war when Alice found me."

"And how did she convince you to rise?"

"By convincing me that it would be safe to love her."

"After all you had been through, how did she ever do that?"

"She promised it would be just the two of us. I could no longer believe in humanity, but maybe—just maybe—I could believe in the goodness of just one person." Joseph eyed his morose reflection in the dull depths of his wine. "Now here I am, betrayed by another saviour."

For a time, the only sound was the thrum of the airship's engines. The eternal engines. The next day they would cease forever, consumed in inferno.

A steward in a white uniform entered and quietly announced to Hoffman that their table for two in the dining room was now ready. Did it suit herr and sir to dine now? Hoffman looked across the table at Joseph with unease in his eyes. "Would you care to join me?"

Joseph downed the last dregs of his wine, then said to Hoffman in the antique French that they and the other Crusaders had spoken before the walls of doomed Antioch, "I attest that the wine and the memories it has unleashed have brought me within a single cup of le Loup de l'Enfer." He set down his glass and rose. "I think I shall return to my cabin to sleep and await the flames in dreams."

Hoffman did not protest.

Alone in the windowless cabin, Joseph slept as a man sealed in a tomb.

After untold hours, the heavy silence was finally disturbed by battle horns blowing deep within the earth. *A raid! A surprise attack!* shouted voices in the land of dreams and memories. *To arms! To the walls!* Twitching back to consciousness, he found himself in his bunk with his ear to the pillow. Awake, he still heard the trumpets. Not from within earth, he realized, but somewhere below the bunk—below the airship itself. Trumpets of an army in the sky? No...not trumpets.

Car horns.

In the darkness, he had no idea what time it was, only that surely it was the last day of the airship's doomed flight. He considered doing exactly what he had told Hoffman he would do: remain in his bed until the end, when the flames of the airship's immolation would transform the cabin's tomblike darkness into inferno.

However, the thought of dying that way reminded him of witnessing Peter Barthomolew's trial in the First Crusade. The priest, who had claimed to have found the Spear of Longinus—the Spear of Destiny, which had pierced the side of Jesus—finally meddled one too many times in crusader politics, so he had been challenged to prove he was a true prophet of God by walking through fire. And the old man had surprised, even unnerved, his critics by accepting the trial. Two walls of fire were constructed by the crusaders and the priest had walked between them with head high. At first. Twelve agonizing days it had taken him to die from the hideous burns. The fool.

Joseph rose in the darkness, dressed, and then went out.

When he reached the lounge, the sunlight was shining brilliantly through the windows of the promenade. Excited Natives were gazing down at the world, chattering and waving. No Wanderers. He joined the crowd and peered down through the panoramic windows.

A city covered the world. The Empire State Building passed by so close that the passengers could see the flashbulbs of tourists taking their picture from the skyscraper's observation deck. An excited girl edged aside to give Joseph a turn at an open window, through which blew a breeze combining the bracing scent of the sea and the exhaust of a busy city. Joseph recognized the girl as Irene Doehner. White lace frills tumbled down her blouse. Later that evening, she would burn to death.

"Can you hear?" Irene asked him. "Half of the city are honking their horns at us."

Indeed, he could see that Manhattan traffic had stopped along the side streets and even some lanes of the main avenues had slowed to a halt. Drivers stood at their open doors, gaping upward at the spectacle of the giant silver airship gliding overhead. Many of the drivers were honking their horns. These had been the chorus of trumpets he had heard.

And inside the Hindenburg, passengers reached their arms out the open windows and waved back with hats or scarves—desperate for the people of the city to understand that they could hear them all the way in the sky. The duty of angels, he reflected: to let the people so far below know that they are seen. Irene Doehner had nothing to wave. Joseph rummaged in his pocket, found a handkerchief, and gave it to her. She smiled a bright thanks and then thrust the handkerchief out into the sunlight, flapping it like a happy wing.

The pure white cloth had a red stain, he noticed, from the previous night, when he wiped away a scar of red wine from his face.

As he stepped back to leave the crowd at the windows to their joy, he became aware of a tall woman similarly standing several paces removed from happy Natives farther along the promenade. Zelfira, the Russian bodyguard. The amazon wore a period dress with padded shoulders that were probably not quite as padded as people assumed, and her makeup did not disguise the smudges under her red eyes. *Someone else sleeping poorly*, he realized. Seeing that he had finally noticed her, Zelfira gave him a weary up-nod and moved closer so that the two of them were standing side by side behind the excited crowd.

"Hoffman say you say to let me out of cabin arrest," she side-whispered.

Joseph shrugged. "I expect you could have broken out of your cabin anytime you chose."

She simply kept staring at the sun-limned Natives with tired eyes.

"O'Connor said you'd have to return to the Prime Line," Joseph said. "Said your chronal wet-ware was designed to require recharging there?"

She nodded.

"It's for the best, maybe," he said. "If you surrender voluntarily, they'll probably do nothing worse than sentence you to doing some propaganda interviews about the decadence of the Wanderer class and how...no?"

Zelfira had started shaking her head. "Is Russia. They don't need real Wanderers for the cameras. They will put actor to pretend to be Wanderer and confess to anything with real tears." She plucked at her muscular forearm as though demonstrating the high quality of a piece of meat. "Me? Back to army."

"Oh?"

"I have wet-ware, I have wandering experience, I am soldier. They will tell me I am volunteer in the new history war." She reached sideward and tapped a thumbnail into his sternum twice. "Maybe next time we meet: bang, bang."

"You and I won't ever meet again. I have no intention of getting involved in any Wanderer rebellion."

She muttered something in Russian.

His Russian was meagre, since the only Russians he had ever met were advisers to the International Brigade in the Spanish Civil War, where they had typically spoken in Spanish, French, or English in front of the volunteers. "What was that?"

"I called you someone who is foolish like child." She said this with no hint of apology for the insult. "When I was first time a soldier, it was the Environment War. UN soldiers hunting down polluters to save the planet, yes? All good. But then, the Environment War becomes the Resource Wars. No longer UN, now country against country for watersheds and fishing grounds."

"I don't think I get what that has to do with the Wall."

"The Wall, it is good. All the countries band together to protect existence from the Wanderers. Yes, why not? But now...now...." She faltered on the English, and her eyes focused on something in the air only inches from her face as she consulted an intraocular translation display. "But now, 'the genie is out of the bottle'. Now, the countries know that history can be changed."

As he finally understood, Joseph felt himself grow chilled despite the sunshine shining through the windows and the laughter of the Natives. "You're saying it won't stop at a police action against the Wanderers. The countries will go to war against each other."

"Back in time, over time. History is now the ultimate resource— to be protected, to be seized. And history shows that battlefields are levelled to the last brick, so what happens when history itself is the battlefield?" Zelfira shook her head with a weariness so very Russian. "Humanity will finally have its war to end all war."

Joseph stared at her for a time, wanting to argue. He did not know how. As he stood there, Irene Doehner flounced away from the windows. Face flushed pink, she gave him back his red-stained handkerchief and then chased off on a mission of vengeance after a brother who had just taken a ribbon from her hair and was dodging away through the adjacent lounge's tables of indulgently smiling passengers, the ribbon trailing in the air over his head like a pennant.

"What will you do?" he asked Zelfira eventually.

"If I go home to Prime Line, I have to fight. But if I hide in history—just let my wet-ware lose power—then what? If I raise family, then family disappears when I die. If I do anything, it is undone when I die. But if I do nothing, then I have no life before I die." She rolled her shoulders in an enormous shrug, like Atlas giving up hope of holding up the world. "So be a soldier or be nothing."

They stood a time longer, but words were of no more use. Eventually, he nodded and turned to leave, but as he did, a final thought occurred to him. "I have a question for you, a military scenario to pose," he told her. "Alice and I arrived on the Hindenburg to save the Wanderers, and we anticipated the presence of an assassin from the Wall. Given that scenario, how would *you* have gone about our mission?"

Zelfira at first gave no indication that she would answer at all. Eventually, she said, "Not at landing. Too hard to control situation, time window too small, maybe even assassin team at airfield." She stroked a finger along her lower lip, then nodded. "Parachutes."

"Parachutes?"

"As cargo in hold. False manifest, sealed crate. Keep secret until last moment."

Joseph stared at her for a few moments, then reached out and squeezed her shoulder. She reacted like the dead. He left the once and future soldier staring bleakly out the sunlit windows at the cheering world.

Joseph found Alice in the writing and reading room. A tiny room with comfortable chairs and four small tables for reading and composing letters, it had been claimed by eight Wanderers. Alice was holding court beneath an improbable wall painting of northern Indigenous folk with a reindeer-drawn sled posed before a tepee. The Wanderers greeted his arrival with stares and silence, and one pointedly closed a journal in which they presumably had been recording plans. One of the Wanderers, the short tech geek who had gushed about the Paris Trove the day before, even rose to stand between Joseph and Alice.

Joseph considered lifting the man and setting him aside, but he'd always had a secret weak spot for little heroes. So he stopped, cleared his throat, and spoke past the man to Alice. "A word, please."

Alice measured him, and he knew she would be looking for signs that he had come to rehash their argument, so he kept his face bland and folded his hands before himself. She clicked her tongue and told the other Wanderers, "I'll hear him out."

The Wanderers moved only as far as the doorway, but that limited amount of privacy would have to do. Joseph sat across from her and leaned across the tiny bistro-style table separating them. Alice leaned forward toward him in a reflex born of their years of secrecy together, until their two heads were side by side, allowing them to whisper in the way of conspirators. Her hair smelled of the lilac shampoo whose scent he had breathed in his sleep for a long time.

"I have an odd confession, given the circumstances," he said. "I've lost track of time."

"An electrical storm is lighting things up over the Naval Air Station at Lakehurst," she whispered back, "so Captain Pruss is taking us on a tour of the east coast until it blows over. We'll make our approach this evening. Then boom."

"Have you told the other Wanderers about the escape plan?"

"We've formulated a plan that calls for—"

"But have you told them about the *real* escape plan?" he interrupted.

Alice hesitated and he sensed that she was waiting for a sign that her followers standing just ten feet away had overheard him. Then she whispered back, "I haven't told anyone the real plan yet, but I was about to."

"Hold off."

"Sooner's better than later. If O'Connor's gone, then why not tell everyone the real plan?"

"O'Connor may not have been the only assassin aboard."

The way their heads were pressed together allowed him to feel the twitch that went through her. "You said the Wall would send only one operative at a time."

"Because I thought there was only one war." He told her about Zelfira's prophecy of a history war. "If she's right," he concluded, "then there might be soldiers from an individual nation or two on the voyage that O'Connor himself would not have known about. As an UNCDA operative, he might have been a target for them even as he was targeting the Wanderers."

Alice considered this for a time, then gave a sideward half-nod, half-shrug. "That will change everything later, but it changes nothing right now. Our immediate goal is to survive the voyage, and to do that we'll still use the same escape plan. Won't we?"

"I asked Zelfira what she would have done to save the Wanderers on board if she were us," he told her. "She considered the problem for all of eight seconds, then said she'd have hidden parachutes in a crate shipped in the cargo hold."

Alice swore like a sailor.

On the trip down into the lowest deck of the airship, Joseph and Alice filled in Hoffman. When Joseph related Zelfira's prophecy, Hoffman was glumly silent for a time. Then he shook his head in despair. "A war over history, for history. As a historian, I should have considered that."

"You think it's likely, then?" Joseph asked as he took a sentry position at the end of the corridor ten feet away, keeping watch for crewmen.

Hoffman contemplated the question as he produced a ring of keys and sorted through them. They were in a restricted hallway narrow as a submarine corridor, and from a door marked *Elektoraum* and *Electrical Room* immediately beside them came the scent of generator diesel and electrical ozone. Speaking over the dynamo whine of this captive lighting, Hoffman said, "Any student of history can think of many instances where the changing of a single event could have altered the destiny of nations. As I understand it, any nation attempting to change such a historical event would have to stage a chronal intervention thousands of times to disrupt the time stream permanently. But what is the cost of such a labour compared to, say, the benefits of reversing the loss of a war?"

"And other countries would have to counter their action thousands of times," said Alice.

"Yes," said Hoffman. "But no."

"Yes but no?" Alice asked.

"Consider an obvious theoretical example in which Germany attempts to reverse their loss in the Second World War by giving their ancestors schematics for atomic weapons," Hoffman suggested. The countries with much to lose could indeed send operatives into the past to stop them, but that's inefficient and uncertain since they would have to uncover and frustrate Germany's clandestine activities over and over again. A more efficient and reliable means of historical defence would be to assail modern Germany to stop them from ever attempting such an intervention program."

"Wars in the past become wars in the present," agreed Joseph.

"A tangle of them." The corridor was dim and a frustrated Hoffman moved to stand under a wan yellow light fixture enclosed in a wire frame, holding the collection of keys up to the malarial light. "After all, such combatants may not be limited to states. Struggles over history might be fought by intra-national political factions, corporations, secret societies, criminal syndicates—anyone with sufficient resources and a will. It may well be that the Wall *is* our only hope."

Joseph and Alice met each other's eyes, their faces the hue of old bone in the yellow light.

Hoffman finally found the right key. He unlocked the cargo hold opposite the electrical room. They entered. Hoffman closed the door. For a moment, they were all in darkness. Then, Hoffman turned on a handheld electric lamp.

The cargo hold was not as Joseph had imagined it, a windowless smooth-walled compartment. Instead, it was a raw space surrounded by exposed girders and naked cables that crisscrossed the air. Above them, wire netting held up hydrogen gas cells. Two of the engine nacelles of the airship were laterally congruent with the space, filling the tangled space with a roar and a cheek-tickling vibration. As Hoffman held the electrical lamp, Joseph awkwardly searched through piles of luggage, crates, and canvas mail sacks until he found the trunk. Sealed with two chains and a heavy padlock, the trunk had a trilingual label *Medical Specimens* that also indicated it had been shipped from the Biology Department of the University of Munich.

Alice produced a key from her pocket and unlocked the padlock. Joseph slipped off the chains and lifted the lid. The electric lamp's beam revealed sealed glass jars containing human organs floating in formaldehyde. As the three of them crouched over the trunk in the close darkness lit only by his lantern, Hoffman whispered, "I am reminded of my tomb robbing days."

Alice stared at him. "'Tomb robbing'?"

Hoffman shrugged. "Other historians may call it 'archaeological excavation', but having actually met many of the tomb inhabitants while they were alive, I cannot discount their views on the matter."

Meanwhile, Joseph had lifted out the top tray of specimens, revealing the trunk contents hidden below: canvas packs stamped with the parasol logo of the parachute factory where he and Alice had purchased them a week before the flight. Joseph started counting the parachutes.

While he did so, Alice explained to Hoffman, "Rather than risk the flames at Lakehurst, Joseph and I reasoned that the Wanderers could simply parachute out once safely over land. To keep the existence of the chutes secret in case of Wall infiltrators, I've given the Wanderers a false escape plan—told them that we would mutiny and guide the airship away from the lightning storm at Lakehurst altogether But as soon as the Hindenburg clears Manhattan's concrete canyons, I'll reveal the existence of the parachutes. The Wanderers will all storm down here to the cargo hold, don their chutes, and whoosh: out a boarding hatch."

"Leaving the minimum possible time for any Prime Line assassin to foil us." Hoffman nodded in satisfaction. "Bon."

"And as soon as we reach ground," Alice continued, "everyone can time-slip to anywhen they want."

Joseph finished the count of the parachutes. "...fourteen, fifteen."

"All intact and accounted for," Alice said.

"Excellent," said Hoffman. "Let's leave before our absence is noticed."

"It's not that simple," Joseph said. "If there is a second operative on the voyage smart enough to anticipate our parachute gambit the way Zelfira did, simply jettisoning the chutes out a window would be a half measure. Once the Wanderers found them missing, we could still attempt some other last-minute survival plan such as the mutiny. But if I were the one trying to kill everyone..." Joseph took out one of the square canvas packs and examined it. It appeared tightly packed and sealed, with a tag still attached to the D-Ring attesting to the date of inspection. He frowned a few moments, then turned the pack over and inspected the rear facing. Still nothing untoward. He prodded the main seam running down the centre of the pack.

His finger slipped through the apparently sturdy double-stitched seam without resistance.

All three of them leaned closer over the pack, their heads almost touching.

The stitching of the parachute pack, they saw, had been carefully sliced beneath the overlap of the canvas, leaving the visible stitching apparently intact. Wriggling two fingers through the compromised seam, Joseph tugged out folds of the creamy silk canopy into the beam of the electric light. Alice and Hoffman groaned. The gossamer material had been slashed.

"Nothing we could have detected until we pulled the D-ring and found ourselves plunging from the sky trailing a comet tail of silk streamers." Joseph quickly inspected two more packs and found them both identically compromised.

"They'll all be sabotaged in the same way, then," said Hoffman. "O'Connor's work perhaps?"

"O'Connor's mission was to recruit the Wanderers on the Hindenburg as unwitting Judas goats," Joseph said, "not kill us out of hand."

Alice nodded. "Besides, whoever did this had to access the cargo hold, search it, pick the trunk's lock, sabotage all the packs, and then replace everything. That would take an entire night. But O'Connor was playing 'hail fellow well met' and 'rebel leader' with Wanderers the whole flight, I'd swear it."

They considered their predicament in the stuffy engine-roaring darkness for a time. Then Joseph said to Hoffman, "This would all be so much easier if you were the second operative."

"Je suis désolé," Hoffman said. " How do you know I'm not?"

"I've seen you fight," Joseph replied. "As an assassin, you make a good historian."

Alice took Joseph by the wrist and moved his wristwatch into the lamp's beam. "I don't know what we're going to do, but we'll need to make a move within the hour. Hoffman—Denis—we need to gather the Wanderers."

Hoffman gave a little click of his SS boots. "I'll assemble them in the writing room. I'll tell them nothing for now." He handed her the electric lantern, then groped his way out of the cargo hold.

Alice waited until Hoffman had left and closed the door behind himself before beginning the interrogation Joseph had been anticipating. "You're helping."

"I am."

"Thank you." She rose up on her toes and kissed his cheek, but her expression remained guarded. "Now make me understand why. Yesterday, you couldn't even find the will to get out of bed."

"As Zelfira mentioned to me just an hour ago, if you've been trained to be nothing but a soldier, you need to soldier or be nothing at all."

"But you made it quite clear you're not interested in fighting the war to save the Wanderers."

"I'm not." He took the lamp from her and held it between them, its beam angled directly upward, so that they could see each other's faces. "But the coming war over history? There is no other kind of war so perfectly suited to destroying everything. Even a nuclear war that destroyed everything that is and that ever would be would still spare everything that ever was."

In the lamplight, her face was both surprised and softened by understanding. "*That's* what you want to do? Stop the war?"

"Don't you?"

"But..." She took him by the hand, her own hand so small that she could only hold three of his fingers. Yet she did so gently, being the only person in existence who knew that decades of violence had broken his hands so often that the resultant calcium deposits caused him chronic pain. "You can't stop something as large as a war, Joe. Not one person. If you come between the countries, they'll grind you to dust like tectonic plates crushing a single stone."

"Nations have tried to destroy me before." He lifted her hand and kissed her little knuckles. "Are you with me?"

"No! I mean, I don't know. It's all too...too vast for me." She shook her head so hard that hair haloed her in the lamplight. "I don't even know how I'm going to save a handful of Wanderers over the next two hours. Do you?"

"No," he admitted. "Not yet."

Joseph, Alice, and Hoffman sprung a trap for the second operative in the writing room, where Hoffman had gathered all fourteen Wanderers. The chamber was so small that nobody could sit. In these cramped conditions, the short Alice had to stand upon a chair to be seen by everyone, keeping a hand on Joseph's shoulder for balance. With the door closed and locked, Alice announced to the Wanderers that all along the true escape plan had been to parachute out of the doomed airship—that the cargo hold had parachutes enough for all.

As Alice spoke, she and Joseph and Hoffman stood studying the faces of the other Wanderers. Alice and Hoffman, two veterans of history, had an understanding of people that few non-Wanderers could match. But it was Joseph, who had spent decades immersed in cauldrons of intrigue embroiling nobles and peasants, soldiers and merchants, across dozens of lands, with personal survival and the fates of nations always at stake, who had an unparalleled eye for the expression of false surprise, the furtive calculation behind a wide-eyed gaze, the hypocritical gasp.

Then Alice announced that the parachutes had been sabotaged and there was at least one more assassin among them. This naturally created a furor. And as the crowd seemed to suddenly become aware of the fellow Wanderers pressed close all around them, Alice, Hoffman, and Joseph studied the tableau of frightened, surprised, angry faces. While the Wanderers were still talking among themselves, the three of them put their heads together.

"I saw nothing," Hoffman admitted. "They all seem sincerely surprised."

Joseph nodded. "The operative must be so well trained that I can't spot them. Or they're not in this room at all."

Someone knocked on the door.

The babble of the Wanderers cut off instantly. Hoffman forced his way through the tight crowd and cracked the door open a bit. Outside stood a steward. "The captain sends his compliments, Hauptsturmführer Hoffman. In fifteen minutes, we will make one more pass over Manhattan and then proceed to Lakehurst for landing. All passengers should prepare for—"

"Danke schoen." Hoffman closed the door, set his back against it, and looked at his fellow Wanderers with desperate eyes.

The Wanderers stood in the thick silence unique to dread and epiphany. They had all boarded the flight prepared for the risk of the fiery final conclusion of the voyage, but that had been before they learned that an operative from the future was on the airship with them and determined that they not survive. They turned away from Hoffman toward Alice.

Atop her chair, Alice looked down to Joseph standing beside her.

"Very well, then," Joseph said to everyone. "The time has come for history to go off script."

Given the acute shortage of time, tools, and expertise at his disposal, Joseph would normally have made the simplest battle plan possible, but the circumstances dictated multiple teams of Wanderers with different tasks. As he tersely explained his plan, he could see the raw doubt in their faces. Nothing to be done for it other than keep his own voice steady as he concluded with, "All teams need to be in position in seven minutes. Godspeed." He inwardly winced a bit as he said this by reflex, having not used that blessing in years.

He and Alice had no time to say a proper goodbye. Wanderers were pressed too close all around them for him to even whisper privately to her, and any one of them could be an assassin. So he just told her, "Remember where it all started for me? If this goes wrong, meet me there."

She embraced him fiercely. "If this goes wrong, neither of us—"

"Enough of that." He uncoupled from her embrace. "Focus on the now. Go."

The Wanderers streamed out of the writing room and spread out through the airship.

Seven minutes later, in the lounge where passengers were taking in a final view of Manhattan from out over the ocean, Alice suddenly asked in a loud and shaking voice if anyone else could smell garlic. "That's the scent they put in the hydrogen, isn't it?" Before her question could be answered, another Wanderer rushed in and shouted that an overpowering stink of garlic had flooded into the aft corridor of B-Deck: "For the love of God, nobody make any sparks!" Simultaneously, other Wanderers positioned throughout the airship raised more false cries of 'garlic'. Hysteria took hold, and soon Native passengers were announcing they could smell it too.

By the time Joseph reached his own team's rendezvous position at a B-deck door marked 'Crew Only' in three languages, two crewmen bearing tool kits had already passed him on the run.

Hoffman was the next to arrive. He reported, "All the riggers and electricians are hunting for hydrogen leaks, the cooking staff will be shutting down ovens and policing the kitchen, and the stewards are busy dealing with frightened passengers." The historian's face had gone pale beneath a sheen of perspiration and he was visibly trembling. "I wish to God we only had a hydrogen leak to worry about."

Joseph took out a small flask and handed it to him, while nodding at the Luger holstered on Hoffman's hip. "Time to be honest. Does that have a firing pin?"

"No."

"You didn't even keep one in your cabin in case of an emergency?"

Hoffman's shaking hand was having trouble unscrewing the flask's cap. "I didn't dare trust myself with one. I feared that eventually some Wanderer would have outraged the dignity of history one too many times and I would shoot them. I didn't want that on my conscience."

Joseph smiled as he reached out and unscrewed the flask's cap for him. "You're a terrible Nazi, Denis. Just terrible."

"I was a terrible Nazi, a mediocre cartographer, and an utter embarrassment as a tomb robber." Hoffman sucked down a swallow from the opened flask large enough to make him cough, then added in a hoarse voice, "Historians are born to study history, not live it."

The next member of the team to arrive was the short tech who earlier that afternoon had attempted to stop Joseph from approaching Alice. The tech's name, Joseph had only learned minutes ago during the frantic planning session, was Marvin. "Thanks for picking me for the team," the young man said as Joseph handed him the flask. "But why? You get I'm not a fighter or anything, right?"

"I've seen your courage. That's all that matters right now." This was both the truth and a lie. Marvin was small-framed yet capable of bravery, and though mild-mannered he had appointed himself a bodyguard for Alice—and Joseph did not trust that combination at all. An assassin might play it just that way. He had decided to keep Marvin close to him and hence away from Alice.

The three of them had drained most of the flask in the sixty seconds it took for the fourth and final member of the team to appear. Zelfira arrived on the run, having gone back to her cabin and changed out of her gown and heels into a shorter dress that left her legs freer and a pair of sturdy shoes. And she had tended to another matter too, Joseph noticed, as she saluted him with flushed cheeks and bright eyes.

"Are you drunk?" he asked.

Zelfira held her head high. "I never get drunk."

He rephrased, "Have you consumed enough alcohol to make a normal person drunk?"

"Da, of course." Then she took the flask from Marvin, emptied it in a single long pull, and side-tossed it away, the flask skittering down the corridor.

The universe suddenly seemed to lose a tithe of its gravity, and the four of them each reflexively set a hand to the corridor wall to brace themselves. Joseph realized that the airship had just executed a pronounced course change. "What just happened?"

Hoffman's eyes grew distant as he concentrated on the silent language of the ship's movement. "We've changed course."

"Why? Where to?"

"I don't know," Hoffman said. "As you said, history is now off-script. Everything that happens now is unwritten."

"Then let's get everything right the first time." Joseph clicked his fingers and pointed at the locked *Crew Only* door. "Go."

But as Hoffman set about unlocking the door, the key danced around the slot in his shaking hand for seconds that stretched maddeningly. Zelfira hissed at his back. "Yes, yes!" the historian snapped back. "All of history at our fingertips, but never enough time."

After passing through the door, the four Wanderers descended to the lowermost of the two axial catwalks that ran the length of the airship's cavernous interior. The catwalk reminded Joseph of a tunnel in a medieval catacomb. Masses of wires and netting surrounded the cramped triangular walkway of duralumin girders, looking like centuries of silver cobwebs. Titanic gas cells pressed against all three sides of the catwalk with a sense of immensity that suggested the unimaginable weight of the earth pressing upon a tunnel deep underground. Their fabric smelled of must, like old shrouds. The inverted triangle of the catwalk left only a thirty-centimetre gangway under their feet, so any resistance by crewmembers could have bottlenecked their progress with ease. But none were about. The catwalk ran so straight and long that the riggers searching with flashlights for gas leaks aft were visible only as winking stars.

Hoffman led the way forward. "Most of the mechanics and elevator men will already have been at landing stations in the nacelles and auxiliary control," Hoffman explained. "Radio room coming up. Careful."

Walking at the rear of the group where he could keep watch on the others, Joseph slipped from his sleeve a knife he had stolen from the dining room the first night of the voyage. In front of him, Zelfira did the same, and like him, she held her knife out of sight on the side of her body opposite the radio room door.

When they passed the open door of the radio room, the single operator manning the several shortwave sets turned and looked out at them with a frown of uncertainty. Hoffman waved him back to his equipment with his best SS imperiousness. Joseph turned his arm to show the man that he was wearing a swastika armband, the one that Hoffman had given him earlier in the voyage so that could masquerade as Hoffman's American fascist henchman. The radio man returned his attention to his shortwave sets.

Soon after, they reached the ladder leading down to their final goal: the airship's control car. Standing at the top of the shaft, Joseph could hear voices speaking in German below. He whispered to Hoffman, "You said five bridge officers, normally?"

Hoffman nodded. "But I passed two of them in the upper decks checking on the emergency. There should only be three left."

"Good. Time's not on our side, but there's something that needs to be said." Joseph motioned everyone to take a knee, and the four of them knelt around the ladder shaft leading down to the airship's control. Light shone up the shaft, illuminating the gloom in which they had gathered. "We're about to fight for our lives. Pretty good motivation. But sometimes, that's not enough. Sometimes good people, strong people, get so hurt or scared they can't go on. I've stepped over their bodies a thousand times."

He paused. Their faces, on the other side of the lit shaft, looked like the faces of listeners at a campfire.

"I survived," Joseph continued, "because I always had a reason to go onward. A crusade. It all turned out to be hollow, but I didn't know that. But right now, right here, I *do* know that Alice is the only

Wanderer to have learned the truth of the Wall, and now the rest of us on this ship who have learned that truth from her are the only free individuals who can act. We are the only ones who can spread the word, and the news of that impending war is the only thing that can possibly stop it. So we need to survive this voyage for the sake of...of everything. Of everyone, everywhen. I can't force you to believe that. I just ask you to face it."

The other three nodded.

He nodded back. "Denis and I will go down alone, then. The crew already thinks I'm Hauptsturmführer Hoffman's aide, but all four of us would look like a mutiny party. Zelfira, Marvin, you two stay up here and keep anyone from interfering. If I call for you, come fast." As he handed Marvin his knife to use, he found himself struck by deja vu. Issuing earnest orders in the cramped gloom while his pulse raced brought back memories of speaking a few final words to attackers inside siege towers in the moments before the gangway dropped open and they flung themselves at the wall defenders. "One last thing you need to understand," he told Marvin and Zelfira. "It's possible that one of you is the saboteur who is trying to kill us all. If so, he or she will likely make a move the moment Hoffman and I go below. You understand what to do then?"

"Of course," Zelfira said with an indifferent shrug, as though he'd asked her if she liked ice cream.

Marvin nodded weakly.

Joseph made Hoffman descend first, and he kept an eye on Marvin and Zelfira as long as possible as he followed Hoffman down the ladder.

After the catwalk's gloom, even the dim sunlight of the overcast sky outside dazzled them. They were alone in the observation room that was the aft-most of the three sections of the large gondola that was the airship's control car. Above them, acres of silver fabric stretched off to the vanishing points beyond the airship's forward and aft horizons. The roar of the mighty engine nacelles not far aft of them made the control car tremble. The panoramic windows surrounding them on all sides showed that the silver airship was flying at a middle altitude between the gray clouds and the gray sea, with the skyline of Manhattan nearby. This skyline seemed in the midst of a very slow orbit of them: the airship was circling in a holding pattern. Hoffman consulted his watch and whispered, "Yes, we would normally have already started down the coast. Everything that is happening is new."

Joseph considered noting that this was the way that humans were meant to live: uncertain and free. But Hoffman had too much tension in his voice already, so he instead just nodded and steered Hoffman forward with a gentle touch on his shoulder.

The second chamber of the control car was a small navigation room, and there a single crewman stood at the gas valve control board. The man's hands flashed over the board's controls and his eyes flickered between the gauges as from his intercom headphones squeaked German voices passing along terse updates on the frantic search for the phantom gas leaks. Far from trying to stop Hoffman and Joseph, the crewman did not seem to even notice them passing.

Hoffman and Joseph entered the control car's third and final chamber, the control room proper.

Given the massive scale of the Hindenburg, the control room was perversely tiny. More of a booth than a ship's bridge. At the moment, only Captain Pruss and a helmsman manning the wheel staffed the bridge, but the vestibule still felt cramped when Hoffman and Joseph entered. Holding a telephone-style intercom receiver to one ear, Pruss spared them a single sour glance and then said in German, "Now is not a good time, Hauptsturmführer. We have a developing situation that demands my attention."

"Sabotage, Captain! That is your developing situation!" Hoffman half-shouted. "The Jewish saboteur my colleague and I liquidated earlier was not acting alone—that much is now clear! You must avert the ship from the planned landing site."

"Avert from...?" Captain Pruss set the intercom receiver back in its socket and turned fully to Hoffman. "If we have hydrogen leaks, accidental or not, proceeding to the airfield as swiftly as possible is in order."

"Landing is absolutely imperative, but we cannot make it all the way to New Jersey. You must find a place to land—now!"

This was the new plan Joseph had hastily devised after the discovery of the sabotaged parachutes. He had briefly considered making real the original fake plan that Alice and he had bruited to the Wanderers: to mutiny and seize control of the airship. But that diversionary plan had never been a real option because he knew that most of the Wanderers would have failed as combatants and the aircrew could have been counted upon to resist vigorously. And even if the crew were somehow incapacitated or taken hostage—well, who among the Wanderers knew how to land the zeppelin? Let alone do so without a docking tower and ground crew. No, they needed the aircrew to land the ship more or less voluntarily. So his new plan was to simply convince the crew to land the airship as quickly as possible anywhere open, potentially a coastal highway, to give the unknown chronal assassin or assassins the least possible amount of time to adapt and strike again.

But Captain Pruss shouted at Hoffman, "This is not an airplane! There is no question of landing it anywhere but the designated airship facility!"

"The saboteurs are bleeding the ship of hydrogen even as we speak!" Hoffman thundered back into the Captain's red face. "You have mere minutes—minutes!—to find a landing spot before gravity selects one for us."

At this, Joseph glanced back through the open door into the navigation room, anticipating that the crewman manning the gas valve control board would protest that his gauges showed no sign of the fictitious hydrogen leaks.

The crewman simply remained hunched over his equipment.

Joseph studied the man. The other crewman in the control car, the helmsman manning the ship's wheel, had reacted to Hoffman's announcement that the ship had been sabotaged by looking back at the ostensible SS officer with surprise and fear on his face. And when Hoffman had demanded an immediate landing, the helmsman's surprise had turned to consternation. All normal reactions. But this other crewman at the gas valve control board seemed not to have heard the conversation at all, though Hoffman and Pruss were arguing at the top of their voices from only paces away. In fact, it struck Joseph that the way the man had kept turning his attention to one gauge after another always seemed to keep his face averted.

Joseph cleared this throat.

Hoffman turned to him with an arched eyebrow, the picture of an SS officer being interrupted by a subordinate.

Joseph inclined his head to the navigation room.

Hoffman glanced into the navigation room at the crewman manning the gas valve control board. He could not see the man's face fully any more than he had seen it when he passed him in the first place, but he studied the general shape of the head, the build, the hair. Switching from German to the antique French dialect of the Crusades, Hoffman declared in a very casual tone, "After so many voyages on this ship of heaven, I know every crewman. But I have never seen that man before."

"I agree, the weather is promising for a landing," Joseph answered in English. "I'll go back and tell the others." Then he turned to leave the bridge as though he would pass through the navigation room to the observation room's ladder and leave the gondola altogether. But when he passed behind the chronal assassin who had infiltrated the voyage disguised as a Native crewman, he would snap his neck.

But for all his show of being absorbed in his instruments, the operative in the navigation room had indeed been paying attention to what was happening on the bridge. Perhaps his training in historical languages allowed him to understand Hoffman's ancient dialect, perhaps his wet-ware was up to the challenge of translating that warning, or perhaps he just had an assassin's instinct for a mortal threat. Whatever the reason, before Joseph could take a single step in his direction, the fake crewman yanked open a chart drawer and darted a hand inside.

"Down!" Joseph shouted, leaping aside from the doorway between the navigation room and control room.

Hoffman froze. Taken even more off guard than the historian, the puzzled Captain Pruss started to step around Hoffman to see what was happening. Then the firing began. A slug from a high calibre handgun took Hoffman in the chest, knocking him from his feet, and then Captain Pruss's face transformed to a mask of surprise as another bullet took off his white commander's cap and the top of his skull. The helmsman was facing forward as he steered the airship, so the third bullet caught him in the spine, his dying body arching against the wheel.

Joseph had dropped down behind the protection of a waist-high instrument console. For a few moments, there was no sound in the gondola except the impersonal thunder of the engine nacelles. He and the assassin were perhaps only eight feet from each other, a thin wall between them.

From the navigation room came metallic clacks of levers being worked.

Joseph located the assassin's reflection in a window on the opposite side of the gondola.

The assassin in the navigation room was holding a heavy revolver he had presumably drawn from the chart drawer, the smoking muzzle trained on the bridge doorway in case Joseph decided upon a charge. The man held the weapon in a military grip suitable for a close-quarters struggle: gun in one hand and that arm tucked back against his side to make it more difficult for someone to wrest the gun away. His free hand worked a final few controls, then he was finished. He turned his attention fully to the bridge, taking a careful glide-step toward the doorway, the gun aimed low at Joseph's hiding spot.

Joseph tore a metal control lever out of an engine telegraph to use as a club. He felt an urge to shout a warning to Zelfira and Marvin: *Don't come down!* But that sort of self-sacrifice would simply get everyone killed, since the assassin would shoot him and then simply seize the wheel and crash the airship. So he said swift and silent prayer for the damned souls of leaders, then shouted, "Now! Now!"

Deck plating thumped in the rear of the control car as Zelfira slid down the access ladder and into the observation room.

Joseph sprang to his feet on the bridge.

In the navigation room between the observation room and the bridge, the operative had indeed turned around to face the most immediate threat: Zelfira, charging at him with knife in hand. Joseph roared a wordless battle cry at the assassin's back, trying to distract him from her, but the man was too well-trained. His first bullet caught Zelfira in the chest, a divot of satin rising from her dress. Still, she came onward. A second bullet struck her above the right eye; behind her, Marvin and the bright duralumin ladder he was climbing down were splattered with blood and brain tissue. Martin froze in horror, then another bullet took him in the back of the head, switching him off so instantly and completely that his body dropped from the ladder like laundry when a clothesline snaps.

Then Joseph was through the doorway into the navigation room and on the assassin. Rather than trusting in any single blow, he tackled the man from behind and drove him to the floor. His every action artless and ruthlessly effective, Joseph straddled him and rained down a savage barrage of blows with his control-lever club, caving in the man's skull.

Swearing viciously, Joseph rolled off the twitching corpse. A glance at Zelfira and Marvin lying crumpled in the observation room confirmed they were dead. He'd known they'd be killed if he called for them—and he had done it anyway. He rose, slipped on a smear of blood, and fell to a knee, then rose again and returned to the control room.

The panoramic windows of the Hindenburg's bridge were a horror of blood splatters. Captain Pruss lay on his back, his dead face surprised and a pool of crimson spreading in all directions from his head. The dying helmsman had collapsed onto his knees, one hand still on the airship's spoked wheel and the other hand reaching around behind himself to explore his back out of an animal instinct to understand the source of his agony. The rear of his uniform jacket was already soaked in glistening blackness.

Hoffman had come to rest on the floor in a sitting position. He had drawn his knees up and was hugging the wound on his chest with both arms, seized by a child's need to hide the horror. He was looking to Joseph with a face twisted into an expression of terror.

"I'm sorry, Denis," Joseph told him. He reached up, drew the ship's intercom handset from its resting place, and held it toward Hoffman. "But I need you to get on the ship's intercom."

"L-listen," Hoffman said through red-tinted lips.

Joseph shook his head emphatically and tried to force the intercom receiver into Hoffman's hand. "You need to call more crew to the bridge. Someone—anyone—who can pilot the ship."

"Listen!" Hoffman repeated, this time so urgently that blood flecks flew from his mouth. "Listen to the *ship*!"

Joseph held still. At first, he could only hear the roar of the engines. Then he noticed that the engines' familiar calm thunder had taken on a new timbre. Rising. And now he heard a harmonic starting to rise from the ship's duralumin frame. Like a power line starting to hum in the stirring wind of an approaching storm.

"Speed." Hoffman pointed a crimson-slicked hand at an indicator panel. "Speed."

Still kneeling before the dying man, Joseph had to crane his neck to read the speed indicator. "Uh, one hundred and thirty-five kilometres per hour."

Blood bubbled at the corner of his mouth as Hoffman groaned, "Too fast. Too...fast."

"Too fast?" Suddenly, Joseph understood the ship's strange new symphony of sounds: the engines were roaring and the metal skeleton was humming as the airship picked up speed. He checked the engine telegraph, fearing that he had locked the ship into full speed when he had torn off its lever to use as a club. But he could see by the socket inside the housing that the telegraph was still at the 'half speed' setting. Yet, the airspeed indicator's needle was continuing to creep upward. "Why are we accelerating?"

Hoffman raised a bloody hand and pointed at him. This had happened to Joseph many times before, the final accusation by the dying. But suddenly, he realized that Hoffman was not pointing at him—Hoffman was pointing at something behind him.

Still on one knee, Joseph looked over his shoulder.

Beyond the blood-streaked windows at the front of the gondola, a gigantic metal spire hung in the sky. It shot toward them. As he stared at the bizarre sight of the approaching spire of green metal, Joseph saw that it was rising even as it approached. And, rising, it became recognizable as a torch...then came a titanic hand...an arm...

Dazed by understanding, Joseph rose to his feet so that he could better gape through the blood-smeared windows.

The Statue of Liberty's impassive face passed by the port side of the airship so closely that rivets were visible in the patina of its antique copper. Inside the viewing windows of the statue's crown, visitors with black holes for mouths stared in terror as the titanic airship roared past them—missing so closely that the ship's slipstream tore a dust-storm of grime off the statue's upper surfaces and sucked hats off the tourists' heads. The torch that had been at the level of the control car was now above them and still rising.

"We're going down...!" Joseph hauled the dying Hoffman to his feet and thrust him towards the nearest bank of controls. "That's why we're speeding up! We're going down!" The now-howling engines, he understood, were not revving high—they were straining to keep up with the plunging airship.

Blood bubbling from his mouth, Hoffman wrenched free of Joseph, lurched over to a different panel, and clawed at some levers.

Outside, cascades of ballast water plumed downward from the airship's midship tanks, knocking sprawling a crowd of tourists on Liberty Island and flattening swathes of the island's trees. And then they were past the island and shooting over water.

The airship's plunge eased, but did not stop. Mind racing, Joseph recalled that the assassin had been working at the controls in the navigation room. He ran back into the navigation room now and quickly located a panel of toggles and white labels that suggested a vertical piano keyboard. He deciphered the German labels. *Gas board.* "He opened the gas valves!" he shouted at Hoffman. "We're venting hydrogen!"

It was this release of the hydrogen, he understood, that had set the airship plunging downward—and this dive had in turn increased the airship's speed uncontrollably. Even now, the entire gondola was shaking so violently that all loose charts and tools rained down to the floor, instrument panels were visibly shuddering in their housings, and the glass facings of gauges were cracking.

Joseph frantically explored the gas board's controls with his hands, trying to close the vents. But the toggles had no tension on them, and he discovered why: the row of thin control cables that rose from the controls had been sliced through by the assassin. The venting of the hydrogen could not be stopped.

Joseph fought his way forward back to the bridge, slammed back and forth between consoles, the deck slick with blood under his feet.

Through the bloody windows, he saw that the airship's descent had given it a truly terrifying forward momentum. They were soaring low over New York Bay at a speed that blurred the waves. The velocity and size of the airship horrified the harbour shipping, freighters wallowing and smaller craft veering away as panicked navigators spun wheels hard-over. The airship roared so low over a speedboat that the hurricane of its passage plucked the craft up into the air and then disintegrated it into a storm of planks and bodies.

Moments later, the gondola ghosted through the smoke rising from a tanker's stack, blinding his view for a few moments. When the smoke column shot aft, he could see the Brooklyn waterfront bristling with loading cranes ahead of them, like an invasion beach laden with anti-tank obstacles.

Joseph flung the corpse of the helmsman away from the main wheel and spun it over.

The airship's bow eased away from the cranes only ponderously, but finally the zeppelin oriented itself toward open water. He spun the wheel back to what he hoped was a straight course. In the next moment, he realized that the promise of open water was a false hope: the airship was now speeding toward a river mouth, not the open sea. He looked around frantically.

The palisade of cranes was now on one side and growing closer.

On the other side, the skyscrapers of lower Manhattan rose like jagged ramparts—they, too, growing closer as the bay narrowed toward the river mouth.

Joseph froze. The cranes and skyscraper were both too close for him to turn the gigantic airship at such a speed. The ship was now too low for him to hope to fly over the cranes, let alone the skyscrapers. As the naval traffic flashing below evolved from ships to river barges, he started shouting at Hoffman, "Call the engineers! Reverse the engines!" He could barely hear his own voice over the demonic howl of the overstraining nacelles, the avalanche rattle of the equipment panels, and the whale groans descending from the overburdened superstructure above them. "Reverse! Reverse!"

Suddenly, a line appeared across the water directly ahead. It was just a dark streak above the gray river at first, but the airship shot toward it at such a speed that the object quickly became recognizable. A bridge. The Brooklyn Bridge. As the Hindenburg raced toward it, he could see the bridge's lower decks flickering with electrical sparks from passing trains. Its top deck was packed with traffic. This traffic had stopped, and hundreds of drivers and bus passengers now lined the railing of the bridge, staring at the spectacle of the stricken silver leviathan. The dreamlike quality of the event had frozen them, and only now—seconds before death— did some of them grasp that this truly was happening. That the airship truly was heading right at them. Futilely, they started to run from a fate too huge and too fast to escape.

History in a nutshell, Joseph thought, despite the hot haze of fear.

The bridge had a second wheel, an elevator wheel that controlled the ship's height. Joseph leapt over to it and seized the wheel, intending to bring the zeppelin right down to wave height and pass beneath the bridge. But he hesitated as he stared at the approaching structure. Could the airship actually fit under it? As large as the bridge seemed, the Hindenburg still seemed so much more massive.

"H-hydrogen!" Hoffman, slumped against a console, reached out toward him as though he would snatch the wheel away from Joseph. "The hydrogen!"

Joseph understood. The Hindenburg was still venting hydrogen, its immense reservoir of explosive gas rising in deadly clouds.

In the dark cavern of the bridge's lower rail deck, blue sparks continued to rise from the passing trains.

Joseph realized that even if the airship managed to pass under bridge, the venting clouds of hydrogen would be ignited. Nothing would survive the near-nuclear firestorm.

Does it really matter? he asked himself. The thousands of Natives who would die on that bridge and in the airship would live again once the Wanderers were gone and history reasserted itself. The deaths of the Wanderers would matter only in the short term, since most of them would be hunted down by assassins eventually. And those Wanderers who instead chose to surrender? The lives of those who surrendered and forfeited their ability to set their hand to history in favour of mere life did not interest him in the least.

But Alice would die in the flames.

Joseph spun the elevator wheel wildly, but not in the direction he had first intended—in the opposite.

Instead of dipping toward the waves, the airship began to soar toward the sky.

Joseph and Hoffman were slammed to the floor by the G-force.

As the airship ascended, it haemorrhaged velocity. Violent winds flattened the hull fabric outside the control car windows until the ship's skeletal frame visibly stood out. Support wires sang and snapped, and a thousand metal banshees howled in the depths of the vessel. Sunlight leaked between the top of the control car and the airship's underside as the tormented slipstream sought to tear the car away.

The cable spans of Brooklyn Bridge disappeared below the windows, its towers sinking down out of sight on either side of them a moment later. Suddenly, there was nothing ahead of them except the clouds waiting above like the ancient promise of heaven. The airship's momentum slowed, faded. The negative gees starved the engines of fuel and their seemingly eternal roar fell away, never to return.

Silence fell across everything.

When the airship had reached the apex of its climb, the weight left Joseph like a body from a soul. He simply floated from the bloody floor into the air. Tumbling slowly in the air of the control car amid drifting globules of blood and languid corpses, he looked down through the windows and saw the Brooklyn Bridge. Thousands of faces stared up in awe. Then the bridge of witnesses began to slowly drift aft.

"What happened?" Hoffman asked somewhere.

"We made it," he reassured the dying historian in the hush. "We made it."

Then the great airship began its final plunge from the sky. As the Hindenburg once again picked up vertical speed, the slipstream of air under its control surfaces forced the behemoth into forward motion. The hurricane of its passage sucked every speck of grime and every piece of litter from the bridge, drawing it all in its wake like ticker tape.

As weight returned, Joseph twisted in the air so that he slammed back to the deck near the elevator wheel. His head struck a console. Half-blind from the impact, he still reached up and spun the elevator wheel, reversing the airship's trim.

The airship's plunge levelled out as it soared up the river. In the moments before it struck the water, the mighty ship's displaced air pushed a white hurricane of spray before it, a concussive vee-trench briefly taking form in the river. Then the shimmering silver underside of the airship impacted the dirty water.

Darkness blasted through the bridge windows.

By midnight, spotlights transferred from Broadway lined the bank of the East River and the Manhattan Bridge, their beams illuminating the half-submerged Hindenburg from all sides as tugs and Coast Guard boats nuzzled her flanks. Minnows alongside a whale. One of the live on-scene reports playing from a radio announced that authorities estimated a million people were lined up on both banks and on the bridges watching the recovery operation. The voice, Alice was pretty sure, belonged to the radio reporter who would normally have narrated the tragedy of the ship's conflagration in the famous broadcast.

Not this time, she thought. *Not this one time.*

After the Hindenburg had plunged into the river, the Wanderers and Natives had found themselves alive. The airship's frame had held as the oblique angle of approach had allowed the river to slow the airship to a halt. The tidal wave that this created had destroyed moored boats upstream for a half a mile.

Inside the airship, the giant gas cells retained enough hydrogen to slow the sinking of the craft just enough for the passengers and crew to outrace the cold black water rising upward deck by deck. Ultimately, they had been saved by the gargantuan dimensions of the Hindenburg: when they reached the uppermost levels and could find no way out in the darkness and seemed certain to drown, the rising of the water had stopped. The sinking airship's lower hull had settled on the river bottom. The Hindenburg was simply too colossal to drown in a mere river.

They had eventually cut their way through the top hull of the ship, then descended its vast flank to the flotilla of police boats and pleasure craft that had converged upon the scene. Alice had been ferried to shore on a tug whose passengers included the Doehner family, the daughter, Irene, no worse for the accident than a bloody nose cupped in a handkerchief.

With a blanket around her shoulders and her body bruised a hundred places from the airship's wild final minutes, Alice had remained at the scene for hours, even as the other Wanderers who had not yet left urged her to flee with them. Now that they were back on dry land, they could flee to anywhen they wanted. But she had refused to leave, grimly watching the recovery operation. Fearing the arrival of Wall operatives or other chronal assassins, the Wanderers had all abandoned her.

Standing on the riverbank through the cold dark hours, Alice realized that any assassins waiting for the airship at its landing field would have heard the news of the crash and abandoned the operation, leaving her as the last living Wanderer in the divergent historical timeline. When she left, all would be as it once was. The huge rescue operation she saw before her would be no more, and many of the survivors of the airship now in hospital or in hotels or toasting their close escape in Manhattan bars would instead be corpses in the gargantuan tangle of scorched wreckage still smouldering at the Lakehurst Naval Air Station. But still, she waited.

Eventually, a coast guard officer arrived on a launch. He held his hat in his hand as he came to her. "We've located the control car, ma'am. It was torn away on impact, and we just found it floating half-submerged out in the bay. No bodies. They must have drifted out to sea. If your husband was inside, he's gone."

She nodded her thanks, then strode away from Broadway's borrowed lights into the night and vanished.

Remember where it all started for me? Joseph had said to her before they parted for the last time. *If this goes wrong, meet me there.*

After leaving the site of the Hindenburg crash, Alice time-travelled to the 1970s. She went through the familiar routine of acquiring funds and fake ID in an agony of impatience, then took the Concorde across the Atlantic. Rented a car in Paris. Drove to Clermont. The tourists who saw her making her way through the streets in the medieval dress and veil she had picked up at a Paris costume shop probably took her for an actress on her way to a theatre performance. Arriving at the coordinates provided by her wet-ware database, she time-slipped back to 1095 CE.

The Council of Clermont, as Joseph had described it to her, had entailed two parts. The formal announcement of the First Crusade to a crowd of bishops and other dignitaries had occurred inside a cathedral. Joseph, an eighteen-year-old time-slipping for his first time, had attended the second part of the Council, in which the Pope had harangued a larger outdoor crowd of laymen with descriptions of the predations of the Muslims and exhortations to save the Christians of the Holy Land. This event, she discovered, was actually held in a field.

She stood among this rapt crowd, dressed in a widow's black dress and face-concealing veil, listening to the speech that would lead to the falls of nations and slaughters that would stain history itself for a thousand years. She didn't understand the language well, but caught snatches. The Pope was promising that this crusade would wash away all sins. Redeem all souls. As she listened, she knew she was stalling before instructing her wet-ware to send out the homing signal. In the way of Wandering, any response to the signal would either be immediate or never. And in the way of Wandering in shadow of the Wall on the eve of a chronal war, the response might very well be the sudden thrust of a knife into her back. She sent the signal anyway.

One heartbeat. Two. Three.

Someone came up behind her in the crowd. She waited for the intimate horror of a knife. Instead, a voice said in English, "You remembered."

Smiling, she discontinued the beacon signal and turned.

When Joseph had first attended the Council of Clermont as a youth, he had worn sackcloth and sandals. Now decades older, he wore a knight's surcoat of mail, carried a helmet under one arm, and rested his other hand upon the hilt of a sword. The armour had a red cross upon its chest. She had so often imagined him this way that it was strange to think that this was the first time she had actually seen him clad in steel. He had apparently made better subjective time to the rendezvous than she had, for his face was still bruised from what she assumed to be Hindenburg injuries. He had gotten off lucky, she knew. Time-jumping the moment before the control car had impacted the river surface, he still would have impacted the river at high speed no matter what timeframe he had jumped to. But he smiled at her all the same, his battered features crinkling up in fondness.

A knight and a widow among the faithful, they did not kiss. They leaned forward and touched their foreheads together. Somewhere, an old man was thundering about sins and God's will. Only eventually did they raise their heads from this silent communion.

"Have you considered my invitation?" he asked.

"To join you in your war?"

"To join me in a struggle for peace," he said. "I mean to stop humanity from waging a war over history. And I will succeed."

"How? How, Joe? How exactly would you fight a war against a war?"

"With truth. The Wall isn't just about creating a DMZ between the future and the past, it's a lockdown of information. The people of the future will be told that their governments are fighting to protect their existence, so they won't even know that the governments are also struggling to bend reality to their will. It'll be the ultimate secret war. But we'll change that. We'll lay siege to that Wall—tunnel under it, climb over it, or smash through it—to spread the truth that history is to become a battleground."

"And if the truth doesn't matter?"

"If humanity can't care enough about the destruction of history to rein in our governments, then let's hope that the next species to inherit the earth says a kind word or two about us in their museum exhibits of our bones. If we leave them any world at all." He touched his hands to her shoulders. "Are you with me?"

"It just sounds so...eternal."

"The war against poverty, the war against racism, the war against climate destruction—all such wars are never-ending. But does that mean we should lay down our arms?" His mail rustled with the music of steel as he shook his head. "No, those are exactly the wars that need to be fought."

"They're crusades. That's what you're starting, Joseph. A crusade."

His battered features lightened, and suddenly Joseph looked somehow young. It was something in the eyes. "A crusade to save all things that ever were and ever will be. A Prime Crusade."

Behind her widow's veil, she lowered her eyes. "We'll be killed, Joseph."

"That goes without saying. Nobody who starts a crusade lives to see its end." Joseph offered her his steel-clad arm. "Are you with me?"

She took his arm.

We had hit a roadblock in the writing of our latest novel when Murandy suggested we take a break from it and write something just for fun as a cure to writer's block. She wanted to write a story about two lovers with destinies intertwined from opposing cultures. A sort of opposites-attract, star-crossed lovers situation. I picked up the idea and ran with it, doing the research needed to set our story in a fantasy version of ancient rome, where the gods are literal and magic of all kinds is possible. Deneige and Alton are each told they are destined for greatness, yet their two worldviews seem completely at odds. So the question becomes, must one best the other to achieve their destiny or are they stronger together?

J.A. Dowsett

Justine Alley Dowsett and Murandy Damodred write together. They've completed eight novels, two novellas, and a few short stories. They also attended the University of Windsor, attained BAs in Dramatic Arts, and founded Mirror World Publishing together. They both love role-playing and living vicariously through their characters, and they live in Windsor, Ontario, Canada.

You can learn more about them at:
http://www.mirrorworldpublishing.com

Fatestorm

by J.A. Dowsett & Murandy Damodred

In loving memory of Lincoln Valentine Kell

221 BC - Somewhere North of the Great Roman Empire...

Deneige felt the water in the cloth beneath her hand crystallize, tiny pinpricks of cold stabbing into her flesh.

Instinctively, her eyes sought those of her mentor. Ignes' careworn face carried a gentle smile. "See now, I told you it was simpler with something cool and wet to direct your focus. You've got it now, Javvar's fever is as good as broken."

With renewed focus, Deneige returned her attention to her patient, dabbing at his steaming brown skin with her now ice-cold cloth, when sounds coming from outside the tent intruded on her concentration. Her ears pricked. She heard screams, a distant yell, and the unmistakable clang of weapons over the pounding of horses' hooves. Along with it all, she felt a stirring in her blood, the kind that always warned her when the weather was about to take a turn for the worst. But if the sounds she was hearing were any indication, this wasn't a natural kind of storm.

Instinct drove Deneige to her feet. She reached for her medicine bag, then fished around her sleeping area for her larger travelling sack. It had been a few weeks now since they'd settled in for the winter, and her belongings were mostly unpacked in the tent she shared with Ignes and sometimes those who were injured or sick, but she started shoving anything she thought she might need into the pack.

The stillness within the tent, in contrast to the rising sounds of chaos from outside, slowly alerted Deneige that all was not as it should be. She whipped her head around to stare at Ignes, who knelt unmoving in the centre of their living space. "Can you not hear that? Ignes," Deneige snapped, losing patience in the face of the fear that gripped her, "they are coming. They have come for us. Your visions were wrong. They are here!"

"I should have told you." She spoke calmly, but the old woman's icy blue eyes snapped upwards and locked with Deneige's own. Her words seared into Deneige's soul as if driven into her on the tip of a cold, steel blade. Outside, the storm drew nearer.

"Should have told me what?" Deneige reached for her mentor's hands and found them colder than her own, and brittle, more like lifeless objects than the warm, steady tools she used to comfort those given over to her care.

Ignes curled her fingers around Deneige's hands up to the wrists and then clamped down hard. "*You* will be the one to lead us from this black night and into the bright light of day. *You* will save us. Only you can-"

Ignes words cut off like her life did, without warning.

Deneige had been so focused on her mentor that she hadn't heard the tearing of the tent fabric behind her as a sword slid through it, and neither had she noticed the faceless armoured soldier who followed the point of his weapon into the tent's softly lit interior. She did, however, scream as the blood-soaked tip of his blade emerged unexpectedly from Ignes' middle. The bitingly cold air and the sudden feeling that the storm had arrived cut her scream short, and she whirled from the horrific sight to find yet another man staring at her.

This one was as faceless as the first in his helmet, but with one undeniable difference.He *was* the storm. The wind and early season snow swirled around him, but he was the storm's centre; Deneige could feel it in her bones. The man sat atop a black horse with a striking white mane, wearing full plate mail and a cape the colour of the blood beginning to pool beneath her. He was death itself, come to claim her, but there was also no doubt that he stood very much among the living. He hadn't moved, but to Deneige's otherworldly senses he was a force in and of himself, as chaotic as a whipping wind. She found herself staring. Beneath his featureless helm, she felt him staring back.

"This one lives," the storm thundered. "See that she's tied with the others."

"Wait! I-" Deneige began, fighting to compose herself. "Who are you to come in here and bark commands?!"

"Sir Rendall, Praefecti of Apollo's Legion."

"I'm the Dea of my people," Deneige answered desperately, climbing to her feet and lifting her chin. Her mentor's death meant she had inherited her position by default. "I am Deneige Audra."

His response was impassive, despite the swirling power she still felt rolling off of him. "The Lumen are no more. Your rank is no longer relevant."

She faced the storm head on. "You could take all I own, but you cannot take my identity from me."

"We shall see," he stated flatly, nodding to the other legionnaire in the tent, and before Deneige had a chance to react she was grabbed forcefully from behind.

"I do not fear the storm!" she shouted as she was dragged to her feet, her ears filled with the sound of his horses' hooves striking the ground as he moved away. "I do not fear you!"

The burning of the last Lumen village, if the word 'village' could even be used to describe the loose collection of tents and lean-to's, took most of the night, but that was only because he wanted to be thorough. Having long ago left his horse in favour of taking to the ground himself, Rendall kicked at a pile of muddy, snow-covered furs. *This is what passes for shelter among these people? For walls? We're doing them a favour bringing them to Rome, to civilization.*

In truth, the Lumen as a whole hadn't been defeated all that easily. Their population consisted mostly of small nomadic bands, which made them harder to find and even harder to kill. They didn't gather all in one place, they didn't own property or buildings that could be taken, and they simply scattered when threatened or overwhelmed. It was maddening.

But we've done it, Rendall reminded himself, *or, more accurately, I've done it. The Governor will see me lauded for this. I may even be given charge of my own legion.*

Thoughts of the elderly Vestal Virgin he'd met in his youth returned to him, as they often did whenever he achieved some sort of success which would move his career forward. On that fateful day, during the festival of Vestalia, he had wandered into the temple seeking shade, and had the fool-headedness of youth to blame for thinking no one would take issue with his taking a drink from the fountain within.

A hand with the grip of bones snapping together locked around his wrist and despite the age-spotted and wrinkled nature of it, he didn't have the strength needed to break out of its grasp. Rendall gasped, spilling the water of the gods back into the fountain as he sprung to his feet.

"I didn't mean nuthin' by it."

The grip on his wrist only tightened in response and he found himself looking into ice blue eyes. They bored into his soul and chilled him, despite the heat of mid-summer.

"Who...are you?" he stammered.

"It's you who matters, young man." The old voice was at the same time tremulous and full of conviction. "Not so much yet, but you will. I have seen your destiny, boy. You will lead Rome to a great victory, and in turn become great yourself. Beware the night, though, my boy. The sun is your domain. The moon...the moon will be your undoing."

"You there!" Rendall looked up to find a priest staring at him. He turned to gesture at the old woman and protest that it was her fault he had lingered where he wasn't supposed to be, when he realized she was already shuffling away. He rubbed at his wrist; he could still feel the woman's bones digging into his flesh.

He'd repeated the woman's words in explanation for his presence within the temple, or at least the positive parts, and doing so had changed his life. The woman, as he was to later learn, was the eldest of the Vestal Virgins still living, gifted with prophecy from the goddess herself. Taking her pronouncement with the utmost seriousness, the priest had seen that he was taken into the ranks of

Apollo's Legion, where he swiftly rose to prominence, as if the gods themselves willed it so. Now he was a Praefecti, a knight-general of cavalry, with five hundred men under his command, charged with the task of eliminating the last of the Lumen people in Rome's name.

He'd spent the last hour reining in stragglers. He rounded up those who were able-bodied enough and had them strung together like a line of cattle to be sold at market. The rest, he simply let fall off his blade, telling himself it was a mercy. Without the ability to work, they would never find a place in Roman society, not even as slaves, and so they would forever find themselves outsiders. Better to be dead, really. The empire didn't need more beggars.

Having completed his circuit of the former Lumen territory, Rendall found himself surveying the prisoners. Most were huddled together with their heads down, trying to use one another's body heat to keep warm and stay alive. Some weren't even capable of that, lost either to shock or grief. Those ones might not make it through the night, but Rendall wasn't overly concerned; there were too many of them, anyway.

One prisoner in particular stood out in stark contrast to the others. It was the woman from before, the 'Dea' as she'd called herself. Unlike the others, she did not huddle. She sat cross-legged on the ground, her ice blue eyes open and clear, and her long white hair cascading wildly around her. *She's staring right at me,* Rendall realized with a start. *Why do I feel as if she's been staring at me this whole time?*

He unconsciously closed the distance between them until he was standing no more than a few feet from her. If she had a weapon hidden and managed to move quickly enough, she could maybe get between the plates of his armour, but he was confident, firstly, that his men had done a thorough job in both searching and securing her, and secondly, in his own ability to disarm her if she so much as tried to raise a hand against him.

"Deneige, was it?" His voice rumbled past his helmet.

"Praefecti, was it?" she echoed.

"I believe I did you the courtesy of using your name, but if you'd rather titles…I expect to see you in my tent later this evening, slave. It's the large one at the center of camp."

"Were you talking to me? My title is Dea."

Rendall smirked inside the relative privacy of his helmet. *She's got spirit, this one, I'll give her that.*

He knelt before her and swiftly cut her loose from the others. She was still bound, her wrists tied together behind her back, but she was no longer attached to the line of other slaves. He let her go.

"Is this supposed to make me trust you?"

"Not at all. It's merely that any one of your people attempting to flee this place now will be killed on sight, so I have no need to worry that you'll get away. As I said, I expect you in my tent before morning. I'll give you some time to *warm* to the idea." He gave a pointed look to the people shivering all around them.

"I would never leave my people to suffer while I sought warmth without them. I am not cruel or selfish like you."

He smiled, though she couldn't see it. "I'm counting on it," he told her, then walked away, continuing his rounds.

Warm up to the idea, huh? Rendall's words gave Deneige an idea. She waited until the legionnaire was out of sight and then shuffled toward the nearest of her people. "Siobhan," Deneige whispered the woman's name, "listen to me. I'm going to take the cold away from you."

Dark-eyed Siobhan met her gaze, a glimmer of hope showing, which was immediately replaced by fear. "Don't waste your gifts on me, girl...I mean, Dea...and don't let them see what you can do. You think they want you as a slave now..." she trailed off ominously.

"Are you a prophet now, Siobhan?" Deneige admonished and Siobhan lowered her eyes. "Alright now, just keep still."

She concentrated, taking the woman's hands between her own. She'd never done this sort of thing before, but then again, her need had never been greater and the spirits always responded when the need was greatest. "Come on..." Deneige muttered beneath her breath.

Unlike Ignes, Deneige had never had the gift of fire, or of light. She knew she would not be able to summon the warmth Siobhan and the others would need to survive this night. She could, however, she thought, make the cold...*less.* She concentrated on taking the cold into herself, on neutralizing its effects.

"I can't feel my fingers." Siobhan shivered beneath her grasp and Deneige opened her eyes to see that the woman's fingers had turned an alarming shade of blue.

Oh no. She panicked, letting go of Siobhan. Deneige got swiftly to her feet. "I'm so sorry. I'll be right back. Hold tight."

She scanned the area immediately around them and her gaze lit on a pile of nearby furs. Unfortunately, a legionnaire stood between her and her goal. She looked the other direction, but didn't see much other than scattered belongings, namely pots and pans. She found herself regretting not having held tight to her pack full of clothing and medical supplies during her initial imprisonment, but she saw no trace of her former shelter anymore. For all she knew, they had burnt it to the ground like so many other tents. Gritting her teeth, Deneige prepared herself for whatever might come; she had to try.

She squared her shoulders and walked forward. The soldier turned, noticing her at once, and he raised his weapon. She stopped, recalling the Praefecti's threat, and gestured to make herself understood. "I'm taking the furs. We need them. You wouldn't want to lose your slaves before you even got them home, would you?"

Deneige seethed. *I hate these people. The only value we have to them is as property. But if I want them to listen, I have to speak words they understand.*

There was a tense moment before the soldier nodded, then Deneige was able to let out a breath of relief and bend to her task. A good half the furs were wet with mud and snow, but a few were still usable. She took these, though it was difficult with her hands tied behind her back. The legionnaire ignored her instead of offering to help.

She made it back to Siobhan, and covered the woman's hands and lap with the largest and driest of the furs, then she went down the line until she found the next person who looked like they needed her help to survive.

It's just like triaging patients. As much as I'd like to give furs to everyone, there just simply aren't enough to go around. I have to concentrate on treating those who need it most.

All too soon she was out of furs and there were far too many more 'patients' suffering. She scanned the area around her for more clothing, blankets, furs, or anything that might help her people survive, but the only things near the Lumen were the charred remains of their former lives. Deneige felt her heart squeeze just taking in the sight of all that they had lost, but at the same time, another idea sparked. "The spirits provide when the need is greatest," she whispered, eyeing a piece of canvas that was still on fire.

She headed toward the flames determinedly. This time the legionnaires didn't stop her, they merely watched. Finding an unlit corner, she turned around and then squatted to feel around for her prize. Once the canvas was in her hands, she stood.

She heard one of the legionnaires laugh, but she did her best to ignore him as she dragged the burning canvas back toward the line of 'slaves'. It took a great deal of effort, but eventually she brought the flaming cloth close enough that her people could huddle near it for warmth. Feeling proud of her accomplishments, Deneige stood and straightened her spine, looking out over what was left of the Lumen.

Never again, she vowed, *will I allow this to happen to anyone else, if it is within my power.*

To her left, a legionnaire cleared his throat, intruding on her thoughts. She turned to look at him.

"Sir Rendall desires your presence in his tents…my lady…" the soldier stammered. By the sound of the voice beneath his helm, he was likely very young.

"Desires?" Deneige found herself smirking. *Has he learned that he can't compel me, so he's decided the only way to get what he wants is to force himself upon me? Romans are such savages.*

Beneath her bravado, however, was fear. She shivered, and not because of the cold, which she was aware of, but could not hurt her. *Thank the spirits for that.* There was nowhere to run, and even if she wanted to fight, she was not stronger than even this Roman child who stood before her. She had little choice but to obey Rendall's orders, even if he did intend to gviolate her. Against every instinct she nodded, and the legionnaire gestured for her to precede him deeper into the hastily erected Roman encampment.

Rendall paced the length of his sparsely furnished military tent. It was brisk without his armour, but the brazier was lit and starting to do its job of heating the space. *That's one downside to having the largest tent on the field, it takes longer to warm up.*

He passed the brazier once more, trying to convince himself that he was pacing because he was cold, not because he was anxious. But he was anxious. *Why did I summon that woman to my tent? Not that I would turn down a warm body right now, but I can't imagine she'd be willing...*

He got no further before the tent flap opened, admitting the very person he'd been thinking about. He made himself stop pacing and face her. It was all he could do not to stare at her intense, ice blue eyes, which seemed wise despite her youth.

He cleared his throat. "That will be all, Lucius."

Despite himself, Rendall couldn't take his eyes off her. The former Dea was at once both elegant and wild; her clothing was no more than rough-cut animal furs, but clearly stitched together by someone with skill. Her hair fell loose around her in tangled waves, pristinely white and not the kind of white one associated with age, either. She was technically a prisoner and a slave, and yet she stood with her back straight and her chin lifted proudly. It was no wonder Rendall stared, and yet he wished he didn't feel as if he was giving her so much power by doing so.

"So how am I supposed to act?" she demanded, the fire of her spirit no more dampened than it had been upon their initial meeting. She was scared, however much she seemed to want to hide it behind bravado. "The scared girl willing to do anything to save her people, the spitting viper who needs to be subdued, or should I just play the willing whore and get this over with?"

"Well I have to admit I would prefer you willing, though I'd rather it was genuine," he said at last, clearing his throat to cover how startled he was by her words.

"Such a gentleman," she commented snidely, looking him up and down appraisingly and then lifting her chin once more, as if to say she wasn't impressed. "How *do* you defend yourself against all the eligible women back in Rome?"

He allowed himself a slight smile. "I spend little time in the capital, actually," he admitted, warming his hands at the brazier in earnest now. "My daily life is more often spent in the company of men, and before you turn that into some kind of joke, don't bother. Having lived around soldiers for most of my adult life, I've heard them all."

"Then you prefer to rape women after you're done pillaging."

He opened his arms wide to gesture around himself. "I don't see the results of pillage here, do you?"

Her icy eyes flashed. "Don't play games with me, you know exactly what I mean."

He took a single step around the brazier, closer to her. "I don't play games, Deneige, and I don't steal from the disenfranchised."

"You stole our livelihood! You stole our people's souls! Killing and destroying everything they ever knew *is* stealing from them. You're worse than a common thief, you're a monster."

"Stealing souls," he mused, "that's a new one. Think of me what you will, Apollo knows I've probably earned it, but regardless of your opinion you've been brought here to serve me and that's what you will do until I decide I've had enough of you, do you understand?"

She started forward and Rendall took a step back before he caught himself. Two steps later she was within kissing distance, but instead of something so desirable, she spat in his face. Instinctively, he caught her by the wrist before she could whirl away in triumph. With his other hand, he wiped the spittle from his cheek, then he spun her about and pulled her in close.

"You're mine now, Deneige, whether you like it or not," he growled, baring teeth.

"Don't you dare say my name! To you, I'm the Dea of the Lumen and you will address me with respect!"

Where his hand gripped her flesh, he suddenly felt a piercing chill, as if he was holding on to frozen metal. With a start he let her go, pushing her away from him and sending her stumbling. With her off balance, his height advantage made him feel as if he were towering over her, abruptly reminding him just how fragile she really was. Despite her harsh words and unyielding demeanor, she was still a woman, not a trained Legionnaire. He had the strength and the power here, and it was time she acted more aware of that fact.

"You will sleep in this corner," he commanded. "I will post guards to make sure you don't try anything during the night. If you do, you'll spend the next night tied to the tent posts, and the night after that tied out with the horses."

"Anywhere is better than warming your bed," she spat, brushing at her fur clothing unnecessarily.

He nodded. "Sleeping beside a venomous snake isn't my idea of a good time, either."

She narrowed her eyes. "That's only because you fear the snake instead of embracing its power."

"Think what you wish."

He turned his back to her without a care, striding back across the tent to where his cot lay waiting for him. Outwardly, he was calm, nonchalant, even, but inside, Rendall was in turmoil. *Who does this woman think she is?!*

It took Deneige a long time to fall asleep, but when she did she slept surprisingly soundly. The ground beneath Rendall's tent was even, the carpet thick enough to ward away the cold, and her clothing sufficient enough to keep her comfortable. Considering the way he'd acted toward her, she also felt confident enough that Rendall wasn't going to take her into his bed, not without her consent, anyway. *And it's not like I would give him that!*

She awoke early, feeling well rested despite the continued horror of her circumstance, and she immediately turned to meditation to help calm herself in the way her mentor had shown her. Thoughts of Ignes brought her uncomfortably close to a memory she didn't want to relive, but she was disciplined enough to focus on her task and push aside the need to grieve, for now. *I will see myself and my people through this. Ignes said I would be the one to save us…and Ignes' visions always come true.*

"What are you doing?" Rendall's deep, commanding voice cut through her meditation like the sword that had so easily cut through the wall of her tent the night before.

She flinched, her eyes snapping open. "What does it look like I'm doing?"

"Talking to yourself while seated in an extremely uncomfortable position."

"How astute of you," she muttered, trying to reapply herself to the task, but finding herself unable to concentrate with him so close. His presence was much like a powerful wind rattling everything nearby.

"Yes, well, you have your first task," he stated. "I require breakfast."

"Excuse me?" She found herself studying his impassive features a moment, trying to ignore the intriguing turquoise of his eyes and the subtle way a smile played about his mouth. She tried not to think about how his two-day-old growth of stubble might feel beneath her fingers or, spirits-forgive, against the softer parts of her flesh. She set her jaw and deliberately turned away from him, but it did nothing to change the fact that she could feel his eyes on her.

"Let me rephrase. Slave, I command you to fetch my breakfast and bring it here, posthaste."

Deneige's eyes went wide, her attention snapping back in his direction. His smile was much wider now. *I hate this man. Fetch him his breakfast? I'll fetch him breakfast. You know what's really refreshing in the morning? Moss. Pinecones really clear out the system, too. I bet I can find some nightshade if I look hard enough.*

Deneige stood and strode from the tent mostly just to get away from his mocking grin when the scent of the cookfires hit her nostrils and she realized just how hungry she was. Last night had been a terror and a whirlwind, and even before that she'd been too busy tending to Javvar in his illness and learning to use her spirit-given skills to worry about something as commonplace as dinner. Her stomach rumbled.

Despite her intentions, her feet led her over to the nearest cookfire. *Nothing says I can't get myself some food before I find Rendall something poisonous in the forest.* She sniffed at the cookpot. The legionnaire stirring the pot stopped to stare at her, mouth open. He was young, she realized, maybe only fourteen or fifteen.

"Uhh," he stammered and Deneige recognized him as the young soldier who'd escorted her to Rendall's tent the night before.

"Sir Rendall requires his breakfast, *posthaste*," she informed him, amused by the way his mud-coloured hair stuck out in every direction like some animal had licked it dry.

"Of course!" The legionnaire almost saluted her before he thought better of it and applied himself to the task of filling a bowl with the contents of the stewpot. "Here you are." He handed her a steaming helping and then bent to fill a second bowl before handing that to her as well.

Deneige took the second bowl without meaning to, too startled by the gesture to refuse him. She looked down at the two equally filled steaming bowls in her hands in a mild state of shock. *I honestly didn't think they were going to feed me, let alone feed me the same thing they'd feed their commander. I was going to steal Rendall's breakfast...but now I don't have to.*

"Uh, thank you," Deneige stammered just as awkwardly as the legionnaire.

A wide grin split the boy's face. "You're most welcome, my lady. My name's Lucius, if you ever need something."

Bewildered, Deneige juggled the two bowls as she headed back to Rendall's tent. Once there, she placed one of the bowls on the ground and sat down next to it to consume the contents of her own. She didn't have any utensils and the meaty stew was piping hot, but she did her best to shovel it out of the bowl and into her mouth. Unfortunately, this took long enough that Rendall came out of his tent when she was only about half finished. He raised a questioning brow in her direction and she quickly swallowed. "That one's mine too," she stated, following his gaze.

"Answer me truly," he said. "Are you really that hungry?"

His sincerity caught her off guard. "No," she answered.

He nodded and sat down beside her, scooping up the untouched bowl. "I trust you haven't placed any of your venom in here?"

"I was going to do that when I finished," she admitted. "Next time, I guess."

He let out a small huff of breath and shook his head, bemused, before starting in on his breakfast. They ate in silence for a time and when Deneige finished first, she found herself studying him once more. He was quieter than she'd expected him to be, after all his blustering about power the night before. The man, now out of his armour, was a different beast altogether. Not tamer, exactly, but calmer, more relaxed. Perhaps it was just because he was surrounded by his own people. He knew he had nothing to fear from her or anyone else.

"How are you so sure of yourself? It goes beyond normal confidence."

"I could ask you the same thing," he countered. His greenish-blue eyes glittered in the early morning light as he stared into her own icy blue irises. "I suppose it's because of a prophecy I was told when I was younger. A woman with eyes like yours promised me greatness. She told me the Sun is my domain, and here I am, a Praefecti of the Legion of the sun god, Apollo."

"So there are the spirit-touched among your people? Deas, like me?" Deneige questioned, taken aback. As far as she knew, her people were the only ones who revered the spirits and made use of their gifts. With the rest of her people scattered or dead, she had started to believe she might be the last one.

"Deas? No, she was a Vestal Virgin, dedicated to Vesta, the Goddess of the Hearth. She's a feminine god, mostly, but we all pay her mind during the festival of Vestalia and on most feast days."

"I don't know who that is, but I do know that only those touched by the spirits can read the future and give prophecy."

"Spirits?" he questioned, seeming genuinely interested instead of patronizing.

"There are spirits all around us, in everything," Deneige explained, even while wondering why she was being so open with this Roman stranger. "A Dea can speak to them and call on them when in need."

He nodded thoughtfully. "That's similar to what we believe, actually, except we call them gods. There's a god of the earth, for example," he said, picking up some dirt and letting it fall between his fingers, "and a god of the plains," and he gestured around them. "Some gods we simply acknowledge. The more important ones, we worship. Like Apollo."

"So we are similar, but not similar enough to let us be who we are. Am I to be shipped off as one of your 'Vestals'?"

He laughed, an unexpectedly deep, rich sound. "No. One, you're mine, remember? And two, Vestal Virgins are given into service at a young age. It's a very prestigious position that requires quite a bit of training. I hate to be the one to tell you this, but you're too old for the job."

"It's almost like how you require a lot of training to be a Dea, and I started that as soon as I was able to speak. It is also a prestigious position."

He looked her up and down appraisingly, as if seeing her with new eyes. "I suppose you're right."

They didn't speak again while Rendall finished off his breakfast and he left her to her own devices as he saw to his troops. She tried to snoop, but there really was nothing worth looking at or taking within Rendall's tent except for his armour, which she had no use for, and his sword, which if she was being honest she could barely lift, let alone wield. She thought about making a run for it or checking on her people, but Lucius' presence just outside the tent kept her where she was. She wasn't afraid of the boy-soldier, not really, but something in her didn't want to disappoint him, which was silly, but she couldn't shake the feeling. So she stayed and took the time to work the tangles out of her hair and wish for the means to wash herself. Not for Rendall's sake, of course, but for her own.

Two days later, she was granted her wish, but in the most unexpected way possible. On the afternoon of the second day, the legion crested a rise and were treated to the sight of what Rendall called the Castra. If she had thought the camp they made each night was large, she was mistaken. The Castra was a semi-permanent encampment that put her own people's winter village to shame. It filled the valley below, spreading as far as the eye could see in either direction, and around it all stood a wall just high enough that a man would have trouble climbing it, with towers at each of the corners and over each of the entrances.

Within the wall were buildings, not tents. Deneige didn't understand it; her people had been by this way less than a year ago, and there was no hint of development then, nor even any Roman presence. *How did they manage to build all this in such a short time?*

And it wasn't just the size of it or the permanent nature, but the sheer orderliness of it all. The buildings were in distinct rows, with meticulously straight dirt roads between them, and not a person, thing, or construction was out of place. Looking at it from a distance, she also noted that each collection of buildings had a courtyard or a space nearby where men trained or horses grazed. Her old tent, no, her whole village, could have comfortably fit inside one of the compounds.

Without hesitating, their line of legionnaires and their 'slaves', though Deneige hated to use the word, headed down into the encampment, and as soon as they crossed the threshold of the orderly line of tan-coloured tents, they were swallowed by the gaping maw of Roman society. Deneige fought back the sudden panic at the thought that she might never find her people again, let alone manage to free them like she so desperately wanted.

Rendall, Lucius, and the few others who formed the Praefecti's personal entourage, including herself, she realized, headed toward the centre of the Castra as her people were led away elsewhere. She locked eyes with Siobhan as the woman was hauled away and kept watching after her long after she was out of sight.

"We're here," Rendall announced, snapping her out of her dark thoughts by swinging down from his horse and crossing in front of her field of vision. She followed him with her gaze, unsure of what else to do, and he stopped at a door, opening it for her before stepping back. "I took the liberty of having a bath prepared for you. I thought you would appreciate the chance to get clean."

Deneige looked through the opening and her jaw dropped. Unlike the sparse tent where she'd spent the past few nights sleeping on the floor, this structure was at least three times its size, had other walled off rooms besides, and was almost luxuriously furnished with tables, chairs, worn pillows and rugs, and yes, a copper bathtub set in the center of it all, filled with water, steaming in the chill air.

She cautiously entered the building and drifted toward the bathtub, reaching for the cinch of her belt. Halfway there, she stopped and turned back, but Rendall was nowhere to be seen. He'd quietly shut the door and left her finally, blessedly, alone. She slid out of her layers of furs and undergarments and slid gratefully into the warm embrace of the tub.

With two tray-laden servants trailing behind him, Rendall returned to his rooms not knowing exactly what he would find there. His new slave was turning out to be a handful and he was rapidly learning he might not have what it took to tame her. *Deneige could very well be waiting for me with a weapon in her hand,* he mused with a smirk on his face. *This should be interesting.*

He loosened the dagger on his belt; not that he thought we would need to use it, but it never hurt to be prepared. *Here goes nothing.* He opened the door and stepped cautiously into his own domain, waiting a moment for his eyes to fully adjust to the change in lighting before he made a sound or moved any further. He scanned the room for Deneige but surprisingly she was exactly where he'd left her, in the tub. He crossed to the centre of the room in two strides to find that she hadn't drowned herself in an attempt to escape him, but was simply asleep. And also completely nude.

He gestured for the servants to leave the trays and depart, then stood silently contemplating his new houseguest. She was beautiful, though he had detected that the moment they met and didn't need to see her naked for confirmation. Her hair was no longer a matted nest of tangles, but instead lay floating lightly in the water, delicately outlining some of her finer features. He had to stop himself from tracing some of those delicate strands with his fingers or moving them out of the way. Though Deneige was technically his property now, he didn't feel he had the right to put his hands on her in that way. To violate her trust now while she was vulnerable seemed like the worst kind of barbarism and something he didn't think she'd ever forgive him for.

She stirred and he immediately averted his gaze, though the sight of her long, smooth legs and the patch of white hair between them would stay in his memory forever. He cleared his throat. "I thought you would be finished bathing by now. I brought you supper."

"Thank you," she murmured, and he heard the sloshing of water as she got to her feet.

His eyes lit on the towel laid out for her and he reached for it, thrusting it out behind him so she wouldn't have to cross in front of his vision in order to cover herself. He felt the slight weight of the towel lifted from his hands. "You're welcome," he stated, unsure of how else to fill the silence.

"I wouldn't have guessed you to be so modest."

Rendall felt his face heat but he didn't turn around. *Let her stick a knife into me now and I would have earned it for being foolish.*

"I was respecting your privacy." Outwardly, his words were controlled, even if inwardly he was cursing himself. "Would you rather I didn't?"

"You command me as your personal slave, then try to show respect afterward. Seems strange to me."

"Slave or not, I haven't tried to violate you and you have my word that I won't do so." He turned around to face her then, having managed to compose himself. She was just as alluring, if not more so, in only a towel. "However, you belong to me and I *will* continue to command you. It would be better for you in the long run to get used to the idea."

"I belong to no one but myself, and maybe the spirits, should they see fit to work through me," she stated through clenched teeth.

"You and your people belong to Rome now, and *you*, specifically, belong to *me*. I can protect you, keep you from being sold to someone who wouldn't hesitate to…disrespect you. And if you were as difficult with them as you have been with me, you would end up in the labour camps at best, and at worst flogged daily until your beauty and your will were stripped from you." He couldn't help the anger that slipped into his voice, but he didn't know if it was at her, or on her behalf.

"The only reason you must keep me safe from these men is because you put me in this situation in the first place! You can't destroy my life and then tell me you are saving me."

"What would you have me do, Deneige?" he demanded, raising his voice. "Your people are part of Rome now, your way of life, ended. Yes, I am responsible for some of that, but even if I hadn't been the sword to your people's throats, Rome would have sent another."

"We have always been in these lands. We just did things differently than you, it doesn't make us wrong!" She gestured as she spoke, and the towel covering her threatened to come loose, but in her passion she hardly noticed.

Pretending not to be riveted by this, Rendall shrugged and fought to avert his gaze. "Right and wrong don't come into this. Rome has been guided by the gods to expand, and expand is what we will do. Your people were simply in the way."

"You're a sheep!" She threw her hands up and stepped up until her body was nearly pressed up against his. "Did you ever think that maybe greatness comes from standing on your own two feet and doing something for yourself? Men who create change are remembered, those who follow orders simply live and die for those greater than them."

She was inches from him now and her scent was intoxicating. Her dampness only made her that much more alluring. He wanted to take hold of the loose corner of her towel, and tug on it until it came free and dropped to the floor. Despite his promise to her earlier, he lifted his hand and when her eyes went wide noticing the motion, he simply tucked the loose corner of fabric back into place.

"Well said," he murmured. "I didn't know your people had a propensity for politics."

"There's a lot about my people you don't know."

"Perhaps you are right."

"You don't know a lot about me, either," she continued. "You should know that I don't back down, not ever."

He allowed himself a grin. "I've been beginning to suspect as much. It seems you leave me little choice but to come to an arrangement with you. It's either that, or I have to give you up, as fascinating as you are."

She quirked a brow, her anger dissipating at the sound of an opportunity. "What sort of arrangement?"

"Your oath that you will not attempt to harm me or escape, and mine in exchange that you will have my protection and all I can provide for you. It's a generous offer, I guarantee it. Without my protection, your life in this camp would be quite miserable."

"That sounds kind of like a marriage."

He laughed. "I should hope I would get more out of a wife than simply her agreement not to try and kill me in my sleep!"

"You don't know very many women, do you?"

He chose to ignore that particular barb, and lifted the lid on one of the trays of food, allowing the scent of perfectly roasted pheasant to fill the air. "You will have to at least act the part of subservience to me in public, even if I allow you to speak your mind freely when we're alone."

"Now it's a secret marriage?"

He casually tore the leg off one of the small birds and brought the succulent meat to his lips. "Would you rather I simply brought someone in to train you to be more…obedient?"

"One," she counted on her fingers, "we both know that wouldn't go well for the person you brought in, and two, I told you I wouldn't escape to save my people. To be fair, I was going to bring you pinecones and nightshade for your breakfast that first morning, but since then I haven't tried to kill you. You'd be dead if I wanted you to be, I promise you that."

Even from where he stood he could hear her stomach growl and he noted the way she wrapped her arms around her midsection, as if to hold herself back from the temptation he was offering.

"I don't doubt it," he commented, pinching some cooked grain between two pieces of bread, "but why exactly have you left me alive?"

"Because you feel like a storm," she mumbled, finding the floor suddenly very interesting.

"What are you talking about?"

Her eyes flashed. "I know when storms are coming, bad ones, ones that are needed to create change, ones that take your breath away. You feel like a coming storm, or one that I'm standing in the middle of. Maybe I just want to see what you are capable of."

She crossed the room to him then, reaching for the food. He grabbed her by the wrist before she could touch so much as a single grain of rice. "So," he asked, staring her in the eyes, "do we have an arrangement?"

"What do you think?"

"Not good enough. I require your oath."

"What exactly do you want me to say?" Her eyes refused to meet his, darting this way and that.

"I want it in your own words. Swear by your spirits if you have to but make me believe it, or my provisions and my protection are lost to you."

She met gaze at last, her ice blue pupils searingly intense. "I would love to but I don't even know your full name. How can I swear an oath to you?"

"My name is Alton Marcellus Rendall," he stated without hesitation, meeting her stare for stare and not daring to breathe in her scent again, now that she was within his grasp.

She adopted a very serious expression and lacked her usual mockery when she spoke. "I, Deneige Audra, Dea of my people, swear to you, Alton Marcellus Rendall, Praefecti of Apollo's Legion, that I will cause you no harm nor take my leave of you. This I swear to you by your Gods and my spirits, or may the spirits forsake me and revoke their gifts."

He nodded solemnly, taking her measure and deciding she meant what she said. "And I, Alton Marcellus Rendall, swear by Apollo, the gods of Rome, and the spirits of your people, to protect you and see to your wellbeing for as long as you are by my side, or may Apollo revoke the favour he has bestowed upon me."

"So, now that we are basically handfasted," she noted, her cavalier demeanor returning, "can I have something to eat?"

True to his word, Rendall released her wrist, stepped back, and allowed her access to the tray. "Help yourself. What's mine is yours, after all."

Over the next few weeks as winter fully set in, Deneige reluctantly grew accustomed to life in the Castra and her place within it. She hated to admit it, but as the Praefecti's personal slave she was allowed more freedom than she would have thought possible, and far more than any other Lumen was granted.

She was allowed to wander within the walls of the Castra, for example. If Rendall gave her some business to be about, she could pretty much go where she pleased. She avoided the General's compound, however, and she didn't like spending too much time near the barracks of the common legionnaires as their eyes tended to linger in a way that made her skin crawl. This left her with visiting the stables, the great hall where food was served, and the slave pens.

The pens were where they kept the slaves who had no masters yet, or those who were too sick or injured to work. Deneige tried to visit them as often as she could, bringing what gifts she could smuggle under her clothing, but as she had no reasonable excuse to give when caught by the legionnaires, she couldn't go as often or stay as long as she would have liked.

As for Rendall, he kept true to his word. She was not required to sleep in his bed and she had her own cot in a space off the main room of his apartments in the Praetorium. He did send her on constant errands, and had her fetching his meals and cleaning up after him, but if she was being honest she didn't mind, as the tasks filled her days and gave her the excuses she needed to go where she wished. As an added bonus, the legionnaires got used to her presence so she wasn't questioned as much while she was out and about.

After breakfast one morning, Rendall had sent her with a cart full of spirits-knew-what to deliver to the stables. Deneige dutifully pulled the cart along behind her for quite a distance, but the roads in the Castra were abuzz with activity and the blustering wind kept blowing her hair into her face, making her have trouble seeing clearly. When she almost bumped into another legionnaire for the fifth time, Deneige stopped and dropped the handles of the cart in a huff.

It was then, only halfway to the stables that she belatedly became aware of the sensation. The humming in her blood was back, not that it had ever fully left, living with Rendall. *A storm's coming,* she realized, *and it's going to be a bad one.*

Feeling the storm on her skin and tasting it in the air now, Deneige silently cursed herself for not becoming aware of it earlier. It was obvious the bad weather had been building for some time. The sky wasn't dark yet but it would be soon, and if the wind was any indication this storm would blow in hard and fast.

She whirled around, trying to decide her best course of action and how soon she would need to take cover, when she realized that some of the contents of her cart had spilled to the ground in her near collision with the legionnaire. She hurried to retrieve what she'd dropped; Rendall likely wouldn't punish her, but any other slave would have been whipped for less.

Her fingers wrapped around soft wool and she realized she was holding a blanket. Looking back at the cart, it was clear to her now that the whole thing was filled to the brim with blankets, furs, and other such provisions. She went to replace the fallen blanket when the thought occurred to her. *My people are going to need these more than the horses do when that storm sets in. I've seen the ratty things they call blankets in there, more holes than cloth. If I can get this cart to them before the storm sets in...*

Deneige didn't let herself dwell on her plan, so she didn't give herself time to see its flaws. She knew beyond a doubt that a severe winter storm was coming and that her people wouldn't live through it without help, and so she acted, racing now through the streets of the Castra, swerving around any stray legionnaires in her path.

She knew the fastest way to the slave pens and she made it there in no time at all. Once there, she pulled her cart around the back side of the fenced compound, which she knew from experience was less well guarded. She knocked on the wooden post, rapping out the signal she and Siobhan had devised, and then reached for the first blanket.

Siobhan gasped as her fingers wrapped around the thick wool. "Dea, you can't! They'll notice this is missing, surely they will."

"I don't care. A bad storm is coming. You'll need whatever I can give you."

Siobhan fell silent and Deneige kept feeding the blanket through the fence. Once the first one was past, she fed another, and another. Several blankets and some furs later, she'd uncovered what else was in the little cart. Deneige gasped when she realized what she was looking at. *That's a tent, and Rendall's chest, the one where he keeps his armour when he's not wearing it.*

Her eyes snapped upwards to look in the direction of the storm, but she couldn't see any hint of the sky darkening yet; she still had time. A smaller, but no less distinct, hum drew her gaze in the opposite direction toward her own personal storm. *Rendall. I can still feel him, even in all this. He's going to be so angry when he finds out what I've done.*

"Hey! You there!" A deep, male voice snapped her out of her thoughts. "I've told you not to linger around these pens!"

The legionnaire started forward, far more intent on catching her than worrying about what the slaves may or may not have managed to obtain. Deneige reached for the handles of the cart and she started running, wheels clattering along behind her. A few steps into her mad dash she realized the cart was only slowing her down, so she let it slide from her grasp and kept going, not sparing a glance behind her.

She ran all the way back to the Praetorium's courtyard, where she found Rendall fully dressed and standing beside Lucius and three horses. He looked annoyed.

"Find her, Lucius, I don't care what it takes," he was saying in a voice loud enough to be heard halfway across the courtyard. "We're leaving within the hour. I won't be delayed any further."

"Yes, sir-" Lucius began, then stopped, his eyes landing on Deneige where she stood trying to catch her breath.

Rendall seemed to follow Lucius' gaze. "Deneige, where have you been? The men left nearly two hours ago."

It struck Deneige then what all the bustle and the preparations had been for and why the way back to the Praetorium had been clear, as was the courtyard now. The Legion had left; they were on the march again.

She shook her head as if she couldn't believe what she was hearing. "We can't go. There is a storm coming. Call them back or they will be in great danger."

"Call them back?" Rendall furrowed his brow "We can't call them back. They're expecting us to meet them. It's not just my men, but the whole legion."

"Tell them the truth," she urged. "A storm is coming and it's going to be a bad one."

"Pardon, my lady," Lucius chimed in, "but I don't think the General's going to care about some storm, no matter how bad it is, and that's if he takes your word for it, which I don't expect he will."

"He will when he's caught in it," Deneige muttered.

Rendall shook his head. "We don't have a choice. Even if I were to send Lucius to warn them, my men might listen, but the General? The Legion as a whole? Never."

"Well, we can't go anyway," Deneige stated, struggling to think of anything that might stop him from wandering out into the coming storm, dragging her and Lucius along with him. She knew a bad storm when she felt one and this one was worse than most. Her own people would have sought shelter in a cave or some ruins, or worst case hunkered down together as best they could. She thought of the Lumen now, and how they were trapped in an open air pen with only a few warm blankets between them and perhaps one wall to huddle behind. "I gave away all of our supplies."

Rendall's eyes went wide. "You did what?"

"My people will die without them. I had to do something."

"If the storm is as you say, the slaves will be brought inside," Rendall started to say, but then the truth began to dawn on him, "or they would be if the majority of the Castra wasn't already empty." He growled. "Fine, we stay, but if the General is to have my head over this, I will see that you are brought to the executioner alongside me. Lucius, ride as hard as you can and see if you can get the men to turn around. Once you reach them, have one of our messengers sent to the General with the same warning. If he doesn't heed it, at least it will be his decision."

Lucius saluted Rendall, then mounted his horse and expertly spun it about.

"I dropped your armour," Deneige admitted.

Rendall shot daggers from his eyes at her. "We'll talk about that later." He grabbed her by the arm and started walking, then seemed to think better of it. "Can you ride?" She nodded and he gestured to the second horse. The stark white mare with small black flecks along its flanks was about as opposite as one could get to Rendall's own black stallion, but it was still a beautiful creature. "Mount, then, and follow me."

Having grown used to his commands by now, and with her mind still hovering anxiously on the storm she knew would strike any moment, Deneige did as she was told. The mare skittered a little under her weight, but quickly settled; the Romans knew how to train their beasts.

And then they were off, cantering quickly through the now empty streets of the Castra.

"Where are we going?" Deneige shouted to Rendall over the rising wind, but he didn't answer her.

Soon enough, Deneige realized their destination as Rendall seemed to be retracing her steps from before. They stopped and dismounted in front of the slave pen, tying their horses to the posts inside the small stable where they would be safe from the coming weather. The guard from before was still on duty, along with a second one, dressed similarly in light armour. He recognized her immediately. "Hey, you-" he began, but Rendall cut him off.

"Open the slave pen and help me lead these people to the great hall."

The man's eyes narrowed suspiciously as he looked from Deneige to Rendall and back again. "I caught her sneaking blankets to the slaves not too long ago," the guard reported.

"I don't care what you saw," Rendall growled dangerously. "I gave you an order and last I checked I outrank you by a considerable margin."

"Uh, yes sir, sorry sir!" The guards did as they were told and started opening the gates of the slave pen. "Uh, did you want them shackled together, sir?"

"Never mind that," Rendall said, hand-waving them away as the wind picked further and flurries began to fill the air. Behind him, Deneige danced nervously from foot to foot, much like her mare; it was like the creature also knew what kind of danger they were facing. "We don't have the time. Round them up and follow me. Those that run will die on their own, so don't worry about chasing them down."

To the immense surprise of both Rendall and the guards, her people fell into line and came meekly enough once they set eyes on Deneige. Together, Deneige and Rendall were able to lead them away from the cruel open pen and deeper into the Castra, though it soon became clear that if it was the great hall they sought, they wouldn't make it in time.

The snow grew as thick as a whiteout within minutes and with the swirling wind it quickly became hard to tell up from down, let alone distinguish the person nearest to you. Deneige lost even the sound of Rendall's bellowing voice on the wind. Soon she was all alone in the whiteout and she'd completely lost track of where she was headed or which way lay shelter, or even her fellow Lumen.

Deneige fought hard to control her panic. She'd been feeling this storm building for the past few hours and the feeling had gotten under her skin, making her fearful when normally she would feel empowered and in control. Her thoughts immediately turned to Ignes, whom she would have sought for comfort at a time like this, only to remember like the cold shock of the wind whipping at her face that Ignes was no longer among the living.

If Ignes isn't here to lead us, then it falls to me, Deneige realized. *I'm the Dea of my people now. I must see them to safety.*

She reached out to the spirits of the storm. At first they were only noise, like the hum of the storm had been in her blood, but after a moment of listening, their voices became clearer. The cold she could do nothing about, but the wind? She called out to the wind with its own song and asked it gently if it would calm for her. She sang silently and soothingly to the wind-spirits and soon enough the air around her began to clear, not entirely, but enough so that she could see at least as far as the person nearest to her. Her hand clamped down on Rendall's forearm and he startled, his green-blue eyes lighting on hers.

"How did you find me?" he mouthed, but the song of the wind was still too loud and it took his words away before they could reach her ears.

She continued soothing the wind spirits and soon Siobhan became visible, and after her another Lumen and one of the guards. Using her power all the while, she gathered her people to her and led them toward the nearest shelter. With the wind not fighting them every step of the way, it didn't take long before they were safely within one of the barracks. Deneige stopped singing to the wind as the door shut solidly, locking them within and the storm outside, except for the ever-present storm that was Rendall, of course.

Rendall whirled on Deneige, his jaw dropping open. She seemed oblivious to his stares as she straightened herself and tried to tame her windswept hair. He struggled to control himself, but the truth staring him in the face was too obvious, too real. *She commanded the winds out there. She lessened them somehow. Not to mention that she knew the storm was coming long before anyone else and not just because she could read the signs...it was like she had some kind of* foretelling.

Those blue eyes... He found himself staring at them once more and recalling those of the Vestal Virgin who'd proclaimed his fate in his youth. *They're the same. She must be touched by the gods. Is that why I'm so drawn to her? Why I can't let her go?*

Deneige, seeming to take notice of his fascination at last, locked eyes with him and raised a brow in question. He broke away, turning back to look at the people he'd risked his neck for. They were a sorry-looking bunch, dirty and foul-smelling from their time wallowing in the slave pen. Some were able-bodied enough, but the rest were women and children, and a few were elderly. He frowned. *These are the people Deneige was so concerned for?* Then he had to mentally remind himself. *Of course, these are* her *people, her extended family as my fellow legionnaires are mine, no matter what state they may be reduced to now.*

"Okay everyone, you have the run of this building," he spoke loud enough for the bunch of people crowded in the common area of the barracks to hear him. "There are sixteen rooms besides this one, so divide them as you see fit and use what supplies you find. I suggest you make the most of this opportunity to rest and recover as trying to escape in this weather would be suicide. Do I make myself clear?"

"Where will you be setting up, then, so I can help you get ready for the evening?" Deneige offered.

Rendall raised a brow of his own in her direction. *Where's this coming from? She accepts my orders only grudgingly and now she's offering to make up my rooms? Is this some sort of trap?*

"Make that fifteen rooms. as I'm taking this one," he announced, pointing to the first door on the right. "And I don't want to be disturbed. If you have any questions," he indicated to the one guard who seemed to have made the trip with them, "you go to him."

And with that, he took Deneige by the wrist and pulled her into the room behind him, shutting the door once they were inside and almost immediately regretting the action. The room was dark and no larger than a closet, really, with two beds built into one wall, leaving only enough room for him and Deneige to stand to either side of a small brazier taking up the centre. The barracks of the common soldier was not a place of luxury or comfort.

"Do you know how hard it will be to get this room ready with you practically standing on top of me?" Deneige questioned, hands on her hips and her right elbow digging into his side.

"I'm beginning to get an idea, actually," he muttered. "I'd leave, but your people have a somewhat unpleasant odour about them, if you hadn't noticed."

"And whose fault is that?"

"Well, that's hardly worth arguing now. Hopefully they will take this opportunity to bathe themselves."

"Oh, they will. They have their pride and would have been clean the whole time if given the means. Plus, your legionnaires don't exactly smell like a spring day themselves!"

He smiled, despite himself. He liked the way she scrunched her nose when she was angry. "Well, since neither of us are going anywhere, why don't I help you with the room?"

Deneige looked surprised. "Are you feeling alright? Have you taken a chill?"

He ignored the mocking nature of her questions, looking around the room and rubbing his hands together to warm them. "Come to think of it, it is rather chilly in here. Can you heat the room with your thoughts, or must you light a fire like everyone else?"

"If I could heat a room with my thoughts your tent would have burned down that first night."

He chuckled. "I believe you." Rendall turned, moving around the brazier toward a basket set in the corner. Reaching in, he found what he was looking for. "Ah, charcoal. I'll have us warm in no time."

"I get the top bed," Deneige announced, climbing up there and reaching for the blankets the previous occupant had left neatly folded at its base. He nodded and set to work. Before long, the fire was started and Deneige was making the lower bed.

"On nights like this one, if we were lucky enough to have decent shelter like this, it would be a night for couples to come together," she commented in an offhand way as she patted the blanket so it lay smooth against the sheet beneath.

He froze, feeling something stir within him at her words. "Are you insinuating something?"

She stopped what she was doing and turned to face him. "Yes," she said with a smile, "my people are going to be having a good time tonight."

He felt his face heat and he cleared his throat. "Yes, well, it's the least I could do. Slaves or not, their lives would be lost if they were left outside in this."

"Well you may live to regret your decision in nine months when you have more mouths to feed," she commented.

He set his jaw. "I don't see your people multiplying as a bad thing, you know. I'm not trying to exterminate them."

"Of course not," she said with a shrug, as if they weren't speaking of life and death. "Who would make your beds?"

Something about her words sat poorly with him, even though, or perhaps because, they were true. His eyes kept going past her to the delicate work she'd done making up his bed for him, with the corner of the blanket turned down invitingly. As he was lost in his thoughts, he noticed Deneige begin to remove the outer layers of her clothing, revealing the long woolen under-tunic he'd provided for her. Cinched at the shoulders and under the arms, it was a simple garment, but it hung loosely on her feminine form, being meant for a legionnaire twice her size. It was simple enough to recall what she looked like beneath it, even if it had been some time since the day he'd found her sleeping naked in the bathtub.

He cleared his throat again to try and shake the image from his mind, but the loud sound in the small room caused her to turn to look back at him. "Um, did you want something to eat?" he questioned, just to have something to say to those piercing blue eyes of hers.

"We have no food with us," she pointed out.

He shook his head. "Legionnaires always keep some stashed away for days like these. It's not always worth the trip to the great hall."

"Sure, just let me put my coat back on." She started back down the ladder.

It took him a moment to realize what she must be thinking. "Oh, no, I mean you stay here. Get warm. I'll be right back."

Her eyes widened in surprise and she watched him until he was fully out of view. Out in the hall, Rendall let out the breath he hadn't realized he'd been holding. *I sleep in the same apartment as this woman every night and we've even shared a tent, but somehow I think spending the night in this small room is going to be the hardest thing I've ever done.*

He made quick work of raiding the legionnaires' stash and was pleased to note as he was leaving that some of the newly-washed slaves had taken notice of the hidey hole and were going over to investigate it as he left. *Poor sods. At least they'll get a decent meal into themselves tonight.*

Back in the room, Deneige was no more than a lump on the top bunk, snoring lightly. Letting out a small sigh of relief, Rendall put the food down on the lid of the charcoal basket, then proceeded to remove his own outer layers of clothing. Despite the small brazier burning brightly, it was still quite cold and drafty in the room, so he left his woolen tunic on as he climbed into the lower bunk and it wasn't long before he was also asleep.

"Rendall?" He heard his name spoken softly.

"Deneige..." he muttered, half awake and half dreaming.

"Move over, I'm cold."

Icicles pierced his skin in various places and he moaned, shrinking back from their touch, then the entire snowbank pressed up against him. He immediately snapped awake. "Dammit, woman, you're freezing!"

"Then warm me," she murmured, already melting into him, the cold pinpricks turning to sparks against his skin and waking him in other ways.

"Uhhh," he stammered, but there was no deterring her. She burrowed in close until it was difficult to tell where his body ended and hers began. The bed was small; he had to wrap one of his arms around her just to keep his back from pressing against the cold wall behind him.

"Mmmm," she purred, "yes, just like that."

He tried to settle into this new reality, but it was at war with everything he'd come to believe to be true. *Does she want me to...?* He couldn't even put words to the thought. He'd spent the last month of their acquaintance fighting off any attraction he felt towards her and now she was here, in his arms. *But does she want what I want?*

He tried once more to relax, letting his head rest on the pillow of her white hair, but the scent of her kept going to his head. With his free hand, he brought it around to run his fingers through her hair. He'd been wanting to touch it since he'd first laid eyes on her and that seemed innocent enough. *If she has a problem with it, I'll just say I was moving it out of my way.*

But she didn't complain. If anything, she let out a soft sigh of contentment and burrowed more completely into his chest. Soon, her breathing was slow and even.

"Deneige?" he questioned softly.

"Yes?"

Oh, she's awake. I didn't really think she was going to answer me.

"Would it bother you to know I find you beautiful, both your body and soul?" The words escaped him before he'd even realized he'd spoken, but there was no taking them back.

She went silent and stiff for a moment, and Rendall feared he'd crossed a line he'd never be able to uncross, but then the most curious thing happened; he felt her lips moving against his chest. At first, he thought she might be speaking too low for him to hear, but he soon became aware that her movements were more sensual and more deliberate than that. Moving the fabric aside as she went, her tongue caressed his nipple and a small gasp escaped him.

The kisses continued, trailing along his chest from one side to the other. Her hands also came alive, running across his skin under his tunic and eventually lightly scratching the surface of his back.

"Deneige," he said again, and this time she stopped to look up at him. "You're not just doing this because you think you have to, are you?"

He didn't mean his words to come out as vulnerable as they sounded, but this close to his heart's desire as he was, he couldn't help it.

"I think you should know by now, I don't do anything I don't want to do."

He allowed himself a chuckle. "That you don't," he agreed, lowering his mouth to hers. Now that he knew he had her permission, he stopped holding himself back and he gave into her fully, kissing her with all the passion that had been slowly building within him these past weeks.

When they next parted, she was gasping for breath and there was a wild sort of hunger in her eyes. He smiled, seeing it by the light of the brazier behind her. *Now* that *was what I was looking for.* He bent himself again to the task of kissing her, but she put a hand to his mouth instead.

Eyes wide, he stared at her as she twisted so she was straddled atop him, her head just below the floor of the top bunk. Reaching down, she lifted the fabric of her tunic and artfully pulled it from her body in a way that made him suck in air. She was as gorgeous as he remembered, maybe even more so in the soft flickering light.

Looking at her like this, he wanted her with an intensity he'd never felt before. Sure, he'd had lovers, but none like this. None that he'd felt he both had to conquer and lure, seduce and be seduced by them. She felt like his equal, someone worthy of him.

He reached out and cupped one of her breasts with his hand, stroking the nipple with his thumb in a circular motion. She arched her back, enjoying the moment freely. He was a little surprised at her lack of modesty, but then he shouldn't have been; she was as bold in lovemaking as she was with everything else and it was one of the things he loved about her.

She wriggled her thighs, arousing him further as she adjusted her position, and then she reached down and lifted his tunic until it was no longer a barrier between them. He reached for her, but she didn't need prompting. She slid herself into place and pressed down on him until they were as one, a moan escaping her the moment the sweet spot between her legs was parted and his warmth filled her completely. He wrapped his hands around her bottom and guided her motion, rocking her body with his own. She grabbed the wood of the upper bunk and closed her eyes, even as she threw her head back and gave herself over to the feelings he was unleashing upon her.

As for Rendall, he never took his eyes off her, even in the moment of his own climax. He watched her body heave and writhe and sweat, and he fought to sear this moment in his mind; the moment of his greatest conquest.

Deneige woke feeling pleasantly sore in all the right places. *It's been a long time since I've done* that *with anyone.* She stirred and she felt Rendall stir beneath her, like they were still entwined as one being. *He was good, better than I expected, really.*

She forced herself to remain still, wanting more time just to enjoy being wrapped up with him before the day began and she became his slave again. For this night they had been equals and she didn't want that to end. Despite how good laying with Rendall had made her feel, worried thoughts raced across her mind with the first rays of sunlight that filtered through the small, shuttered window. *What if this was all he wanted from me all along? If he only earned my trust to get me to give myself to him willingly?*

She thought about the Rendall she knew in private, the one who seemed to care about her opinions and ask questions of her like he was genuinely curious about the answers, and compared him with the man he was in public, all brooding stares and harsh commands. *Which one is the real Rendall? I've risked a lot believing in the person he's only shown to me, but what if he really is the brutal legionnaire and not the kind, intellectual person I've come to know these past few weeks?*

She felt Rendall stirring for real now beneath her and she knew their night together was coming to an end. Soon they would both have to face the light of day and the truths it might bring. Deneige shuddered. *I hope I haven't made a huge mistake.*

Rendall's arm came around her. "Are you cold?" His deep voice rumbled gently and Deneige felt her heart squeeze at the sound of his concern for her well-being. Despite the daylight, it seemed the gentle Rendall was still with her.

"I'm comfortable," she answered honestly, "though hungry."

She felt him nod against her hair. "I stored the food in the corner, over there," he gestured. "Help yourself."

She rose from the bed and immediately regretted the decision. The bed, and Rendall, had been warm; the rest of the room was not. She scurried across the small space and heard Rendall chuckling behind her. Snatching the cloth-wrapped packet of food up in her hands, she scurried back and practically threw herself at Rendall, which only made him laugh harder. She smiled with a slightly sheepish expression on her face. "It's cold," she muttered.

"I bet," he agreed, reaching around her for a piece of hard cheese.

She tore into the food herself, and could have happily stayed there in the tiny room with the gentle version of Rendall for as long as fate allowed, but it wasn't to last. There was a loud knock at the door, followed by the squeal of hinges as the person who'd knocked decided to let him or herself in without any regard for the occupants. Deneige reached for the blanket and immediately covered as much of herself as she could, as a burly legionnaire stomped into the small space. She felt Rendall stiffen behind her.

"Some of the slaves you freed told me I might find you here," the legionnaire, a man Deneige didn't recognize, rumbled through his helmet. He spoke to Rendall, not her, which was no real surprise. To them, Deneige was no more worth paying attention to than the brazier in the centre of the room. She had her uses, but otherwise she was no more than a fixture of the camp. "I see you kept the finest of them for yourself. Tell me, did she come to your bed willingly or did you have to drag her by her pretty white mane?"

Deneige geared herself up to challenge this man. She was ready to spring to her feet and spit in his face, but Rendall's hand on her shoulder made her hesitate and she missed her moment.

"Who are you to question me?" Rendall's cold, commanding tone was back. Deneige shivered at the sound, glad it wasn't meant for her this time.

The legionnaire should have backed down. Deneige had seen it before. Men parted at Rendall's command and even those who outranked him spoke to him and about him with respect, but this man merely laughed. "Felix Corinius, the General's newest Centurion. You're wanted in the great hall. The General has some questions for you."

The way the man said 'questions' gave Deneige a great sense of foreboding. Rendall was in trouble with his superiors, that much was clear, but how much and what it would mean for him, or for her, was uncertain. She felt Rendall move behind her even as he said. "I expect some privacy as I prepare myself to speak to the General."

Felix smirked. "As you wish. I'll be out in the hall. Don't take too long or I'll have to find some way to amuse myself." He ran his eyes up and down Deneige's form as he spoke to give meaning to his comment, then he let himself out into the hall.

Rendall said nothing; he simply slid past her and started to dress himself.

"Don't go," she said suddenly. "Leave with me."

He was silent a moment, then said, "Which is it, Deneige? Are you asking me to go or stay?"

"Come with me, leave this place. We don't need it, we can build something better. Together."

He met her eyes and when he did she noticed how much more pronounced the blue was in them today. It made him look solemn. "The two of us together, on the run, with no people to turn to…that's not a life. Accept it, we're from different worlds. This one's mine."

"You told me you were destined for greatness. I am too. Maybe together we could build a new world, a better one, a fairer one."

He frowned, looking at her in a way that said he was memorizing her features, like a man going off to war, uncertain if he would return.

"Don't," she turned her face away from him, drawing the blanket tighter to herself. "You used me, didn't you? You got your prize and now I'm not worth anything to you anymore. No more than a slave."

Another bout of silence passed between. Deneige felt tears fill her eyes and she fought them. She didn't want to show weakness in front of him, not now. Another loud knock at the door rang out like the final tolling of the bell.

"I hope you don't really believe that," Rendall said, throwing his cloak over his shoulders as his cold mask slid over his features and he left her alone in the room.

Deneige sobbed sharply, unable to help herself, and she grabbed the nearest thing to her, the blanket, and stuffed it in her face to keep the sound from escaping. Now more than ever, she had to be strong and fearless. She was the last Dea of the Lumen, and without Rendall's protection her people would need her more than ever.

Rendall knew he was in trouble when more of the General's men formed up around him to escort him from the barracks to the great hall. He squared his shoulders and walked as if he was wearing a full suit of armour and not his travelling clothes, which were inadequate to this weather and to the pride of his station. He silently cursed Deneige for having lost his chest of armour.

The walk to the great hall was not a long one, but it felt that way due to the heavy snow they had to trudge through to get there. The wind, at least, had died down so they were able to see their destination and find their way there easily. *If only it had been so simple last night in the storm.* But had they reached the great hall, Rendall suspected his night would have gone very differently, and despite where the result of his actions was leading him now, he found he wouldn't trade last night for anything. *Whatever today brings, it was worth it.*

The great hall was bustling with soldiers, though not many he knew. His own men were elsewhere, it seemed. Felix brought him to the General's ready room, where he found the man himself facing out a window while someone else knelt in the center of the room, his head slumped as if he didn't have the strength to lift it. It took

Rendall a moment to recognize Lucius past the purpling bruises and swelling that made up his once handsome face.

"Rendall," the General acknowledged his presence without turning as Felix took up position just inside the door. "I trust you know our mutual friend?"

"I do," Rendall stated without any sign of emotion, though his heart went out to the young soldier.

"Then you will understand why Lucius needed to be punished."

Rendall set his jaw. "I do not," he stated, knowing it was not what the man wanted to hear.

The General flicked his wrist and all of a sudden Rendall felt something powerful strike the back of his leg. He fell to one knee and snapped his head back only to find Felix staring back at him through his open visor with a hint of eagerness in his dark brown eyes.

"I will enlighten you, then," the General continued as if nothing untoward had occurred. "It is for the same reason that you will be punished. You failed to obey orders and, worse than that, you commanded your men to desert and return to camp."

"I sent Lucius with a warning to-" he began, but Felix striking him about the head set his ears ringing and cut off the rest of what he'd been about to say.

"Ah yes, the storm," the General said, "that's the other thing. You ordered your men to desert, which left the rest of the Legion at the mercy of the storm."

"That's hardly my fau-" Rendall tried again only to get punched in the gut by Felix's gauntleted hand for his troubles.

"Is it not?" the General asked, too innocently. "How is it you knew of the coming storm, when no one else did?"

Rendall's heart froze in his chest. He stayed silent, both because he had no wish to tell them the truth and because he'd learned by now that speaking resulted in physical punishment.

"Well?" the General pushed, and Felix struck him once more anyway.

Rendall spit out blood, turning his head to the side, but still he said nothing. *There's no way to explain Deneige's gift or why I chose to believe what she had to say. And besides, I can't put her in danger.*

The General turned now to face him and the older man narrowed his gaze. "No matter," he said, "I don't need you to answer my questions. I have the truth of the matter already. Felix?" Felix hoisted Rendall by the arms. "Come with me," he urged them both and strode from the room. Hauled by Felix, Rendall had no choice but to obey.

They half led, half dragged him from the great hall with the occasional legionnaire turning to watch as they made their way across the snow-covered road to the small building sandwiched innocuously between the granary and the stables. Rendall tried to steel himself for the worst. If he was to be punished for his actions then so be it, but he would not stand for torture and he would not give away any of Deneige's secrets. Doing so would see her killed, or worse, a tool for the General to use. If she could see storms, it was possible that like the Vestal Virgins she could see other things. A man like the General would do a lot for an advantage like that.

They brought him into the small windowless building and it took a moment for his eyes to adjust to the dim light within after the brightness of outside, but as soon as they did, he knew exactly what they had brought him here to see, and it wasn't the two rows of cells lining the north and south sides of the eastern half of the building. No, it was what filled the other half of the space. An open-concept room, with a row of whipping posts along one wall, and other blank spaces where prisoners or out-of-favour legionnaires could be strung up to be tortured or punished for their crimes. Either way, the result was the same; pain, and plenty of it.

But Rendall only had eyes for one thing in the room and that was the woman he'd thought he'd left safely in the barracks. She was as naked as she had been when he'd left her, but now she was strung up by her hands and ankles, splayed uncomfortably and indecently on the wall in the centre of the worst place in the entire Castra. Rendall felt a deep growl begin somewhere low in his throat, an animalistic sound he couldn't quite control or stop. The sound of it only made the General grin harder, however, and it did nothing to ease the fear in Deneige's eyes.

"Why are you doing this?" Deneige asked and Rendall was at least relieved to note that she hadn't been harmed yet beyond a blackening eye, which he assumed she'd earned by trying to fight for her freedom when they'd come for her.

"Usually, I wouldn't deign to answer a question from a creature such as this one, but in this case I'll make an exception." The General turned to Rendall. "Renounce her and admit to us all that you've been bewitched by this woman, and you'll be spared your punishment and can return to our favour."

Rendall stared at the man, open-mouthed. *He thinks Deneige is a witch. Either that, or he's using it as a clever excuse to take his frustrations out on her instead of me.* He racked his brain for the why of it, until he remembered how many times the General had publicly praised him in front of the men. *He can't stand to lose face over this, but he has to punish someone for the losses the storm wreaked and there's no way he'd take that responsibility on himself. Using his logic, a fey-looking slave would seem like the perfect scapegoat.*

"Stop this, it's barbaric!" Deneige demanded.

She's right, it is, but he'll have his scapegoat no matter what I do and I made a vow to provide Deneige my protection.

Rendall straightened his spine and the General regarded him expectantly. He took a single step forward, still wary of Felix's presence behind him and the fact that he wouldn't get within two feet of the General before Felix either slammed him to the ground or ran him through with his sword.

"Not that the truth matters here," Rendall stated as clearly as he could, "but the slave is innocent. She is not a witch and I acted of my own free will. I sent the message to the troops to turn around and I freed the Lumen slaves to protect them from the storm. If my actions deserve punishment, then so be it."

The General nodded, seeming to accept this, but there was a sad resignation behind the older man's eyes as he looked to Felix and then flicked his wrist one more time in Rendall's direction. This time Rendall knew what to expect, but it didn't make it hurt any less when Felix's gauntleted hand struck him in the jaw.

He fell to the ground from the force of the blow, spitting blood on the ground where a hundred men had spat blood before him.

"Stop!" Deneige cried, but it made no difference. Another blow came, then another, and another. Some to his ribs, his back, his face, and even his legs.

"It was me! I bewitched him! I called the storm! I did it all." Deneige kept screaming, listing all manner of crimes, but still the blows kept coming until at long last Rendall lost awareness of his circumstance and he fell into the darkness of unconsciousness, glad at least that he never gave Felix the satisfaction of hearing him cry for mercy.

Deneige sobbed and fought against the leather straps that bound her long after the men had gone. Not for herself, but for Rendall, whose form lay unmoving on the cold dirt floor not ten feet from her, though it might as well have been a thousand.

"Please, Rendall, don't leave me! Wake up! Spirits help him, heal him! Rendall!"

Whether the spirits were listening to her or not, she didn't know. Shut up in this windowless room, she couldn't see or feel the outside world. All she had was the dirt at her feet; strung up as she was, her toes only barely reached the earth's surface, and she doubted there was any life left in this place the Romans had conquered.

"Rendall," she cried, once more, begging him now. "I need you. You promised me!"

Rendall began to stir, as if he'd heard her. Deneige snapped to attention, willing whatever strength she could to him to help him stand, though the sight of him told her how difficult he must have been finding it to just even breathe. "It's going to be okay, we'll be okay. Just make it to me and I can help heal you."

On his hands and knees now, he lifted his head in her direction, but his eyes and face were so swollen, she wasn't sure he could see her. "I'd be careful how loudly I say that if I were you." He coughed, spitting up blood. "They already think you're a witch."

"I don't care what they think of me." She shook her head. "I only care about you right now."

"Don't be foolish," he said, making his way toward her as quickly as he was able, which mostly involved crawling and dragging one of his legs behind him.

"Don't you be stubborn! Just follow my voice. I'm sorry you have to come to me and not the other way around."

He shook his head, misunderstanding her. "I would never have let them touch you."

"I know," she said softly, feeling tears well in her eyes again. *I believe you now,* she thought in his direction, *I believe in you. The person I thought you to be, the one I came to love. That's the real you, I know it now.*

"Keep talking," he told her, shuffling closer.

"I'm cold and they didn't let me put any clothes on before they took me, those bastards," she said, the first thing that came to mind.

He grunted, moving past the pain to try and reach her. "Uhh," she searched for something, anything to fill the silence and guide him to her. "I won't lie; you look awful."

A half chuckle, half cough escaped him and she winced at the sound. "I've been better," he admitted as his hand closed around her ankle; he'd reached her at last.

"Good," she guided him, "the straps are leather, like belts. The clasp is just by your thumb."

"Unfortunately, I know how these work. Just give me a minute." He made quick work of her bindings for someone half-blind and in as much pain as Rendall no doubt was; soon he was slumped over in her arms, and she was free and able to support his weight.

Spirits, I need you now, she called out in the silence of her mind, feeling outwards with her gift for the spirits she knew to be out there somewhere. *Help me heal him. Help me, please.*

But the spirits didn't answer her. In fact, she couldn't feel them at all. It was like they didn't exist in this man-made place of torture and hate, or perhaps they simply avoided it. Deneige fought to control the emotions trying to drag her back into despair. *Rendall needs me to be strong for him right now. I can't fall apart.*

Despite his injuries, she felt him draw away from her to stand under his own power. He wobbled in an unsteady fashion, but past the swelling and the bruising, she could see his expression was set in a determined fashion. He unclasped his cloak and pulled it off, holding it out to her. "Take it," he commanded, and when she did as she was bid, he began unlacing the front of his shirt.

"What are you doing? We have to get out of here."

He shook his head. "Only one of us is getting out of here and that's going to be you. I can barely stand and you…" he trailed off and then swallowed with difficulty. "They'll kill you if you stay. They've already decided you're guilty."

"I can make it snow, we can get out with cover. Please don't leave me."

"I would only be a burden to you," he said, pulling at his shirt and then giving it up when he didn't have the strength to lift it over his own head.

"You're not a burden," she said, shaking her head and wrapping her arms around him. He winced at the contact and the pain it caused him, but didn't ask her to stop.

"Deneige, listen to me. They won't kill me, they've already had their fun. But you, your life is in danger. I don't know why they've spared you this long other than to make me think that I've paid for your life with the punishment they've just given me, but I know them. I know how they think. Even if they let you be for a day, or a month, the next time something goes wrong that doesn't have an immediate explanation, they'll come for you and I *can't let that happen.* So go. Take my cloak, take whatever you can steal, and use your gifts to leave this place and get as far as you can."

"I'll come back for you," she promised, setting her jaw and lifting his shirt over his head. It was sweaty and blood-soaked, but large enough to cover her, at least. And besides, it smelled of him. He offered her his boots as well; she stuffed his socks into them to make them fit her much-smaller feet. While she dressed, he used the rest of his strength to slump up against a whipping post. She hated to admit it, but he was right; there was no way he would be able to flee the Castra with her in his condition and she couldn't heal him without the spirits to help her.

"Thank you," she whispered, leaning in to say her goodbyes. "I know ours was only a marriage of convenience, but I was starting to fall for you, you know."

Rendall managed a chuckle. "If I could," he told her, "I'd marry you for real."

"You already have," she managed, her voice cracking on the words, because she wished so badly for them to be true. *If we were really married, there would be nothing to keep us apart.*

Holding back the storm of tears that threatened to overwhelm her, she kissed him gently on the lips and then pulled away swiftly, knowing that if she didn't leave now, she would never leave without him. "I love you," she said, fleeing his side and throwing the door to the outside wide open, where the wind and snow reigned.

As hard as it was to command her to leave, it was even harder watching her go, not that Rendall had the strength to do anything about it. Spent from even the simple task of helping Deneige to escape, he slid to the floor, his head leaning uncomfortably against the whipping post. *Some protector I am,* he cursed his own weakness. *I just have to hope she can do as she says and makes it out of here alive.*

Anxiety gnawing at his empty stomach, Rendall kept his ears trained on the door for sounds to indicate Deneige had returned either under her own power or dragged there by a legionnaire. Either way would mean she had failed to escape, and he wished just as hard to never hear those sounds as he did to one day see her again. Time dragged on, but Rendall didn't have the means to count it. At some point he must have lost consciousness, but when he woke again it was to the sound of the door opening.

"Deneige?" he questioned, but heavy footfalls immediately dissuaded him of this notion.

"Are you fucking kidding me?" Felix's loud voice boomed. "You let her go? Of course you did." A heavy hand grabbed him by the hair and dragged him several feet from the whipping post. "The General's going to hear about this," Felix thundered more than hissed into his ear before something hard and familiar struck him about the face, and Rendall blacked out once more.

When he came to again, it was to the higher, smoother pitch of the General's voice and a cool, moist cloth on the tender flesh of his jaw. "There, now," the General cooed, "it's a shame what Felix did to your face. I shall have to reprimand him for it."

"Why do you care?" Rendall spat.

A slight pause and then he said, "There's no need to be vulgar. I know you're mad at me right now, but you'll see the necessity of my actions in time. I know what you did, Rendall. I know you freed the witch and I'm not pleased."

Rendall fell silent. There was nothing he could say in his own defense.

The General continued. "But I also know it's not your fault. She's a witch. You're under her spell. No doubt she lured you to her side despite your injuries and she used you for her own nefarious purposes, isn't that right?"

Rendall again, stayed silent, but his thoughts were jumbled. *What is he playing at?*

"Yes, well, you don't need to speak. Save your strength. I'll make sure the men know that none of this was your fault and maybe when you're feeling better..." he trailed off and then Rendall felt a long, cool finger trace the line of his throbbing jaw. "Well, hopefully you will look upon me with more kindness considering all that I'm going to do for you, hm?"

Bile rose in Rendall's throat, but some instinct told him to remain still and silent or the General's 'kindness' might easily turn to cruelty.

"That's my boy," the General finished, and Rendall felt him stand and move away. "You rest now and I'll have a stretcher brought in to see you back to your rooms. I regret Felix's…enthusiasm. It's going to be a long recovery for you, I'm afraid. I'll let you know if we recapture your witch. I'm sure you'll be relieved to know when we've hung her."

Deneige was grateful for the icy wind stinging her face. Every pinprick of falling snow heightened her courage and strengthened her resolve. *My storm. This is my storm and I control it.* She wrapped the weather around herself like a cloak and prayed it would keep her safely hidden.

Thankfully, she knew her way through the Castra. In fact, she knew every path and had intimate knowledge of which ones were more thoroughly used and which ones might be empty. It was this knowledge that allowed her to safely reach the spot where she'd toppled Rendall's cart, which seemed like months ago when it was really only yesterday. She found the cart just as she'd left it, though covered in significantly more snow.

She dug her hands into the icy depths, locating what she wanted by feel. She found Rendall's trunk and opened it, pleased to find that her spare clothes were inside along with his. She pulled them out and made a bundle, then she reached back into the snow.

"Deneige? Deneige is that you?"

Letting out a small gasp, Deneige snapped her head upwards, but it had been a woman's voice calling her and she was relieved to recognize Siobhan squinting at her, as if trying to make her out in the swirling wind.

"Quick, help me find supplies," Deneige instructed. "We're getting out of here."

Nodding, and quickly scanning the area around them to make sure they weren't spotted, Siobhan ran as best she could through the thick snow. "Did something happen? Did they punish that man of yours for letting us loose?"

Deneige nodded, feeling hot tears sting her cheeks, and Siobhan frowned in sympathy. "I tried to warn the others that our good fortune wouldn't last, but they didn't believe me. They took your man's warning seriously about not surviving the weather if they left, but I knew I had to take my chances out here. Nothing good can come of trusting the Romans."

Deneige frowned, thinking about leaving her people in the hands of that vile General and his Legion, but in her heart she knew she wouldn't be able to save them all. *The barracks will be guarded and such a great number of us would be noticed, even if I can convince them to leave. Besides, Rendall was right, this weather is dangerous. It's bad enough Siobhan and I have to be out in it. I will return for them when I return for Rendall, I swear it.*

"I agree about the rest," she told Siobhan, "but Rendall is different. He saved me, set me free." She pulled out the small sack of emergency foodstuffs Rendall had tucked away with their belongings. She grinned, showing teeth, and Siobhan smiled back at her.

"We really are doing this, then?" Siobhan asked, hope and wonder in her voice.

Deneige nodded, getting to her feet as she gathered the storm around them to protect them on the next leg of their journey. "Yes," she told her, "we are. And I know just where we can find some unattended horses. Come on."

In the end, Deneige decided to only take the one horse and to have Siobhan climb up behind her. She tried to convince herself that it was because the horse Rendall had chosen for her was white and therefore easier to hide in the snow than his black stallion, but in her heart she knew it was because she couldn't bear to take his horse and leave him without it. She kept that part to herself, however, as she and Siobhan used the cover of her storm to slip unnoticed through the southern gate.

They rode through the wind for what seemed like an eternity, the blank canvas of their surroundings slowly darkening as the sun set behind a seamless bank of cloud cover. Neither of them spoke much, but when Siobhan's shivering slowed and finally stopped, Deneige stopped the horse for fear her friend was dying from exposure.

"Siobhan?" Deneige questioned, trying to twist far enough to see behind her.

"Huh?" The other woman started awake.

"Oh, thank the spirits. Are you very cold? I think we've gone far enough that we can stop for the night. As long as no one has followed us, we should be safe enough in those trees over there." She pointed.

"I am cold," Siobhan admitted, "but not as cold as I should be. I feel…numb. Maybe we should stop, it's possible I'm losing my toes to frostbite and don't even know it." She let out a weak laugh.

Deneige realized belatedly that she felt the same. Despite the fact that she was hardly dressed for the weather, and wasn't even wearing any pants, she hadn't felt the cold at all since she'd called the storm to protect her. *Is this a gift from the spirits? And am I really able to share it with Siobhan?* She thought of the way she'd wrapped the storm around the both of them and realized it must be true.

She guided Snowflake, for that was what she'd decided to call the mare Rendall had given her, toward the treeline. "We'll stop, if only because I don't know how much longer I can keep this up."

Before long, they were safely within the cover of the evergreens. Deneige dismounted and helped Siobhan down beside her, but before she could look about to find an appropriate spot to set up camp and hopefully start a fire, a sharp whistle drew her attention. Deneige and Siobhan both recognized the whistle immediately. They turned to look at one another. "You don't think-" they said at the same time, when the sound repeated itself.

Deneige put her fingers to her mouth and returned the call, and before long a familiar figure came toward them from between the trees.

"Javvar!" Siobhan recognized him first and ran forward to throw her arms around him. It took Deneige a moment longer to put the face to the name as it felt like a lifetime ago that she'd walked freely among her people and tended to Javvar in the tent she'd shared with Ignes.

Images of that last night flashed in her mind's eye and Deneige shuddered. "I thought they'd killed you, Javvar. How do you come to be here?"

"I'm sorry about Ignes," he said instead, "but they didn't lay a hand on me. I was still a little out of it when it all happened, but they must have thought I was dead. Good thing, too. Is it just the two of you? Did you manage to evade the Romans?"

"Oh, Javvar, it was awful-" Siobhan began.

"We had to leave the others behind. I will go back for them when I can, but without help…" Deneige trailed off, realizing for the first time since fleeing the Castra how bleak her chances were of ever getting her people out, let alone Rendall. "We were in their camp for a little over a month."

Javvar shook his head sadly. "Well, I'm glad to see you safe. Come on, we've got a camp a little ways into the forest. It's not much, but we'll share what we have, and we'd be really glad to have you back among us, Dea. A few of us are wounded and sick," he added with a sad smile.

Deneige and Siobhan followed Javvar back to the camp he'd mentioned and if Siobhan was dismayed at how few free Lumen awaited them, she didn't show it. She greeted each of the dozen or so with open arms and wide smiles. For Deneige, her arrival in camp was the beginning of a long night of work tending to the needs of her people. When she had finally seen to everyone and was able to take her supper by the fire, she was exhausted.

"Spirits!" Siobhan exclaimed, staring at Deneige open-mouthed. "Who died? Did you have to cut into someone?"

"What?" It took Deneige a moment to remember the blood-stained shirt she was wearing under the cloak she'd kept closed until now, the one Rendall had given her off his own back. "Oh, this is Rendall's blood."

Her explanation didn't seem to appease Siobhan. The woman put a hand to her mouth. "Oh, Deneige, I'm so sorry. I get it now, why you had to flee and where you got that black eye. Wait," she stopped, "why did you kill Rendall? I thought he was on our side?"

"I…I didn't kill him. He's not dead. They beat him." Deneige sighed, putting aside her dinner to explain everything to Siobhan and Javvar, who came over part way through to join them. Her people needed to know what they were up against; they needed to know the truth if they were going to help her break back into the Castra and free those they'd left behind.

Rendall's recovery took longer than anyone expected, but that was only because he took it upon himself to train as much as he could each day in secret. He wanted them to think him weaker than he was. It was the only way he could be sure they didn't ever catch him off guard again. *The next time Felix goes to take a swing at me,*

I'll be ready, Rendall vowed as he did his daily exercises in the privacy of his rooms in the Preatorium.

He made sure he was in his chair, reading and trying not to look like he'd just been exerting himself, when the General came around for his usual visit. Against Rendall's better wishes, the General came by nightly to share dinner with him. It was a tradition that had begun as soon as Rendall's jaw had healed enough to take in more than broth and before speech had been comfortable. Rendall had very quickly discovered that he disliked the General's company and his high-pitched nasal voice even less, but there was nothing he could do as the man outranked him by a significant margin and had direct say over Rendall's very position within the legion.

"So," the General was saying, "I trust the food is to your liking. I took the liberty of having the cook prepare the quality of food he usually only reserves for me."

Rendall nodded, his eyes on his soup. The food really was several cuts above the common fare the average legionnaire received, but he didn't want to appear to like it too much in case he encouraged these dinners to continue.

"You're a quiet man," the General stated. "I admire that in you."

Rendall grunted, putting another spoonful of soup in his mouth. *Maybe if I finish quickly he will leave all the sooner.*

"As I was saying," the General continued whether Rendall was listening to him or not, "I need a man like you by my side. Someone I can trust to know when to keep his mouth shut and when to offer his opinion. I believe you are that man. What would you say to me naming you one of my Centurions?"

This brought Rendall up short. "That's very generous of you," he said carefully, "but I'm still recovering, and besides, you have Felix."

The General waved his hand. "Felix can stay for the time being, as my muscle. It's your mind I'm after, my boy. You're a great strategist, the kind this legion can make use of."

Rendall swallowed around the lump in his throat the soup had become. Over these past few months he'd been doing little more than regaining his strength and plotting his escape from the Castra. He'd thought his career with the Legion was over and done with, and he ached for Deneige daily; he'd been intending to leave and find her if he could.

"I, uh…"

"Oh, don't be modest!" the General beamed. "I've already made the arrangements and sent word of your promotion back to Rome. You're destined for great things, my boy! Great things."

The Vestal Virgin's words echoed in his mind and Rendall found himself nodding along to the General's proposal. *That's right, my destiny. I'm supposed to lead Apollo's Legion to greatness. How can I do that if I desert my post?*

She also said, 'Beware the night'. Could she have been talking about Deneige and that one night we spent together? It's the one thing that almost ruined my entire career…

"Excellent, excellent," the General slapped Rendall amiably on the shoulder. "Eat up, Alton. We'll have you back to your old self in no time!"

Rendall applied himself to his dinner with renewed vigour, genuinely enjoying the prime cut of meat the cook had supplied and washing it down with the highest quality of wine one could ask for while on campaign. *I could get used to this,* he allowed. *It's certainly better to have the General's favour than to face his ire.*

"To Alton Rendall, my right hand man."

Rendall lifted his own glass to salute the General when the door to his apartment opened, admitting a legionnaire. "General, you wanted to be notified immediately if the white-haired witch was spotted?"

Rendall's head snapped upwards as the General dropped his napkin on his plate and lowered his glass to the table. "Well, what is it, boy?"

"She was spotted with a band of Lumen, raiding Alder's Keep, sir."

"Did they catch her?"

"No, sir, but they caught a few of her fellows."

The General ground his teeth. "Have the captured Lumen brought back here for questioning." He stood as he spoke, "Alton, I'm afraid I seem to have lost my appetite. I expect you at your post tomorrow at first bell."

Rendall nodded slowly, his mind a swirl of unwanted thoughts, and the General left with the legionnaire. Rendall stood and paced the length of his apartment until he came to a decision. He would take the General up on his offer; there was little reason not to accept and a lot of reasons to do so, the least of which being it would give him the trust and freedom he needed to move about the Castra without suspicion. Then, in a few weeks when the prisoners arrived, he would question them to learn what he could about Deneige's whereabouts and what in the world she was playing at.

In the five months since Deneige's escape from the Castra, she'd grown in many ways. She was no longer the kind of woman who could watch her own mentor die in front of her and not do something about it, and she was also no longer the kind of woman who could pretend to be less than she was for the sake of a man. She was the Dea of the Lumen and she was intent on fulfilling the task destiny had set before her: freeing her people from the cruel grasp of Apollo's Legion.

And she'd made strides toward that goal. With Siobhan and Javvar's help, their little camp had grown from a dozen to nearly five hundred. They weren't all Lumen, but all had reason to want to fight back against the Romans. Deneige had separated them into smaller camps, giving each group instructions on where to hide and how and when to contact one another. They were careful and organized, and so far that had kept most of them alive and out of the Legion's hands.

Until now. The raid on Alder's Keep had not gone entirely to plan. They'd still managed to free the slaves brought to market there, but a few of Deneige's own band had gotten caught and she'd been forced to leave them behind, Javvar included.

That was a week ago and now Deneige found herself on a familiar ridge looking down on a familiar sight. The moonlit Castra lay spread out in the valley before her, much as she remembered it, except the streets were filled with mud rather than snow or packed dirt. The other oddity was that the camp was nearly silent; only a few men with lit torches wandered within and the barest amount of soldiers needed to man the gates.

"Something doesn't feel right," Deneige whispered under her breath.

"You're not wrong," Siobhan agreed, "but this is what you wanted, a time when the camp was nearly empty. Perhaps they're simply out pillaging somewhere else."

"Perhaps. I guess we will see. Let's go in."

Siobhan gave the call, which sounded like a kind of bird only found much further north of here, and their small group started forward, confident that the others would hear the signal and know it was time to act.

From every direction, the Lumen and the Freefolk, as they'd taken to calling themselves, spilled down into the valley to fall upon the Castra. From Deneige's position they were no more than shadows moving in the night, but she knew the truth. The other groups reached the walls first, far from the manned towers. There they lit torches of their own, which they then left near the bottom of the wooden wall, or tossed strategically over the top of it to where Deneige knew the Romans kept hay and other supplies for themselves and their horses.

That's the signal. Deneige was up and running at the first sight of flames licking the walls, with Siobhan and the others at her heels. They tore down into the valley and went straight for the southern gate, the same one they'd so painstakingly snuck out of all those months ago.

There was a brief clash. People on both sides lost their lives, but when the night fell silent around them, Deneige's people were the ones left standing. She left a few in the guard tower to watch their rear in case this was a trap of some kind and then she led the others deeper into the compound.

"Siobhan, take the others and go to the slave pens. I'm going to find Rendall."

Siobhan nodded, taking the lead, as Deneige veered off down familiar paths she'd long since put out of her mind.

No one stopped her from reaching the Praetorium. She'd half-hoped to run into Lucius, just to see how the young man would react to her presence now, but no one was waiting for her outside Rendall's door. The courtyard was eerily quiet and dark. Deneige couldn't help the feeling that something was wrong, and her anxiety prevented her from sensing whether or not Rendall was nearby. A storm could have struck her over the head right now and she wouldn't have seen it coming.

Deneige put her hand on the door and quietly nudged it open. Within was just as dark as without, and just as silent. She slipped in, relying on her keen senses and her memory of the place to navigate her way around the apartment. It didn't take long to ascertain that it was empty and by all evidence seemed to have been that way for a while. *Have they moved him since I left? Did he get demoted over what happened and assigned to a common barracks?*

If they did, there was no way for Deneige to know. She balled her fists in frustration. She racked her brain for places in the Castra to search for signs of where Rendall might be. *The room in the barracks where we waited out the storm? No, he wouldn't get to choose where they put him if he was demoted.*

Hoping Rendall had thought to leave her some kind of sign, Deneige scoured the apartment. She'd almost given up when she noticed the oddity in the centre of the room. She'd been avoiding walking there because there was usually a table where Rendall would take his meals, but now, in its place stood a copper bathtub she immediately recognized from the many times Rendall had had it brought in for her use.

She reached into the tub and found a small note stuffed in the drain.

Your friend is in the last place you'd want to go.

That was it. No signature, no words of love or encouragement, just one cryptic sentence. It was in Rendall's hand at least, she could tell that much.

Suspicion stabbed at her. *How was he able to leave this note for me? When I left, he was in disgrace, not in a position to set up elaborate messages or know where prisoners are being kept. This isn't right.*

Despite her misgivings about his intentions, she didn't think Rendall was lying to her about Javvar's whereabouts. She left the apartment and raced across the Castra until she reached the scene of her last moments with Rendall and the place she'd almost been tortured by the Legion. She found the door unlocked and unguarded, with Javvar tied to the same whipping post she'd left Rendall slumped against five months ago.

She rushed to her friend's side and fell to her knees, rapidly checking him over. He came awake at her touch, but he was weak and delirious with fever. Beside him, just in his reach, was the remains of a meal that looked like it had been picked over by rats at some point.

"Shh," Deneige soothed him, putting a hand to his forehead to gauge his temperature.

"Deneige," he mumbled. "Knew you would come…left me…a warning. They wanted to know where you were. I wouldn't tell, but Rendall…" he trailed off, not making much sense.

"What have they done to you? What did you tell Rendall?"

But Javvar was beyond her grasp now. Having held on long enough to deliver his message, he let go and let the fever take him. Her healer's instinct told her there was nothing more she could do for him. His wounds were obviously infected and taking the fever away would only allow them to fester more quickly. As Deneige considered her options, she heard the all-too familiar sound of a death rattle. She winced as Javvar's body went cold beneath her fingers. She sighed sadly and let him go with the spirits.

A sharp gasp filled the room along with a short burst of wind as the door opened. Deneige whirled to find Siobhan standing there, her hand covering her mouth. "Is he...?"

"I'm sorry," Deneige said simply and Siobhan sobbed once, her whole body shaking with the force of it. Deneige stood. "I'll give you a moment to say goodbye."

As Deneige waited outside for Siobhan, she pored over the events of the night while watching the nearby fires and keeping a sharp eye on her surroundings. *If this is a trap, it hasn't been sprung yet.*

But even if it isn't...how could Rendall have been a part of this? Was I wrong about him after all? If...no, when *I see him again, I won't fall for his tricks. I can't let him hurt anyone else. This is what I get for trusting a Roman. I thought...I thought he loved me.*

She wrapped her arms around her middle and held herself tight as she waited for her friend. Soon they would leave this place behind for good and then the real hunt for Rendall would begin. *But for now...* she thought as Siobhan joined her once more, *there's one more thing I have to do.*

Crossing to the nearest source of fire, she lit the unused torch she still carried and brought it back to the cursed place where Rendall had left his final message to her. Lowering the torch to the ground, she left it at the door to the Roman's torture chamber, knowing it would catch and burn the whole windowless wooden structure to the ground in short order; releasing Javvar's spirit from this awful place.

"Come on, Siobhan," she said without looking back, "let's get the others and get out of here. Our plans have been compromised. We can't go back to the way things were before, we can only go forward now."

"Javvar wouldn't have told them anything," Siobhan protested.

Deneige shook her head. "He told Rendall. He trusted Rendall because I did and he told him everything. I've been a fool."

Rendall thought he would be relieved to be back on the road campaigning, but riding at the General's side was nothing like he was used to. They continued their tradition of dining nightly together, the fare he received in the General's tent far beyond that which was provided to the common soldier. They travelled in near luxury instead of sleeping on hard ground and roughing it with the soliders. It made Rendall feel like he was betraying his men somehow, but the General seemed to expect such treatment as his due and Felix revelled in it.

The entire experience, combined with thoughts of what he'd left behind at the Castra for Deneige, left Rendall feeling moody and out of sorts. And so when they took the town of Whelan, it held no joy for him. In fact, the unnecessary violence sickened him.

Choosing not to partake in the exercise himself, Rendall was glad enough for his position at the General's side, as it meant he didn't even need to draw his sword unless the man was threatened. Felix, meanwhile, was chomping at the bit, eager to get his chance to add to the destruction around him and forcing the General to keep him on a tight leash.

"You'll get your chance, Felix. For now, though, your place, like Rendall's, is at my side."

Rendall fought down his disgust at the fact that he and Felix were considered equals in any way.

They paraded through the town like heroes when it was clear to Rendall, at least, that they had become the villains. *This town was governing itself just fine. It didn't need the guidance of the Empire and it certainly did not ask for it. These people are not our enemies and they shouldn't be our subjects just because we choose it.*

The General led their small party to the town's keep. A modest-sized building, it boasted only a single tower and it was to the top of this the General took them so he could oversee his new domain. Rendall had conquered his share of territory in the past, but he had never gloated like this. The General seemed to want to bask in what he saw as proof of his own greatness. He stood at the large open-arch windows of the keep's tower and watched the chaos continue below, as townspeople attempted to hide or flee and the men of Apollo's Legion butchered or captured them in the streets. Some of the houses even burned.

Rendall concentrated on breathing steadily in and out, so as not to betray his thoughts by any outward reaction. A brief chill on the wind drew his attention out the window where, past the General, he noted dark, warning clouds on the horizon. Rendall furrowed his brow. *A storm? Please tell me that's just a coincidence and not some sort of sign. Deneige…*

"Perfect timing," the General noted, causing Rendall to start, but it wasn't the clouds he was looking at.

"What is?" Rendall asked.

"Taking this town. We have done so quite efficiently, don't you think? Just in time for the visitors we're expecting."

Rendall said nothing.

"Oh, come now. We both know what this whole exercise has been about. I have laid a trap for your witch and soon it shall close around her."

The silence stretched even longer this time.

"Felix, why don't you step outside and guard the door a moment?"

From his place against the wall, looking bored, Felix suddenly snapped to attention and nodded to his General, said, "Yes, sir," and then took himself from the tower room, closing the door behind him.

"Alton, my dear," the General began, "it's clear to me that you still have…lingering feelings for this witch." Rendal stiffened. "No, no, it's quite alright, I understand. Willingly or unwillingly, she put a spell on you and such things can be hard to overcome. I had hoped that putting her to death would cure you of any affection for her, but I am beginning to suspect that will not be the case.

"To put it simply," he continued, "I'm willing to make a deal with you."

Rendall raised a brow, even if beneath his helmet the General could not see it. *What is he playing at now?*

The General turned to him then, searching with his eyes as if to try and see past his helmet, though he didn't ask him to take it off. "I should think it obvious by now that I have…feelings for you, Alton. Without overstepping myself, I have tried to make that quite plain."

Though he supposed deep down he had suspected the truth of the matter, the words struck him like a spear made of ice. His insides went cold and his heart started beating faster. The General was a dangerous man and Rendall didn't know if his affection made him safer, or more at risk. He decided right then and there: he didn't want to know.

"Ah," the General said, "so you will give me no indication of how you take this news. Very well, I have decided to confess and so I'm going to. I would very much like you by my side and in more ways than you are now. Preferably in my bed," he added softly with a slight smile touching his lips. "So I make you this offer. Say yes, be with me, and I'll let your witch go, with a stern warning of course. She can't go completely unpunished."

Rendall's thoughts swirled. *He seems so confident that Deneige is coming, but if I successfully warned her away, then this game of cat and mouse continues and she will live another day. If, however, she didn't get my message, or chooses to ignore it, which would be perfectly within her character to do...*

He eyed the storm clouds, which were only getting darker and more violent by the minute. *Either way, I need to give the General an answer. Could I be what he wants me to be for the sake of Deneige's life and freedom, and for my position within the legion? I love her and I made a vow to keep her safe, but...*

He never reached the end of his thought and the General never got his answer before the door slammed open and Deneige herself, the Dea of her people and the dreaded 'white-witch' who had hounded the Romans for months, was dragged into the tower room by her hair.

Beneath his helm, Rendall's jaw dropped as he took in her pregnant belly, made all the more prominent by the way she had to arch her back to keep Felix from tearing her hair from her skull. By the look of her she was at least five or six month's along. *Is that...is she carrying my child?*

Deneige strained against her captor's hold, seething at the injustice of having come so far only to be caught at the very last when she was so close to her goal. There he was, not ten feet from her, perfectly impassive in his suit of armour with his helm in place so only his eyes were visible. She sneered at Rendall, hoping he understood how much she'd come to hate him and exactly what she would do to him if she wasn't held back by Felix's gauntleted hand.

"Well, well, well," the General beamed, obviously pleased by this turn of events, "it looks like our guest of honour has arrived.

Thank you, Felix, for having escorted her to us. And, oh look, she's with child, that's quite a twist. Almost a two-for-one bargain, if you ask me."

"I'm still capable of destroying you," Deneige spat, "all of you!"

The General laughed. "Oh, she's a feisty one. I can see what you liked about her, Alton."

"You're murderers! You killed Javvar, and all these innocent people. What gives you the right?"

The General grinned. "Apollo, my dear. We follow the sun and we go where it leads. With our God behind us we have the right to anything we want, and with his might we bring enlightenment to the uneducated peasants of this land. In fact, you should thank us. Without our intervention, you would still be living in a mud hut with no one but your fur-covered savages for company. Now, instead, you'll be the mother to a son of the empire!"

"None of you have any claim over my child! Just like you don't have any say over the way I or any of the Freefolk choose to live." And having said what she'd come here to say, Deneige bent, ignoring the pain in her skull, to retrieve the dagger she'd hidden in her boot. Standing once more, she lifted her arm and in one fluid motion she spun and sliced through the silvery thickness of her hair.

She didn't stop moving once she was suddenly free. Instead, she raced from Felix's grasp, straight toward the object of her hatred: the General. She watched his eyes go wide as she charged him, but at the same time she heard the thunderous footfalls of Felix behind her. He was gaining on her and drawing his sword as he went; she knew in that instant she would never reach the General alive.

Sudden motion to her left caught her eye as the statue that was Rendall came to life. He surged forward, leaping over the worn desk that was the only real piece of furniture in the room. For a split second, Deneige thought he was coming for her, that he intended to knock her down and take her as his prisoner once more, but instead he put himself between her and Felix, and she heard the sharp clang of the heavier man's sword on Rendall's armour.

Continuing her forward motion, Deneige slammed bodily into the General, sending him flying through the open arch that constituted the tower's window. Genuine surprise flashed across the man's face as he lost contact with anything solid and he windmilled his arms in the air, grasping at nothing. Deneige watched in satisfaction as the man fell to his demise, lightning cracking in the air above them as the sky opened and the rain began to fall in sheets.

Repeated clanging sounds drew her attention back towards what was going on behind her. In the small tower room, Felix and Rendall faced off, each armed and armoured similarly, with only their relative sizes to tell them apart. At a glance Rendall looked outmatched, but it quickly became clear he was the better fighter.

Deneige frowned, watching them, her heart warring with her head over how she wanted this conflict to end. On the one hand if Felix won, her life was forfeit because the heavy-set man would come for her next, but on the other she was still angry with Rendall and didn't know if she could trust him. She wanted to, but she also knew that his actions had led her here to risk it all, putting her child and her people in danger to try and take this town back from the Romans. In the distance, she could hear that conflict ring out from far below. Rendall's and Felix's fight wasn't the only one taking place right now. Her people were fighting to liberate Whelan at her command.

Felix swung his heavy blade in a downwards arc, but Rendall was quick on his feet, which caused Deneige another bout of confusion. *When I last saw him, he was barely able to stand under his own power. He had broken bones and more. I know it's been nearly six months, but there should still be some lingering complications from those injuries.*

The fight continued, each man taking blows that would have felled lesser men. Deneige found herself holding her breath, unsure of who to root for and if she should interfere, or try to make her escape while they were preoccupied with one another.

But then Rendall went down, hard. Thinking the fight was basically over, Felix tore off his helmet to reveal a wicked grin. He tossed the metal aside and circled his victim, as if deciding how best to finish him off. Rendall threw off his own helmet to reveal a scarred face with a nose that was just slightly out of alignment. He was breathing hard and sweating profusely in his armour; Felix had him just where he wanted him.

Deneige found her heart suddenly in her throat. She'd spent the past while hating Rendall for his part in what had happened to Javvar, but seeing him like this she realized how much she still loved him and that, whatever he had done, she didn't want him to die. They'd been through so much together and though they were both so different from one another, they complemented one another well. She brought out the best in him and he tempered her rough edges.

"No!" Deneige screamed, drawing the attention of both men for the barest of instants, just long enough for Rendall to reach for something on the floor behind him. Deneige furrowed her brow, trying to figure out what Rendall was thinking, when Felix turned back to the fight and lifted his sword, ready to end Rendall's life.

Rendall threw what he'd picked up. Silver-white strands flew in every direction, but most headed for Felix's face, causing the man to cough and splutter while he backed up and waved to clear his vision, and in that very moment Rendall had him.

Her lover surged to his feet and lifted his sword as he went, using his momentum to strike upwards in a long, smooth motion. His aim was true, the sword struck where Felix's neck met his torso, and the sharp, heavy blade slid through flesh, sinew, and bone, cleaving his head from his body instantly.

Deneige's stomach heaved as Felix's head rolled across the floor to join his discarded helmet and she retched as the rest of him struck the ground, crimson blood pooling everywhere.

"Deneige?" Rendall's voice came to her slowly as if she was underwater. "Deneige?" He was gripping her shoulders now and leading her away from the seeping pool of blood and toward the window where she could breathe.

She managed to tear her gaze away from the carnage. "Don't…don't touch me," she said sharply, slapping his hands away.

"I'm sorry," he said, lowering his gaze.

"You're sorry that the entire time I was trying to find a way to save you, you were betraying me? Living life like you did before and moving up in the ranks, while I struggled out there."

His brow furrowed. "Betray you? I-"

Whatever Rendall's explanation was, it was cut short by a familiar figure filling the open door. "Rendall, she's here -" Lucius stopped, mid-sentence. "Oh, Deneige, you've found him already. I was worried when I lost track of you."

"You were following me?" Deneige questioned.

Lucius nodded. "The General ordered a contingent of legionnaires to track you. Sir Rendall wanted to keep you safe, so he had me tail them. I killed them with the help of a few of your people just outside of town. That Siobhan woman is something else with a blade…" he trailed off at their expressions. "Well, anyway, I'm glad you found each other…hey, wait, is that Felix?"

Rendall let out a small sigh. "Lucius, is the town secure?"

"If you're asking if the fighting has stopped, then yes," he answered. "If you're asking if we won, then that depends on your definition of 'we'." He grinned. "Most of the fighting stopped when the storm got so bad no one could see past their own noses anymore, but from what I could tell the Lumen have Whelan under their control now."

Rendall nodded. "Lucius, will you give us a moment."

The young legionnaire nodded and saluted professionally before leaving and shutting the door behind him. That left the two of them alone with Felix's corpse, but Deneige found herself staring at Rendall instead.

"Why did you leave Javvar to die?"

"He's dead then? I had hoped…" he trailed off. "Nevermind. I did what I could for him, leaving him food and medicine, but I suspected he might not make it. I would have helped him escape, but he insisted on staying to wait for you and he was in no condition to make it out alive on his own."

"He said he'd told you everything and I thought…"

"You thought I betrayed your location to the General?" Rendall asked and Deneige nodded. "I did give the General a few tidbits to make him think I was loyal, but your people were never in any danger from me, Deneige. I did what I could to keep them safe. Javvar was supposed to warn you never to come here, that Whelan was the General's trap. He wanted to make you angry enough to come in here blind. It looks like he underestimated your capabilities."

"I was more mad at you than the General," Deneige told him honestly.

He nodded. "And that's what I'm sorry for. I never meant to make you doubt me. And I hate the man the General was trying to make me become. Prophecy or no, I don't want greatness for Rome if this is what it means," he said with a gesture to the town of Whelan outside and the state it had been reduced to, even if it couldn't really be seen in the dark and through the thick sheet of rain.

"What if you joining me to fight against Rome is what makes it great? We could stop the horrible practices they've adopted and show them the value that other people and other cultures have to offer. There are other ways to be great. We could find them…" She looked up into his eyes, tentatively. She knew she was risking a lot asking him this, but she had realized his place in her heart and now that she had she knew she couldn't walk away from him again. "We could do it together…the three of us."

Rendall smiled, placing a hand on her outstretched belly. "I'd like that," he said. "I'd like that very much."

"On one condition," Deneige said, holding up a finger before he drew her into a kiss, "in private, we can be as loving as we want, but in public, *you* answer to *me*."

He chuckled and drew her close, pressing his lips against hers, "Any way you want it, my love."

Why Mirror World?

We publish escapism fiction for all ages. Our novels are imaginative and character-driven and our goal is to give our readers a glimpse into other worlds, times, and versions of reality that parallel our own, giving them an experience they can't get anywhere else!

We offer free delivery within Windsor-Essex in Canada, an all-you-can-read membership program, blind-dates with books, and you can order our novels from our online store, or from your favorite major book retailer.

We appreciate every like, tweet, facebook post, and review and we love to hear from you. Please consider leaving us your comments online or sending your thoughts or questions to info@mirrorworldpublishing.com

Thank you.